Secret Fire

Johanna Lindsey

AVON BOOKS ◆ NEW YORK

SECRET FIRE is an original publication of Avon Books. This work has
never before appeared in book form. This work is a novel. Any similarity
to actual persons or events is purely coincidental.

AVON BOOKS
A division of
The Hearst Corporation
1350 Avenue of the Americas
New York, New York 10019

Copyright © 1987 by Johanna Lindsey
Published by arrangement with the author
Library of Congress Catalog Card Number: 87-91598
ISBN: 0-380-75087-2

First Avon Books Printing:December 1987

AVON TRADEMARK REG. U.S. PAT. OFF. AND IN OTHER COUNTRIES, MARCA
REGISTRADA, HECHO EN U.S.A.

Printed in the U.S.A.

RA 20 19

For Grandma Rosie,
a very special lady that I love

SECRET
FIRE

Chapter One

London 1844

Another spring shower was in the offing, but Katherine St. John took little note of the overcast sky hanging heavily above her. She moved absently about the little garden, snipping pink and red roses that she would later arrange to her satisfaction, one vaseful for her sitting room and one for her sister Elisabeth. Her brother Warren was off in his typical endeavor of enjoying himself somewhere, so he didn't need flowers to brighten a room he rarely slept in. And her father George disliked roses, so she cut none for him.

"Give me lilies or irises or even wild daisies, but keep those cloying roses for you girls."

Katherine wouldn't think to do otherwise. She was adaptable in that way. So a servant was sent out each morning to find wild daisies for the Earl of Strafford, never mind that they weren't easy to find in the city.

"You're a wonder, my darling Kate," her father was fond of saying, and Katherine would accept the compliment as her due.

It wasn't that she needed praise; far from it. Her accomplishments were for her own sense of pride, for her own self-esteem. She loved being needed and she was needed. George St. John might be head of his household, but it was Katherine who ran the household, and it was to her that he deferred in all things. Both Holden House here on Cavendish Square and Brockley Hall, the Earl's country estate, were her domains. She was her father's hostess, housekeeper, and steward. She kept domestic trivialities and tenant troubles at bay, so the Earl was free from worry and free to dabble in politics, his passion, to his heart's content.

"Morning, Kit. Come have breakfast with me? Do."

Katherine glanced up to see Elisabeth leaning precariously out her bedroom window, which overlooked the square. "I've had breakfast, love, several hours ago," Katherine called back in a voice just loud enough to carry. It wasn't in her character to shout when anything else would do.

"Coffee, then? Please," Elisabeth entreated. "I need to talk to you."

Katherine smiled in agreement and carried her basket of roses inside. She had in fact been waiting patiently for her sister to awaken so that she could have a talk with her. No doubt they both had the same subject in mind, for they had both been called into the Earl's study last evening, separately, but for the same reason—Lord William Seymour.

Lord Seymour was a dashing young man of devilishly good looks, who had taken the innocent young Elisabeth by storm. They had met at the start of this year's season, Beth's first, and the poor girl had looked at no other man since. They were in love, that universal emotion that made fools out of the most sensible people. But who was Katherine to scoff just because she thought the emotion silly and a waste of energy that could be better put to some useful endeavor? She was happy for her younger sister, at least she had been until last night.

In the time it took her to cross the back hall to the stairs, she had servants running to do her bidding: a breakfast tray to be sent upstairs, the mail delivered to her office, a reminder sent to the Earl that Lord Seldon had an appointment this morning and was due in half an hour, two maids dispatched to the Earl's study to make sure it was in order to receive a guest (her father was not known for his neatness), and vases of water carried to Beth's sitting room. She would arrange the roses while they had their talk.

If Katherine had been one to put things off, she would have avoided Elisabeth like the plague. That wasn't her way, however. Even though she wasn't sure yet exactly what she intended to say to her sister, she was certain she wouldn't fail her father in his request.

"You're the only one she'll listen to, Kate," her father had told her last night. "You have to make Beth understand I wasn't just making idle threats. I won't have my family associated with this bounder."

He had laid the whole dismal tale in her lap by that time, but her calm "Of course, Father" had only made him more defensive over his decision.

"You know it's not my way to be autocratic. I leave that to you, Kate." They both smiled over this, for she really could be domineering when warranted, though that was rare, since everyone did their best to please her. George St. John continued his defense. "I want my girls to be happy. I don't lay down the law, like some fathers."

"You're very understanding."

"I like to think so, 'deed I do."

It was true. He didn't interfere in his children's lives, which wasn't to say he lacked concern. Far from it. But if one of them got into trouble—more accurately, when Warren got into trouble—he left it to Katherine to sort out the mess. Everyone depended on her to keep things running smoothly.

"But I ask you, Kate, what else could I do? I know Beth thinks she's in love with this chap. Probably is, for that matter. But it makes no difference. I've had it from the best of sources that Seymour is not what he claims to be. He's just one step ahead of debtors' prison. And what did the girl tell me to this? 'I don't care,' she says. 'I'll elope with William if I have to.' Of all the impertinent misses." And then on a quieter note, one full of uncertainty, "She wouldn't really elope, would she, Kate?"

"No, she was just upset, Father," Katherine had assured him. "Beth just said what she needed to say to appease her pain and disappointment."

Elisabeth had gone to bed last night in tears. Katherine had gone to bed saddened for her sister, but too practical to let this turn in events depress her. She felt partly responsible, because she had been her sister's chaperon and had in fact encouraged the growing affection between the two young people. But she couldn't let that influence her. It came down to one simple fact. Beth couldn't marry Lord Seymour now. She had to be made to see that and accept it and go on from there.

She knocked only once before entering Elisabeth's bedroom. The younger girl was still in dis-

4

array, wearing a pink silk wrapper over her white linen nightgown. She sat before her vanity, where her maid was pulling a brush through her long blond hair. She looked exquisite in her melancholy, with her soft lips pulled down at the corners. But then there was little that could detract from Elisabeth St. John's dazzling beauty.

The two sisters were alike only in height and in the color of their eyes, neither green nor blue, but a subtle blending of the two. All the St. Johns possessed these light turquoise eyes ringed with a darker blue-green. The servants were fond of swearing that Katherine's eyes lit up with an unholy light when she was displeased about something. Untrue. It was just the lightness of color and the fact that her eyes, her only really good asset as far as she was concerned, tended to make the rest of her features fade away to nothing.

For Elisabeth, the lovely turquoise color complemented her light blond hair, the darker gold brows, the soft lines of her face. She had a classic beauty inherited from their mother. Warren and Katherine favored their father, with dark brown hair; a proud, patrician nose; forceful, stubborn chin; cheekbones high and aristocratic; and full, generous lips. On Warren these features produced a handsome countenance. On Katherine they were too severe. She was much too tiny at just over five feet to carry off their haughty effect. Passing pretty would have been a generous compliment.

But what Katherine lacked in beauty she made up in character. She was a warm, giving woman with many facets to her personality. Warren liked to tease her by saying that she was so versatile that she should have taken up the theater. In a quite natural way she could adapt herself to any situation, whether to take charge or to cooperate humbly if others were leading. Hers were not all inherent traits, however. Many she had learned during the year she had been one of Queen Victoria's ladies-in-waiting. If court life teaches anything, it's versatility and diplomacy.

That was two years ago, after her own first season, which had been such a resounding failure. She was twenty-one years old now, soon to be twenty-two, and considered quite firmly on the shelf. A distasteful term that, just as bad as old maid. It was whispered about her, but it wasn't what she considered herself. She fully intended to marry one day, a staid, dependable older man, not handsome and dashing, like the men sought by all the young debutantes, but not ugly either. No one of her acquaintance could deny she would make a superb wife. But she just wasn't ready yet to be that wife. Her father still needed her, her sister needed her, even Warren needed her, for without her he would have to own up to his responsibilities as the Earl's heir, which he had no desire to do at present.

Elisabeth waved her young maid away and met Katherine's eyes in the mirror above her vanity. "Kit, did Father tell you what he did?"

Such a woebegone expression. Beth's eyes were even glistening, very close to tears. Katherine was sympathetic, but only because it was her sister who was suffering. All this emotion expended on such a silly thing as love she just couldn't understand.

"I know what he did, love, and I'm sure you've had a good cry over it, so buck up now. No more tears, if you please."

Katherine didn't mean to sound so heartless. She really did wish she could understand. She supposed she was too pragmatic, and being realistic to boot didn't help either. She firmly believed that if you couldn't win after all your resources were depleted, you gave up and looked on the bright side. No one would catch her beating her head against a wall.

Beth swung around on her little velvet stool, and two fat tears did indeed trickle down the creamy expanse of her cheeks. "That's easy for you to say, Kit. It wasn't your fiancé that Father refused and showed the door to."

"Fiancé?"

"Well, of course. William asked me before he came for Father's blessing and I said yes."

"I see."

"Oh, please don't take that tone with me!" Beth cried. "Don't treat me like one of the servants who's displeased you!"

Katherine was taken aback by this heated attack. Good Lord, was she really that condescending?

"I'm sorry, Beth," she said sincerely. "I know I've never been in this sort of situation myself, so it's not easy for me to comprehend—"

"Weren't you ever even a little bit in love, just once?" Beth asked hopefully. Katherine was the only one who could persuade her Father to change his mind, but if she didn't realize how important it was . . .

"Honestly, Beth, you know I don't believe in
. . . What I mean is . . ."

That pleading expression on her young sister's
face was making this very difficult. The maid arriving with a breakfast tray saved her from saying the truth, that she felt herself immensely
fortunate to be one of the few women of her day
who could look at love in a practical manner. It
was a silly and useless emotion. It produced
highs and lows of feeling that had no business
cluttering up one's life. Look what it was doing
to sweet Beth. But Beth didn't want to hear that
what she was feeling at this moment was ridiculous. She needed sympathy, not ridicule.

Katherine took the steaming cup of coffee the
maid handed her and moved over to the window. She waited until she heard the door close
on the servant before she turned to face her sister, who hadn't moved toward her breakfast tray.

"There was one young man I thought would
do," Katherine offered lamely.

"Did he love you?"

"He never even knew I was alive," Katherine
said, remembering the young lord she had
thought so handsome. "We saw each other the
whole season, but each time we spoke, he always seemed to look right through me, as if I
wasn't even there. It was the prettier young ladies he danced attendance on."

"Then you *have* been hurt?"

"No, I—I'm sorry, love, but you see I was realistic even then. My young man was much too
handsome to be interested in me, even though
he wasn't that well off and I am quite a catch,
financially, that is. I knew I didn't have a chance

to snag him, so it didn't bother me that I didn't."

"Then you didn't really love him," Beth sighed.

Katherine hesitated, but finally shook her head. "Love. Beth, it is the one emotion fated to come and go with remarkable regularity. Look at your friend Marie. How many times has she been in love since you've known her? A half-dozen times at least."

"That's not love but infatuation. Marie isn't old enough to experience real love."

"And you are, at eighteen?"

"Yes!" Beth said emphatically. "Oh, Kit, why can't you understand? I love William!"

It was time for the hard truth to be thrust home once again. Obviously Beth had not taken her father's lecture to heart.

"Lord Seymour is a fortune hunter. He gambled away his inheritance, mortgaged his estates, and now needs to marry for money, and *you*, Elisabeth, are money."

"I don't believe it! I'll never believe it!"

"Father wouldn't lie about something like this, and if Lord Seymour tells you differently, it's he who will be lying."

"I don't care. I'll marry him anyway."

"I can't let you do that, love," Katherine said firmly. "Father meant what he said. He'd cut you off without a shilling. You and William would both be beggars then. I won't see you ruin your life over this scoundrel."

"Oh, why did I ever think you might help?" Beth cried. "You don't understand. How could you? You're nothing but a dried-up old prune!"

9

They both gasped together. "Oh, God, Kit, I didn't mean that!"

The accusation hurt nonetheless. "I know, Beth." She tried to force a smile, but it wouldn't come.

Another maid arrived with the two vases of water she had requested. Katherine directed her to her own sitting room and moved to leave the room, picking up her basket of roses.

She paused at the door. "I don't think we should talk any more about this for a while. I only want what's best for you, but you can't see that right now."

Elisabeth wrung her hands for five seconds before she jumped up and followed Katherine across the hall. She had never seen such a stricken look on her sister's face. At the moment William was forgotten. She had to make amends to Kit.

She shooed the maid out of the large room filled with Chippendale furniture, handsome with covers that Kit herself had embroidered. She then commenced to pace across the thick diamond-patterned carpet that covered the floor from wall to wall. Katherine ignored her as she began to arrange the roses.

"You're not dried up!" Beth exclaimed. "And you're certainly not old!"

Katherine glanced up, but she still couldn't manage to smile. "But I am occasionally a prune?"

"No, not a prune, just—just prim and proper, which is as you should be."

Now Katherine did smile. "I got this way having to entertain all those old German and Spanish diplomats at the palace. As soon as it was learned I spoke both languages so fluently, I never lacked for dinner partners.''

"How boring," Beth sympathized.

"Never say so. It was fascinating, learning about other countries at first hand, almost as good as traveling, which Father refused to let me do.''

"Didn't you ever get to entertain any dashing Frenchmen? You speak French as well as a native.''

"But so does everyone else, love.''

"Of course," Beth said, continuing her pacing.

It wasn't enough. Kit had smiled, but there was still hurt in her eyes. Oh, those horrid, horrid words! If only she had Kit's control. Kit never said anything she didn't mean.

A turn about the room brought her close to the window facing the street. The coach drawing up below looked familiar.

"Is Father expecting Lord Seldon?''

"Yes. Has he arrived?''

Beth turned away from the window, nodding. "I never did like that pompous old goat. Remember when we were children and you poured that pitcher of water out the window onto the old fellow's head? I laughed so hard—''

Beth stopped, seeing that mischievous look enter Kit's eyes. God, it had been years since she had seen that look. "You wouldn't!''

Katherine picked up the second vase of water and walked slowly to the window. Lord Seldon was just being helped out of his coach by a liveried groom.

"Kit, you shouldn't," Beth warned, but she was grinning from ear to ear. "Father had a fit the last time. We both got the birch.''

Katherine said nothing. She waited until the unsuspecting Lord Seldon had reached the door just under her window, then tipped over the vase. She drew back, a second passed, then she burst into giggles.

"Good Lord, did you see his face?" Katherine said between gasps. "He looked like a dead fish."

Beth couldn't answer at first, for she had thrown her arms around Kit and was laughing too hard.

Finally: "Whatever will you tell Father? He's going to be furious."

"Yes, undoubtedly. And I will assure him I will dismiss the clumsy servant responsible for such an outrage."

"He won't believe you." Beth giggled.

"Of course he will. He won't know the difference. He doesn't concern himself with domestics. And now I must go see to Lord Seldon. I can't have him dripping all over my foyer. Pray for me, love, that I can deal with him with a straight face."

Lady Katherine St. John sailed out of the room to do what she did best: soothe and manage. She had also managed to relieve the tension between her and her sister.

Chapter Two

"Grandmère, he's coming!"

The young woman flew into the room in a white blur of lace and silk. She didn't even look at her grandmother, but ran straight across the room to the window where she could view the procession of elegant coaches moving swiftly up the long drive. A small drop of blood appeared on her lower lip where her teeth were set so tightly. Her knuckles turned white from gripping the windowsill. Her dark brown eyes were wide with a very real fear.

"Oh, God, what am I to do?" she cried. "He'll beat me!"

Lenore Cudworth, Dowager Duchess of Albemarle, closed her eyes with a sigh. She was too old for these theatrics. Well, not really too old, but such drama was not needful at her age. And her granddaughter should have thought of the consequences before she disgraced herself.

"Do compose yourself, Anastasia," Lenore said quietly. "If your brother does beat you, which I seriously doubt, it's no more than you deserve. Even you must admit that."

Princess Anastasia swung around and stood stiffly wringing her hands. "Yes, but—but he will *kill* me! You just don't know, *Grandmère*. You've never seen him in a rage. He has no control over what he does. He will not mean to kill me, but I will be dead before he finishes with me!"

Lenore hesitated, remembering Dimitri Alexandrov as she last saw him four years ago. Then, even at twenty-four, he was an immense man, just over six feet and with a musculature well honed by the Russian army. Yes, he was strong. And yes, he was capable of killing with his bare hands. But his sister? No, not his sister, no matter what she had done.

Lenore shook her head firmly. "Your brother might be angry with you, as well he should be, but there will be no violence."

"Oh, *Grandmère*, why won't you listen?" Anastasia cried. "Dimitri has never lived with you as I have. In his whole life you have seen him only a half-dozen times and never for very long. I live with him. He is my guardian now. I know him better than anyone."

"You have been with me this last year," Lenore reminded her. "You haven't even written to Dimitri in all this time."

"So you suggest he is not the same man, that he will have changed in only a year? No, men like Dimitri never change. He is a Russian—"

"Half English."

"He was raised in Russia!" Anastasia persisted.

"He travels extensively. He spends only half the year in Russia, sometimes not even that."

"Only since he left the army!"

They would never agree on Dimitri's personality. His sister would have him a tyrant, just like their Tzar Nicholas. Lenore knew it just wasn't true. Her daughter, Anne, had contributed to his character. Petr Alexandrov had not had exclusive development of his son.

"I suggest you calm down before he walks in," Lenore said now. "I'm sure he won't appreciate these hysterics any more than I do."

Anastasia glanced back out the window to see the first coach stopping in front of the huge country mansion. She gasped and rushed across the room to kneel at Lenore's feet.

"Please, *Grandmère*, please. You must talk to him. You must speak for me. It will not be so much what I did that he will be furious about. He is no hypocrite. It will be that his plans were interrupted to come for me. He sets goals for himself, you see, and he plans everything far in advance. He can tell you where he will be next year to the day. But if something gets in the way of his plans, he is impossible to live with. You sent for him. You made him put aside whatever he was involved in to come here. You must help me."

Lenore finally saw the motive for this little drama. *And she waits until the last moment so I won't have time to think about it.* Very ingenious. But then Anastasia Petrovna Alexandrov was an intelligent young woman. Spoiled, pampered, with a highly volatile personality, but intelligent.

So she was to soothe the wild beast, was she? She was supposed to ignore the fact that this young chit had disobeyed her at every turn, had flouted convention, had made her own rules? Anastasia had even refused to return to Russia after the last scandal had broken. If not for that, Lenore wouldn't have had to send for Dimitri.

She stared down at the exquisite face full of such anxiety. Her Anne had been lovely, but the Alexandrovs were incredibly handsome people. She had gone to Russia only once, when Petr had died and Anne needed her. She had met Petr's other offspring then, his three children by his first marriage and his many illegitimate children as well. They were all exceptionally beautiful. But the two that were her grandchildren she loved. They were her only grandchildren. Her son, the present Duke of Albemarle, had lost his first wife before she gave him children. He never remarried or showed any signs of doing so. Dimitri was in fact his designated heir.

Lenore sighed. This chit could wrap her around her little finger. Anastasia needed to leave England until her most recent scandals had time to be forgotten, but Lenore knew she would invite the girl back again. Life might be hectic with her in residence, but it was always interesting.

"Go on, go to your room, my girl," Lenore said now. "I'll talk to the lad. But mind you, I don't promise anything."

Anastasia leaped up and threw her arms around her grandmother's neck. "Thank you. And I'm so sorry, *Grandmère*. I know I've been a trial to you—"

"Better for me than for your brother, I suppose, if he's as difficult to live with as you say. Now go, before he's shown in."

The Princess rushed out of the room, and none too soon. A minute later Prince Dimitri Petrovich Alexandrov was announced by the butler. At least the poor man attempted to announce him. Dimitri did not wait for such trifles, but entered the room the moment the door was opened and filled it with his presence.

He gave Lenore pause. Good Lord, was it possible he was even more handsome than when last she saw him? Yes, he was indeed. The golden hair; the piercing, deep-brown eyes; the dark, slashing brows: these were all the same. But at twenty-four there had still been something of the boy in him. Now he was a man, and like no man she had ever seen in her sixty-nine years. He even surpassed his father in looks, and she had thought no man better looking than Petr.

His long-legged stride carried him swiftly across the room, and then he was bowing quite formally. His manners had improved at least, but such imperious bearing—was this really her grandson? And then his teeth flashed in an engaging grin, and his hands gripped her shoulders. She grimaced as he lifted her completely out of her chair for a resounding kiss.

"Put me down, rascal," the Duchess nearly shouted. "Have a care for my age, if you please."

She was flustered. Such strength! Anastasia had every reason to be nervous after all. If this towering giant did decide to give her the thrashing she so richly deserved . . .

"*J'en suis au regret.*"

"Never mind that French rubbish!" she snapped. "You've a good English tongue. I'll thank you to use it while you're in my house."

Dimitri threw back his leonine head and laughed, a deep, rich sound, so very masculine. And he was still grinning as he set Lenore back in her chair.

"I said I was sorry, *Babushka*, but you utterly destroyed my apology. You are still as feisty as ever, I see. I have missed you. You should come to live in Russia."

"My bones could never withstand one of your winters, and well you know it."

"Then I will have to come here more often. It has been too long, *Babushka*."

"Oh, do sit down, Dimitri. It hurts my neck to have to look up at you. And you're late." He had thrown her for such a turn that she couldn't resist putting him on the defensive.

"Your letter had to wait until the spring melting on the Neva before it could reach me," he said as he grabbed the nearest chair and pulled it closer to her.

"I knew that," she replied. "But I also know your ship docked in London three days ago. We expected you yesterday."

"After weeks on my ship, I needed a day to recuperate."

"Good Lord, that's the nicest way I've ever heard it put. Was she pretty?"

"Immeasurably."

If she had hoped to disarm him with her frankness, she failed. No blush, no excuses, just a lazy smile. She should have known better. According to his Aunt Sonya, who wrote Lenore often, Dimitri never lacked for feminine company, and half that company was married women. Anastasia was correct. He would be hypocritical to upbraid her for her few indiscretions, when his own numbered in the hundreds.

"What do you intend to do about your sister?" Lenore ventured while he was in this pleasant mood.

"Where is she?"

"In her room. She's not too happy that you're here. She seems to think you're going to be rather harsh with her for having been called here to fetch her home."

Dimitri shrugged. "I admit I was annoyed at first. This was not a convenient time for me to leave Russia."

"I am sorry, Dimitri. None of this would have been necessary if that silly woman hadn't made such a scene when she found Anastasia in bed with her husband. But there were at least a hundred guests at this particular party, and half that number rushed to the rescue when they heard the woman's screams. And Anastasia, foolish girl, didn't have sense enough to hide her head under the sheets so she wouldn't be recognized. No, she stands there in her shift and argues with the woman."

"It is unfortunate Anastasia was not more discreet, but do not mistake me, *Babushka*. Alexandrovs have never let public opinion influence their actions. No, my sister's offense is that she did not follow *your* dictates."

"She was just being stubborn and refusing to run from censure, another trait you Alexandrovs have in common, Dimitri."

"You defend her too much, Duchess."

"Then relieve my mind and tell me you don't intend to beat her."

It took a moment for Dimitri's bland look to change, but suddenly he burst into laughter. "What *has* the girl been telling you about me?"

Lenore had the grace to blush. "Obviously nonsense," she said disagreeably.

He continued to chuckle. "She's too old for a spanking, not that I didn't relish the idea for a while. No, I will simply take her home and find her a husband. She needs someone who can keep a closer watch over her than I can."

"She'll balk at that, my boy. She's told me more than once that marriage isn't for her and that her views on the subject come entirely from you."

"Well, perhaps she will change her mind when she learns that I intend to be married before the year is out myself."

"Are you serious, Dimitri?" Lenore asked in surprise.

"Completely," he replied. "It was my courtship that was interrupted by this trip."

Chapter Three

Katherine placed another cool compress on her forehead and leaned her head back on the chaise. She had retired to her room after her morning meeting with the servants to assign their tasks. And this dreadful headache just wasn't letting up. But she supposed she had drunk too much champagne at her ball last night. That wasn't like her at all. She rarely drank spirits at parties, and never when she was the hostess.

Her maid, Lucy, moved about in the bedroom, putting it to rights. The morning tray she had brought remained untouched. She couldn't stomach even the thought of food just yet.

Katherine sighed long and loudly. Fortunately, the ball last night had been a success, despite her slight intoxication. Even Warren had managed to make an appearance. The evening itself had nothing to do with her present headache. It had been caused by Elisabeth and the message her maid had delivered just as the first guests began to arrive: that because William hadn't been invited to the ball, she would not attend either.

It was incredible. Not a word out of Beth all week since their talk, not a sigh, not a tear. Katherine had truly thought Beth had accepted the situation, and she had been so proud of her, of how well she was handling this broken-heart business. And then, out of the blue, this about-face, this message that proved only too well that

Beth hadn't forgotten about William at all—which made her wonder now why there hadn't been any more tears if that *was* the case.

What the devil was she to think? Oh, she couldn't think at all right now, not with this throbbing head.

A loud knock at the door made her grimace. Elisabeth came in, dressed in a lovely watered-silk gown of moss green, a going-out dress. She held a silk bonnet in her hand by the ties, and a lacy parasol was tucked under her arm.

"Martha said you weren't feeling well, Kit."

No mention of her absence last night, not even a guilty look. And after all the trouble Katherine had gone to for the ball, selecting only the most eligible bachelors in the hope that one might catch Beth's interest. Well, the ball hadn't really been any bother. Entertaining two hundred people was a trifling thing when you knew how to make things run smoothly.

"I'm afraid I imbibed a little too freely last night, love," Katherine said truthfully. "Nothing that won't right itself by the afternoon."

"That's nice."

Beth was distracted. Why? Katherine wondered. And where was she going?

She wasn't prepared to mention Lord Seymour again just yet, but she had to know Beth's destination. An uncomfortable premonition raised its head.

"You're going out?"

"Yes."

"You'll have to ask John to drive you then. Henry took sick yesterday."

"That—that won't be necessary, Kit. I'm just going for a—a walk."

"A walk?" Katherine said stupidly.

"Yes. If you've noticed, it's an absolutely lovely day, just perfect for a walk."

"I hadn't noticed. You know I rarely take note of the weather." Good Lord, a walk? Beth never walked. She had such high arches that walking any distance gave her sore feet. And what was all this uncertainty, this stammering? "How long will you be, love?"

"Oh, I don't know," Beth said evasively. "I might venture over to Regent Street and do a little shopping before the afternoon crowds arrive. You know how dreadful it can be there between two and four."

Katherine was speechless, and before she could recover, Beth had waved and closed the door. And then Katherine's eyes flared and her headache was momentarily forgotten as the most astounding thought occurred to her. *My God, she wouldn't be that foolish, would she?* But her unusual behavior, that ridiculous statement about going for a walk, the even more absurd suggestion that she might shop—without a carriage to carry her parcels. She was meeting William! And if she had to be so sneaky about it, they had to be going to elope! There had been ample time for him to obtain a license. And the city abounded in churches.

"Lucy!"

The red-haired maid appeared almost instantly in the bedroom doorway. "Lady Katherine?"

"Quickly, call my sister back here!"

The maid fairly flew out of the room, alarmed by the harried note in her mistress's voice. She caught Lady Elisabeth descending the stairs, and they both returned to Katherine's sitting room.

23

"Yes, Kit?"

A definitely guilty look this time, Katherine thought wildly, her mind already racing ahead. "Be a dear, Beth, and confer with Cook over tonight's menu for me. I really don't feel up to making any decisions just now."

Obvious relief. "Of course, Kit."

Elisabeth closed the door behind her, leaving a confused Lucy staring at Katherine. "Didn't you already—"

Katherine leaped off the chaise. "Yes, yes, but going to the kitchen will delay her for a few minutes while I change. Now, if only Cook won't mention that I have already spoken with her, I'll pull this off neatly."

"I don't understand, Lady Katherine."

"Of course you don't. I don't expect you to. I've got to prevent a tragedy from occurring. My sister is going to elope!"

Lucy's mouth simply dropped open at that. She had heard the gossip among the servants concerning Lady Elisabeth and the young Lord Seymour as well as what the Earl had threatened to do if she should marry against his wishes.

"Shouldn't you stop her, my lady?"

"Don't be a ninny. I can't stop her now without any proof of her intentions," Katherine said impatiently as she unbuttoned her morning gown. "Quickly, I need your dress, Lucy!" Then back to her first thought: "It would be too easy for her to sneak out again when I'm not expecting it. And I can't very well have her locked permanently in her room. I've got to follow them to the church and put a stop to it there. Do hurry, Lucy! Then I'll take her home to Brockley Hall where I can better keep an eye on her."

The maid didn't understand at all, but she quickly stripped off her black cotton uniform and handed it over. "But why do you need—"

"Here, help me put it on, Lucy. You can change into my dress after I've gone. So I won't be recognized, of course," she said in answer to the maid's question. "If she sees me following her, then she won't meet Lord Seymour, and then I've no proof, and then I can't do anything until she tries again. Understand?"

"Yes, no, oh, Lady Katherine, you really can't mean to go out looking like a servant!" Lucy exclaimed even as she helped to button up the stiff dress.

"That is the whole idea, Lucy, to be in disguise. Even if Beth should see me, she'll never recognize me in this," Katherine said, trying to pull the skirt down over her many petticoats. It stuck at the waist. Lucy's dress was more form-fitting. She wore only two petticoats. "This won't do. I'll have to remove some of these flounces and especially this bulky horsehair petticoat. There, that's better."

Four petticoats dropped to her feet, and the black skirt slid over her hips easily. A trifle long now, since Lucy was a few inches taller than she, but that couldn't be helped.

"You don't wear that long apron when you go out, do you, Lucy?"

"No."

"I didn't think so, but I wasn't sure. Oh, why haven't I ever taken notice of these things? What about a parasol?"

"No, my lady, just that reticule in the pocket—"

"This?" Katherine pulled out a little camel's-hair bag with long tie strings. "Perfect. You don't mind if I use it, do you? Good, I do want to look my part. I suppose these rings should go too," she added, stripping off a large ruby solitaire and a cluster of pearls. "Now for a bonnet, quickly. A poke bonnet, I think. That will help to hide my face."

The maid rushed in her petticoats to the wardrobe and returned with Katherine's oldest bonnet. "This really is too nice, my lady."

Katherine grabbed the thing and swiftly ripped off every embellishment. "Well?"

"As you say, my lady, perfect. You no longer look like a—"

Katherine grinned when Lucy blushed, unable to finish. "A lady?" she supplied, then chuckled as the girl's blush deepened. "Never mind, my girl. That was the point."

"Oh, my lady, this—this worries me. Men can be awfully cheeky on the street. You will take several of the footmen—"

"Heavens, no!" Katherine exclaimed. "Beth would recognize every one of them."

"But—"

"No, dear, I'll be fine."

"But—"

"I must go!"

Lucy stood wringing her hands after the door closed on her mistress. What was she a party to? Lady Katherine had never in her life done anything like this. She didn't really know what she was doing either. Why, just last week Lucy had been accosted by a big brute of a fellow only two blocks away, and she had been wearing that very dress. If a gentleman passing in a fine carriage hadn't come to her rescue, she didn't know what might have happened. But that fellow wasn't the first to make indecent propositions to her. A working girl had no protection. And Lady Katherine was leaving the house looking like a working girl.

Katherine didn't exactly look like a working girl. In her appearance, yes, but in her bearing, no. She was still an earl's daughter no matter what she wore. She wouldn't know how to act like a servant even if she tried. She didn't try. That wasn't necessary. All that was necessary was that Elisabeth not recognize her if she should happen to look back. And she did look back every few minutes, confirming Katherine's suspicion that she was worried about being followed. Katherine had to lower her head quickly each time. But so far, so good.

She followed her sister down to Oxford Street, where Beth turned left. Katherine kept well back, the green silk gown ahead of her easy to keep track of even when the sidewalks became more crowded.

Beth was indeed heading for Regent Street, in the next block, but that didn't allay any of Katherine's suspicions. It was as good a place as any to meet William, not nearly as crowded as in the afternoon, but congested nonetheless with clerks rushing to work, servants shopping for their employers, wagons making deliveries; and being a main thoroughfare, the street was quite crowded with carriages and coaches and advertisement wagons, those dreadful vehicles that caused so many traffic tie-ups in the afternoon.

Katherine lost sight of Beth when she turned onto Regent Street and had to hurry to the corner. But there she stopped. Beth had halted three shops down and was examining the display in one of the windows. Katherine didn't dare get any closer, so she stayed where she was, impatiently tapping her foot, ignoring the people who passed her. It was a busy corner.

"Hello, luv."

Katherine didn't hear him, never dreaming the fellow would speak to her.

"Don't be snooty, now." He grabbed her arm to gain her attention.

"I beg your pardon." She looked down her nose at him, which wasn't easy when he was a half-head taller than her.

He didn't let go of her. "Hoity-toity, ain't you? But I like that."

He wore a suit, even carried a cane, but his manners left much to be desired. He was rather good-looking, but Katherine didn't take that into account. Never in her life had a stranger laid a hand on her before. There had always been grooms or footmen surrounding her to keep that from happening. She was at a loss how to deal with this, but instinct made her jerk her arm back. His grip held.

"Go *away*, sir! I don't wish to be bothered."

"Now don't put on airs, luv." He was grinning at her, liking the sudden challenge. "You're just standing here with nothing better to do. It won't hurt you to pass the time."

Katherine was appalled. Was she supposed to argue with him? Not likely. She had already made her wishes known.

She drew back the hand that clutched Lucy's sturdy little reticule by the string and let fly at him. The fellow let go of her to jump back. He avoided being hit, but in doing so, collided with another man waiting to cross the street. That man shoved him away forcefully, with a sharp oath that stung Katherine's ears and brought vivid color to her cheeks.

The moment her accoster righted himself, he glared at her. "Bitch. A simple no would have sufficed."

Katherine's nostrils flared angrily. She very nearly stooped to his level to tell him what he could do with his misplaced indignation. But she had too much breeding for that. She gave him her back, then groaned when she saw that Elisabeth had moved on during the commotion and was nearly half a block away now.

Chapter Four

Anastasia fretted at the delay. It seemed as if their coach had been stuck on this busy corner for a half-hour, waiting for an opening in the heavy congestion on Regent Street so that they could cross over and continue on their way. Their uncle's townhouse was only a few blocks away. She could have got there quicker if she had walked.

"I hate this city," Anastasia complained. "The streets are so narrow and always so crowded compared to St. Petersburg. And no one ever hurries here."

Dimitri said nothing, not even reminding her that this was where she said she wanted to stay. He simply sat staring out the window. What did she expect? He had hardly said two words to her during the entire journey to London. But then he had said more than enough before they left the Duke's country estate.

Anastasia shivered, remembering his rage. He hadn't beat her. She almost wished he had. His anger had been just as nerve-racking.

After he had ranted and called her every kind of a senseless fool, he had said scathingly, "What you do in bed, and whose bed you do it in, is not my concern. I have allowed you the same freedom that I enjoy myself. But that is not why I'm here, is it, Nastya? I am here because you had the temerity to scorn *Grandmère's* wishes."

"But it was unreasonable for her to send me home for such a minor thing."

"Quiet! What is minor to you is not minor to these English. This is not Russia!"

"No, in Russia Aunt Sonya monitors my every move. I have no freedom there."

"Then I will do well to put you in the care of a husband, who will perhaps be more lenient."

"Dimitri, no!"

The matter was not open to discussion. He had made his decision. And even that was not the blow she had been anticipating in retaliation for the inconvenience she had caused him. It came just before he turned to leave her.

"You had better hope to God that my plans have not been ruined by this unnecessary trip, Nastya," he told her brutally. "If they are, you can be sure the husband I find for you will not be to your liking."

And then he had been most congenial for the four days he had stayed to visit with the Duchess. But Anastasia could not forget the threat hanging over her future. It was too much to hope that he hadn't meant it, that it had been said only in anger. A husband wasn't too bad if he allowed her freedom and ignored her indiscretions. And at least she would be out from under Sonya's rigidity. But a man who would demand fidelity, who would cruelly enforce his wishes on her, set his servants to spy on her, beat her if she defied him, that was another thing entirely, and that was exactly what her brother was threatening her with.

She had never suffered his wrath before. She had seen it fall on others, but with her he had always been indulgent and loving. It only showed how mightily she had displeased him in this instance. She had known he would be furious. She had known she had gone too far in disobeying the Duchess. And Dimitri's cold silence since they had left the country was proof that he had not forgiven her.

They shared the coach alone, which only made the silence that much more unbearable. The dozen servants that he traveled with were in coaches behind them as well as those she had brought to England. There were also eight Cossack outriders who always accompanied the Prince when he left Russia, a necessity, she supposed, considering Dimitri's wealth. They were a curiosity to the English, these savage-looking warriors with their flowing mustachios and Russian uniforms, fur hats, and numerous weapons. They never failed to attract attention to the Prince's entourage, but they aptly discouraged anyone from bothering him.

Oh, she wished the coach would move. If she had to go home, she wanted to get it over.

"Can't you have your men open a path for us, Mitya?" she asked finally. "So much inconvenience, just to cross a stupid intersection."

"There is no hurry." He didn't look at her as he answered. "We do not sail until tomorrow, and we do not leave the townhouse this evening. There will be no scandals here in London to greet the Tzar when he visits the English Queen this summer."

She fumed at the warning, meant entirely for her. It was the first she had heard that Tzar Nicholas was coming to England. And she had in-

deed thought to go out tonight, possibly her last
night of freedom for a long time to come.

"But Mitya, this coach is stifling. We've been
sitting here—"

"Not even five minutes." He cut her off
tersely. "Do stop complaining."

She glared at him, then was amazed to hear
him suddenly chuckle. But he was still staring at
something out the window, so she wasn't offended, just furious.

"I'm glad to see you're enjoying this boring
ride," she quipped sarcastically. But when she
got no response, she snapped, "Well, what is so
amusing?"

"This wench fending off an admirer. She's a
fierce little thing."

Dimitri was intrigued, but he wasn't sure why.
She had a pleasing enough figure, but unremark-
able. Full breasts pushing against a too-tight bodice, a small waist, rather narrow hips, all encased
in an unbecoming black dress. He saw her face
for only the briefest moment, and that at some
distance, for she was on the opposite corner
across the street. No beauty, but a certain character, huge eyes in a small face, a determined little chin.

If not for that swinging reticule, he would
never have noticed her. She was not the type of
woman who usually caught his interest. She was
too petite, almost childlike, except for those
thrusting breasts. But she amused him. Such
haughty indignation in such a little package. And
when was the last time a woman had actually
amused him?

Sheer impulse had him call Vladimir to the window. His man of all jobs, indispensable to him, Vladimir saw to Dimitri's comfort in all things. He didn't ask questions, he didn't pass judgment. He obeyed to the letter any and all requests.

A few words to the trusted servant, and Vladimir was off. A few moments later, and the coach was again moving.

"I don't believe it," Anastasia said from the opposite side of the coach, well aware of what he had just done. "Procuring whores right off the street now? She must have been exceptionally pretty."

Dimitri ignored her sardonic tone. "Not particularly. Let us say my vanity was piqued. I like to succeed where others have failed."

"But from the street, Mitya? She could be diseased or worse."

"You would like that, wouldn't you, my dear?" he replied drily.

"At the moment, yes."

Her rancor got her only a bland smile.

Across the street, Vladimir was met with the difficulty of securing a carriage and at the same time keeping an eye on the little figure in black moving steadily up Regent Street. There were no carriages in the vicinity to hire, his English was not so good, and his French not well understood. But money solved most problems and this one as well. After several tries he was able to induce the driver of a small, enclosed private carriage to desert his post, where he was waiting for his employer. What amounted to nearly a year in wages was well worth the risk to his job.

Now to catch up with the woman. Clearly the carriage could not overtake her on such a crowded street. The driver was told to follow behind Vladimir as quickly as he was able. The driver just shook his head at the eccentricities of the wealthy, which he assumed the bloke to be, to hire a carriage and then not make use of it. But with so much money in his pocket, who was he to disagree?

Vladimir caught up with the woman near the end of the street, but only because she had stopped, and for no apparent reason. She just stood in the middle of the walk, staring straight ahead.

"Mademoiselle?"

"Oui?" she said in some distraction, barely glancing up at him.

Excellent. She spoke French. Most of the English peasants did not, and he had been afraid he would have difficulty communicating with this one.

"Attend me, please, miss. My master, Prince Alexandrov, would like to hire your services for the evening."

The mention of Dimitri's title was usually all that was required to conclude transactions such as this. Therefore Vladimir was surprised when all he got was a look of annoyance from the woman. And seeing her face clearly now surprised him further. She was not at all to Dimitri's taste. What could the Prince be thinking of, to want this little wren in his bed tonight?

Katherine was indeed annoyed to be bothered again, and for employment this time, a party or gathering, no doubt, that required extra servants. But to hire them right off the street? She had never heard of such a thing. But the fellow was a foreigner, so she had to make allowances.

Nor did she dismiss him out of hand, as she had that other fellow. She had realized her mistake there. She was disguised as a servant. She needed to at least try to act the part. By not doing so earlier, she had come close to creating a disturbance with her thoughtless attack on that other man. Causing a scene in which she might be recognized by one of her acquaintances was out of the question, yet she had foolishly nearly done so before.

One thing Katherine would never allow was scandal attached to her name. She prided herself on the most impeccable behavior, far above reproach. So what was she doing here? She could only blame that nasty headache for fogging her thinking. Clear-headed, she would have come up with a better plan than to masquerade as a servant.

The man was waiting for her answer. He must be an extremely well-paid servant, for his coat and pants were of a superior quality. He was tall, middle-aged, and not bad-looking, with brown hair and pale blue eyes. What would Lucy reply to him? The girl would probably flirt a little to make her refusal more palatable. Katherine couldn't quite bring herself to do that.

With an eye on Elisabeth, who had crossed the street, but had gone no further, she said, "I'm sorry, sir, but I don't require an extra job."

"If it's a matter of money, the Prince is extremely generous."

"I don't need money."

Vladimir began to worry. She had not been impressed by the Prince's title. Nor did she seem even remotely interested in this honor being bestowed on her. If she actually refused—no, impossible.

"Ten pounds," he offered.

If he thought that would conclude the haggling, he was mistaken. Katherine stared at him incredulously. Was he mad to offer such a wage? Or didn't he realize the going rate for servants here? The only other possibility was that he was desperate. And she realized uncomfortably that there probably wasn't a maid in the whole of England who wouldn't quit her job to accept this one night's work at such a price. And yet she couldn't accept. He would no doubt think *her* mad.

"I'm sorry—"

"Twenty pounds."

"Absurd!" Katherine snapped, becoming wary of this fellow now. He *was* mad. "You can hire a whole legion of maids for less than that. Now excuse me." She turned her back on him, praying he would go away.

Vladimir sighed. All this ridiculous haggling wasted on a mistake. A maid? She had utterly misunderstood.

"Miss, forgive me for not making myself clear at the start. My master does not require the services of a maid. He has seen you and wishes to share your company for the evening, for which you will be generously paid. If I need to be more explicit—"

"No!" Katherine faced him again, her cheeks hot. "I . . . ah, quite understand now."

Good Lord, how had she got into this insane position? Her instinct was to slap his face. The insult was extreme. But Lucy wouldn't be offended. Lucy would be thrilled.

"I am flattered, naturally, but not interested."

"Thirty pounds."

"No," she snapped. "At any price. Now do go away—"

A man's voice interrupted. "I made it, gov'ner, if you're ready to ride now."

Vladimir glanced behind him to see the carriage only steps away. "Good. You will drive us around this block. I will tell you when to stop." And with that he put his hand over the woman's mouth and dragged her into the carriage. "A runaway servant," he explained to the gawking driver.

"Run away? Now see 'ere, gov'ner, if she don't want to work for you, that's 'er business, ain't it? You can't force—" Several more pound notes shoved into his hand changed the driver's tune. "Whatever you say."

Katherine's scream had died abruptly in her throat. Had no one witnessed this abduction besides the carriage driver? But there was no call to halt. The man had moved so fast, had taken only seconds to push her into the carriage, that it was doubtful anyone had noticed.

Her face and chest were shoved down onto the seat immediately. As the carriage began to move, her bonnet was yanked off and a handkerchief whipped about her mouth and tied behind her head. A hard elbow in her back prevented her from resisting, and then her arms were pulled behind her and held tightly at the center of her back with enough pressure to keep her shoved down against the seat. Twisted sideways in this position, she could barely move her legs, but a leg was thrown over hers anyway to keep her still.

The man was strong enough to hold her arms with only one hand, which he changed after a moment, and she realized why when his coat was draped over her. The windows, of course. The carriage might be enclosed and dark inside, but if it stopped, anyone walking past could see in through the windows.

She had been right to be wary of the fellow. He really was crazy. Things like this just didn't happen to Katherine St. John. But as soon as she told him who she really was, he would be forced to let her go. He would, wouldn't he?

He leaned over her, his voice coming softly through the cloth of his coat. ''I am sorry, little wren, but you left me no choice. The Prince's orders must be obeyed. He did not consider that you might refuse his request. No woman has ever refused him before. The most beautiful women in Russia fight for this honor. You will see why when he comes to you. There is no man like Prince Dimitri.''

Katherine would have dearly loved to tell him what he could do with this honor. No man like his prince indeed! She didn't care if he was the most handsome man alive, she would have none of him. To listen to this man, she should feel gratitude for being abducted. The very idea!

The carriage stopped. She had to get away from this lunatic. He gave her no chance. His coat was wrapped around her rather like a sack, effectively locking her arms at her sides. He picked her up. He began walking, carrying her in his arms, one arm held tightly under her knees, keeping them firm against his chest and useless. She couldn't see anything through the coat, which also covered her face.

She suddenly smelled food, however. A kitchen? So he was bringing her in through the back door, was he? There was hope in that. He didn't want his prince to know what he had done. He had said this Dimitri hadn't considered that she might refuse. A prince would never resort to such measures to obtain a woman. She wouldn't have to embarrass herself by explaining who she was, after all. She had only to speak to the Prince and tell him she wasn't interested. She would be released immediately.

His knees brushed her backside as he mounted stairs, and then more stairs. Where was she? The carriage hadn't driven far, no farther than it would have taken her to reach home. Good Lord, was this some house in Cavendish Square near her own home? How ironic! But she knew of no prince who had moved into the neighborhood. Or did a prince exist at all? Was this just some wicked fellow who abducted young women for his own amusement, creating outlandish tales to make his task that much easier?

Her captor spoke again, but in a language she didn't recognize, and she was familiar with nearly all the European languages. A woman was answering in the same strange . . . Russian! He had mentioned Russia. They were *Russians*, the barbarians of the North! Of course—that country abounded in princes. Didn't all of the old aristocracy there bear such titles?

A door was opened. A few more steps and she was set carefully on her feet. The coat was removed. Katherine immediately yanked down her gag. Her first impulse was to let her temper loose on the fellow, who just stood staring at her in a curious way now. It took every effort not to give in to the impulse.

"Get hold of yourself, Katherine. He's just a barbarian, with a barbarian's mentality. He probably doesn't even know what he's done is a crime."

"We are not barbarians," he said in French.

"You speak English?" she demanded.

"Only a few words. Barbarian I know. I have been called that before by you English. What else did you say?"

"Never mind. I was speaking to myself, not to you. A quirk of mine."

"You are prettier with your hair down. The Prince will be pleased."

So that was why he was staring at her now. Her back bun had come undone when he gagged her, yet the hair caught up at each side of her head still held; the tail ends, forming ringlets, still framed her face.

"Flattery will avail you nothing, sir."

"Your pardon." He bowed slightly in deference, then caught himself doing it and was chagrined. She was a haughty wench for a servant. But then she was English and he must make allowances for that. "My name is Vladimir Kirov. I tell you this because we must speak—"

"No, I don't have anything else to say to you, Mr. Kirov. You will kindly inform your master that I am here. I will speak to him."

"He will not come until tonight."

"Fetch him!" She was appalled at how high her voice rose, and yet he simply shook his head. "I am very close to screaming my head off, Mr.

Kirov,'' she warned in what she considered a very reasonable tone under the circumstances. ''You have insulted me, abused me, yet I am still calm, as you can see. I am not some ninny to fall to pieces under a little adversity. But I am reaching my limit. I am not for sale at any price. A king's ransom wouldn't change that fact. So you might as well release me now.''

''You are stubborn, but it changes nothing. You will stay—no.'' He held up a hand when she opened her mouth. ''I do not recommend screaming. There are two guards outside this door who will immediately come in to quiet you. That would be most uncomfortable for you, and so unnecessary. I will give you a few hours to reconsider.''

Katherine didn't believe him for a moment about the guards until he opened the door to leave and she saw them both standing there, vicious-looking men in identical uniforms; long tunics, baggy pants tucked into high boots, wicked swords hanging from their hips. Incredible. Was the whole household to be a part of this crime? Apparently. Her only hope was still the Prince.

Chapter Five

"*W*hat am I to do, Marusia?" Vladimir asked his wife. "He wants her. She is refusing to share his bed. I have never before met this dilemma."

"So find him another woman," she replied easily, thinking the solution was that simple. "You know what will happen if he is disappointed tonight. There will be no pleasing him the entire voyage home. If his grandmother had not scolded him for his excessive wenching, it would not be so bad. But she warned him away from her maids, and he complied in deference to her. He has had no sexual relief since we docked, an incredibly long time for the Prince to willingly deny himself. He must have a woman tonight before we sail, or we will all suffer for his frustration. It will be ten times worse than on the way here, when that stupid countess changed her mind at the last moment and did not sail with him."

Vladimir knew all of that. His problem was not only that he had never failed the Prince before; it was a matter of guaranteeing a pleasant voyage for them all as opposed to weeks of living with Dimitri in one of his dark moods. Not that the Prince could not remain celibate out of necessity, as he would on the voyage home. But when there was no necessity, as tonight, heaven forbid he should not get what he wanted, for when Dimitri was not happy, no one in his household was happy.

Vladimir poured another shot of vodka and gulped it down. Marusia continued to stuff a goose with *kasha* for Dimitri's dinner tonight. She thought the matter settled. He had told her only that the woman he had procured for the Prince was giving him trouble.

"Marusia, why would a woman—now, this is no lady, but an English peasant, a servant—why would she not be pleased that a prince found her desirable?"

"She must be flattered. No woman alive would not be at least flattered, even if she didn't want to sleep with him. Show her his picture. That will change her mind."

"Yes, I will, but—but I do not think it will make a difference this time. She was not flattered, Marusia. She was insulted. I saw it in her face. I just do not understand. No woman has ever refused him before, virgins, wives, princesses, countesses, even a queen—"

"Which queen? You never told me this!"

"Never mind," he replied sharply. "That is not for gossip, and you, dear wife, love to gossip."

"Well, every man should be refused at least once. It does him good."

"Marusia!"

She laughed delightedly. "I jest, husband. Every man except our prince. Now stop worrying. I told you, go and get him another woman."

Vladimir looked dismally down at his empty glass and filled it again. "I cannot. He did not tell me, 'I want a woman tonight. Find one.' He pointed out this petite wren to me and said, 'That one. Arrange it.' She is not even beautiful, Marusia, except for her eyes. I could find him a dozen women more to his taste before this evening. He wants this one. He has to have this one."

"She must be in love," Marusia said thoughtfully. "That is the only reason a woman of low class would refuse such an honor. No peasant in Russia—"

"This is England," he reminded her. "Perhaps they think differently here."

"We have been here before, Vladimir. You never had this trouble before. I tell you she is in love with someone. But there are drugs that can make her forget, make her memory fuzzy, make her more agreeable—"

"He will think she is drunk," he replied sternly. "That will not please him at all."

"At least he will have her."

"And if it does not work? If she remembers enough to fight him?"

Marusia frowned. "No, that will not do. He would be furious. He does not need to take a woman by force. He would not. They fight each other to throw themselves at him. He can have any woman he wants."

"He wants this one, who does not want him."

She gave him a disgusted look. "You begin to make me worry now. Do you want me to talk to her to see if I can find out what she objects to?"

"You can try," he agreed, willing at this point to do anything.

She nodded. "In the meantime, go and speak to Bulavin. It may be nothing, but he was bragging last week that he knew a way to make a woman beg him to make love to her, any woman. Maybe he has some kind of magic potion." She grinned.

45

"Nonsense," he scoffed.

"You never know," she teased. "The Cossacks have ever lived close to the Turks, and you never hear of those sultans having trouble with their slave girls, and most of them innocent captives."

He dismissed that notion with a wave of his hand and an annoyed scowl, yet he would speak to Bulavin. He was that desperate at the moment.

Katherine couldn't sit still. She walked circles around the room, every few minutes glaring at the huge wardrobe that had been shoved in front of the only window by the two guards. Her small weight couldn't budge it, even empty as it was. She had tried for half an hour to no avail.

It was a fairly large bedroom she was being detained in, a room not in use. Even the large bureau was empty. Pink-and-green wallpaper (the Queen approved of that combination) covered the walls. The furniture was in the Hope design, the rather clumsy style that favored Greek and Egyptian influence in decoration. An expensive green satin spread on the bed. Wealth. Cavendish Square, she was sure. If she could just get out of this room, she could be home in no time—but to what good? Elisabeth, last seen waiting alone on the corner, would have met William by now. *She'll be married before I get home.*

This stupid masquerade, this appalling predicament, all for nothing. Elisabeth married to a fortune-hunting blackguard. That and that alone made Katherine furious with these Russians. That barbarian, that pig-headed idiot who had brought her here—because of him Beth's life was now ruined. No, not him. He had only followed orders. His prince was really the responsible one. Who the devil did he think he was, sending a servant after her for such a salacious reason? What arrogance!

He'll get an earful from me, and then some, Katherine thought. I ought to have him thrown in gaol. I know his name. Dimitri Alexandrov—or would it be Alexandrov Dimitri? Whatever. How many Russian princes can be in London at the moment, Katherine? He won't be hard to find.

The idea was nice to think about, but she wouldn't do it. The scandal would be worse than the crime. That was all she needed: the St. John name dragged through the mud.

"But if Beth isn't home when I get home, and isn't still unmarried, I will do it, by God."

There was a hope, however slim, that Elisabeth was meeting William today only to talk to him, to make plans. She needed to cling to that thought. All would not be lost then, and this would be just an irritating experience that she would do her best to forget.

"I bring you lunch, miss, and another lamp. This room is so dark with the window blocked. You speak French, yes? I speak it very well, because it is the language of our aristos. Some of them, they don't even speak Russian."

This flow of words came as a woman hurried across the room with a heavy tray and dropped it on a low, round table between two chairs. She was half a head taller than Katherine, middle-aged, with brown hair in a tight bun, and kindly blue eyes. She hadn't knocked. One of the guards had opened the door for her and closed it as well.

She straightened the things on the tray. A thin vase holding a single rose had fallen over. Fortunately it contained no water. The lamp she moved to the marble mantel. It was already lit, and the extra light welcome. Then she moved back to the tray and began lifting covers.

"*Katushki*," she explained, revealing a plate of fish balls in a white wine sauce. "I am the cook, so I know you will like it. My name is Marusia."

She wasn't at all what one would expect of a cook, being slightly on the thin side, Katherine thought, as she glanced at the food. There was a little loaf of rye bread next to the *katushki*, a chicory and fruit salad, a piece of cake for dessert, and a bottle of wine. A very appetizing lunch. The *katushki* smelled delicious. And Katherine had missed breakfast. A shame she was too stubborn to eat it.

"Thank you, Marusia, but you can take that away. I won't accept anything in this house, including food."

"It's not good that you don't eat. You are so small." Marusia said this with awe.

"I am small because . . . I am small," Katherine said stiffly. "It has nothing at all to do with food."

"But the Prince, he is so big. See?"

She practically shoved a little picture beneath Katherine's nose, so she couldn't possibly avoid looking at it. The man in the miniature was . . . impossible. No one could really look like that.

Katherine pushed the woman's hand away. "Very amusing. Is this little ruse supposed to make me change my mind? Even if that really were your Prince Alexandrov, my answer would still be no."

"You are married?"

"No."

"You have a lover then that you love very much?"

"Love is for idiots. I am no idiot."

Marusia frowned. "Then tell me, please, why you say no. This is truly my prince." She tapped the picture. "I would not lie, since you will meet him tonight. If anything, this picture does not do him justice. He is a man full of life, energy, and charm. And for all his size, he is gentle with women—"

"Stop it!" Katherine snapped, her control slipping. "My God, you people are incredible. First that brute who abducts me, now you! Can't your prince find his own women? Do you realize how disgusting this is for you to pander for him, as if I were for sale? Well, I am not, and there is no amount of money that can buy my affection."

"If it is the money you object to, you need only consider a man and woman enjoying each other's company. And my master does usually court his own women. There is just no time today. He is at the docks, seeing that everything is in order with the ship. You see, we sail tomorrow for Russia."

"I am delighted to hear it," Katherine said dryly. "The answer is still no."

Vladimir was right. The wench was worse than stubborn. She was impossible. Sweet Mary, she had the disdain of a princess but the stupidity of the lowest serf. No one in their right mind would turn down a night with Dimitri Alexandrov.

There were women who would pay for such a privilege.

"You still have not said why you refuse," Marusia pointed out.

"You people have made a mistake, that's all. I am not the type of woman who would even remotely consider going to bed with a perfect stranger. I am simply not interested."

Marusia let out a string of Russian words as she left the room, shaking her head. In the hall she met her husband, who was waiting expectantly. She hated to disappoint him, but she had no choice.

"It is no use, Vladimir. I think she is either frightened of men or she does not like them. But she will not change her mind. This I can swear to. You might as well let her go and inform Prince Dimitri so he can make other arrangements for tonight."

"No, he will have his first choice," Vladimir said stubbornly, handing her a little string-tied pouch. "Mix some of this in the food for her dinner."

"What is it?"

"Bulavin's magic potion. From what he claims, the Prince will be most pleased."

Chapter Six

The bath was delivered late in the afternoon, or was it early evening already? There was no clock in the room. And the little watch Katherine always carried in her pocket was still in the morning gown she had tossed to Lucy so many hours ago.

She had watched warily as a trio of servants had come and gone. They had carried in the porcelain tub and filled it with steamy water and oil from a small vial, which permeated the room with the scent of roses. No one had asked her if she wanted a bath. She certainly didn't. Not a stitch of clothes was she going to remove in this house.

But now Vladimir Kirov came into the room. He tested the water, smiled. Katherine did her best to ignore him. She sat stiffly in a chair, her fingers sounding an angry tapping on the arms.

He came to stand in front of her, his bearing as commanding as his tone. ''You will bathe.''

Katherine slowly looked up at him, and then in the most condescending way, glanced away again. ''You should have asked before going to all this trouble. I do not bathe in strange houses.''

Vladimir had had enough of her arrogance. ''It was not a request, wench, but an order. You will make use of the bath on your own, or the men outside this room will assist you. While they might enjoy that, I do not think you would find it a pleasant experience."

He was pleased to see how quickly he had regained her attention. Her eyes, large and oval, flared enormously. They were her best feature by far, brilliant in color. Beautifully unique, they dominated her small face, giving her a look of quaint innocence. Could that be what had appealed to Dimitri? But no, he couldn't have noticed the eyes at such a distance.

The unbecoming dress would have to go. Its severe black washed out her coloring, leaving her face a sickly white. The pink tinge suffusing her cheeks at the moment was an improvement, but it wouldn't last. She had good skin, smooth and unblemished, almost translucent, but she could benefit from a little makeup. He would order it if he didn't think she would have to be restrained to have it applied. He wanted no bruises on her body that the Prince would object to.

The soft lighting and the lime green bed sheets would have to be her only enhancements. Vladimir was satisfied he had everything in order. The woman perfumed from her bath, drugged from her dinner soon to arrive, and left vulnerable without her clothing.

"Avail yourself of the water while it is still hot," Vladimir continued with his orders. "I will send in a maid to assist you. Your dinner will arrive shortly, and this time you will eat, or you will be helped to do so. It is not our intention you go hungry while you are here."

"And how much longer must I be here?" Katherine said through her teeth.

"When the Prince leaves you, I will have you taken wherever you wish to go. It would be unusual for him to require your company for more than a few hours.''

It would take only a few minutes for her to upbraid the lecher, Katherine thought furiously, and then she could go. ''When will he come?''

Vladimir shrugged. ''When he is ready to retire for the evening.''

Katherine lowered her eyes as warm color stained her cheeks again. She had heard sex discussed more today than in all her twenty-one years, and all in such a natural, unembarrassed way. These servants of Alexandrov's must do this sort of thing all the time to have no shame whatsoever. It was as if they saw absolutely nothing wrong in kidnapping an innocent woman off the streets to serve up to their master.

''You do realize, don't you, that what you're doing is criminal?'' she asked quietly.

''But such a little offense, for which you will receive recompense.''

Katherine was too stunned to answer, and he was gone before her temper had a chance to explode. They thought they were above the law! No, perhaps not. They simply thought *she* was of the lower classes, and the law favored the gentry here, no doubt in Russia too. As far as they were concerned, abusing her was nothing, for what could she do against a powerful prince? But she hadn't told them they were mistaken. She hadn't told them who she really was and that it was quite a different matter to abduct an earl's daughter.

She supposed she should have made a clean breast of it. But the thought of confessing to such a foolish charade was just too embarrassing. And it wouldn't be necessary to secure her freedom. Showing Alexandrov her antipathy would be enough.

It was a young maid who came in to help her with her bath. Katherine didn't want any help, but the girl obviously spoke only Russian, for she ignored all of Katherine's protestations and chatted away in her own language as she folded each piece of clothing Katherine dropped on the floor in her haste to get her ordeal over. And then the moment she stepped into the tub, the girl walked out of the room with every stitch of Katherine's clothing, including her shoes.

Blast and damn! They thought of everything! And there was nothing in the room, save the bedding, to cover herself with. It was the last straw! She had tried to be calm. She had tried her best to overlook each offense and treat the whole thing as a simple mistake. In the end she would have been civil to the Prince when she explained his servant's highhandedness. But not now. No, by God, now he would suffer her wrath.

Katherine scrubbed herself with a vengeance until every inch of her skin was glowing pink. It was the only way she could immediately let off a little steam. Before she was done, her dinner arrived, delivered by Marusia again.

"I want my clothes back!" Katherine demanded immediately the door opened.

"All in good time," the woman replied calmly.

"I want them now!"

"I must warn you not to raise your voice so, little one. The guards have their orders—"

"To hell with them, and to hell with you! Oh, what's the use?"

Katherine stomped out of the tub, whipped a towel around her, and marched to the bed before they thought of removing even those coverings from the room. The heavy spread was too thick and bulky to do, so she threw it back and yanked off the top sheet, tossing it around her shoulders like a cape. The green satin quickly soaked up the moisture from her skin.

Marusia was more than a little surprised. Such a little bundle of fury, all glistening pink from her bath. Anger made her eyes sparkle, her cheeks bloom, and her body . . . la, such perfection had been hidden beneath that ugly black dress. The Prince would find no fault there.

"You eat now, yes, and then perhaps you have time for a little nap before—"

"Not another word!" Katherine interrupted sharply. "Leave me. I will speak to no one but Alexandrov."

Marusia wisely left. There was nothing left to do anyway except wait and hope that there was some truth to Bulavin's bragging.

Visions of those burly guards holding her down and shoving food down her throat forced Katherine to the table. The fact that she had been experiencing hunger pangs for the last three hours had little to do with it. But the food was delicious: chicken in a creamy sauce, boiled potatoes and carrots, little honey cakes. The white wine was excellent too, but she was really too thirsty to appreciate it, having drunk nothing all day, and had finished off two glasses before the young maid returned with another tray. This one held a pitcher of iced water, too late, since she had already quenched her thirst, as well as a large decanter of brandy and two glasses. It was set by the bed.

So was the time finally approaching when the great prince was going to show himself? Obviously. Good, let him come while she was still at the height of her outrage. But he didn't come soon, and the time continued to drag by as it had all afternoon.

Katherine finished the meal, then began pacing again. But after about a dozen circles around the room, when every moment she expected the door to open on the elusive prince, she felt her skin begin to tingle where the satin rubbed against it. Nerves. Imagine that! She, who was always steady as a rock, experiencing nerves.

She stopped beside the brandy and poured herself a glass. The great fortifier, brandy. She gulped it down, unwisely, but there was no time to waste. He would be here any minute, and she needed to relax, to be in control. She sat down, willing herself to calmness. Her method didn't work. The tingling continued, in fact was getting worse.

Katherine leaped up and poured another brandy. This one she sipped. She wasn't foolish enough to get drunk over a case of nerves. She began to walk again, but the satin, the blasted satin sheet, was so irritating where it brushed against her legs. And yet she couldn't throw it off, as she had the urge to do. It was her only claim to modesty.

She stopped in the middle of the room, standing perfectly still. That didn't work either. It was as if every nerve in her body screamed with energy, urging her to move, to do. Standing still was impossible.

She began to fidget, to stretch—God, she had never in her life felt such restlessness. And then there was something else. She thought she could actually feel the blood rushing through her veins. Impossible, and yet she felt so strange and— warm.

The door opened, but it was only the young maid, come to take the dinner tray away. No point in talking to her when the girl couldn't reply in anything but Russian. God, she needed another drink. She went to pour another one as soon as the girl left, but stopped herself. She didn't dare. She already felt a little light-headed, when she definitely needed to keep her wits about her.

She sat down on the bed, then heard herself groan. Her eyes flared wide at the sound. What was wrong with her? It had to be the blasted sheet. She had to get rid of it, if only for a few moments.

Katherine let the sheet fall, then shivered as it slid down her arms and back to pool around her hips. Reflexively she crossed her arms over her bare breasts, then felt a shock clear down to her toes. She gasped. Her breasts had never been so sensitive. But the shock had been pleasurable. She had never felt that before either.

When she looked down at herself, she was amazed to see her skin flushed to match the warmth she was feeling. And her nipples were hard little nubs, tingling, the tingling was everywhere. She rubbed her arms, then groaned again. Her skin was sensitive everywhere too. Something was definitely wrong. She hurt, no, not hurt—she didn't know what it was, but it was rushing through her in waves and culminating in her groin.

Unconsciously Katherine fell back on the bed, squirming restlessly. She was sick. She must be sick. The food. And then she realized, suddenly, horribly, that something must have been put in the food.

"Oh, God, what have they done to me?"

But they couldn't have wanted her to be sick. She must be having a bad reaction to whatever drug they had given her. It was almost funny. For her to be consumed with fever certainly couldn't be the effect they wanted to produce. But what else could be making her so hot and so furiously restless, so much so that she couldn't seem to control the movements of her own body?

She curled up on the bed in a moment of frightful despair. The sheet was cool against her burning skin. She stretched out on her stomach, and for a few blessed moments she felt some relief. A pleasant lassitude enveloped her, and she started to hope the crisis was over—but it didn't last. She could feel hot surges of sensation beginning again, building in strength, and an insistent throbbing in her groin, an ache. *Oh, God!*

She twisted over onto her back in the middle of the bed, her arms thrown out at her sides. Her head tossed back and forth, her breath came in little gasps. She was losing control completely, her body arching, twisting, thrusting, and she didn't even realize she was doing it. She had no conception of time. Her nudity, the situation she was in, all were forgotten in the raging fever consuming her.

Twenty minutes later, when Prince Alexandrov entered the room, Katherine was beyond thinking about anything except the burning heat in her body. She didn't hear him come in. She didn't know he stood watching her, dark, velvet eyes fascinated by her every movement.

Dimitri had been arrested by the erotic picture she presented. Her body, undulating and arching, gyrating on the bed, seemed in the throes of sexual passion. He had always been aware of these motions in his more passionate bed partners, had felt such movements under him, delighted in them, but never had he observed them from a distance. The scene was immediately effective. He could feel his manhood springing to life beneath the loose robe that was all he wore.

What *had* this little English rose been doing to herself to bring about this feverish pitch of excitement? What a surprise she was! And here he had been regretting all evening the impulse that had sent Vladimir after her. After all, there was really nothing about her to arouse his passion. So he had thought until now.

When Katherine finally became aware of his presence, he was standing at the foot of the bed, leaning casually against the bedpost.

That picture . . . Adonis come to life. Impossible. He couldn't be real—she was delirious. But no, this was flesh and blood.

"Help me. I—I need—" Her throat was so parched from the heat that she could barely get the words out. She ran her tongue slowly over her lips. "A doctor."

Dimitri's half-smile turned to a frown. He had been shocked when he finally looked into her eyes. Another surprise. Such color, and smoldering with passion. He had been so certain she had meant to say she needed him. A doctor!

"You are—ill?"

"Yes . . . a fever. I'm so hot."

His frown turned into a black scowl. Sick! Damnation! And after she had made him want her.

Unreasonable anger shot through him. He started for the door. He would have Vladimir's head for this. Her voice stopped him.

"Please . . . water."

The pathetic plea stirred his compassion for some reason. Ordinarily he would have left her in the care of his servants. But he was at hand, and to give her water would take only a moment. It wasn't her fault that she was ill. Vladimir should have informed him before he had come to her. She should have been taken to a doctor immediately.

He didn't consider the possibility of contagion and that getting near her might postpone his sailing tomorrow. He poured the water and lifted her head to bring the glass to her lips. She took a few sips, and her cheek turned toward his wrist and rubbed against it. Then her whole body turned toward him, as if drawn by the contact.

He let go of her, but she groaned at the loss of his cool skin. "No . . . so hot . . . please."

She was trembling. With cold? he wondered. Her cheek hadn't been hot. He put his hand to her forehead; it was cool. Yet she acted as though she was burning with fever. What kind of sickness was this? And damned if he still didn't want her!

His anger returned and he slammed out of the room, bellowing for Vladimir. The servant appeared instantly.

"My prince?"

Dimitri had never struck a servant in anger. To do so would have been the height of unfairness, because his servants belonged to him. They could not retaliate, could not leave his employ, could do nothing to protect themselves. But his present frustration nearly made him lose sight of all that.

"Damn you, Vladimir, the woman is sick! How could you not know it?"

Vladimir had anticipated this, had known he would have to explain. But better now that the dose had taken effect than earlier, when he would have had to admit to failure.

"She is not sick," he said quickly. "She was given cantharides in her food."

Dimitri stepped back in amazement. Why had he not realized himself what ailed the woman? He had seen a woman given that powerful aphrodisiac before, during the year he had spent in the Caucasus. She had been insatiable. Fifteen soldiers hadn't been enough to satisfy her. She still demanded more, and the effect had lasted for hours.

Dimitri was disgusted, knowing that he alone wouldn't be able to take care of the woman, that he would probably have to call his guards to help relieve her suffering, and suffering it was. She was burning to have a man between her legs, aching with need. But despite his disgust, his manhood throbbed in anticipation. She wasn't sick. He would have her, and she would beg for more. A unique situation that produced all manner of pleasurable thoughts.

"Why, Vladimir? I was looking forward to a relaxing evening, not a sexual marathon."

The crisis had passed. Vladimir could see that the Prince had accepted the idea, even if it

61

wasn't what he had had in mind. And he would be well pleased in the end. That was all that mattered.

"She was difficult to persuade, my lord. She could not be bought and insisted she did not bed strangers."

"You mean she actually refused me?" Dimitri was amused at the thought. "Didn't you tell her who I was?"

"Of course. But these English peasants have a high opinion of themselves. I think the wench wanted to be wooed first. I explained there was no time for that, not that you need to exert yourself for someone like her," he added, with a touch of disdain. "Forgive me, Prince Dimitri, but I could think of nothing else to do."

"How much of the drug did you give her?"

"We were not sure how much to use."

"So it could last for hours or all night?"

"For however long you wish to amuse yourself, my lord" was the simple reply.

Dimitri grunted and waved Vladimir away. He reentered the room, rather surprised at how eager he was to see the woman again. She was still thrashing about on the bed and moaning quite audibly now. When he sat down beside her, her eyes turned to him. She quieted a bit, but she couldn't still her body.

"A doctor?"

"No, little dove, a doctor can't help what ails you, I'm afraid."

"I'm dying, then?"

He smiled gently. She really didn't know what was happening to her, or that there was only one cure that would give her relief. But he would be happy to show her.

He leaned over and softly brushed his lips against hers. Her eyes opened wide in surprise. Dimitri couldn't help laughing. Such a combination of innocence and sexual allure. He found her delightful.

"You didn't like that?"

"No, I . . . oh, what is wrong with me?"

"My man took it upon himself to overcome your shyness with an aphrodisiac. Do you know what that is?"

"No, but it . . . it's made me sick."

"Not sick, little one. It's doing exactly what it's supposed to do—arouse your sexual desire to an unbearable degree."

It took her a moment to accept that she hadn't mistaken his meaning before she cried, "Nooo!"

"Shh," Dimitri soothed, cupping her cheek in his hand. Her face immediately turned into his palm again. "I would not wish this on any woman, but it is done, and I can help you if you will allow it."

"How?"

She was wary of him. He could see the mistrust in her eyes. Vladimir was right. She really wanted no part of him. If not for the drug, he would have failed with her, just as that lout on the street had failed. How intriguing. Even if he were to put all his considerable charm to use, he had the feeling it would avail him nothing. What a challenge! If only there were more time . . .

But there was the drug. The cantharides would deliver up what human efforts could not. He would have her. And his vanity was pricked enough to take full advantage of the situation and humble this little English flower.

Dimitri didn't answer her question. He continued to caress her cheek, which was flushed a delicate rose, like the rest of her lovely body.

"What is your name, sweet?"

"Kit—no, Kate—I mean, it's Katherine."

"So, Kit and Kate for Katherine." He smiled. "An imperial name. You have heard of our Catherine, Empress of all the Russias?"

"Yes."

"And have you no last name?"

She turned her face away. "No."

"A secret?" He chuckled. "Ah, little Katya, I knew you would amuse me. But it is no matter, last names. We will be much too intimate for them anyway." As he spoke, his free hand dropped to her breast. Her cry was sharp and agonized. "Too sensitive, sweet? You need immediate relief, don't you?" He moved the hand to the dark triangle of brown curls between her legs.

"Don't! Oh, no, you mustn't!" But even as she protested, her hips thrust up against his fingers.

"It is the only way, Katya," his deep voice assured her. "You just don't realize it yet."

Katherine moaned as the throbbing accelerated with his touch. Her mind balked at what he was doing with his fingers, but she was powerless to stop him, just as she had been powerless to cover herself when he first appeared. She needed the coolness of his soothing hands. She needed . . .

"Oh, oh, God!" she screamed as pleasure erupted in shuddering, pulsating waves that went on and on, flooding her senses, washing away the unbearable heat.

Katherine floated down into a sea of blissful lassitude. The tension had all drained away, leaving her sated and infinitely relaxed.

"You see, Katya?" His voice robbed her peace. "It was the only way."

Katherine's eyes flew open. She had forgotten about him. How could she forget? It was he who had brought her relief from that molten heat. Oh, God, what had she let him do? He was sitting there watching her, and she was naked!

She half sat up, looking about frantically for the top sheet, but it had long ago slid to the floor beyond reach. She started after the cover at the foot of the bed, but he anticipated her intention and his arm shot across her stomach, keeping her in place beside him.

"You expend useless energy, when you have only a few minutes of respite. It will all begin again, little one. Conserve your strength and relax while you are able."

"You're lying!" Katherine said in horror. "It— it can't start again. Oh, please, let me go! You have no right to keep me here!"

"You are free to leave," he said magnanimously, though he was quite sure she would never get off the bed. "No one is stopping you."

"They did!" She remembered her anger. It swelled and exploded. "That—that barbarian Kirov abducted me and has kept me a prisoner in this room all day!"

She was adorable in her fury. Dimitri felt an overwhelming desire to kiss her blended with a desire to take her in his arms. She was potent, this surprising little gem, and he was on fire to have her after watching her reach her climax. But he must be patient. He didn't have to take from her what she would willingly give soon enough.

"I'm sorry, Katya. My people sometimes exceed what is reasonable in their efforts to please me. What can I do to make amends?"

"Just—just—oh, no, no!"

The fever was starting, the warmth flowing through her veins, swiftly getting hotter. She looked at him for a moment in abject misery before turning away with a groan. The ache had returned so swiftly. He hadn't lied. And now she knew what she needed, what her body was craving. Morals, shame, pride, all slid away like rain down a gutter.

"Please!" She squirmed, seeking those velvety eyes of his again. "Help me!"

"How, Katya?"

"Touch me . . . like before."

"I cannot."

"Oh, please—"

"Listen to me." He caught her face between his hands to hold it still. "You know what must be."

"I don't understand. You said you would help! Why won't you help me?"

She couldn't be that naive, could she? "I will, but you must help me as well. I need relief too, little one. Look at me."

He opened his robe. He was naked beneath it, and Katherine sucked in her breath, seeing his manhood thrust boldly forward. Understanding dawned, and with it hot color flooded her cheeks crimson.

"No . . . you can't," she whispered brokenly.

"I must. It is what you really need, Katya, me inside you. I am here for you. Use me!"

This was the closest Dimitri had ever come to pleading with a woman. That he did so now proved the extent of his desire—he couldn't remember ever wanting a woman this much. And it was so unnecessary for him to argue with her at all. She couldn't resist for long. The drug wouldn't allow it.

He said no more, waiting, not touching, watching her welter in an agony of need. Watching her needless suffering was almost painful. She had only to ask, and relief would be hers. But she was resisting the drug and resisting the cure. Was it pride? Could she be that foolish?

Dimitri almost took matters into his own hands—her protests be damned—when she turned to him, her eyes beseeching, lips parted enticingly, hair all bedraggled, and flesh quivering. God, she was beautiful like this, so incredibly sensual.

"I can't bear it anymore. Alexandrov, do what you will, please, anything—just do it now."

Dimitri smiled with amazement. The little wench had managed to turn a plea into an order. But it was a command he was quite willing to obey.

Shaking off his robe, he stretched out on the bed next to her and drew her close. She sighed at the cool contact of his flesh, but the sigh quickly turned to a whimper. She had waited too long. Her skin was too sensitive again, everywhere, but especially her breasts. Damn. He wanted to feel her exquisite body under his hands. He would have to wait.

"Next time, Katya, don't wait so long." His voice was sharp with frustration.

Her eyes rounded. "Next time?"

"This will last for hours, but there is no need for you to suffer through any of it. Do you understand? Don't deny me again."

"No—I won't—only please, Alexandrov, hurry!"

He smiled. No woman had ever called him Alexandrov, at least not in bed. "Dimitri," he corrected. "Or Your Highness." He chuckled. She beat her tiny fists against him. "All right, little one. Easy. Relax."

He could wait no longer. Her hips were thrusting wildly against him, firing his passion to an alarming height. He rolled on top of her, resting on his elbows, his long upper arms keeping the massive width of his chest well above her. He bent to taste the sweetness of her parted lips, and they were sweet, distracting, but the gyrations of her lower body would not let him forget the matter at hand.

He released her lips to move into position, cupping her face between his large hands. He wanted to watch again as she received her pleasure, to see ecstasy reflected in her eyes. He thrust deep—and she screamed. But it was too late. Her maidenhead was breached.

"Sweet Jesus!" Dimitri hissed. "Why didn't you tell me, woman?"

She didn't answer. She had closed her eyes, and a single tear slid from the corner of one. Dimitri swore silently. She was no blushing girl, but a woman! What the devil was she still doing with her virginity intact? It was not something usually valued by servants. Only the nobility used it as a commodity when arranging important marriages.

"How old are you, Katherine?" he asked gently now, brushing the moisture away from her eyes.

"Twenty-one," she murmured.

"And you managed to stay a maiden that long? Incredible. You must work in a household sorely lacking in men."

"Mmmm."

Dimitri laughed. She wasn't listening anymore, but was availing herself of the hard shaft embedded deep within her, undulating provocatively, drawing him in even more—exquisite. He groaned, gritting his teeth, letting her have her way as long as possible, but it didn't take long before she soared over the edge. And although he would have prolonged his own pleasure, the throbbing pulsations he felt within her were his undoing. He joined in her climax, grinding his hips fiercely against her and hearing her cry out as she exploded yet again.

With his heart still pounding erratically, Dimitri moved to sit on the side of the bed and poured himself a brandy. He offered one to Katherine, but she shook her head without looking at him. He would have to wash the stains of her virginity from her, but he would wait until she would better appreciate it. He smiled, contemplating that. Already he was anticipating bringing her to another climax.

He moved back, sitting sideways, resting one arm on the other side of her hip. She still wouldn't look at him until he brought the cool, round base of the brandy goblet to play across one pointed nipple. He chuckled, delighting in the way her eyes flared.

"You will have to appease me, Katya. I like to play with my women."

"I'm not one of your women."

The rancor in her tone made it a pleasure to insist. "But you are—for tonight."

He bent forward and flicked her other nipple with the tip of his tongue. Katherine jerked in response and then groaned when he took her breast fully into his mouth. Instinctively her hands moved into his hair to pull him away. He responded to this resistance by closing his teeth gently on her nipple until she gave in and allowed him his way. But soon she was ready for him again.

Dimitri left the bed to retrieve the washcloth from her bath, dipping it in the cold water. When he returned to her, he applied it to her body first, waiting until her inner heat was near raging, then he doused the cloth with ice water from the pitcher and pressed it between her legs.

Katherine went wild with the combined pleasure of icy cold to quench the heat and stimulation where she most needed it. She came almost instantly and continued on and on until he was finally done cleaning her.

He left her once again to wash himself and when he came back, he settled himself between her legs to suckle at her breasts. She didn't have the will to protest. She needed him. That had been proved beyond a doubt. If he insisted on "playing" with her between each crisis, that was her cross to bear. But she actually derived pleasure from that too, so how could she complain?

Katherine reached another peak by grinding herself against his pelvis while he continued to caress her breasts. And then he used his fingers again, while his tongue explored every inch of her mouth. The double stimulation each time added to her pleasure, magnifying the intensity to an almost unbearable pitch. Yet nothing was as completely satisfying as when he finally used his body, the deep penetration fulfilling a baser need, leaving a blessed contentment.

And so it went throughout the night. What he said proved true. She didn't suffer again. As long as she obeyed his every command, he was there to soothe and relieve and give her hour after hour of the most incredible ecstasy, with his hands, his mouth, his body. All he asked in return was that she allow him to play with her, to caress her as he would. She was sure that he now knew every inch of her body intimately. But she didn't care. This night wasn't real. It had no basis in reality. It would dissolve like the drug, to be forgotten come morning.

Chapter Seven

"*V*ladimir, wake up. Vladimir!" Marusia shook his shoulder roughly until he finally opened one bleary eye. "It's time. Lida heard him moving about in his room. You had best see about sending the poor girl on her way."

"Poor girl? After what she put me through?"

"Yes, but what did we put her through? Look outside, husband. It is dawn."

He squinted at the window, and sure enough, the sky was tinted violet. He came instantly full awake and threw off the light spread Marusia had covered him with before she had gone down to the kitchen to light the fires. He was still dressed in yesterday's clothes. He had stayed up half the night waiting for the Prince to leave the woman's room. He had not meant to fall asleep at all, only to rest on the bed a few moments.

"He is probably just rising early," Vladimir said. "You know he needs little sleep. He can't have stayed the whole night with her."

"Whether he did or didn't, Lida says he is awake, and you had best get the woman out of the house before he leaves his room. You know he doesn't like to encounter these casual women of his after he is done with them."

He gave her a look that said "You don't have to tell *me* that" before he swept up a bundle of clothes and started up the stairs to the third floor. The hallway was empty. The guards had been dismissed last evening before Dimitri arrived. It had been imperative then that he not suspect anything until after he had seen the woman. Now if the unguarded wench had managed to vacate the premises on her own, Vladimir wouldn't find it amiss, even though he owed her something for her trouble.

Quietly he opened the door. There was a chance that Lida had been mistaken and had only heard Dimitri's valet moving about in his room. Yet the odds against finding the Prince still here were so likely that Vladimir chided himself for being this careful. And the room was empty, save for the woman. *She* was still there, sound asleep under the satin cover.

Dropping her clothes on a chair, he crossed to the bed and shook her.

"No more," she groaned.

Vladimir felt a momentary twinge of pity. She had been well and truly used. The odor of the night was overpowering in the enclosed room. In fact, that was the first order of business: letting in some fresh air.

He shoved the heavy wardrobe away from the window, panting with the effort, then welcomed the early-morning breeze that wafted in.

"Thank you, Vladimir," the Prince said from behind him. "I was dreading the thought of putting my shoulder to that clumsy thing."

"My lord!" Vladimir swung around. "Forgive me. I was just going to wake her and—"

"Don't."

"But—"

"Let her sleep. She needs it. And I have an urge to see what she's like when she has her wits about her."

"I . . . don't recommend it," Vladimir said hesitantly. "She's not a very pleasant young woman."

"Isn't she? Now I find that fascinating, considering how pleasant she has been all evening. In fact I can't remember when I last enjoyed myself so."

Vladimir relaxed. The Prince wasn't fencing with words, as he sometimes did in his sardonic way, but was truly well pleased. The gamble had paid off. Now if they could only sail without any mishap to disturb this good mood. But the woman—no, surely Dimitri had charmed her and she wouldn't be disagreeable this morning.

Dimitri turned toward the bed, where just a slim arm and a pale cheek were visible on the pillow, her abundant brown locks in utter disarray hiding everything else. He had been compelled to come back to this room. He had meant to bathe and get a few hours' sleep before the hectic preparations for departure began. The bath he had had, but he had been unable to dismiss the woman from his thoughts.

He had spoken the truth to Vladimir. He didn't think he had ever spent such an unusual and yet delightful evening. By rights he should have been as exhausted as the woman was. But then he had paced himself, held back his own pleasure, deliberately conserving his strength by satisfying her in other ways. The thought of having to summon a few of his men to take over if he should grow weary had disgusted him. And then too, he simply hadn't wanted to share this treasure.

It was incredible, but he had actually been disappointed when she had finally succumbed to sleep. He still wasn't tired, was in fact feeling quite vigorous.

"Did you know she was a virgin, Vladimir?"

"No, my lord. Did it matter?"

"I think to her it did. How much were you going to pay her?"

Considering this new information, Vladimir doubled the figure he had in mind. "A hundred English pounds."

Dimitri looked sideways at him. "Make it a thousand—no, two thousand. I want her to be able to splurge on some pretty clothes. That rag she was wearing was atrocious. In fact, have we nothing more suitable she can wear when she wakes?"

Vladimir shouldn't really have been surprised. The Prince's generosity was renowned. And yet this woman was no more than a simple English peasant.

"Most of the servants' belongings were taken to the ship yesterday, my lord."

"And I don't suppose Anastasia would agree to give up one of her dresses? No, of course she wouldn't. She was in a pout all evening because I wouldn't let her carouse in London last night. I think right now she would relish any reason to spite me."

Vladimir hesitated, but if it was Dimitri's wish to clothe the wench in finery . . . no, he couldn't bring himself to mention that Countess Rothkovna's clothes had sailed from Russia with them even if she hadn't. Dimitri might appreciate the subtle revenge of giving away *all* of the Countess's things, since he was undoubtedly through with her after the way she had disappointed him, but Vladimir just couldn't bring himself to gift this thoroughly disagreeable peasant with such an expensive wardrobe. A more becoming dress was one thing, an exceedingly costly one quite another.

"I will send one of the women to obtain something suitable once the shops open," Vladimir suggested, but added, "if you think she will be here that long."

"No, don't bother. It was just a thought, and the pleasure of ordering that rag thrown away." Dimitri waved his hand in dismissal. "I'll call you when she is ready to leave."

So he was staying in this room with her? His interest was still that piqued? Vladimir hesitated again. He had never put his wishes before the master's, as he had just done. Yet he did not have to appease the Prince. Dimitri was still in an excellent mood. But Vladimir disliked the woman too much after all the frustration and anxiety she had caused with her stubbornness, even if she had pleased Dimitri in the end. She was being given much too much, in his opinion, as it was. She wouldn't get any extras thrown in if he could help it.

"As you wish, my lord."

Vladimir left, closing the door softly, and went down to tell Marusia about this latest quirk of the Prince's. But she would probably be amused and remind him that Dimitri's father had also been fascinated by an Englishwoman, enough to marry her. Thank God *this* English wench was not royalty, as the Lady Anne had been.

In the room, Dimitri turned off the lamps that had burned all night, then stretched out on the bed he had left only a few hours ago. Katherine lay on her stomach, her face turned toward him. He brushed the hair back from her cheek for a better view. She didn't stir.

In sleep, the severe lines of her face were softened, just as they had been in her passion. Dimitri couldn't forget that passion. Of course it was the drug that had produced it, not him—which was why he wanted her one more time, without the drug controlling her. In part he felt a challenge, a desire to see if he could stimulate the same heights of feeling in her. But perversely, he also felt a need to prove that in reality she could not possibly be as sexy and incredibly sensual as she had been under the influence of the cantharides.

At the moment, however, she needed a few more hours' sleep to replenish her strength. Having to wait was inconvenient. Patience was not one of his better qualities. But he had nothing else to do this morning before he sailed.

Chapter Eight

As the sun rose higher, the activity in the house increased, for the Prince liked to leave a place as he found it. The Duke of Albemarle's servants, dismissed yesterday because the Prince liked only his own staff around him, would find nothing amiss when they returned later that day. But in the room on the third floor, all was still quiet.

Vladimir, waiting patiently at the end of the hall to be summoned, assumed Dimitri had fallen asleep. Three hours more he had spent with the woman. He must be asleep. But there was still time before they were due at the docks. He would wait awhile yet before disturbing him.

Dimitri was quite awake, still not the least bit tired. He had surprised himself by his patience, for the morning was moving by at a devilishly slow rate. And he had managed to keep his hands off of Katherine until now. But at last he drew her into his arms and began to caress her awake. She fought against him peevishly.

"Not now, Lucy! Do go away!"

Dimitri smiled, wondering only vaguely who Lucy might be. Katherine had spoken French to him last night because he had first addressed her in French, and she spoke it superbly. But English suited her much better, and the commanding tone she affected was rather amusing. Still, English was not the language he preferred, so he didn't bother using it.

"Come, Katya, join me," he coaxed her, his fingers playing with the silky skin of her shoulder. "I grow bored waiting for you to wake."

Her eyes opened on a level with his, their noses nearly touching. She blinked once, but couldn't seem to focus clearly. There was no sign of recognition, none of surprise, either, or even of confusion. It was as if she didn't even see him. But she did. She moved back slowly until she was at arm's length. All the while her eyes were moving over him, clear down to his toes, then back up again, in a way that was quite unnerving, for Dimitri had the distinct impression that she found him wanting.

Katherine was in fact having difficulty accepting that he was real. Adonis again, had been her first annoying thought. The fairy-tale prince. Her practical eye truly doubted what she was seeing, for reality didn't create men like this.

"Do you disappear at the stroke of midnight?"

Dimitri burst into delighted laughter. "If you say you have forgotten me so soon, little one, I will be pleased to refresh your memory."

Katherine flushed with flaming color from the roots of her hair to the cover, which she gripped tightly to her breasts as she sat up. She remembered.

"Oh, God!" she moaned, only to demand quickly, "Why are you still here? You could have at least had the decency to let me deal with my shame alone!"

"But why should you be ashamed at all? You have done nothing wrong."

"Well I know it," she agreed bitterly. "The wrong was done to me. And you—oh, God, just go away!"

Her hands slid over her face to cover her eyes. Her shoulders were bent dejectedly. Fretfully she rocked back and forth, giving Dimitri a tantalizing view of her smooth back and a small portion of her derriere.

"You aren't crying, are you?" he asked casually.

Katherine stilled, but didn't lower her hands, so that her voice came out in a mumble. "I don't cry, and why aren't you leaving?"

"Is that why you're hiding, waiting for me to leave? If it is, you may as well give up. I'm staying right here."

Her hands fell away to reveal eyes narrowed and sparkling with rancor. "Then I'll leave!"

And she started to do so, only the cover she attempted to drag with her wouldn't budge. Dimitri was stretched out on top of it and made no effort to move.

Katherine twisted back to face him. "Get up!"

"No," he said simply, crossing his arms at the back of his neck in a thoroughly relaxed manner.

"Playtime is over, Alexandrov," Katherine warned in a frigid tone. "What the devil do you mean, no?"

"Katya, please, I thought we had dispensed with formality," he chided gently.

"Must I remind you we haven't been introduced?"

"So proper? Very well." He sighed. "Dimitri Petrovich Alexandrov."

"You forget your title," she sneered disdainfully. "Prince, isn't it?"

A single dark brow rose questioningly. "That displeases you?"

"It doesn't matter in the least to me one way or another. Now I would appreciate some privacy so I can dress and leave this place, if you don't mind."

"But what is your hurry? I have ample time—"

"I don't! Good Lord, I have been kept here all night. My father will be frantic with worry!"

"A simple matter. I will send someone to let him know you are safe, if you'll just give me the address."

"Oh, no. I'm not about to give you the means to find me again. When I leave here, it will be the very last you will see of me."

He wished she hadn't said that. It struck a chord of regret in him that was wholly unexpected. He realized that if he had the time, he would delight in getting to know this young woman better. She was so totally refreshing, the first woman he had ever encountered who seemed genuinely unimpressed by his title, wealth, and charm. And not to overstate the case, he knew he appealed to women physically. Yet the little dove couldn't wait to fly the coop.

Impulsively Dimitri rolled to face her and asked, "Would you like to visit Russia?"

She snorted. "*That* doesn't deserve an answer."

"Careful, Katya, or I will begin to think you don't like me."

"I don't know you!"

"You know me very well."

"Being acquainted with your body is not knowing you. I know your name and that you're leaving England today. That is the most I know about you—no, I take that back. I also know that

81

your servants go to criminal lengths to please you!''

''Ah, now we come to the heart of the matter. You object to the manner of our first meeting. That is reasonable. You had little choice in the matter. But, Katherine, neither did I. Well, that is not exactly true. I did have a choice. I could have left you alone to suffer.''

She glared at him for that pointed reminder. ''If you expect me to thank you for your assistance last night, I must disappoint you. I'm not stupid. I know exactly why I was given that foul drug. It was for your benefit, because I had refused to go along with your plans for the evening. And that reminds me: I want your man brought before a magistrate. He's not getting away with this.''

''Come now, no harm was really done. True, you are no longer a maiden, but that is a matter to rejoice in, not bemoan.''

If it hadn't been such a horrid situation and she the victim, Katherine might have laughed at such an absurdity, for she had no doubt he was sincere. He actually believed she had suffered no great loss, which stated clearly the extent of his libertinism. But to treat that as she would have liked would only confound him, considering who he thought she was, or rather, what she was. And yet she had the feeling that his opinion would be no different if he knew the truth.

She had to willfully control her temper. ''You conveniently overlook the fact that I was kidnapped, literally dragged off the street, tossed into a carriage, gagged, and then secreted in this house, where I was detained all day in this room. I was abused, threatened—''

"Threatened?" Dimitri frowned.

"Yes, threatened. I was quite ready to scream my head off and was told the guards posted outside my door would not hesitate to restrain me if I did so. I was likewise warned force would be used if I didn't bathe or eat."

"Trifles." Dimitri waved a hand dismissively. "You weren't actually hurt, were you?"

"That is beside the point! Kirov had no right to bring me here or keep me here all against my will!"

"You are objecting too much at this point, little one, considering in the end you enjoyed yourself. Let the matter go. To make a fuss now will avail you nothing. And Vladimir has been instructed to deal with you generously now."

"Money again?" she asked in a deceptively soft tone.

"Of course. I pay for my pleasure—"

"Oh, God!" she shrieked furiously. "How many times must I say it? I was not, am not, nor will I ever be for sale!"

"You would refuse two thousand pounds?"

If he thought the extent of his generosity would effect an immediate about-face in her, he was quickly disabused of that notion. "I not only refuse it, I would be happy to tell you what you can do with it."

"Please don't," he said distastefully.

"Nor can you buy my silence, so don't bother insulting me further."

"Silence?"

"Good Lord, haven't you been listening?"

"To every word," he assured her, smiling. "Now, can't we dispense with this? Come, Katya."

She drew back, alarmed, when he reached for her. "Don't! Please!"

The beseeching note in her voice infuriated her, but she couldn't help it. After last night she was terrified of her own reaction should he touch her. She had never met a man as handsome as he. There was something almost hypnotizing about his beauty. That he had wanted her, that he had made love to her all night, was astonishing. It took a concerted effort to concentrate, to protect herself with her well-founded anger, and not just simply stare at him.

Instead of being annoyed by her response, Dimitri was rather pleased. He was too familiar with women being unable to resist him to mistake her present dilemma. He should press his advantage now, but he hesitated. As much as he still wanted her, she was too agitated at the moment and not likely to calm down any time soon.

He dropped his hand with a sigh. "Very well, little one. I had hoped—never mind." He sat up on his side of the bed, but glanced over his shoulder at her, his beguiling grin devastating. "You are sure?"

Katherine groaned inwardly. She would have liked to pretend ignorance of what he was intimating, but she couldn't. His look was explanatory in itself. Good Lord, how could he possibly still want to make love after the excesses of the night?

"Quite sure," Katherine answered, praying that *now* he would leave.

He stood up, but not to leave yet. He walked over to the chair where her clothes lay, and came back to the foot of the bed, handing them to her.

"You should accept the money, Katya, whether you want it or not."

She was staring distastefully at the black dress. He was staring at the petticoats, noting that she did have better taste, at least in underclothes.

He added gently, "If I offended you by offering too much, it was only with the thought that you might like to improve your wardrobe. It was intended as a gift, no more."

Her eyes rose and rose until they met his. Why hadn't she noted how incredibly tall he was last night?

"I can't accept gifts from you either."

"Why?"

"Because I can't, that's all."

He was finally annoyed. She was impossible! Who was she to refuse his generosity?

"You *will* accept, miss, and I will hear no more about it," he stated imperiously. "Now I will send a maid to assist you, and then Vladimir will take you—"

"Don't you dare send that brute in here again," she cut him off sharply. "You see, you haven't listened to me at all. I told you I'm having Kirov arrested."

"I regret that I cannot appease your wounded sensibilities by allowing that, my dear. I won't leave my man behind."

"You will have no choice, just as I had no choice." How it delighted her to be able to say *that*.

His smile was condescending. "You forget we sail today."

"Your ship can be detained," she retorted.

His lips tightened ominously. "So can you be, until it is too late for you to cause any trouble."

"Go right ahead," she said rashly. "But you underestimate me if you think that will be the end of it."

Dimitri refused to quibble any longer. He was amazed he had stayed to argue this long. What could she do anyway? The English authorities would not dare to detain him on the word of a mere servant. The idea was laughable.

With a curt nod, Dimitri left the room. But halfway down the hall he stopped short. He was forgetting this was not Russia. Russian laws were made for the aristocracy. English laws took commoners' welfare into account. Public opinion was not discounted here. The wench could in fact create a public hue and cry that might well reach the ears of the Queen.

That was all Dimitri needed, with the Tzar to arrive soon in England. Public sentiment here was already decidedly anti-Russian. Tzar Alexander the English had loved because of Napoleon's defeat at his hands, but his much younger brother Nicholas, who had succeeded him, was considered a meddler who wouldn't leave well enough alone, always concerning himself with the problems of other countries. That was true enough, but beside the point. Dimitri was in England now because he hadn't wanted Anastasia's outrageous behavior to be an embarrassment to their emperor.

"Does she leave now, Prince Dimitri?"

"What?" He glanced up to see Vladimir standing before him. "No, I'm afraid not. You were right, my friend. She is a most unpleasant young woman, and she has created a bit of a problem with her unreasonableness."

"My lord?"

Dimitri suddenly laughed. "She wants to see you rot in some English prison."

Vladimir's lack of concern over this news spoke well for Dimitri's ability to look after his own people. "The problem?"

"I don't think she means to give it up, even after we are gone."

"But the Tzar's visit—"

"Precisely. It wouldn't matter, except for that. So what do you think, Vladimir? Any suggestions?"

Vladimir had one in particular, but he knew Dimitri wouldn't approve of doing away with the troublesome wench. "Can she not be persuaded—" At Dimitri's raised brow, he groaned inwardly. "No, I didn't think so. I suppose she will have to be detained."

"My thought as well," Dimitri replied, and then perversely he smiled, as if the solution suddenly pleased him. "Yes, I'm afraid we'll have to keep her with us, for a few months anyway. She can be sent back here on one of my ships before the Neva freezes up again."

Vladimir gritted his teeth in vexation. Months of having to deal with that infuriating woman was not what he had had in mind. Someone could be found here to keep her confined. They didn't *have* to take her with them. But for Dimitri not even to consider that meant he was obviously not finished with her. What *did* he find so fascinating about this particular wench?

He supposed he needn't ask in what capacity she was to be kept, but he couldn't afford any more mistakes. "Her status, my lord?"

"Servant, of course. I see no reason to waste her talents, whatever they may be. That can be ascertained later. For now, get her aboard ship with as little commotion as possible. One of my clothes trunks ought to serve nicely. She's tiny enough to fit. And you'll have to see about some clothes for her after all, at least enough for the voyage.''

Vladimir nodded readily, the position the wench would fill, after what he had previously thought, making the situation much more acceptable. "Anything else, my prince?"

"Yes, she's not to be harmed," Dimitri replied, his tone now carrying a distinct note of warning. "Not even a tiny bruise, Vladimir, so do be careful with her."

And how was he to manage that, when he was to stuff her into a trunk? Vladimir wondered, as Dimitri walked away. Disgruntlement settled in as his opinion changed yet again. Servant, indeed! The Prince was just annoyed with the wench at the moment. His fascination was still strong.

Chapter Nine

"*In* here." Vladimir held the cabin door open for the two footmen carrying the Prince's trunk. "Careful! For God's sake, don't drop it. Very good. You may go."

Vladimir walked over to the trunk and stared at the lock. He held the key in his pocket, but he didn't reach for it. There was really no reason to release the woman yet. They wouldn't sail for another hour. And just to be on the safe side, it wouldn't hurt her to remain where she was until it was too late for any possible escape.

He heard a distinct banging from within, no doubt her feet kicking at the sides. He smiled, not in the least sympathetic to her plight. She wouldn't be at all comfortable, which was no more than she deserved for her temerity. Wanting to put him in prison, indeed! For what? No real harm had been done to her.

Katherine was of a different opinion. She now had one more grievance to add to the others against these barbaric Russians. To truss her up and stick her in a trunk just to get her out of the house was intolerable. But what should she expect after she had been so thoughtless as to warn the Prince what she intended to do. How could she have been so stupid?

No, you can't blame yourself, Katherine. It was simply impossible to think clearly in his presence, with those velvety eyes staring at you.

She had no doubt that *he* was responsible for this last insult. She had warned him not to send Kirov to her again, and yet it was that brute who had entered the room not long after the Prince left, before she was even completely dressed. That he was not alone should have given her warning. The big fellow with him, not one of yesterday's guards, but dressed in the black-and-gold livery of a footman, had circled round behind her, and before she knew it she was attacked, gagged again, her wrists wrapped up behind her back, and even her ankles bound together.

Then the footman, who hadn't said a single word (neither man had, for that matter), had picked her up as if she weighed not an ounce and carried her downstairs. But instead of leaving the house as she had supposed they would be doing, they had taken her into a room on the second floor, and before she had even got a glimpse of it, she was laid down in a trunk, her knees tucked up, and the lid slammed shut.

She was cramped beyond belief. Bent at the waist, with her head just touching one end of the trunk, she was lying on her hands, which had long since lost all feeling, and she could just barely kick her feet at the other end if she inched her knees up to her chest first. But a lot of good kicking did her. They obviously weren't going to let her out until they were good and ready.

She had no idea where she might be now. She had sensed a carriage ride from the jolts and bumps that jarred her, and she knew the trunk had been carried again after that, but where it was set down and left she couldn't guess, unable to hear much of anything beyond her own painful breathing. And it was getting harder and harder to breathe, the air hot and thick with only the barest crack showing around the rim of the lid.

She imagined that if she was kept in here much longer she could well suffocate. But if she dwelled on that possibility she would panic, and it seemed only sensible to remain calm so that the air would last longer. Yet as the minutes passed into hours, she had to consider the fact that this might be the Russians' solution to the problem she had raised. If they thought she would make good on her threat, how could they afford to let her go? They couldn't, and this trunk might well be meant as her coffin. But could Prince Dimitri really do that to her after . . . after—no, she wouldn't, couldn't believe it. But Vladimir certainly would. She hadn't mistaken his antipathy toward her.

Down in the galley, the fellow high in Katherine's thoughts was bending over to reach for a plump *piroshki*, the small pies with meat filling his wife made to perfection. Marusia stopped him just inches from his target with a light slap on his wrist.

"You know those are for the Prince and Princess," she grumbled. "If you want for yourself, husband, you'll have to ask me to make you some."

Beside Vladimir, the ship's cook laughed. "You'll have to make do with my fare tonight, like everyone else." And then in a softer whisper, "What's the matter? Is she mad at you? If so, you're lucky she only thinks to deny you her cooking."

Vladimir glared at the jovial fellow until he moved away to stir his own pots, but he did wonder. When he had told Marusia earlier what had been decided on for the English maid, she had frowned mightily and snapped that no woman should be treated like that. When he had pointed out that the trunk was Dimitri's suggestion, she said something must be wrong with the Prince for him to be so callous toward a woman, but it was at him that she had frowned.

"Is he still sleeping?" Marusia asked now.

"Yes, so there's no need to hurry his dinner."

"Don't worry about his food. It will be ready when he is." Her pale blue eyes narrowed, letting him know she *was* irritated about the wench for some reason. "What did you do with little English?"

Vladimir gathered his resentment about him and snapped, "Put her in the cabin with the extra clothes trunks. I suppose I will have to string a hammock for her."

"What was her reaction?"

"I thought it best to wait until we are far from London before letting her out."

"Well?"

"I haven't gotten around to it yet."

"Then you made holes in the trunk? You know how seaworthy Dimitri's trunks are."

Vladimir blanched. Holes hadn't occurred to him—how could they? He had never locked anyone in a trunk before.

Marusia gasped, correctly interpreting his expression. "Are you crazy? Go, and pray it's not too late! Go!"

He was gone before she finished shouting at him, running out of the galley. The Prince's words came back to him, pounding in his head. She wasn't to be harmed, not even a tiny bruise. And if there would be hell to pay for a tiny bruise, what madness would ensue if his petty vengeance had killed the woman? It didn't bear thinking about.

Marusia was close behind him, and the two of them running with such mad haste through the ship did not go unnoticed. By the time they raced passed Dimitri's cabin, they had collected five curious servants and several members of the crew. Dimitri, having awakened only minutes before, sent Maksim, his valet, to see what the commotion was about.

The man had only to step outside to see everyone crowding into the cabin a few doors down the corridor. "They've gone in the storeroom, Highness." The Prince traveled with so many personal possessions, even bedding and dishes, that an extra cabin was required just to accommodate his belongings. No doubt some trunk had fallen over. "I'll only be a moment."

"Wait." Dimitri stopped him, realizing Katherine had probably been put in the storeroom and was now causing a disturbance. "It would be the Englishwoman. Bring her here to me."

Maksim nodded, not even thinking to ask what Englishwoman. He was not privy to all of the Prince's affairs, as Vladimir was, but had to wait and hear of them from Marusia, who couldn't keep a secret. He wouldn't dream of questioning Dimitri directly. No one questioned the Prince.

Inside the storeroom, Vladimir was too upset even to notice he had an audience as he unlocked the trunk and threw the lid open. Her eyes were closed. There was no movement, not even a cringe from the sudden flood of light. Vladimir felt panic rising up to choke him. But then her chest expanded as it filled with air, and then again and again she took deep gasping breaths to fill her lungs.

Vladimir actually loved her in that moment for not being dead. It was a short-lived feeling. As her eyes opened and locked with his, he watched murderous fury gather in those turquoise orbs. He was again overcome with the desire simply to leave her there, but Marusia jabbed him in the ribs to remind him he couldn't do so.

He grunted and bent to lift Katherine out of the trunk, setting her on her feet. She immediately crumpled, falling forward against him.

"You see what your thoughtlessness has done, husband? The poor thing probably has no feeling in her feet." Marusia threw the lid of the trunk down for lack of a chair. "Well, set her down and help me get these ropes off."

It wasn't just Katherine's feet that were numb, but her entire legs. She discovered this when her knees knocked together as she was plopped down on the top of the trunk, and she felt nothing. Her hands too had long since lost feeling. And she wasn't ignorant of what would happen when the feeling began to return. It wasn't going to be pleasant.

Vladimir untied her wrists while Marusia worked diligently at her feet. Her shoes had been left behind, one of the things she hadn't gotten around to putting on when Vladimir had entered the room. There had been no time to arrange her hair either, and it hung loose and tangled down her back and shoulders. But most embarrassing was her dress, which was partly unbuttoned in

the front, the lacy bodice of her white chemise
stark against the black of the dress. And as she
noticed the crowd in the doorway, staring at her
curiously, bright color swept up her cheeks. No
one had *ever* seen her in such a state of disha-
bille, and yet more than a half-dozen people were
in this tiny room with her.

Who *were* all these people? For that matter,
where in God's name was she? And then she felt
the swaying motion and knew. She had felt it in
the trunk, but had prayed she was mistaken. She
heard a babble of Russian being spoken by the
door (she could recognize the language easily
now) and knew she was on a Russian ship.

Her arms sprang free of the rope, and she
brought them around in front of her with a
moan, carefully flexing her shoulders and elbows. Behind her, Vladimir reached for the gag,
but she felt his fingers hesitate in her hair. Very
perceptive of him. He must know she was not
going to accept this last misdeed silently. She
had such a tongue-lashing ready for him that his
ears would blister before she was done. But still
he hesitated, and she couldn't make her fingers
move yet to yank the gag away herself.

A torrent of Russian came from behind her,
and the group by the door quickly departed. The
gag fell away, but Katherine's mouth was too dry
for her to do anything but croak the word *water*.
Marusia left to get some, while Vladimir came
around and began to massage Katherine's feet.
She would have liked nothing better than to send
him sprawling with a solid kick, but she couldn't
move her legs yet at all.

"I owe you an apology," Vladimir said without glancing up at her. His voice was gruff, as if

he had to force the words out. "I should have made holes in the trunk for ventilation, but I'm afraid it just didn't occur to me."

Katherine was incredulous. What about his putting her in the trunk in the first place? Where was his contrition for that?

"That was not—your only—mistake, you—you—"

She gave up. It simply hurt too much to talk with her parched throat and her tongue feeling like some swollen, rotten intrusion in her mouth. And feeling was returning to her legs, the discomfort increasing by the second. She had to grit her teeth to keep from moaning. Good Lord, she had suffered numb limbs before from lying too long in one position, but nothing of this magnitude.

The water arrived, and Marusia held the cup to Katherine's lips. She drank greedily, without the slightest thought to decorum. At least one part of her had found instant relief. But the rest of her was screaming in protest, a thousand needles attacking her legs and hands until she thought she couldn't bear it, only to have it get worse and worse. She moaned despite her resolve not to.

"Stomp your feet, little *angliiskii*. It will help."

The words were spoken kindly by the older woman, but Katherine was hurting too much to appreciate her sympathy. "I—I—oh, blast and hang you, Kirov! They don't draw and quarter felons anymore, but I'll see the custom revived for you!"

Vladimir simply ignored her, continuing to rub her ankles and feet briskly, but Marusia chuckled as she did the same to Katherine's hands. "At least her spirit was not smothered in that trunk."

"More's the pity," Vladimir grunted.

Katherine was further angered by their rudeness in speaking to each other in Russian. "I know five languages. Yours is not one of them. If you don't use French, which I understand, then I won't bother to tell you why the Queen's navy is going to pursue this ship all the way to Russia if necessary."

"What nonsense," Vladimir scoffed. "Next you will tell us you have the ear of your English queen."

"Not only that," Katherine retorted, "but her friendship as well, ever since I served a year at court as one of her ladies. But even if that were not so, the Earl of Strafford's influence alone would suffice."

"Your employer?"

"Don't humor her, Marusia," Vladimir warned. "An English earl would not concern himself with the whereabouts of one of his servants. She does not belong to her master as we belong to ours."

Katherine noted the contempt with which he said this, as if he were proud to be owned. But the fact that he obviously didn't believe anything else she had said rubbed her raw.

"Your first and most grievous mistake was in assuming I am a servant. I didn't correct you because I didn't want my true identity known. But you've gone too far with this kidnapping business. The Earl is my father, not my employer. I am Katherine St. John, *Lady* Katherine St. John."

The husband and wife exchanged a glance. Katherine didn't see Marusia's expression. It seemed to say to her husband: "You see? Now you can understand the commanding arrogance, the haughty disdain." But Vladimir's expression showed not a whit of concern for what Katherine had revealed.

"Whoever you are, you waste your anger on me," he told Katherine with utter calm. "I did not act on my own this time. I followed orders, specific orders, even to the suggested use of the trunk. The oversight of not properly ventilating the trunk was mine, however. You were not to be harmed. And perhaps I should have released you sooner—"

"Perhaps?" Katherine exploded, wanting to hit him over the head with something.

She would have gone on, but a wave of debilitating pain spread down her legs at that moment, scattering her thoughts and making her double over with a loud groan. She yanked her hands away from Marusia and dug her fingers into her thighs, but to no effect. Full life was returning to her legs with a vengeance.

For the last five minutes Maksim had stood in the doorway, listening to the exchange between the three people in fascinated silence, but he finally recalled his duty. "If she is the Englishwoman, the Prince wants to see her immediately."

Vladimir glanced over his shoulder, his earlier dread returning. "She is in no condition—"

"He said *now*, Vladimir."

Chapter Ten

Dimitri leaned his head against the high-backed chair and lifted his bare feet to the stool in front of it. It was a comfortable chair, firm, but thickly padded, and served to remind him that he was a man who rarely denied himself anything, be it women, luxuries, or even moods. The chair was one of eight he had purchased, all identical, one for each of his bedrooms in the estates he owned across Europe as well as one to travel with him. When he found something that suited him, he made certain he acquired it. It had always been so.

Princess Tatiana was such a goal. She would suit him. Of all the glittering beauties of St. Petersburg, she was the rarest gem. And if he was going to marry, why not the fairest?

Dimitri hadn't thought of Tatiana since he had mentioned his courtship to his grandmother, and she wouldn't have come to mind now if he hadn't just woken from an unpleasant dream of her. She had led him a merry chase, and even in his dream his goal had not been reached.

It was not that he wanted to marry her or any woman. He did not. What did he need with a wife when he never lacked for female companionship? She would just be an added responsibility, when he was already responsible for thousands. And this marriage arrangement wouldn't have been necessary at all if his older brother, Mikhail, hadn't foolishly extended his service in the Caucasus, so enamored with fighting Turks that he had stayed year after year until his luck finally ran out. He had fallen behind the lines early last year, and although his body had never been recovered, too many of his comrades had seen him shot down for there to be any hope he was still alive.

It was a black day for Dimitri when he had been told. Not that he bore this half-brother by his father's first marriage any great love. When he was much younger, he supposed, they had been closer, even though the seven years' difference in their ages made for a lack of like interests. The Alexandrovs had been a close-knit family then, when their father was alive. But the army had always fascinated Mikhail, and as soon as he was old enough, he had made it his life. Dimitri had rarely seen him after that, except for the one year when he had served in the Caucasus too.

Dimitri had seen enough of killing in that year to last him a lifetime. He didn't thrive on the danger, as Mikhail did. He had wanted adventure, as had so many of his young friends in the Imperial Guard, and like them, he found it aplenty. It was enough to make him resign from the army. Not even the distinction of the Guard had drawn him back. He was a younger son, but he didn't need the army for a career, as most other younger sons of the aristocracy did. He had wealth of his own, apart from the vast wealth of his family. And he had better things to do with his life than risk it needlessly.

If only Mikhail had felt the same way. Barring that, if only he had found the time to marry and leave an heir before he died, then Dimitri wouldn't have been the last legitimate male Alexandrov. He had five other half-brothers, but they were bastards all. And his father's sister, Sonya, had made it perfectly clear that it was now his *duty* to marry and produce an heir before something happened to him as it had to Mikhail. Never mind that Mikhail had put his life in jeopardy every day and Dimitri did not. Aunt Sonya had been so shaken by Mikhail's death that she wouldn't hear of any delay.

Dimitri's life had been carefree up until then. Mikhail had been head of the family ever since their father had died in the cholera epidemic of 1830, and he had made all major decisions. Dimitri had overseen most of the family's holdings, but only because finances had become a fascination, a safe way to take risks, and he was willing to do so. But now *all* responsibilities fell to Dimitri, the vast holdings, the serfs, the bastard siblings, even Mikhail's half-dozen bastards. And soon a wife too.

A thousand times he had cursed his brother for dying and leaving him to control it all. His life no longer seemed to be his own. This trouble with his sister was a prime example. If Mikhail had been alive, the Duchess would have written to him. The problem would have been his, even though Anastasia was only Mikhail's half-sister. He would undoubtedly have turned the problem over to Dimitri, but the difference was that Dimitri wouldn't have been in the middle of a courtship and wouldn't have minded a trip to England at all. Traveling, which he loved, was another thing curtailed now.

At least his sister was one responsibility that he could soon turn over to another when he married her off. Yet there would be another responsibility to take her place when he married himself. If he had been willing to accept failure to reach a goal he had set himself, he would have given up on the beautiful Princess Tatiana as his choice.

Tatiana Ivanova had surprised him by proving most difficult to win. Courting her had taken time and considerable effort on his part, more than he had ever devoted to any woman, and he had had to exert the greatest control over his temper more than once in enduring the infuriating dance she led him. She might be flattered by his suit, but she was a young woman totally aware of her own desirability. She knew she could have any man she wanted and was in no hurry to make a choice from her dozens of suitors.

But no woman had ever been able to resist Dimitri for long. He was not vain about this fact; it was just the simple truth. And just when he had finally been making headway with the Princess, just when the ice seemed to be melting around her frigid heart, the Duchess's letter had arrived. It was the damnedest luck. And yet he wasn't worried that Tatiana would choose another while he was gone. It was the delay involved that irritated him and the fact that he had lost ground by his absence and would probably have to begin his court all over again, when all he wanted was the matter settled so that he could devote himself to other things.

The knock at the door was a welcome distraction. Dimitri didn't want or need to be thinking of his impending married state when he could do nothing about it until he reached Russia, and that was many weeks away.

Maksim entered, holding the door wide for Vladimir, who followed with Katherine in his arms. At first glance, she appeared to be sleeping. But then Dimitri noticed the white of her teeth gripping her lower lip, the tight scrunch of her eyes, and her hands squeezing the fabric of her skirt.

He shot to his feet, the swiftness of his action making both servants freeze in alarm. "What is wrong with her?" The question was directed to Vladimir in the most chilling tone.

"Nothing, Highness, truly," Vladimir hastened to assure him. "She has merely lost the feeling in her limbs, and now the feeling returns—" He paused, for Dimitri's expression was growing blacker by the second. "It was a precaution to leave her in the trunk until we reached the sea. On the river she could have escaped, swimming to the bank. I thought to take no chance, considering the importance—"

"We have not left the Thames yet, and need I point out there are other ways to insure she couldn't escape? Do you mean to tell me you've only just released her?"

Vladimir nodded guiltily. "In truth, I had forgotten how long it takes to reach the coast, and in the confusion of sailing, with the wench under lock and key, I—I didn't give her another thought, until Marusia reminded me of her."

The half-truths seemed to appease Dimitri to a degree. His expression relaxed somewhat, but not completely. Vladimir knew the Prince couldn't tolerate incompetence, and he had made more mistakes since he had met the Englishwoman than ever before. Yet Dimitri was a reasonable man, not a tyrant. And he did not punish for simple human failings.

"She is to be your responsibility, Vladimir, so you will not be so forgetful in future, will you?"

Vladimir groaned inwardly. Being responsible for the woman was a punishment in itself. "No, my prince."

"Very well, set her down."

Dimitri moved aside, indicating the chair he had vacated. Vladimir quickly deposited his burden there and stepped back, praying the woman would display no more dramatics. He was not so lucky.

Katherine's gasp was quite loud as she bent forward over her knees. Her hair fell forward too, dangling down to her feet, and the lacy chemise dipped open from the weight of her breasts in this position, revealing a tantalizing swell of flesh to all three men.

Seeing Dimitri's scowl return, Vladimir said quickly, "Her discomfort will pass, Highness, in a few moments."

Dimitri ignored this. Dropping down on one knee in front of Katherine, he gripped her shoulders gently but firmly, forcing her to sit up. He then tossed her skirt up over her knees, and taking one slim calf in both hands, he began to knead it.

Katherine's natural reflex was to kick. She had listened to their exchange in silence, only because she was afraid she would scream if she opened her mouth. But the dreadful tingling was on the wane now, just as Vladimir had predicted, still annoyingly present, but bearable. Yet she didn't kick. Her simmering temper needed a better outlet, one that wouldn't be misconstrued, and she took it. Her hand cracked soundly against the Prince's cheek.

Dimitri stilled. Maksim blanched, horrified. Words tumbled out of Vladimir without thought. "She has made a claim to nobility, Highness—an earl's daughter, no less."

Silence still reigned. Vladimir wasn't sure if the Prince had heard him, and if he had, whether the claim mattered. Why he had thought to explain such an incredible outrage, and with what was certainly a lie, he wasn't sure. If he had said nothing, the wench might have been tossed overboard, with his eternal thanks.

Dimitri had looked up instantly, only to meet the turquoise tempest in Katherine's eyes. That had been no light slap of affront to make a point. A potent fury had been behind that blow, and it so surprised him that reaction was suspended for the moment. And she was not done.

"Your arrogance is beyond contempt, Alexandrov! That you would dare—that you ordered me to be—oh!"

If steam could have come out of her ears, it would have. Her fingers curled into tiny fists in her lap. She was straining with every fiber of her being for control, which was maddeningly elusive. And he just knelt there staring at her in amazement!

"Blast you, you will turn this ship around and return me to London! I insist—no, I *demand* that you do it immediately!"

Dimitri stood up slowly, forcing Katherine to crane her neck to keep eye contact. He fingered his cheek absently as he continued to look at her, and then suddenly, a glint of humor appeared in his dark eyes.

"She makes demands of me, Vladimir," Dimitri said without looking at the servant.

Tension drained out of the older man upon hearing the amused tone. "Yes, my prince," he sighed.

A single glance over his shoulder. "An earl's daughter, you said?"

"So she claims."

Those velvety brown eyes slid back to Katherine, and she found that even in her fury she could blush, for they came to rest not on her face but on her opened bodice, which she had forgotten about until now. And if that audacity was not enough, they moved down her slowly, stopping finally to admire her stocking-clad legs, which she had also forgotten about.

With a gasp, she shoved her skirt down and then began to fumble with the row of buttons lining the front of the dress. For her modesty she gained a deep chuckle from the man standing only a foot in front of her.

"Scoundrel!" she hissed, not looking up until the last button closed at her throat. "You have the manners of a guttersnipe who knows no better than to gawk, but then that shouldn't surprise me in the least, since your morals are equally decadent."

Vladimir's eyes rose to the ceiling. Maksim hadn't recovered from his first shock when he was shaken again by these words. But Dimitri was only further amused.

"I must commend you, Katya," he finally said to her. "Your talent is remarkable."

She was momentarily thrown off guard. "Talent?"

"Of course. Tell me, did you have to work at it, or does this ability come naturally to you?"

Her eyes narrowed suspiciously. "If you are insinuating—"

"Not insinuating," Dimitri cut in with a smile. "I applaud you. You mimic your betters to perfection. Was it a part you played on the stage? That would explain—"

"Stop it!" Katherine cried, jumping to her feet, her cheeks hot with understanding.

But standing next to him unfortunately put her at a distinct disadvantage. This was the first time she had done so, and it was intimidating in the extreme. He was so tall compared to her small height that she felt ridiculous. The top of her head just barely reached his shoulders.

Katherine stepped hastily to the side until she was well out of his reach, then swung around so fast that her hair flew out in a wide arc. At this safe distance, she gathered her dignity about her. Squaring her shoulders, her chin thrust forward, she gave the Prince a look of utter disdain. And yet she had lost some of her fury. He hadn't been mocking her. He had been sincere in his appreciation of her "talent," and that frightened her.

She hadn't considered that he wouldn't believe her. She had given way to her temper because she had never doubted for a moment that once he knew who she was, he would fall all over himself to make amends. That wasn't happening. He thought she was putting on a performance and he was amused by it. Good Lord, an actress! The closest she had ever come to one was in her father's box at the theater.

"Dismiss your lackeys, Alexandrov." On second thought, realizing that she couldn't afford to antagonize him, she amended herself: "*Prince* Alexandrov." The blasted man held all the cards, and although that was utterly galling, she knew how to be flexible—to a degree.

That she had issued an order didn't occur to her. It did to Dimitri. His brow rose sharply for the breath of a second, then smoothed out, intrigued.

With the wave of a hand he dismissed the two men standing behind him, but he didn't speak until he heard the door close. "Well, my dear?"

"It's Lady Katherine St. John."

"Yes, that would fit," he replied thoughtfully. "I recall meeting a St. John on one of my visits to England many years ago. The Earl of—of—Stafford, was it? No, Strafford. Yes, the Earl of Strafford, very active in reform, very much in the public eye."

The last was said with meaning, insinuating that anyone in England would know the name. Katherine gritted her teeth, but that he had met her father gave her hope.

"In what capacity did you meet the Earl? I can likely describe the setting as well as you, if not better, since I am acquainted with all of my father's friends and their homes."

He smiled tolerantly. "Then describe to me the Duke of Albemarle's country estate."

Katherine winced. He *would* have to name someone she had never met. "I don't know the Duke, but I have heard—"

"Of course you have, my dear. He is also much in the public eye."

His attitude rubbed her raw. "Look you, I am who I say I am. Why won't you believe me? Did I doubt that you're a prince? Which by the way does not impress me, since I'm not ignorant of the Russian hierarchy."

Dimitri chuckled. He had only sensed it before, but now she had come right out and stated it: that she found him singularly lacking. He should be piqued, and yet it did so suit this role she was playing. He had known at first sight that he would find her amusing, but he had never guessed she would be this full of surprises.

"So tell me then what great truths you know, Katya."

She knew that he was only humoring her, yet she had to get her point across. "All you Russian nobles carry the same title, though the old aristocracy does rank higher than the new, or so I've been told. Very democratic, really, and yet the truth is a prince in Russia is merely the equivalent of an English duke or earl or marquis."

"I'm not quite sure I approve of 'merely,' but what is your point?"

"We are equals," she said emphatically.

Dimitri grinned. "Are we? Yes, I can think of one instance when we might be." His eyes slid over her body to leave her in little doubt of what he referred to.

Katherine clenched her fists desperately. To be reminded of what had passed between them last night was disarming. Her anger had been focused on his arrogance and condescension, not on the actual man standing before her. Until this moment, her enraged emotions had kept her from being aware of him as anything except an object of her scorn. But now his presence shook her as it had this morning.

She noticed for the first time his dress, or lack of it. He wore only a short velvet lounging robe belted over a pair of loose white trousers. His feet were bare. His chest, revealed by the open neck of the emerald robe, was also bare. The golden waves of his hair, rather long in this day of shorter styles, was tousled as if he had just come from his bed. His casual attire indicated the same.

Any retort Katherine might have made to his last statement was forgotten in the realization of where she must be: his bedchamber. She hadn't looked at her surroundings. Since she had opened her eyes she had looked only at Dimitri. She didn't dare look around now either, fearing the sight of a rumpled bed would be her undoing. He had ordered her brought *here*. And ninny that she was, *she* had insisted they be left alone for this important confrontation.

Her previous dilemma was overridden by this new one. He had wanted her here and it could be for only one reason. He had been humoring her all along, using charm and subtle insinuation instead of force. But force would come next, and she knew she wouldn't have a chance. Just looking at his size made her feel weak and helpless.

So many alarming thoughts converging on her at once made Katherine overlook the fact that she was on a ship, and that this cabin must serve all of Dimitri's needs, pleasure as well as business. But fortunately, that bit of knowledge wasn't needful at the moment, for she was saved from finding out what might have happened next when the door opened and a swirl of bright fuchsia taffeta glided into the room.

The tall, golden-haired young woman was beautiful. Stunning would be a better word, at least for Katherine, who was in fact stunned to see this vision in such dramatic colors appear so suddenly. But the woman's unannounced entrance accomplished two things, for which Katherine was exceedingly grateful. She drew Katherine's eyes away from Dimitri at last, so that her mind could return to its normal logical processes. And she likewise claimed Dimitri's full attention.

She had spoken the moment the door opened, in a clear though petulant tone. "Mitya, I have waited hours while you sleep the day away, but I will wait . . . no . . . longer." The last two words fell slowly as she halted, finally seeing that he was not alone. She dismissed Katherine with a glance, but her whole demeanor changed when she saw Dimitri's annoyance as he rounded on her. "I'm sorry," she offered quickly. "I didn't realize you were conducting business."

"Which is beside the point," Dimitri said sharply. "It is no wonder the Duchess washed her hands of you, Anastasia, if this lack of manners is another of the new faults you have recently acquired."

The woman's manner changed again, becoming defensive at this set-down in front of a stranger. "It is important, or I wouldn't—"

"I don't care if the ship is afire! In future you will obtain permission before you disturb me, no matter the hour, no matter the reason!"

Katherine, viewing this autocratic display of temper, was almost amused. Here was a man who had let nothing else disturb him, not even her slap, which had been as forceful as she could make it, now blustering over a minor interruption. But then she had met Russians at court and had also heard numerous stories from the English ambassador to Russia, who was a close friend of the Earl's and knew Russians to be inherently volatile, with quick changes of temperament and mood.

Until now, the Prince had shown no tendency toward such a variable disposition. At least this display of temper was comforting in that it was more what Katherine might have expected from a Russian. Predictability was always easier to deal with.

Quickly assessing her options, Katherine decided to gamble. Assuming a subservient manner that was alien to her, she jumped into what was on its way to being a heated exchange, if the woman's now-angry expression was any indication.

"My lord, I don't mind waiting while you attend the lady. I'll just step outside—"

"Stay where you are, Katherine," he tossed over his shoulder. "Anastasia is leaving."

Two commands, one for each of them. But neither woman had any intention of obeying without a fight.

"You will not put me off, Mitya," Anastasia insisted, stomping her foot to make sure he noted how upset she was. "One of my maids is missing! The little bitch has run away!"

Before Dimitri could respond to this, Katherine, moving slowly but steadily around him and toward the door, said firmly, "My business can wait, my lord." Mistakenly she added, "If someone has fallen overboard—"

"Nonsense," Anastasia cut in, not even acknowledging Katherine's assistance. "The sly creature slipped off the ship before we sailed. She was deathly ill on the voyage to England, just as my Zora was. She simply didn't want to sail again. But I refuse to give her up, Mitya. She belongs to me. I want her back."

"You expect me to turn this ship around for a serf, when you know I have offered them all their freedom any time they want it? Don't be a fool, Anastasia. You will have any one of a hundred women to replace her."

"But not here and now. What am I to do now, with Zora sick?"

"One of my servants will have to suffice, don't you agree?" The question was in fact an order.

Anastasia knew that was the end of it; he wouldn't change his mind. She hadn't really expected him to turn the ship around. She had simply needed an excuse to vent some of her frustration with this forced voyage on him, to make him a little more sympathetic to her feelings, and the runaway maid gave her that excuse.

"You are cruel, Mitya. My maids are well trained. Your servants would not know the first thing about being lady's maids. They only know how to serve you."

While they argued over domestics, Katherine took advantage of their distraction to inch her way to the door. She didn't bother to repeat once more that she would wait outside until the Prince was free to finish their own discussion. She opened the door quietly and slipped through it, closing it just as quietly.

Chapter Eleven

*T*he narrow corridor was dimly but adequately lit. A lantern hung at one end, and daylight spilled down the stairs at the other end from the open door leading onto the deck above. The corridor was also empty, a fact that gave Katherine pause. This was too easy. All she had to do was make her way up those stairs to the deck, reach the railing, and quickly slip over it. But for a full twenty seconds Katherine did nothing but stand outside Dimitri's door and hold her breath.

After two days of such rotten luck, it was natural to doubt that an opportunity like this was suddenly within her grasp. Her heart began to pound. There was still danger. She couldn't really feel safe until her feet touched the riverbank and she could watch this ship sail on until it was no more than a dark speck on the water and a bad memory.

Get a move on, Katherine, before he realizes you've flown while he argued with that gorgeous creature.

If she had thought she could persuade the Prince to have the captain turn this ship around for her, his refusal to indulge that beautiful woman in the same request dashed her hopes entirely. Not even for a member of his own party would he return to London, so he certainly wouldn't for her, when it was by his order that she was on this ship to begin with. Why? Why?

Not now, Katherine! Wonder about it later, after you're safely out of that man's reach.

The voices raised in anger inside the room were indistinguishable, but served to remind her that at any moment Dimitri could notice her absence. She had no time to lose. She could only be grateful that this opportunity for escape had come before the ship reached the mouth of the Thames and left the coast of England behind. Once out to sea, there would be no escape.

She pushed away from the door and ran toward the stairs, tripping on the first two steps in her haste. But that moment of lost balance saved her from rushing pell-mell into the arms of one of the crewmen who passed the head of the stairs just then. Foolish to forget the deck wouldn't be deserted at this time of day. She didn't know what time it actually was, but it had to be quite late in the afternoon; closer to evening would be a likely guess. If only it were evening already and dark above, she would have one less worry. But by evening the opportunity would be lost, the river would be behind her. She just had to take her chances on being seen.

Her heart was galloping away now as she took the steps one at a time, slowly. *Don't be obvious about it, old girl. Just act naturally, as if you're just coming up for a stroll on the deck. Nothing to it.*

The only trouble with that reasoning was that she didn't know if a stroll on the deck would be a natural thing for her to do or not. If she was a prisoner, as she uneasily suspected, it wouldn't be natural at all. But would everyone know that? Dimitri's servants, yes, but the sailors, the captain? How could the Prince possibly justify his abduction of her to the captain of this ship? He couldn't. He had probably meant to keep her secreted away during the whole voyage, and that would be an easy enough thing to do with the help of his many servants.

One of those servants came into Katherine's line of vision as she stood nervously in the doorway. It was the young maid who had attended her last night, talking and laughing with one of the sailors about a dozen feet away, and in French no less. The deceitful little chit, speaking only Russian each time she was in Katherine's presence, undoubtedly so that she wouldn't have to answer any questions. Well, never mind that now. Fortunately, the maid's attention was raptly caught up in her mild flirtation and she didn't glance once toward the companionway.

The deck was busy with activity, shouts, laughter, even singing could be heard. No one seemed to notice Katherine as she moved casually toward the railing. That was all she kept her sights on, those wooden planks that signified a return to freedom. So when she gripped the top rail and finally looked up, it was with dismay that she saw how far away land actually was. They had reached the mouth of the Thames, that ever-widening body of water that embraced the sea. It looked as though miles and miles now separated her from the freedom she had thought was only a short swim away. And yet what choice did she have? Sailing to Russia was out of the question when England was still in sight.

She closed her eyes and offered a brief prayer for the extra strength she knew she would need, closing off the terrifying thought that she could well be courting a watery grave instead of imminent freedom. But lurking in the back of her mind also was the possibility, which she had considered while locked in the truck, that a watery grave could be her fate anyway, that the Prince could have had that in mind all along to solve the problem she had presented. It was this that brought out the determination that was so much a part of her character. As far as she was concerned, her options were down to do or die.

Her chest now hurt, her heart was pounding so wildly. She had never been so frightened. And yet she hiked her skirt and petticoats up out of the way to climb over the railing. It was in the instant her bare foot found purchase on a middle plank to hoist herself over that an arm slipped around her and a hand hooked itself under her upraised knee.

She should have exploded in a rage at the unfairness of being stopped at the last second, but Katherine didn't. In fact she felt such relief at having the matter taken out of her hands that she was almost giddy. Later she would bewail the fates that kept conspiring against her, but not right at this moment, as all fear washed away and her heart returned to a normal rate.

The contrary feeling of being saved instead of defeated lasted only a few seconds until she glanced down and saw the green velvet covering the iron arm circling her ribs, just under her breasts. And if that wasn't enough to tell her whose chest her back was molded against, she recognized the hand that was gripping her thigh so firmly she couldn't lower her foot to the deck.

She knew that hand intimately, had kissed it countless times last night in pleasure, in pathetic entreaty, in gratitude. The memories of it were shameful, yet she had instinctively known that to feel his touch again would devastate her.

Hadn't she tried to keep her distance from him? It was too soon, the experience too fresh in her mind for her to have formed the necessary defenses. It was as if the drug were still in her system, its magic working against her. Perhaps it was. Of course it was.

That's a good one, Katherine. Deceive yourself, why don't you. It's him! It's that blasted face of his which you see even when you're not looking at him, and that blasted body which ought to be in a museum instead of walking around destroying the composure of the female population.

Chastising herself did little good when his arm moved an inch upward, and she was mortified to feel her nipples tingling as they hardened. And he wasn't even touching them, just pressing his arm beneath her breasts!

Dimitri was just as aware of the gentle weight resting on his arm as was Katherine. He was having difficulty resisting the urge to put his hands to those soft mounds, to feel again the way they filled his palms so perfectly. But he was also aware that they weren't alone, that dozens of curious eyes were no doubt trained on them. Yet he couldn't bring himself to release her. It felt so damn good to hold her again. Images kept flashing through his mind: the smoldering eyes, the soft lips parted in a cry of pleasure, the thrusting hips.

Heat shot through his loins, worse than it had in the cabin when he had gazed at her open bodice and the creamy ridges of her breasts peaking above the lace of her chemise. If he hadn't been so pleasantly aroused then, he wouldn't have been so annoyed with Anastasia for her untimely interruption. And if he hadn't been so annoyed with her, he would have noticed sooner this little bird's flight, or realized from her words alone what she was up to.

Neither Dimitri nor Katherine noticed the passing of minutes with no word spoken between them. Others did. Lida was shocked to see the Prince appear on deck dressed as he was, even barefoot, and approach the Englishwoman. She hadn't even noticed her there by the rail, but then she wasn't a very noticeable person.

The sailors on deck would have disagreed with this opinion. With Katherine's long hair tossing wildly about in the wind, and no adornment on her plain bodice to distract the eye from the sharp, upthrust breasts, they found her very noticeable indeed. And when the Prince joined her at the rail, knowing grins split more than one hardened face for the intimate picture they presented. It was actually an erotic picture, with Katherine's foot up on the rail, her skirts hiked above her knee displaying the shapely turn of a trim calf, the Prince boldly caressing the exposed leg, or so it seemed, her leaning back into him, his chin resting on the top of her head as he held her close.

Katherine would have died of shame if she could have seen herself at that moment, or worse, if she had known of the lust she was generating among the crew. Her impeccable manners, her sense of self-worth, her modest taste and style (no plunging necklines for her!), had brought her only respect from the men of her acquaintance. At home she was the voice of authority—again nothing but respect, if laced with a little fear.

She might come in a little package, but she could have the disposition of a general when necessary. She had been known to intimidate men, unman them with a haughty look, make them feel inferior. On the other hand, she could also put them at their ease, soothe ruffled feathers, bolster egos. She had prided herself on being able to handle any situation with a man—until she met Dimitri. But never would she have thought she could stir a man's lust.

What had happened with the Prince didn't count, because of the drug. Nothing about last night seemed real, even with the memories so potently clear. And what was happening right now was strictly one-sided—or so she thought. She was so enmeshed in her own turmoil that she was completely unaware of his.

It was Dimitri who recalled their position first and why he had rushed up here in the first place. Bending his head, his voice sounded a husky caress by her ear. "Do you come back with me, or do I carry you?"

He almost wished he hadn't spoken. He hadn't wondered why she had said nothing, why she hadn't even moved a muscle all this time, but he should have. This quiet acceptance of her foiled escape was out of character, just as her final performance in the cabin had been, if only he had been paying attention.

It was unfortunate that he hadn't been able to see her face while he held her, or he would have realized the cause of her acquiescence and been delighted to know she was not as immune to him as she pretended. But now as he felt her stiffen at the sound of his voice, felt her try to draw away from him, he was reminded that this was no empty-headed wench but a very clever woman, and he attributed her silence to some new subterfuge.

"If I hadn't been distracted, I would have been immediately suspicious of those meek 'my lords' you handed out so prettily in my cabin." The huskiness was gone from his voice, but it was still deeply caressing. "But I'm not distracted now, little one, so no more tricks."

Katherine tried once more to break his hold on her, but it was utterly useless. "Let go of me!"

No sweet entreaty. It was a command. Dimitri grinned. He rather liked this haughty role she assumed and was pleased she hadn't decided to abandon it just yet, simply because it wasn't working in her favor.

"You haven't answered my question," he reminded her.

"I prefer to stay right here."

"That was not one of your choices."

"Then I demand to see the captain."

Dimitri chuckled, squeezing her slightly without realizing he was doing so. "Demands again, my dear? What makes you think this one will gain you any more than the others?"

"You're afraid to let me see him, aren't you?" she accused him. "I could scream, you know. It's not very dignified, but it does have its uses."

"Please don't." He was shaking with laughter now, unable to help himself. "I give in, Katya, if only to save you the trouble of plotting a way to reach the man later."

She didn't believe him, even when he called to one of the sailors nearby and she turned to see the fellow hurry away to do his bidding. But when she saw an officer come around the quarterdeck and make his way toward them, she gasped, recalling her position at last, that her skirt was still hiked up and her petticoats wantonly displayed.

"Let go, will you?" she hissed at Dimitri.

He too had forgotten that he was still grasping her leg, which had been a purely impulsive hold, unnecessary to detain her. He took his arm away, but did not immediately remove his hand, letting the fingers trail up her thigh as she put her foot down. He heard her sharp intake of breath at the deliberate liberty, but didn't regret it in the least, even when she swung around to glare furiously at him.

A brow arched innocently, yet he was grinning when, turning to the man who stopped before them, he made brief introductions. Sergei Mironov was a medium-sized man, stocky of build, perhaps in his late forties. There was gray mixed with the brown in his neatly trimmed beard, deep lines around his brown eyes, which showed not the least irritation at being called away from his duties, and his blue and white uniform was impeccable. Katherine had little doubt that he was in fact captain of this ship, but she didn't like the deference he showed to Dimitri.

"Captain Mironov, ah, how shall I put this?" She glanced hesitantly at Dimitri, realizing suddenly that it wouldn't do to come right out and accuse a Russian prince of wrongdoing, at least not to a Russian captain. "A mistake has been made. I—I find that I cannot leave England at this time."

"You will have to speak slower, Katya. Sergei understands French, but not when it is spoken so fast."

She ignored Dimitri's interruption. "Did you understand me, Captain?"

The older man nodded. "A mistake, you said."

"Exactly." Katherine smiled. "So if you will be so kind, I would greatly appreciate being put ashore—if it wouldn't be too much trouble, of course."

"No trouble," he said agreeably, only to look at Dimitri. "Highness?"

"Continue on your present course, Sergei."

"Yes, my prince."

And the man walked away, leaving Katherine staring after him with her mouth open. She quickly snapped it shut and rounded on Dimitri.

"You bastard—"

"I did warn you, my dear," he said pleasantly. "You see, this ship and everything in it belongs to me, including the captain and his crew."

"That's barbaric!"

"I agree," he returned with a shrug. "But until the Tzar can reconcile himself to going against the majority of his nobles and abolishing serfdom, millions of Russians will continue to be owned by only a select few."

Katherine held her tongue. As much as she would have liked to tear into him on this issue, she had already heard him tell the beautiful Anastasia that he had offered his own serfs their freedom. And if he was against serfdom, as that indicated, they would only end up agreeing on any arguments she might raise, and she was in no mood at the moment to agree with him on anything. She took another tack.

"There is one thing on this ship that doesn't belong to you, Alexandrov."

His lips turned up at the corners, and in that smile was the knowledge that even though she was correct in principle, she was nonetheless at his mercy. Katherine didn't need to hear it said to understand this subtle message. The problem was in accepting it.

"Come, Katya, we will discuss this in my cabin over dinner."

She drew her arm out of the way when he reached for it. "There is nothing to discuss. Either put me ashore or let me jump ship."

"To me you make demands, to Sergei you make sweet requests. Perhaps you should change your tactics."

"Go to hell!"

Katherine stalked away, only to realize belatedly that she had nowhere to go, no cabin of her own to retreat to, no place on the entire ship, *his* ship, where she could hide. And time was running out, England receding more and more into the distance with each passing second.

She stopped just as she reached the companionway and turned back toward the Prince, and found herself nearly knocked off her feet as he bumped into her, having been close at her heels. His quick reflex in grabbing her was the only thing that kept her from tumbling down the stairs, and now she was in the same position she had been in earlier, only facing him this time.

She had been ready to swallow her pride. She could have swallowed her tongue in that moment of pure physical sensation and not known it.

"You had something more to say, Katya?"

"What?" He stepped back, releasing her, and her thoughts came rushing back. "Yes, I—"

Good Lord, this wasn't easy. *How do you humble yourself, Katherine, when you'd rather kick his shins?*

She looked up, then quickly down. The dark, velvety eyes were as potent as his embrace had been. And at this close proximity, she didn't dare meet such a challenge.

"I apologize, Prince Alexandrov. I'm not usually so short-tempered, but under the circumstances . . . never mind. Look, I am willing to be reasonable. If you will put me ashore, I swear I will forget we ever met. I won't go to the authorities. I won't even tell my father what happened. I just want to go home."

"I'm sorry, Katya, I truly am. If Tzar Nicholas weren't visiting your queen this summer, it wouldn't be necessary to remove you from England. But your English newspapers would love to have a reason to attack Nicholas Pavlovich. I won't give them that reason."

"I swear—"

"I can't take the chance."

Katherine was angry enough to look him in the eye now. "Look, I was upset this morning. I said a lot of things I didn't mean. But now I've told you who I am. You must see that I can't afford to exact retribution, that I can't do anything without embroiling my family in a terrible scandal, and that I would never do."

"I would agree, if you were in fact a St. John."

She made a sound that was half a groan, half a scream. "You can't do this! Do you know what it will do to my family, the anguish they'll go through not knowing what happened to me? Please, Alexandrov!''

She could see that his conscience was pricked, yet it didn't make any difference. ''I'm sorry.'' His hand came up to caress her cheek, but dropped when she flinched away. ''Don't take it so hard, little one. I will return you to England as soon as the Tzar's visit is over.''

Katherine gave him one last chance. ''You won't change your mind?''

''I can't.''

With nothing left to say, she did what she had wanted to do in the first place: drew back her foot and gave his shin a solid kick. Unfortunately she forgot she wasn't wearing any shoes. His grunt of pain wasn't quite as satisfactory as she had hoped, and her toes were throbbing, but she gave him her back anyway and limped down the stairs. Hearing him bellow for Vladimir didn't stop her. She passed the Prince's cabin, found the storeroom, and sat down on the trunk she had been locked in earlier. There she waited; for what, she didn't know.

Chapter Twelve

"*S*weet Mary and Jesus!" Vladimir exploded. "What did I say? Tell me! All I asked was for you to take the new clothes to her and extend Dimitri's invitation to dinner. But you look at me as if I suggested you do murder!"

Marusia lowered her gaze, but her mouth was set mulishly, and her knife chopped with excessive force, mutilating the spinach for the salad she was preparing. "Why do you ask me anyway? You said he made her your responsibility. Just because I'm your wife doesn't mean I'll share that responsibility."

"Marusia—"

"No! I won't do it, so don't ask again. The poor thing has been through enough."

"*Poor* thing! That poor thing snarls like a she-wolf."

"Ah, so now we have it. You're afraid to face her after all you've done."

Vladimir sat down heavily at the opposite side of the table. He glared at the cook's back, whose shoulders were shaking suspiciously. His two galley helpers peeling potatoes in the corner were doing their best to pretend they lacked ears. This was no place to have an argument with his wife. Everyone aboard ship would know of it before morning.

"How can my request do anything but please her?" he demanded, but softly.

"Nonsense. You know she won't accept the clothes or his invitation. Yet you have your orders, don't you? Well, *I* won't be the one to force more grief on her." Her voice lowered and was tinged with self-disgust. "I did enough already."

His eyes widened, finally understanding what had turned her into a shrew. "I don't believe it. What have you to feel guilty about?"

She glanced up, all hostility gone from her expression. "It's all my fault. If I hadn't suggested you drug her—"

"Don't be a fool, woman. I had heard Bulavin's boasts too. I would have gone to him eventually without your suggestion."

"That doesn't change how callous I was, Vladimir. I gave no thought to her. She meant nothing to me, just another one of the nameless women he avails himself of between his more lofty conquests. Even after I met her and saw how different she was from all the others, I'm ashamed to say I still didn't consider anything except pleasing him."

"Which is as it should be."

"I know that," she snapped. "But that changes nothing. She was a virgin, husband!"

"So what?"

"So what? She wasn't willing, that's what! Would you take me, if I weren't willing? No, you would respect my wishes. But no one has respected her wishes since you dragged her off the street. Not one of us has."

"He didn't force her, Marusia," he reminded her quietly.

"He didn't have to. The drug took care of that, and *we* gave her the drug."

129

Vladimir frowned. "*She* hasn't complained of her loss. All she does is hiss and snarl and make demands. And you forget she will be well compensated. She will be returned to England a rich woman."

"But what about now? What about forcing her to come with us?"

"You know it was necessary."

Marusia sighed. "I know, but that doesn't make it right."

After a moment of silence, he said gently, "You should have had children, Marusia. Your mothering instinct has been aroused. I'm sorry—"

"Don't." She leaned across the table to reach for his hand. "I love you, husband. I have never regretted my choice. Just—just go easy on her. You men, you never consider a woman's feelings. Consider hers when you deal with her."

He made a long-suffering face, but he nodded.

Vladimir hesitated before he knocked on the door. Behind him Lida stood shamefaced, her arms full of packages. He had given the girl a sound scolding for carrying the tale of the stained sheets to Marusia and no doubt anyone else who would listen. If it weren't for that cursed virginity, his wife would never have been so sympathetic toward the English wench, or so he thought. And her guilt had rubbed off on him. Despite all the difficulties the wench had caused, Marusia had managed to make him feel sorry for her. His pity lasted as long as it took for the door to open.

She stood there, a picture of arrogant defiance and withering malice. Nor did she move aside to let him in.

"What do you want?"

He had to stop himself from automatically bowing in deference to her, her tone was so imperious. It prodded his temper, just as it had from first meeting her, this superiority of hers. No Alexandrov serf would dare put on such airs, even those elevated to new enviable positions. The ballerinas, opera singers, ship captains such as Sergei, architects, actors who had performed for the imperial court, they all still knew their place. Not Little English. No, she put herself above them all.

She needed a good slap to bring her down a peg, and every instinct cried out for Vladimir to deliver it. He didn't. Instead he steeled himself to recall Marusia's entreaty. How *could* his wife feel sorry for this bitch?

"I have brought you a few necessities you will need for the voyage." He took a step forward, forcing Katherine to move out of the way so that Lida could carry in the packages. "Over there," he told the girl, indicating the top of one of the many trunks in the cabin.

It annoyed him that the wench would undoubtedly be pleased with these many new clothes. He should have attended to the purchasing himself, what with the four women in the Prince's entourage too busy putting the Duke's house back in order to go shopping. But he had been unable to bring himself to buy anything for *her*.

He had sent Boris instead, who had helped him load Katherine into Dimitri's trunk and so could at least judge her size. He had secretly hoped the fellow would fail and return empty-handed, with no time left to send anyone else. But Boris was smarter than Vladimir gave him credit for. Afraid to make a mistake, he had coaxed Anastasia's maid, Zora, along to help him. And Zora was unfortunately accustomed to buying for the Princess, so everything the two had bought was of a better quality than Vladimir had intended. Nothing fit for royalty, but nothing appropriate for a servant either.

"There is one dress that is finished and appears near your size." Vladimir addressed Katherine again, but avoided looking at her until he had said what he had to say. "The others are all in different stages of completion, according to the dressmaker, but Lida here will help you if you have no talent with the needle. We were lucky to find anything at all at such short notice, but there are still some things money can buy if the price is right." He smiled to himself when he heard her gasp, his barb hitting its intended mark. "You should have everything you will need. The Princess's maid was quite thorough. If not, you need only tell me."

"You've thought of everything, haven't you? Did you buy me a trunk too?"

"You may use that one, since it is now empty."

Katherine followed his nod and grimaced, seeing the trunk she knew so intimately. "How did you guess I was sentimental?"

He couldn't help himself. He smiled at such blatant sarcasm. But she didn't notice. She was still staring at the trunk.

And now for the last of his immediate duty. "Lida will help you change since there isn't much time. The Prince is expecting you, and he doesn't like to be kept waiting."

Katherine turned to him, her expression bland for the moment. "For what?"

"He has invited you to dine with him."

"Forget it," she replied curtly.

"I beg your pardon?"

"You're not deaf, Kirov. Extend my regrets, if you must. Word it however you like. The answer is unequivocally no."

"Unacceptable," he began, but it was as if Marusia were there jabbing him in the ribs. "Very well, we will compromise. Change, go to his cabin, and *you* tell him you don't wish to accept his invitation."

She calmly shook her head. "You've missed my point. I'm not going anywhere near that man."

With a clear conscience Vladimir could tell Marusia he had tried, but now he smiled with particular pleasure.

Chapter Thirteen

*B*athed, shaved, and donned in one of his more elegant formal coats, Dimitri waved Maksim away when he approached with a frilly white cravat. "Not tonight, or she'll think I'm trying to impress her."

The valet nodded, but spared a glance for the candlelit table set for two, the gold-rimmed china and sparkling crystal, the champagne sitting in a bucket of ice. And she wasn't to be impressed? Perhaps not. If she really was an earl's daughter, and Maksim was inclined to believe she was from what he had seen so far, she would be used to such luxury.

The Prince was another matter though. He was at his best tonight, and not just in looks. It wasn't often that Maksim saw him like this. Undoubtedly the stimulation of a new challenge, the sexual tension had its effect, but there was something else too that Maksim couldn't define. He might call it nervousness if he didn't know better, but mixed with a lighthearted exuberance that had been sorely lacking in the Prince for many years. Whatever it was, it made those dark brown eyes sparkle with anticipation as never before.

She was a lucky woman, this Englishwoman. Even if the seductive atmosphere in the cabin didn't impress her, the Prince couldn't fail to.

But when she arrived a few minutes later, Maksim's opinion changed drastically. He learned quickly what it would take Dimitri longer to learn: never to assume anything about this particular woman.

Vladimir was not escorting her. He delivered her, trussed up and tossed over his shoulder. With a single apologetic look in Dimitri's direction, he set her down and quickly untied her wrists. That done, she ripped off her gag—the reason Dimitri had had no prior warning of what was going on before this startling arrival. She took only a second to throw the cloth at Vladimir before swinging round to impale Dimitri with the hot fury in her eyes.

"I won't have it! I won't!" she screamed. "You tell this churlish brute of yours he is not to lay his hands on me again, or I swear—I swear—"

She stopped, and Dimitri gathered that she was too upset for simple verbal threats as she looked wildly around for some kind of weapon. When her eyes lit on the well-laid table, he leaped forward, unwilling to sacrifice a fortune in crystal and china to this tantrum, not to mention possible wounds, at least not when he didn't yet know what had caused it.

His arms were as effective as thick ropes, wrapping around her and locking her own arms firmly to her sides. "All right," he said tightly by her ear. "Calm down and we will unravel this little drama—"

"To my satisfaction," she hissed.

"If you insist." He felt her relax then, if only slightly, and looked toward the supposed culprit. "Vladimir?"

"She refused to change her dress or join you, my lord, so Boris and I assisted her."

Dimitri felt her anger return full force in the straining of her small body against his hold. "They ripped my dress—tore it right off me!"

"You want them flogged?"

Katherine stilled completely. She was staring at Vladimir standing only a few feet away. His expression didn't change. He was a proud man. But she saw that he was holding his breath as he waited for her answer. He felt fear. She didn't doubt it. And she took a moment to savor the power Dimitri was unexpectedly giving her.

She envisioned Vladimir tied to a mast, his jacket and shirt stripped away, and she herself holding a whip poised above his naked back. It was not just for his having dressed her as if she were a child and couldn't do it herself, her arms thrust into tight sleeves, her stockings changed and shoes shoved on her feet. Nor was it for gagging her and tying her up again while her hair was brushed, even while perfume was applied behind her ears. She wielded the whip in her imagination for everything this man had done to her, and he deserved every revengeful stroke.

The picture was nice to contemplate for those few moments, but Katherine wouldn't order it done, no matter how much she might hate the man. That Dimitri would, however, disturbed her.

"You can let go, Alexandrov," she said quietly, still staring at Vladimir. "I believe I have my dreadful temper under control now."

She wasn't surprised that he hesitated. She had never made such a shameful spectacle of herself before. But she wasn't embarrassed. Enough was enough. They had simply pushed her too far.

When Dimitri did let go, she turned slowly to face him, one brow raised in question. "Do you make a habit of flogging your servants?"

"I detect censure."

Wary of his sudden frown, she lied. "Not at all. Mere curiosity."

"Then no, I never have. Which isn't to say there aren't exceptions to that rule."

"For me? Why?"

He shrugged. "Everything said and done, I believe I owe you that much."

"Yes, you do, and much more," she agreed. "But I wasn't demanding blood."

"Very well." He turned to Vladimir. "In future, if her wishes differ from mine, don't argue with her. Simply bring the matter to me."

"And what does that solve?" Katherine demanded. "Instead of him forcing me to do something I don't want to do, you will."

"Not necessarily." The sternness of Dimitri's expression lightened at last. "Vladimir follows my orders to the letter, even when met with difficulty, as you have discovered. On the other hand, I can listen to your arguments and rescind my orders, if need be. I am not an unreasonable man."

"Aren't you? I'm afraid I haven't seen anything to indicate otherwise."

He smiled. "This is all premature, you know. You were invited to join me for dinner so that we could discuss your status among us and come to an arrangement agreeable to us both. There will be no need for any more battles, Katya."

Katherine wished she could believe that. But the fact was that she had guessed the reason for this dinner invitation and had refused it because she was afraid to have her situation spelled out in clear-cut terms. She would rather wonder than have her worst fears confirmed.

But now that she was here and there could be no more avoiding it, she might as well have done with it. "So," Katherine said with forced evenness, "am I a prisoner or a reluctant guest?"

Her directness was refreshing, but it didn't suit Dimitri's plans for the evening. "Sit down, Katya. We will eat first and—"

"Alexandrov—" she began warningly, only to be cut off with a disarming smile.

"I insist. Champagne?"

Observing the slight gesture of his hand, both servants left the room. Dimitri moved to the champagne bucket himself. Katherine watched him with a feeling of unreality. Did he say he was a reasonable man? What a laugh. He wasn't even waiting for her answer but was filling the two crystal glasses on the small dining table.

Very well, she would play it his way, for now. After all, she had had nothing to eat all day and only one meal yesterday. And she was no hypocrite when it came to food, as so many ladies of her class were, only nibbling at dinners in company because too-tight corsets made it impossible to do otherwise. She didn't wear her corsets to the point of discomfort. With such a tiny waist she didn't have to. And she enjoyed good food. The trouble was that she didn't think she would enjoy this meal no matter how good the food, not with such a distracting dinner companion, and not with her immediate future so in question.

Stay on your toes, Katherine. He thinks to wine and dine you and perhaps get you drunk so you'll agree to anything. Just keep your wits about you, don't look at him too much, and you'll do fine.

She picked the chair farthest away from where he was standing and slid into it. A thick plush velvet seat and back. Comfortable. Exquisite lacy tablecloth. Soft candlelight. There were other lamps on in the room, but far enough away not to detract from this intimate setting. It was a large room. Luxurious. How could she have missed all of this before? The enormous white fur rug. One whole wall of books. The bed. *Don't stare at it, Katherine!* A lovely sofa and matching chair in white brocaded satin and dark cherry-wood and the big chair she had sat in earlier were grouped around an ornate stand-up stove. An antique desk. More cherrywood in tables and cabinets. More fur rugs. The room really *was* big. Perhaps it had once been two or more cabins. It was his ship; perhaps he had designed it this way.

He sat down across from her. Thank God for the three-foot width of table. She looked anywhere but at him, but knew he was watching her.

"Try the champagne, Katya."

She reached automatically for the glass, but caught herself and drew her hand back. "I would rather not."

"You prefer something else?"

"No, I—"

"You think it's drugged?"

She looked at him then, eyes flaring. She hadn't thought of that at all, but she should have. Stupid! She was supposed to keep one step ahead of him.

She shot to her feet, but Dimitri reached over quickly and caught her wrist, proving the table wasn't a safe enough width after all.

"Sit down, Katherine." His voice was firm, an order. "If it will make you feel better, I will be your food taster for the evening." She didn't budge, but he let go. "You have to eat sometime. Will you worry about the food for the whole voyage, or will you trust me that you won't be drugged again?"

She sat down stiffly. "I didn't think you would, but Kirov thinks for himself and—"

"And he was duly chastised for the first time. I tell you it won't happen again. Trust me," he added more softly.

She wished she hadn't been looking at him all this time. Now she couldn't tear her eyes away. His white silk shirt was opened at the neck, giving him a rakish look despite the elegance of his black evening coat. The shoulders were so wide, the arms powerful. He really was big, this fairytale prince, so utterly masculine in size, in looks.

No matter how Katherine tried to get around it, she was attracted. And without her anger to protect her, she had no defense against such potent attraction.

Lida saved Katherine from making a fool of herself with her staring by arriving with the first course. From then on Katherine concentrated on her food with a vengeance, only vaguely aware that Dimitri was talking to her as they ate, telling her a little about Russia, anecdotes about court life there, about someone named Vasili who was apparently a close friend. She supposed she made appropriate comments when necessary, since he didn't stop talking. And she knew he was trying to put her at ease. It was nice of him to try. But she would never, ever be at ease in his presence. It just wasn't possible.

"You haven't really been listening, have you, Katya?"

He had spoken louder to gain her attention. She glanced up, blushing slightly. Annoyance seemed to war with amusement in his expression. She imagined he wasn't accustomed to anyone ignoring him.

"I'm sorry, I—I—" She cast about for an excuse. Only one came readily to mind. "I was famished."

"And preoccupied?"

"Yes, well, under the circumstances . . ."

He threw down his napkin and refilled his glass. He had consumed nearly all of the champagne by himself. Her first glass was still untouched.

"Shall we adjourn to the sofa?"

"I—would rather not."

His fingers tightened on his glass. Fortunately Katherine didn't notice. "Then by all means let us dispense now with what concerns you so you can enjoy the rest of the evening."

Too late she became aware of his irritation. And what the devil did he mean by that? She had no intention of remaining in this cabin any longer than necessary. If she was to enjoy the rest of the evening, she would have to be alone, but she doubted that was what he had in mind. But first things first.

"Perhaps you will answer my earlier question now. I feel like a prisoner, and yet you invite me here tonight as if I were only a guest. Which is it to be?''

''Neither, I think, at least not in the strictest sense. There is no reason for you to be confined during the length of the voyage. You can't escape at sea, after all. Yet idleness breeds unrest and is also a bad example for my servants. You will need to do something to occupy your time while you are with us.''

Katherine clasped her hands in her lap. He was right, of course, and this was more than she could have hoped for. She couldn't remember the last time her life hadn't been filled to the brim with activity of one kind or another. There was his library, but much as she loved to read, she couldn't see herself doing nothing but that day after day. She needed stimulation for her mind, to be planning, arranging, doing something useful or challenging. If he had something to suggest, she would be grateful, especially since what she had feared was that she *would* be confined to a cabin the whole voyage.

''What did you have in mind?'' Her eagerness was unmistakable.

Dimitri stared at her for a moment in surprise. He had expected her to balk immediately at the idea of working. He had planned then to offer her the position of being his mistress, so she could continue playing this role of Lady to her heart's content. Perhaps she had misunderstood. Yes. After all, he had never met a woman yet who would not prefer a pampered, idle existence to one of menial service.

''The possibilities are limited aboard ship, you understand?''

''Yes, I realize that.''

"In fact, there are only two positions available for you to consider. Which one you select is up to you, but you must choose one or the other."

"You have made your point, Alexandrov," Katherine said impatiently. "Do get on with it."

Had he thought her directness refreshing? More fool he.

"Do you recall meeting Anastasia here earlier?" he asked tightly.

"Yes, of course. Your wife?"

"You assume I am married?"

"I don't assume anything. It was mere curiosity."

Dimitri frowned. He wished she would be more than merely curious about him. Her question had reminded him of Tatiana, and he made a mental note never to take that one traveling with him. If this evening had been difficult, with him having to carry the conversation, evenings with Tatiana would be much worse since she dominated a conversation by talking about nothing but herself. But there was one great difference in his preference of companion. Tatiana didn't excite him. Little Katherine did. Even her annoying frankness didn't change that. Nor her haughty indifference. And especially her unpredictable temper.

She didn't have the kind of superficial beauty that made men worship at Tatiana's feet, but Katherine was fascinating nonetheless. Her unusual eyes, which he could only think of now as sexy, the sensual lips, her hard, stubborn chin. There was character in every line of her face. And since she had been carried into the room, he had been unable to take his eyes off her.

143

The new dress was a definite improvement. A blue patterned organdy with tight sleeves and scooped neckline that curved to the edge of her shoulders. Those were creamy white, as was her lovely neck. Sweet Christ, he wanted to taste her! But here she was as standoffish as she had been that morning. There was no provocative entreaty now, unlike last night. And yet he couldn't stop remembering.

He wanted her in his bed. He didn't care at the moment how he accomplished it, as long as he didn't have to force her physically. The plan he had come up with was perfect in that it would make succumbing to him easy for her to accept. As long as she didn't desert the role she was playing, it would work. If he was annoyed with her current abruptness, it was because he had hoped to win her by seduction instead, but that door had been closed to him all evening.

''Princess Anastasia is my sister,'' Dimitri told Katherine now.

She didn't even blink, though that little fact made her feel—what? Relief? How absurd. It was nothing more than surprise. She had thought mistress first, wife second, sister not at all.

''So?''

''If you recall meeting her, then you'll recall also that she finds herself in supposedly dire need of a new lady's maid, at least until we reach Russia.''

''Come to the point.''

''I just have.''

She stared at him, not a muscle moving in her face to indicate shock, surprise, anger. He stared at her, eyes studying, intense, waiting.

Easy, Katherine. Don't fly off the handle yet. He's up to something. He must know how you would react to such a suggestion, and yet he made it anyway. Why?

"You mentioned two choices, Alexandrov. Is the second as ingenious?"

Much as she had hoped to sound unaffected, sarcasm had crept into her tone. Dimitri detected it, delighted in it, and relaxed considerably. He felt suddenly like the hunter closing in for an assured kill. She would refuse the first suggestion, and that left only the second.

He stood up. Katherine tensed. He rounded the table, stopping at her side. She didn't look up, not even when his hands closed on her upper arms and gently lifted her to her feet. Breathing became impossible as her throat closed off in panic. His arm came around her. The other hand raised her chin. She kept her eyes lowered.

"I want you."

Oh, God, God, God! You didn't hear that, Katherine. He didn't say that.

"Look at me, Katya." His voice was mesmerizing, his breath caressing her lips. "We are not strangers. You already know me intimately. Say you will share my bed, my cabin, and I will treat you like a queen. I will love you so thoroughly you will not notice the passing weeks. Look at me!"

She closed her eyes tighter. His passion was devastating her senses. In another moment he would kiss her and she would die.

"Will you at least answer me? We both know you found pleasure in my arms. Let me be your lover again, little one."

145

This isn't happening, Katherine. It's just a fantasy, more real than others, but fantasy nonetheless. So what harm in playing along with it? If you don't do something fast, you're lost anyway.

"What if there is a child?"

That was not what Dimitri was waiting to hear, but he was not displeased by the question. So she was cautious. She could be as cautious as she liked, as long as she said yes in the end. But he had never been asked about children before. In Russia, it was taken for granted that the father would provide for his bastards. It was not something that he thought about, as careful as he always was about *not* fathering any unwanted offspring. Unlike his father and brother, he wanted no child of his labeled bastard. And yet he hadn't been careful last night. He would not so forget himself again, but that was neither here nor there. She wanted the truth.

"If there is a child, he will lack for nothing. I will support you both for the rest of your life. Or if you prefer, I will take the child and raise him myself. It would be your choice, Katya."

"That's very generous, I suppose, but I wonder why you don't mention marriage. But then you never got around to answering if you were married or not, did you?"

"What has that to do with it?"

The sudden sharpness in his voice broke the fantasy. "You forget who I am."

"Yes, I forget who you *say* you are. A lady would expect marriage, wouldn't she? But that, my dear, I must decline. Now give me your answer."

The dam on her temper broke and a full flood was released by these latest insults. "No and no and no and *no!*" She shoved away from him and flew around the table until she could look back with that safe barrier between them. "No to everything! My God, I knew you were up to something with that first suggestion of yours, but I didn't think you were this contemptible. And to think I believed you were sincere in offering an 'acceptable arrangement.' "

Frustration cut a keen edge through Dimitri's own temper. His body throbbed in need while she indulged in another tantrum. Damn her, and damn this charade of hers.

"You have been given your options, Katherine. Choose one, I don't care which." And he didn't at the moment. If he never laid eyes on her again, it would be too soon. "Well?"

Katherine straightened to her full height, her fingers gripping the edge of the table. She was calm again, but the calm was deceptive. Her eyes gave the lie to it.

"You are detestable, Alexandrov. Be your sister's maid, when I run not one household but two; when for the past several years I have been my father's estate manager as well as his business advisor? I help to write his speeches, entertain his political cronies, monitor his investments. I am well versed in philosophy, politics, mathematics, animal husbandry, and I'm proficient in five languages." She paused, deciding to gamble. "But if your sister is even half as well educated, I will agree to your absurd proposal."

"Russia doesn't believe in turning its women into bluestockings, as the English apparently do," he sneered. "But then very little of what you claim can be proved, can it?"

147

"I don't have to prove anything. I know who I am. Consider well what you're putting me through, Alexandrov. The day is going to come when you'll find I'm telling the truth. You ignore the consequences now, but you won't be able to then. You have my word on it."

His fist slammed down on the table, making her jump back from it. Candlelight flickered. His empty glass fell over. Hers, still full, sloshed champagne onto the lovely tablecloth, staining it.

"That for your truth, your consequences, and your word! It is here and now that you had best be concerned with. Make your choice, or I will make it for you."

"You would force me to your bed?"

"No, but I will not see a waste of your talents when you can be useful. My sister needs you. You will serve her."

"And if I don't, do you have me flogged?"

"There is no need for such dramatic measures. A few days' confinement, and you will be happy to serve."

"Don't count on it, Alexandrov. I was prepared for that."

"On bread and water?" he tested her.

She stiffened, but her answer was automatic and a measure of her contempt. "If it pleases you."

Sweet Christ, she had an answer for everything. But stubbornness and bravado would go only so far. His patience was gone, his plans come to naught. Anger decided him.

"So be it. Vladimir!" The door opened almost instantly. "Take her away."

Chapter Fourteen

*H*er cabin had been rearranged while she spent the evening with Dimitri. The many trunks were still there, but they had been moved back against the walls out of the way. A washstand had been brought in, a rug found, and a hammock strung up between two beams. Her wardrobe was a trunk, her chair was a trunk, her table was a trunk. A very uncomfortable cell indeed.

If Katherine didn't yet despise her prison, she did come to hate that hammock in the following days. Her first encounter with it had been a disaster. Four times she had landed on the floor before she gave up and slept where she had been dumped. But aching muscles made her tackle the monster again the second night. She conquered it after only two spills this time and was able to relax enough to fall asleep to the gentle swaying, only to fall out in the middle of the night while sound asleep. Black and blue with bruises, she was angry enough to keep trying, and by the fourth night she had succeeded in staying in the damn thing until morning.

Those were the frustrations of her nights. Her days were another matter.

Katherine had always dreamed of traveling, ever since she was ten years old and had sailed with her family to Scotland for the wedding of some distant cousin. She had discovered then that sailing agreed with her. Unlike her sister and mother, she had thrived aboard ship, feeling healthier than ever before. By ten she was already well immersed in the wide range of studies her father allowed her to undertake. She had wanted to visit the countries she was learning about. It was a dream she never outgrew.

She had even seriously considered the marriage proposals of several foreign dignitaries she had met at the palace, just because of her desire to travel. But an acceptance would have meant leaving England for good, and she wasn't quite daring enough to do that.

Those were her only offers of marriage. There could have been others, but she didn't encourage any courtship. And without any encouragement, Englishmen found her too formidable, too competent—perhaps they were afraid to compete. It wasn't that she didn't see herself married eventually. The time had simply not been right for it. She had had her one frivolous season, then served the Queen for a year. She might have continued to enjoy court life if her mother hadn't died. But she had, and Katherine took her place as the one person in the family that everyone brought their problems to, including her father. But even though the household would have fallen into chaos without her, she had intended to marry. She had only wanted to get Beth properly wed first and Warren reined in enough to carry some of the load. Then she would have made an effort to find a husband.

Now she would probably have to settle for a fortune hunter for a husband, thanks to her loss of virginity. That was all right though. Buying a husband was commonplace. If she had been hoping for a love match, she would probably be devastated. It was fortunate that she was too practical for such silly dreams.

But her one dream had come true. What she had never had time for was now being forced on her. She was traveling. She was on a ship sailing for a foreign land. And she wouldn't have been normal if she hadn't felt some degree of excitement mixed in with all her other emotions. Russia might not have appeared on her imaginary itinerary, but then she wouldn't have chosen to travel virtually as a prisoner either.

If she viewed her situation with an open mind, putting emotions aside, she knew there was room for improvement. She accepted that she was going to Russia—nothing was going to change that. The practical thing to do would be to make the best of it. It was in her nature to do just that. And she could, if it hadn't been for these foolish emotions that were fighting her natural inclinations.

Pride had become her worst enemy. A close second was this unreasonable stubbornness that even she hadn't realized she was capable of. Injustice made her inflexible. Anger served only to spite herself. After all, it would cost only a little pride to give in. She needn't even do so gracefully. Surrendering under duress, it was called. People did it all the time, in all walks of life.

If she had to be forced to do something, good Lord, why not something she could have found immense pleasure in? Why did the Prince have to choose for her, taking away the one option she would have gladly given in to in the end? Why did she deny him in the first place? Other women took lovers. A love affair, they called it. It should rightly be termed an affair of the flesh.

Lust, wrapped in a pretty package. But whatever it was, she had all the symptoms. She was so attracted to the man that she couldn't even think straight in his presence.

And he wanted her. Incredible fantasy. This fairy-tale prince, this golden god wanted her. *Her.* It boggled the mind. It defied reason. And she said no. Stupid ninny!

But you know why you had to refuse, Katherine. It's morally wrong, sinful, and besides, you're just not mistress material. You were raised to respect the sanctity of the home, and he did not, repeat, did not offer a respectable proposal.

All valid reasons, but they made cold bedfellows. Yet even if she was given a second opportunity, her answer would still have to be the same. She was, after all, Lady Katherine St. John. And Lady Katherine St. John could never take a lover, no matter how much she might secretly want to.

These thoughts filled her waking hours and only increased her sense of frustration. But she knew how to end it. All she had to do was play maid for the beautiful Princess. Nothing challenging in that. Then she would have the freedom of the ship, be able to catch glimpses of foreign coastlines, watch the sun rising and setting into the sea, in effect, enjoy the voyage.

Much as she despised the notion of acting the servant, she knew she would do it eventually. The Prince was clever in that respect. There was just so much she could take of her own company and having absolutely nothing to do. Even the clothing she was supposed to alter had been removed and given to others to work on. Hands idle, mind idle, she was bored silly.

But she wasn't climbing the walls yet. And she wasn't starving on her bread and water, since Marusia managed to sneak fruit and cheese in to her each day, and some of her meat-filled pastries, without the two guards stationed outside her door being the wiser. But that wasn't why Katherine was still holding out. It was because Dimitri's servants were begging her to give in. It seemed the Prince wasn't taking her confinement by his order any better than she was, and *that* gave her the incentive to hold out longer than she might have otherwise.

Lida was the first to make her aware of Dimitri's attack of conscience. At least that was what Katherine assumed it must be, what with the girl swearing the Prince's black mood would lift if Katherine would just be reasonable and do as he wanted. Lida didn't know what it was he wanted, but as far as she was concerned, nothing could be so terrible or worth rousing his anger for, because when he was angry, everyone suffered.

Katherine said nothing to this. She didn't defend herself, offer reasons, or make excuses. She didn't scoff either. She heard the silence the first day of her confinement and knew something was definitely wrong. It was eerie, as if she were the only one alive on the whole ship. And yet she had only to open her door to see her two guards sitting in the corridor, quite alive, if utterly silent.

Marusia was even more enlightening later that same day. "I don't ask what you did to displease the Prince. If it was not one thing, it would have been something else. I knew it was inevitable."

That was too intriguing to let pass. "Why?"

"He has never met anyone like you, *angliiskii*. You have a temper to equal his. This is not so bad, I think. He loses interest very quickly in most women, but you are different."

"Is that all I have to do, then, to make him lose interest in me? Keep my temper under control?"

Marusia smiled. "You want him to lose interest? No, don't answer. I won't believe you."

Katherine took exception to that. "I thank you for the food, Marusia, but I really don't care to discuss your prince."

"I didn't think you would. But this has to be said, because what you do affects not only you, but all of us."

"That's absurd."

"Is it? We are all aware that you are the cause of Dimitri's present bad temper. When he gets these dark moods at home, it doesn't matter so much. He takes himself off to his clubs, to parties. He drinks, he gambles, he fights. He releases his ill humor on strangers. But on ship, there is no outlet. No one dares raise their voice above a whisper. His mood affects everyone, depressing everyone."

"He's just a man."

"To you he is just a man. To us he is more. We know in our hearts there is nothing to fear. He is a good man and we love him. But hundreds of years of serfdom, of knowing that a single man has the power of life and death, the power to make you suffer cruelly at a whim, are fears not easily ignored. Dimitri is not like that, but he is still the master. If he is not happy, how can any of us be happy who serve him?"

Marusia had more to say each time she came. And Katherine welcomed the stimulating arguments that relieved the boredom. But she wasn't willing to accept responsibility for what was happening outside her small cabin. If Dimitri's servants were fearful of becoming the outlet for his ill humor because he had no other, what was that to her? She had stood up for her rights. She could have done no differently. If that put the great Prince out of sorts, she was secretly glad. It was too bad of him, however, to frighten his servants so much that they would come beseeching her to make things right with him. Why must she forsake her principles for virtual strangers?

But then Vladimir came on the third day, forcing Katherine to reevaluate her position. If he could humble himself, however stiffly, when she knew how much he disliked her, how could she continue adhering to her pride so selfishly? Truthfully, however, he gave her the excuse she needed to compromise.

"He was wrong, miss. He knows it, and this is the reason his anger is self-directed and growing worse instead of improving. Since he never had any intention of treating you like a prisoner, he undoubtedly assumed the threat of such treatment would be all that was necessary to bend you to his will. But he underestimated your resistance to his requests. Yet it is a matter of pride now, you understand. For a man to relent and admit he is wrong is harder than it is for a woman."

"For some women."

"Perhaps, but what can it cost you to serve the Princess, when no one of your own acquaintance will ever know?"

155

"You were listening at the door that night, weren't you?" she accused him.

He made no effort to deny it. "It is my job to know my master's wants and needs before he makes those needs known to me."

"Did he send you here?"

Vladimir shook his head. "He has not spoken two words to me since he gave the order for your confinement."

"Then how do you know he regrets that order?"

"Each day you remain in this cabin his mood grows blacker. Will you please reconsider?"

It was a magic word, please, especially coming from him, but Katherine wasn't ready to let him off the hook yet. "Why can't *he* reconsider? Why must *I* be the one to give in?"

"He is the Prince," he stated simply, but he had already lost his patience with her. "Sweet Mary, if I had known that your behavior could have such an effect on him, I would have risked his displeasure in London and found him some other woman. But he wanted you, and I wanted to spare us this very thing happening. It was a mistake. I am truly sorry. But what's done is done. Can't you see your way clear to being at least a little cooperative? Or is it that you feel you would fail at the job?"

"Don't be absurd. What the Princess would require of a maid cannot be so different from what I would require of one of my own."

"Then where is the problem? Did you not say you served your Queen?"

"That was an honor."

"It is an honor to serve Princess Anastasia."

"The devil it is! Not when I am her equal."

His face had flushed with anger then. "Then perhaps you are better suited to the Prince's other suggestion."

He left her with that, as red-faced as he.

Chapter Fifteen

"I want to see Mr. Kirov." Katherine looked from one guard to the other. The blank, uncomprehending faces were identical.

Each day a different pair of guards sat outside her unlocked door. Today it was two Cossacks, who obviously didn't understand French. She repeated her request in German, then Dutch, English, and lastly, in desperation, Spanish. Nothing. They just stared at her, not budging from their stools.

"Typical." She was frustrated enough to speak aloud. "They all want you to give in, Katherine, but do they make it easy for you?"

She ought to just forget it. So what if she had agonized all night reaching this decision? This was only the fourth day of her confinement. She could hold out much longer, even if Marusia didn't sneak her food. But then there was the excuse she was holding onto. She was giving in not for herself but for the sake of others.

Liar. You want out of that cabin. It's that simple.

She gave it one more try before her pride reasserted itself. "Kir-ov." She used her hands to describe him. "You know? Big fellow. Alexandrov's man."

Both men came to life on hearing the Prince's name. Smiles split their faces. One stood up so quickly that he knocked his stool over and nearly fell over with it. He immediately set off down the corridor toward Dimitri's cabin.

Katherine panicked. "No! I don't want to speak to *him*, you idiot!"

Whether she could have stopped him or not didn't matter. Before he reached Dimitri's door, it opened and the Prince stepped out.

Over the head of the Cossack, Dimitri's eyes locked with hers while he listened to the man's spate of words, not Russian, but some other language Katherine had never heard. The urge was great for her to retreat behind her door. She had *not* intended to speak to Dimitri. She had meant to give her decision to Vladimir, so that *he* could tell the Prince and she wouldn't have to see him again herself. He had won. And she didn't care to see him gloating over his victory.

But she wasn't a coward. She stood her ground as he approached her.

"You wanted to see Vladimir?"

Her eyes flared. "Why those—those—" She glared at the two guards now standing a respectful distance away. "They understood me all along, didn't they?"

"They know some French, but not enough—"

"Don't tell me," she sneered. "Just like the captain, right? Never mind."

His expression was totally void of emotion as he gazed down at her. "Perhaps I can help you?"

"No." Too quick. "Yes. No."

"If you can make up your mind—"

"Oh, very well," she nearly snapped. "I was going to give Mr. Kirov the message, but since you're here, I might as well tell you myself. I accept your terms, Alexandrov." He simply stared at her. Hot pink began to heat her cheeks. "Did you hear me?"

"Yes!" The word was expelled on a breath. His surprise was quite evident now, his smile nearly blinding in its brilliance. "I just wasn't expecting . . . I mean, I had begun to think . . ."

He fell silent, being tongue-tied a whole new experience for him. And he was still at a loss for words. Sweet Christ, here he had been on his way to speak to her, to tell her to forget his stupid demands, and she did this. He still ought to tell her to forget it, that he had been a cad to try and force her to do anything, and yet—and yet it felt too good, winning this battle with her. And it did seem as though he had been through a battle these last four days, with his conscience, with his temper.

He had never dealt with a woman so ruthlessly before, and all because he wanted her while she wanted no part of him. Yet she was giving in, when he had convinced himself she never would and that there was no point in continuing to try and bend her to his will. So perhaps there was still hope after all that she would eventually succumb to his more personal requests.

"I do understand you correctly, Katya? You are now willing to work for me?"

Well, you knew he was going to rub it in, didn't you, Katherine? This was the very reason you didn't want to see him—well, one of them. Listen to your heart racing and you know the other reason.

"I don't know if I would call it work," Katherine answered tightly. "I will help your sister because she appears to be in need. Your sister, Alexandrov," she emphasized, "not you."

"It is all the same, since I pay her expenses."

"Expenses? You aren't going to mention money again, are you?"

He had been going to. Working for him, she would earn ten times what she could have earned in England for the same job. Any other woman would want to know that. But the slant of her eyes warned him not to mention it to this one.

"Very well, no talk of wages," Dimitri conceded. "But I am curious, Katya. Why did you change your mind?"

She countered his question with one of her own. "Why have you been in such a foul temper these last days?"

"How did—what the devil has that to do with anything?"

"Nothing, probably, except I was told I was the cause. I didn't believe *that* for a minute, of course, but then I was also told that everyone on the ship was walking around on eggs because of this temper of yours. That's really rather insensitive of you, Alexandrov. Your people do so try to please you, even to the detriment of others, and here you don't even notice when you're frightening them out of their wits. Or did you know, and just not care?"

He was frowning long before she finished. "Are you through criticizing me?"

Her eyes widened with mock innocence. "You did ask why I changed my mind, didn't you? I was only trying to explain . . ."

He knew then that she was taunting him deliberately. "So you have capitulated for the sake of my poor servants, have you? If I had known you were going to be so noble, my dear, I would have ignored my sister's needs and insisted you attend to mine instead.''

"Why, you—''

"Now, now," he admonished, his humor restored enough to tease her. "Remember your sacrifice before you say anything that might provoke my temper again.''

"Go to the devil!''

He threw back his head and laughed delightedly. How her fury contradicted her demure appearance. Sweetly innocent she looked in her watered-silk dress of pink and white, modestly high-necked and unadorned, her hair tied back with a simple ribbon as a young child would wear it. And yet her lips were compressed tightly, her eyes sparkled with rancor, and her square little chin jutted out mutinously. Had he really worried that her refreshing spirit might be broken by his callous treatment? He should have known better.

Laughter gone, but still smiling, Dimitri met her furious gaze and found himself caught once again by the curious effect she always seemed to have on him. "Do you know this temper of yours excites me?''

"I can't say the same of yours—'' Katherine began, only to fall abruptly silent as his meaning dawned on her.

Her heart seemed to flip over. Her breath stopped. She was mesmerized, watching his eyes turn more black than brown. And when his hand gently slipped under the hair on her neck and slowly drew her toward him, she was powerless to prevent what she knew was coming.

Every single erotic sensation she had felt while under the influence of that exotic drug returned to Katherine the moment his lips touched hers. Her limbs turned to jelly, her mind to mush. His tongue slid unhindered between her teeth to leisurely explore her mouth and heat ignited in her loins. Her hips thrust forward instinctively without any encouragement from him. In fact he still only held her neck. It was she who pressed her body close, needing the contact, needing . . .

Dimitri was utterly amazed by her response to him. He had expected arms to flail and legs to kick, not for her body to turn soft and yielding. Instead of trying to coerce her into his bed, as her firm resistance to him indicated was the only way he would get her there, he should have kissed her sooner.

What a fool he had been. He had not placed her in that well-known category of women who said no when they really meant yes. And yet— and yet there was no coyness about Katherine. There was no pretense to her fiery emotions. She didn't belong with the artful, deceptive women he was used to, and that left him floundering in confusion even as he delighted in his sudden good fortune.

Katherine felt bereft when the kiss ended. Dimitri's hand slid around to the side of her face, and just as she had done that fateful night, she turned her cheek into his palm, unaware that she was doing so. It was hearing his sharply indrawn breath at this tender gesture that brought her back to her senses. Her eyes opened to reality and she groaned miserably, even as she sprang into motion.

She placed her hands flat on Dimitri's chest and pushed hard. He didn't budge, but because he hadn't been restraining her in any way, she nearly stumbled from her own impetus, falling back into her cabin. The distance between them now was all she needed to regain control, even though her pulses were still racing.

She glared at him and threw up a hand when he took a step toward her. "Don't come any closer, Alexandrov."

"Why?"

"Just don't. And don't you dare try that again."

"Why?"

"Blast you and your *whys*. Because I don't want you to, that's why!"

Dimitri went no further than the doorway. There he leaned against the frame, crossing his arms over the wide expanse of his chest as he studied her thoughtfully.

She was flustered. Good. She was also nervous and perhaps a little frightened too, which gave him a sense of power he had not felt in her presence before. Was it possible she was as surprised as he was by her warm response to his kiss? Was she afraid now that it could happen again?

Little fool. Why was she so loath to enjoy the pleasures of the flesh? But he had learned something from this encounter that would satisfy him for the time being. She wasn't indifferent to him after all. There was passion in this woman that needed no aphrodisiac to bring it to the surface. It just needed a gentle touch, and there would be other opportunities—he would see to that.

"Very well, Katya, you have convinced me of your abhorrence of kissing." There was laughter in his tone, for they both knew how ridiculous that statement was. "Come along, then, and I will introduce you to my sister." When she didn't move, he added, "You aren't really afraid of me now, are you?"

She bristled, because he hadn't moved yet either. "No, but if you want me to come with you, it might help if you led the way."

He laughed, but as she followed him down the corridor, she thought she heard him say, "You win this round, little one, but I make no promises to always be so obliging of your wishes."

Chapter Sixteen

"*H*er, Mitya? You think I haven't heard about her? You think I don't know she is the little whore you picked up off the street that afternoon in London? *This* is who you give me for a maid?"

This is how Katherine was greeted by Anastasia Petrovna Alexandrovna after Dimitri had introduced them and explained Katherine's presence. The younger woman had given her only a single glance before ignoring her and attacking her brother as if he had dealt her the most horrendous insult.

Katherine was the one insulted, and yet when she recovered from the shock of having her character maligned, she reacted to the Princess's contempt in a most unusual way. She stepped in front of Dimitri, who was showing every sign of losing his temper in a matter of seconds, and now that Anastasia could no longer ignore her, she smiled.

"My dear young woman, if I weren't a lady *and* of moderate temperament, I might be tempted to slap you silly for your offensive manners, let alone your disparagement of me. But since you have obviously been misinformed about me, I suppose I must be tolerant and forgiving. But let us be clear on one point. I am not a whore, Princess. And I am not being *given* to you, as you so arrogantly put it. I agreed to help you because apparently you can't seem to help yourself. But I understand that perfectly. Why, look at me. Without my own maid along on this voyage, I haven't been able to do a thing with my hair, and dressing is most tedious without a little help. So you see I do understand your dilemma, and since I have nothing better to do . . .''

Katherine could have gone on with her subtle sarcasm, but she was too close to laughing at the Princess's shocked expression, and besides, she had made her point. Whether it would do any good remained to be seen.

Behind her Dimitri leaned close to whisper, ''Tolerant temperament, Katya? When do I get to meet this woman you have described?''

She stepped quickly away from him before turning to bestow on him the same false smile as she had given the Princess. ''You know, Alexandrov, I don't believe your sister is as helpless as you implied. She appears quite capable—''

''Do not be so hasty,'' Anastasia cut in, fearing she had gone too far and was now going to lose a supposedly competent maid, which she did desperately need. ''I thought I would have to train you, as I would Mitya's servants, but if you are a lady, as you say, that won't be necessary. I accept your help. And, Mitya . . . I thank you for thinking of me.''

It galled Anastasia to have to say even that much to either of them. She was still furious with her brother for dragging her home and for his threats about a future husband. Having to thank him for anything at this time went against the grain. And the Englishwoman! Anastasia's blood boiled. Dimitri was no doubt tired of the little whore, and that was why he was foisting her off on her. Lady indeed! But it was possible that she knew more about attending a lady than Dimitri's other servants, and so she could be useful. Yet Anastasia would not forget the insult she had been dealt by this *peasant*.

"I will leave you, then, to become better acquainted," Dimitri said.

Anastasia's smile did not reach her eyes. Katherine's expression would have been bland except for the tight line of her mouth. Dimitri knew his sister could be difficult to get along with. And Katherine's temper he had witnessed firsthand. Perhaps he shouldn't have brought these two together, but it was done. If it didn't work, then there was still the second position for Katherine to fill.

The look Dimitri gave her just before he left warned Katherine of what he had been thinking. He wanted her to fail. He looked forward to it. The scoundrel! Well, she wouldn't. If it killed her, she would be pleasant to this spoiled, unpleasant child who was his sister.

That determination wore thin after listening to the long list of duties Anastasia had in mind for her. She was to attend to the Princess's bath, her toilet, her clothes, her meals. The girl wanted to monopolize her every waking moment, even— and Katherine was truly surprised at this—having her sit for a portrait. It appeared Anastasia considered herself a talented artist, and her painting was the only thing she had to keep herself occupied with on the voyage.

"I will call it *The Daisy*," Anastasia said, speaking of the portrait.

"You liken me to a daisy?"

Anastasia delighted at the opening given her, a chance to belittle the creature. "Well, you are certainly no rose. Yes, a rather sun-browned daisy, with that dull hair—but you do have nice eyes," she conceded, seeing them widen.

She had beautiful eyes, actually, Anastasia admitted to herself, and a face that might not be pretty in the classical sense, but was certainly interesting. It would, in fact, be a challenge to paint. The more Anastasia looked at her with an artist's eye instead of with rancor, the more excited she became by the challenge.

"Do you have a yellow dress?" she asked. "It must be done with a yellow dress, for the daisy effect, you understand."

Keep your calm, Katherine. She's goading you, and she's not really very good at it. You've cut better than her down to size with little effort.

"No yellow dress, Princess. You'll have to improvise, I'm afraid, or envision—"

"No, I must see it . . . but of course! You will use one of my dresses."

She was serious. "No, I will not," Katherine said stiffly.

"But you must. You agreed to let me paint you."

"I did not agree, Princess. You assumed."

"Please."

The word surprised them both. Anastasia looked away to hide a telltale blush, amazed not so much that she had pleaded with the woman but that the portrait had become suddenly so important to her. It would be the most challenging thing she had ever done, not like bowls of fruit or meadows strewn with wild flowers, where one scene was so much like another, nor the few portraits she had done of her friends, where the blondness and prettiness was a sameness too. No, here was an original for a subject. She just had to paint her.

Katherine, seeing the blush, felt like a petty bitch. She was refusing to do the one thing she actually wouldn't mind doing. What spite. And why? Because the Princess was spoiled and said things she probably didn't mean? Or because she was Dimitri's sister, and saying no to her was like saying no to him, a pleasure?

"Very well, Princess, I will sit for you a few hours each day," Katherine consented. "But I must insist on a like time to myself."

The other duties she would deal with as they arose. There was no point in getting into an argument now (she would *not* be scrubbing any backs), when she had this opportunity to get to know Anastasia while her claws were sheathed.

Chapter Seventeen

The first of several storms that the ship would encounter in the weeks ahead arrived that afternoon. It wasn't a violent storm, just a nuisance to most of those on board, Anastasia in particular. She took well to sea travel, except under these circumstances, as she readily admitted. The increased motion of the ship sent her straight to bed.

Katherine left the Princess's cabin, determined to see what she could do about laundering several gowns, including the golden one they had decided would do nicely for the portrait, and then she would have the rest of the afternoon to herself. The trouble was that she didn't know the first thing about laundering clothes. But Anastasia had insisted that Dimitri's servants, accustomed only to attending a man, knew nothing about women's apparel and they would ruin anything they put their hands to.

"As I will."

"My lady?"

Katherine stopped short, amazed to hear herself addressed so. And by Marusia? The older woman was waiting for her in the doorway of her own cabin. She was grinning from ear to ear and beckoning Katherine to come ahead. She did, quickly, when she realized the corridor was no place to linger, not with Dimitri's cabin just a few doors away. She didn't intend to encounter him there again.

"What did you call me?" Katherine asked before stepping into her room.

Marusia ignored the sharpness of her tone. "We know who you are, my lady. It is only the Prince and my husband who doubt you."

It was such a relief to have someone believe her, anyone, and yet nothing was changed as long as Dimitri was still doubtful. "Why doesn't *he* believe me, Marusia? Clothes and circumstances don't change who a person is."

"Russians can be intractable. They stubbornly adhere to first impressions. For Vladimir, there is even more reason, because in Russia, death would be his reward for abducting an *aristo*. So you see why he does not dare admit you are more than he first supposed."

"We are not in Russia, and I am an Englishwoman," Katherine reminded her.

"But the ways of Russia are not ignored simply because we are out of the country for a time. The Prince, now"—Marusia shrugged—"who can say why he does not accept what is obvious? Possibly he chooses not to consider it because he doesn't want it to be true. It is also possible that the temptation you represent to him clouds his judgment."

"In other words, he's so busy figuring out ways to seduce me that he has no time to think of anything else?"

The resentful tone surprised Marusia, but after a moment she couldn't help laughing. She knew by now not to think of Little English in terms of other women, yet she still found it incredible that Dimitri had finally met a woman who wasn't instantly enamored of him. Even the Princess Tatiana was madly in love with him, as everyone knew except Dimitri. According to Tatiana Ivanova's servants, she had decided to pretend indifference to him so that he would better appreciate her once he had won her.

Marusia sobered, seeing that Katherine didn't appreciate her humor. "I'm sorry, my lady. It is just that . . . do you truly feel nothing for the Prince?"

"On the contrary," Katherine replied without hesitation. "I loathe him."

"But do you mean that, *angliiskii*, or is it only your anger that prompts you—"

"Again my integrity is questioned?"

"No, no, I only thought . . . never mind. But it is too bad that you feel this way, because he is much taken with you. But of course you already know this."

"If you are referring to his effort to entice me into his bed, I assure you, Marusia, I'm not stupid. A man can desire a woman he doesn't respect, doesn't know, and doesn't even like. If that were not so, the word *whore* would never have come into being. And don't you dare pretend to be shocked at my bluntness, because I won't believe it!"

"It's not that, my lady," Marusia hastened to assure her. "It's this conclusion you have mistakenly come to. Certainly the Prince is as lusty as any young man his age, and most often his liaisons do mean little or nothing to him. With you it has been different since he first saw you. Do you think it usual for him to pick a stranger from the street to share his bed? He has never done this before. He likes you, my lady. If he didn't, he wouldn't still want you. If he didn't, his emotions would not be so close to the surface where you are concerned. Have you not noticed the difference since you agreed to his demands? It is why I am here, to thank you on behalf of all of us for whatever sacrifice you had to make.''

Katherine could hear the difference—voices no longer whispering, shouts and laughter coming from above, even in the midst of a storm—and she couldn't deny it felt good to think she was responsible for this return to normalcy. Nor could she deny the little thrill that had gone through her on hearing Marusia's claim that Dimitri liked her. But that was neither here nor there, nor to be admitted to anyone but herself. As for her sacrifice, Anastasia wasn't so difficult to get along with—as long as her brother wasn't around. The other hints, well, these people needed to understand that her position hadn't changed simply because she was no longer a virgin. She would not tolerate a campaign of matchmaking, as she had their efforts to get her out of her cabin.

''I don't know how things go in Russia,'' Katherine said, ''but in England, a lady does not expect to be propositioned for anything except marriage. Your prince insults me each time he . . . when he—''

Marusia was amused. ''Has no man ever asked to be your lover before, my lady?''

''Certainly not!''

''A shame. The more you are asked, the less it seems like an insult.''

''That will do, Marusia.''

A loud sigh, then a half-smile told Katherine that Marusia was not one to give up so easily. But she retreated for the moment.

"Did the Princess give you those?" She indicated the dresses draped over Katherine's arm.

"I'm to clean and press them."

Marusia almost laughed at the look of disgust mingled with determination that crossed Katherine's features. "That is one thing you need not concern yourself with, my lady. I will give them to Maksim, Dimitri's valet, and he will return them to you here. Anastasia need never know."

"I'm sure he has enough to do already."

"Not at all. He will also see to your own clothing, and you will let him, yes, because he is the one who had to attend the Prince these last four days, and he is the one who is most grateful to you for making peace with him. It will be his pleasure to help you in any way he can."

Katherine grappled with her pride for about two seconds before handing over the dresses. "That yellow one is to be trimmed down to my measurements."

"Oh?"

"The Princess wants to paint me in it."

Marusia grinned to hide her surprise. Anastasia was presently mad at the world and taking it out on everyone. Marusia would have wagered she would have been particularly unpleasant to Little English and wagered too that a battle royal would have been the result.

"She must have taken to you," Marusia commented, still grinning. "And her painting is really very good. It is her passion, second only to men."

"So I understand."

Now Marusia laughed. "So she told you about her numerous lovers?"

"No, just the one who got her banished from England, and the unfairness of it all."

"She is young. To her, everything she disagrees with is unfair, especially her brother. All her life she has done as she pleases. Now suddenly her reins are pulled, and naturally she objects."

"It should have been done sooner. Such promiscuity is unheard of in England."

Marusia shrugged. "Russians look at such things differently. You have a queen who would frown on such things. We had a tzarina who set the mode by flaunting her lovers before the entire world. So did her grandson Alexander. And Tzar Nicholas was raised in the same court. Little wonder then that our ladies are not as innocent as yours."

Katherine held her tongue, reminding herself that Russia was a different country, a different culture, and she had no right to judge. But good Lord, she felt like a babe being thrust into Babylon.

She had been shocked into speechlessness when she had listened to Anastasia's complaints about being in disfavor with her grandmother over her little affair, as she called it, so much so that the Duchess had sent for Dimitri to take her home. It was then that Katherine had realized just who Anastasia was: the Russian princess who had been on every gossipmonger's tongue earlier in the year. She had heard the story herself. She just hadn't made the connection when Dimitri had mentioned the Duke of Albemarle to her.

The Duke was their uncle on their mother's side. They were half English. Katherine should have felt better for knowing that. She didn't. Blood counted for nothing when you were raised to barbarity.

Chapter Eighteen

"Katya?"

Katherine's heart skipped a beat. She should have known better than to try sneaking past Dimitri's open door. Blast him for leaving the door open.

Katherine smoothed the grimace off her face and glanced inside. He was seated at his desk, a stack of papers before him, a glass of vodka at his elbow. He had removed his coat, and the white shirt he wore lay open at his neck. He had lit the lamp on his desk because of the gloominess of the day, and the light cast his face in sharp relief, making the gold of his hair seem almost white. She made a point of looking away after that quick glance.

Katherine's voice was impatient, clearly indicating that she didn't appreciate being delayed by him. "I was going up on deck."

"In the rain?"

"A little rain never hurt anyone."

"On land, perhaps. On a ship, the decks will be slippery and—"

Her eyes flew to his. "Look, Alexandrov, either I have the freedom of this ship, as you promised me, or I might as well remain locked in my cabin. Which is it to be?"

Hands on hips, chin thrust out, she was prepared for battle, perhaps even hoping for one. Dimitri grinned, not about to oblige her.

"By all means go and get wet. But when you return, I would like to speak with you."

"What about?"

"When you return, Katya."

His gaze returned to his papers. She was dismissed summarily, subject closed. Katherine gritted her teeth and stalked away.

" 'When you return, Katya,' " she mimicked in a furious undertone as she stomped up the stairs. "You don't need to know ahead of time, Katya. No, then you might be able to prepare yourself, and that wouldn't do, would it? Worry about it instead. What the devil is he up to now?"

The rain hitting her in the face captured her full attention the moment she stepped on deck, and Dimitri's arrogance was temporarily forgotten. Katherine moved to the railing, gripped it, and stared out at the turbulence of sea and sky, nature at its primal best. And she had almost missed it. Even now she could see the sun peeking through the clouds in the far-off distance as it descended toward the horizon. The ship would soon leave the storm behind.

But for now she could enjoy what she would never dream of indulging in at home: being wind-tossed and soaked without running for cover, without worrying about a ruined bonnet or dress or who might see her. It was a childish pleasure but so exhilarating that she felt like laughing, and did when she tried to catch rain in her cupped palms to drink and succeeded, and when the wind played lecher with her skirts.

Her spirits were still high when the cooler winds of approaching evening finally forced her to go below. And she was undisturbed when she neared Dimitri's door, still open, and recalled that he wanted to see her. She had kept him waiting for nearly two hours. If doing so had managed to annoy him, the advantage would now be hers.

"Did you still wish to speak to me, Alexandrov?" Katherine inquired pleasantly.

Dimitri was still seated behind his desk. At the sound of her voice, he tossed a quill down and leaned back in his chair to glance at her. That she looked like something a cat might drag home didn't seem to surprise him. Hair wet and stringy, a few strands stuck to her brow and cheek, her dress transparent and clinging—watered-silk took on a more exact meaning—with a puddle forming at her feet.

If his expression didn't show his annoyance, his voice did, though not for the reason Katherine was expecting. "Must you still be so impersonal when you address me? My friends and family call me Mitya."

"That's nice."

She could hear his sigh clear across the room. "Come in, Katya."

"No, I don't think I ought to," she continued with the same irritating nonchalance. "I wouldn't want to drip all over your floor."

A sneeze ruined the effect she was striving for, and if she had bothered to make eye contact, she would have seen Dimitri's returning humor. "So a little rain doesn't hurt? Go and change your clothes, Katya."

"I will, just as soon as you tell me—"

"Change first."

She started to insist he get his talk over, but clamped her mouth shut instead. What was the use? She had played this scene already. And as he had earlier, he again had managed to prod her into exasperation. But this time—this time she slammed his door shut before marching away. She wanted to have the pleasure of pounding on it when she returned. Blasted door. What the devil was he doing leaving it open anyway?

"So that he could stop you, Katherine, which he did. What kind of freedom is it if you can't go on deck, can't even go to the dining salon, without his knowing about it?"

Good Lord, now she had his every motive revolving around her, when it was more than likely that he was just hot and trying to catch some of the cooling breeze that wafted down the corridor. After all, he was from Russia, the land of eternal winter. What was cool to her would be warm to him.

"Deluded, that's what you are, Katherine, when you know very well you're not that important to him. He probably doesn't give you a thought once you're not around. Why should he? And his door won't be open every time. And even if it is, he wouldn't stop you every time."

As reasonable as that sounded, it didn't relieve even half her exasperation in being treated like a child; and that's what he had done, dismissing her summarily as though she were a child or a servant, ordering her to change, as if she didn't have the sense to do so without his telling her to.

Katherine slammed her own door shut and immediately attacked the buttons on her bodice, the task made difficult because of the wet material. She would have given her eyeteeth to have Lucy

present for just one minute, and the fact that she didn't made her all the madder.

She kicked her dress away once it fell to the floor, then followed and kicked it again just for good measure. Shoes, petticoats, and the rest of her underclothes dropped into the same pile before she realized that it was too dark in the room now to find new clothes in her trunk. She stubbed her foot trying to reach the washstand to grab a towel. More fuel for the fire.

"Your talk had just better be essential, my high and mighty prince, that's all I have to say." Her voice was a comfort in the gloom and a hot spur once she got a candle lit. "Keeping me in suspense might be your idea of—"

"Do you always talk to yourself, Katya?"

Katherine froze. Her eyes closed, her fingers tightened on the towel she held around her, and her mind balked. *He's not there. He's not. He wouldn't dare.* She wouldn't turn around to look, even when she heard his footsteps moving up behind her. *Grant me just one favor, Lord, please. Put some clothes on me. One small miracle.*

"Katya?"

"You can't come in here."

"I am in here."

"Then leave now, before I—"

"You talk too much, little one. You even talk to yourself. Must you always be defensive and on guard? What are you afraid of?"

"I'm not afraid," she insisted weakly. "There are proper ways of doing things, and your coming in here uninvited is not one of them."

"Would you have invited me in?"

"No."

"Then you see why I didn't knock."

He was toying with her, taking advantage of her dilemma, and she didn't know what to do about it. There was no dignity in standing in nothing but a towel. Some brave front she was presenting. How could she rail at him when she couldn't even turn around and face him down?

She *was* afraid. He was directly behind her. She could feel his breath on her head. His scent surrounded her. To look at him would be her undoing.

"I want you to leave, Alexandrov." She was amazed that she sounded so calm, when her whole nervous system was racing toward panic. "I will join you in a few minutes, after I—"

"I want to stay."

He said the words so simply, yet they said it all. She couldn't make him leave if he wouldn't, and they both knew it. Her nervousness exploded in unreasonable rancor as she finally turned to face him.

"Why?"

"A foolish question, Katya."

"The devil it is! Why me? And why *now*? I've just been drenched in the rain. I look like a drowned rat. How can you possibly . . . why would you—"

Dimitri chuckled at her difficulty. "Always you pick everything apart with your hows and whys. You want the truth, little one? I sat at my desk and I imagined you removing those wet clothes, and it was as if you did it in front of me, the image was so clear. You see, my memory of you is as tantalizing as the real thing. I can close my eyes and see you again framed in green satin—"

"Stop it!"

"But you wanted to know why I could want you now, didn't you?"

The touch of his hands just then kept Katherine from replying. In fact her thoughts became so thoroughly jumbled that she gave them up. His touch was whisper-soft, moving slowly over the bare skin of her shoulders until finally his hands circled the slender column of her neck.

With his fingers at her nape, his thumbs stretched up under her chin to tilt her head up to him. "I shouldn't have undressed you in my mind." His lips brushed her temple, then her cheek. "But I couldn't help it. And now I need you, Katya. I need you," he whispered passionately, just before his mouth captured hers.

Katherine's fears were realized, but she did not, could not resist his kiss. Like honey, sweet, sweet wine, he tasted so good, made her feel so deliciously wicked. . . . *But the consequences, Katherine. You have to resist. Use your imagination, as he did. Pretend it's Lord Seldon holding you in his arms.*

She tried, but her body knew the difference and begged her to reconsider. Why must she resist? Why? At that moment, she couldn't remember the reason, didn't really want to.

Just a few minutes to savor him, Katherine. What harm can a few minutes do?

The moment she fitted her slim body to his, Dimitri gave his passion free rein. Triumph soared in his blood, heightened his senses as never before, because success had never seemed so important before.

He had been right. Katherine was susceptible only to a direct assault on her senses. But he wasn't forgetting what had happened that morning. He didn't dare pause even for breath, didn't dare give her a moment's respite, or she would throw up her shield of indifference again, and this golden opportunity would be lost.

But what she was doing to him . . . Sweet Christ, he was not going to be able to proceed slowly. It was all he could do not to crush her with the power of his desire. Her small hands moved frantically over his back, into his hair, gripping, urging. Her tongue was dueling with his, not hesitantly, but with bold aggression. He could not be mistaken. She was as eager as he. But he still wasn't taking any risks.

Without breaking the kiss, Dimitri opened his eyes to find the direction of her bed. He should have taken note of it when he first came in, but he had been too enraptured by the sight of her in nothing but a loosely draped towel to notice anything else. But now, as he looked about her room and found no bed, his eyes flew back to what he had disdained to accept at first glance. A hammock!

It was like a splash of cold water. Doomed for lack of a bed? Inconceivable. There was the rug. It was thick and—no! He couldn't take her on the floor. Not this time. This time had to be perfect to give him ammunition to use for persuasion the next time.

Katherine was so attuned to Dimitri's passion that his momentary distraction was like an alarm bell going off in her head. She didn't know what caused it. That didn't matter. But she was abruptly jolted back to an awareness of what she was doing—and what he was doing. He was lifting her in his arms. He started toward the door, slowly, not once severing the contact of their lips.

But there was a difference in his kiss, a bruising increase of ardor, as if—as if . . . *He's figured you out, Katherine. He knows what it takes to turn you into a mindless shell.*

But it was too late. Her senses had returned whether she wished it or not.

She turned her head aside to break his power. "Where are you taking me?"

He didn't stop. "To my room."

"No . . . you can't take me out of here like this."

"No one will see you."

Her voice had been unsteady. It now cracked like a whip. "Put me down, Dimitri."

He stopped, but he didn't set her down. His arms tightened painfully, and she guessed that he was not going to relinquish his advantage so easily this time.

"I helped you in your hour of need," he reminded her. "Do you deny it?"

"No."

"Then you can do no less for me."

"No."

His body stiffened, his tone was sharp. "Fair is fair, Katya. I need you now, at this moment. This is no time to recall your absurd virtue."

That made her angry. "Absurd virtue? Don't compare me with your Russian women, who apparently have no virtue at all. I'm English! My *absurd virtue* is quite normal, thank you, and it won't change by association. Now put me down, Dimitri, right now."

He had the urge simply to drop her, he was so furious with her. How could she switch from one extreme to another with such ease? And why was

186

he even talking to her? He already knew that words couldn't pierce her defenses.

Dimitri let Katherine's legs slide to the floor, but his other arm around her back dropped lower to bend her into the curve of his hard body. The friction loosened the towel tucked in at her breasts, and only the tight fit of their bodies kept it from falling.

"I'm beginning to think you don't know what you want, Katya."

Katherine groaned as his other hand gripped her chin in preparation of a new assault. She wouldn't be able to withstand it, not again, not now. She had yet to recover from the first. But he was wrong, so wrong. She knew exactly what she wanted.

"Would you force me, Dimitri?"

He let her go so suddenly that she stumbled several feet back. "Never!" he fairly snarled.

She had unwittingly insulted him. She hadn't meant to. She had only made a last desperate effort to retain a measure of herself, for she was afraid that once she gave herself to him, he would so dominate her, mind and body, there would be nothing left of Katherine St. John.

There was no mistaking his utter frustration. When she glanced at him after a frantic bid to secure her towel, he was raking his hands through his hair as if he meant to pull out every golden strand. And then he paused, impaling her with a look that was confused and enraged at the same time.

"Sweet Christ, you are two different women! Where does the wanton go when the prude returns?"

Was he blind? Couldn't he see that she was still trembling with desire, her body screaming for his? *Blast you, Dimitri, don't be such a gentleman. Listen to my body, not my words. Take me.*

He didn't hear the unspoken plea. He saw only the lost opportunity, felt only the agony of passion unfulfilled.

After a last heated look, Dimitri left, slamming the door in his anger. But once outside, he regretted his deliberate taunt and the stricken look that had flashed over Katherine's features because of it. No woman who kissed as she did could be termed a prude. She wanted him. And if it was the last thing he did, he would make her admit it.

He had lost his chance this time by disdaining a rug. It wasn't as if he hadn't made love in unlikely places before. Once, on a dare from Vasili, he had made love in his theater box, during intermission, no less, when he was most likely to have been discovered. Damn, he wished Vasili were here now to talk to. He had a knack of breaking down problems so they seemed simple.

Seduction had failed, every direct approach had failed, including an appeal to Katherine's sense of fairness. She had none. So it was time to change tactics, perhaps take a leaf from her own book of supposed indifference. Women loved to say no, but they didn't like to be ignored. That might work. Of course it would require patience, which he sorely lacked.

He sighed heavily as he walked away. At least she had called him Dimitri. Small compensation.

Early the next morning, a bed was delivered to Katherine's room.

Chapter Nineteen

"What are your plans when we reach St. Petersburg, Katherine?"

Katherine deserted her pose to look sharply at Anastasia, but the younger girl had asked this question, like so many others, without glancing up from the canvas on which she was working. Katherine noticed that Zora, in the corner, had stopped sewing to await her answer. The middle-aged maid wasn't completely recovered from her seasickness, but she did have spells of feeling well enough to resume some of her duties.

Was it possible Anastasia really didn't know that Katherine was a prisoner? Zora knew. All the servants knew. But of course if Dimitri had made it understood that he didn't want his sister to know, none of the servants would go against his wishes, not even Anastasia's personal maid.

"I haven't given it much thought," Katherine lied. "Perhaps you should ask your brother."

The evasive answer broke through Anastasia's concentration long enough for a single glance, which brought a quick frown. "You've moved. Tilt your head back to the side, chin up—that's it." She relaxed again after comparing Katherine's pose with the likeness on the canvas. "Ask Mitya? What has it to do with him?" And then she forgot the portrait for a moment, startled by the thought. "You aren't still hoping . . . I mean, surely you realize . . . Oh, dear."

"Realize what, Princess?"

Anastasia quickly pretended to be engrossed in her painting, too embarrassed to answer. She hadn't wanted to like Katherine. She was the perfect target for Anastasia to relieve some of her rancor on, but it just hadn't worked out that way. She had also wanted to portray her on canvas as an earthy peasant, a coarse, common woman, an embodiment of rusticity. That hadn't worked out either. She had started the portrait three times before she had finally given up and painted what she saw instead of what she had wanted to see.

The fact was that Anastasia *did* like Katherine, her forthrightness, her calm control—so different from the Russian temperament—her quiet dignity, her dry sense of humor. She even liked her stubbornness, so like her own. There had been several near-confrontations in the beginning over what Anastasia thought were appropriate duties for Katherine to perform, but when she flatly refused and wouldn't argue about it, or give in, Anastasia developed a certain respect, which led to admiration, especially after she had stopped thinking Katherine was less than she claimed to be. She had actually begun to consider her as a friend.

Now suddenly she felt pity for the English-woman and was embarrassed because of it. Usually, she didn't empathize with women who moaned and complained over lost loves, as her friends so often did. She didn't understand the hurt of rejection, because she had never been rejected or ever had a man lose interest in her. She was the one who broke off affairs of the heart, flitting from one to another as the whim took her. In that, she was very like her brother.

The difference between them was that there was never any involvement for Dimitri. He loved women in general, none in particular, and favored any and all that attracted him. Not so Anastasia. She had to feel she was in love, and did often. It was just unfortunate that the feeling never lasted very long. But that was not to be confused with the melancholy of women who loved men who didn't return the sentiment.

Anastasia hadn't thought that Katherine, who had shown herself to be so pragmatic in nature, could fall into that category. But why else should she think Dimitri would care what she did once they reached Russia? He had obviously realized his mistake in bringing her along. Not even a week passed before he had lost interest and brought her to Anastasia, and he hadn't concerned himself with her since then. Didn't Katherine know what that meant?

"Realize *what*, Princess?"

Anastasia blushed at the repeated question, and then more, seeing that Katherine noticed her discomfort. "It was nothing. I don't know what I was thinking of."

"Yes, you do." Katherine wouldn't let her off the hook. "We were speaking of your brother."

"Oh, very well." Persistence was another trait of Katherine's that Anastasia had noted and admired, until now. "I thought you were different, that you weren't like all the other women who fall in love with Mitya when they meet him. After all, you haven't been upset or shown any signs of suffering from his lack of attention. But it just occurred to me that you might not realize that he's . . . well, that he . . ." This wouldn't do.

191

She was embarrassed enough. Katherine would be even more so if she thought Anastasia was feeling sorry for her. "What am I thinking? Of course you know."

"Know *what*?"

"That Mitya is not a man to become involved with for any length of time. I don't think he is even capable of loving one particular woman. He never has, you know. In fact, it is rare for any woman to hold his interest for more than a fortnight. His few mistresses are the only exception, but he doesn't *love* them. They are mere conveniences, no more. Wait . . . Princess Tatiana is another exception, but he's going to marry her, so she doesn't really count either."

"Princess—"

"No, no, you don't need to say it. I knew you were wise enough not to become enamored of him. You would be amazed if you knew how many women are not so wise. But it is easy to fall in love with Mitya. He appreciates women. Each one he favors, he devotes himself to fully for as long as his interest lasts. And he never makes promises that he will not fulfill, so none can say he deceives them."

Katherine hardly heard the last of what Anastasia was saying. Her ears were still ringing with the word *marry*. Her stomach had constricted and now she felt rather nauseous, which was utterly ridiculous. It was nothing to her that Dimitri was getting married. She had even thought at one point that Anastasia might be his wife. So what if he had a fiancée?

Blast Anastasia for bringing up this subject. And she was sitting there waiting for some kind of reply. To explain her situation, to explain what she really felt about Dimitri, would only prolong the conversation. And Anastasia, being his sister, might not believe her anyway.

"You were right, Princess," Katherine managed nonchalantly. "I am wise enough not to be enamored of your brother or any man for that matter. In fact, it delights me that he has all but forgotten that I am here."

Anastasia didn't believe her for a minute. The tone was indifferent, but the words were definitely defensive. They made her think that Katherine was indeed in love with Dimitri. But after being made to see how hopeless such a passion was, perhaps she would start to forget him now. Having done at least that much for her, and assuming she had helped her, Anastasia felt better.

It was fortunate that Dimitri didn't choose that moment to intrude on them. Fifteen minutes later, when he did, Katherine had tamped down her annoyance, gone through several arguments with her inner voice, and was composed again and satisfied that Anastasia's little revelations hadn't disturbed her in the least. But Dimitri did. After weeks of not seeing him, the sight of him now was too much.

Katherine had forgotten the devastating effect he could have on her—no, not actually forgotten. It was more that she doubted what she remembered. But she had deceived herself. He was still the fairy-tale prince, too handsome to be believed.

He was dressed somberly in black and gray, but it didn't matter what he was wearing. Was his hair longer? Yes, a little. Was that mere curiosity in the brief glance he gave her? Probably not even that.

Katherine had spoken the truth when she said Dimitri had all but forgotten her. Since that stormy day so long ago when he had surprised her in her cabin, he had given up his pursuit. And she was glad, of course she was. It certainly made this voyage more tolerable. . . . *But less exciting, Katherine. Be truthful. You miss the challenge of pitting your wits against his. And you have never been more flattered in your life than by his interest in you. You miss that too, and—other things.*

She sighed inwardly. It made no difference what she felt now, any more than it had before. Her position wasn't going to change. Lady Katherine St. John still couldn't take a lover, not even one as exciting as Dimitri. It was enough to make her wish she wasn't a lady.

"What is this?"

That *was* curiosity in his tone. Of course—how would he know that Anastasia had been painting her? Anastasia rarely left her cabin, and he hadn't come to visit her. And Anastasia was not one to give up a pout easily. She was still angry with her brother; had, in fact, been deliberately avoiding him, just as he had been avoiding Katherine.

"Really, Mitya, what does it look like?"

This was no question, just a retort to make her irritation clear. Anastasia didn't appreciate being interrupted, especially by him.

Her sarcasm was ignored, however. Dimitri turned his attention to Katherine, unable to mask his surprise.

"You agreed to this?"

"Really, Alexandrov, what does it look like?"

Katherine couldn't resist making the same retort. She should have. Dimitri laughed heartily.
She had not intended to amuse him.

"Did you want something, Mitya?" Anastasia
asked with a glare.

He didn't. Well, he did, but it was not something he could admit to his sister, and especially
not to Katherine. He had decided yesterday to
find out how his new tactics had worked. This
waiting game had tested his patience to the limit.
Each time he had wanted to seek Katherine out,
he had resisted, but no more. This morning he
had had to wait again, simply because she had
locked herself in here with Anastasia, posing for
a portrait no less. It was the last thing he expected to see.

There had also been the chance, not really anticipated, but a slim possibility, that this obsession with Katherine could have diminished in the
time he hadn't seen her. One look dismissed the
notion. If he had been in Russia, with other
women to distract him, perhaps. No, he doubted
even that would have helped. She was still, to
him, the most sensuous, sexy woman he had
ever seen. Just being in the same room with her
was all it took to stir his loins. He needed to have
his fill of her, to make love to her again and
again until she was out of his system. Boredom,
which came so quickly with other women, was
the only thing that would work. He was convinced of that.

He had never thought the day would come
when he would wish for boredom, not when he
had often bemoaned his inability to form a more
lasting relationship with a woman because of it.

The women of his acquaintance were only that, acquaintances. In fact, the only woman he could actually call a friend was Natalia, and that was only after he had stopped sleeping with her. But he would prefer boredom to this obsession that was monopolizing his thoughts and causing him more frustration than he had ever experienced before.

Dimitri hadn't answered Anastasia's question and didn't intend to. He was still smiling as he approached her, ostensibly to view her work but actually to give him an excuse to look at Katherine without appearing obvious, by comparing the portrait with the model. That was the plan. But like every plan having to do with Katherine, this one failed too. He couldn't take his eyes off the portrait.

He had known his sister was good at her hobby, but not this good. Yet that was not what held him transfixed. The woman in the portrait was and wasn't the woman he lusted after. The likeness was there. They could be twins. But this was not the woman he saw every time he closed his eyes. In vivid color here was the portrait of an aristocrat, regal, dignified, patrician in every nuance of her pose, a veritable blue-blood.

In the shimmering gold gown, her hair braided tightly and cast over one shoulder, a tiara resting on her head like a crown, she could have been a young medieval queen, proud, indomitable, and beautiful—yes, Anastasia had captured a beauty that wasn't easily discernible. . . .

Sweet Christ, what was he thinking? She was an actress! It was all an act, the pose, the pretense.

He touched Anastasia's shoulder to gain her attention. "Has she seen this yet?"

"No."

"She won't let me," Katherine put in, having heard his question. "She guards it like the crown jewels. Is it so awful?"

"No, not at all." He felt Anastasia stiffen at such a bland answer in regard to her masterpiece. "Ah, Katherine, would you mind stepping outside for a few moments? I would like a private word with my sister."

"Of course."

Katherine was miffed that he had treated her with the casual indifference he would show any lackey. But what had she really expected after all this time? His total neglect spoke for itself. Yet Anastasia had come too close to the truth. Katherine had been hoping without realizing it—for what, she wasn't sure. But now there was a great chasm inside her filled with sorrow. Realistically, she knew his indifference was just as well. Emotionally, she felt like crying.

Inside the cabin, Anastasia turned around to face her brother. He was staring again at the portrait. "Well?" She didn't even try to mask her resentment.

"Why haven't you shown this to her?"

Anastasia was distracted by the unexpected question. "Why?" And again, thoughtfully, "Why? Because I have had a subject become impatient when she did not see an immediate likeness and refuse to sit long enough for me to finish." She shrugged now. "It probably wasn't necessary with Katherine. She knows enough about painting to understand not to judge an unfinished work. And she has been an excellent subject, not even minding sitting for hours at a time. I have been able to get so much done. As you can see, it is almost finished.''

Dimitri was still staring at the portrait, wondering what Katherine thought about while she sat so patiently hour after hour. Did she ever think about him? Did she ever remember their one night together? Had his last gambit worked? Not as far as he could tell. She had barely glanced at him.

"I want the portrait," he said abruptly.

"You *what?*"

He looked at her impatiently. "Don't make me repeat myself, Nastya."

"Well, you can't have it."

She picked up her paint brush and stabbed it into the yellow ocher. Dimitri gripped her arm just above the elbow to keep her from ruining the picture in her sudden pique.

"How much?" he demanded.

"You can't buy it, Mitya." She took pleasure in denying him. "It's not for sale. And besides, I was going to give it to Katherine. I have enjoyed her company during this tedious voyage and—"

"Then what will you take for it?"

"Noth—" She paused with a jolt. He was serious. And if he wanted the picture that badly, she could probably ask him for anything and get it. "Why do you want it?"

"It is the best you have ever done," he said simply.

She frowned. "That's not the impression you gave when Katherine was here. 'Is it so awful?' 'No, not at all,' " she mimicked, still annoyed by his bland answer.

"Name your price, Nastya."

"I want to return to England."

"Not at this time."

"Then I want to choose my own husband."

"You are too young to make such a decision. But I will allow you the right to refuse my choice, if your refusal is reasonable, which is more than Misha would have allowed you were he still alive."

That was so true. Their older half-brother had hardly concerned himself with her and would have simply arranged her marriage, probably to someone she didn't even know, one of his army cronies, no doubt. And what Dimitri was offering was more than she could have hoped for, even if they hadn't been at odds over her indiscretions.

"But what if your idea of what is reasonable differs from mine?"

"Such as?"

"Too old or ugly or obnoxious."

Dimitri smiled at her, for the first time in a long while with the old warmth he reserved just for her. "All reasonable objections."

"Do you promise, Mitya?"

"I promise you will have a husband who will be acceptable to you."

Anastasia smiled now, half in apology for her recent behavior, and half in delight. "The portrait is yours."

"Good, but she's not to see it, Nastya, not now and not when it's finished."

"But she's expecting—"

"Tell her it was knocked over, the paint smeared, that it was ruined."

"But why?"

"You have portrayed her not as she is but as she would like us to believe she is. And I don't want her to know how superb her performance actually is."

"Performance?"

"She's no lady, Nastya."

"Nonsense," Anastasia protested with a short laugh. "I have spent time with her, Mitya. Are you suggesting I can't tell the difference between a lady and a common peasant? Her father is an English earl. She is highly educated, more than any woman I know."

"Nikolai and Konstantin are also well educated, as well as—"

"You think she's a bastard like them?" Anastasia gasped in surprise.

"It would explain her education and lack of social position."

"Very well, but so what?" Anastasia came to the defense of her friend as well as of her half-brothers. "In Russia, bastards are accepted—"

"Only if they are acknowledged. You know as well as I that for every noble bastard raised a prince, there are a dozen raised as serfs. And in England it is much worse. There they always carry the taint of their birth and are scorned by the nobility, no matter who claims them."

"But she spoke of family, Mitya, of living with this Earl of Strafford."

"Perhaps only wishful thinking on her part."

Anastasia frowned. "Why don't you like her?"

"Have I said I don't?"

"But you don't believe her."

"No. But she intrigues me. She is consistent in her lies, if nothing else. Now will you do as I ask?"

Anastasia continued to frown, but she nodded.

Chapter Twenty

The ship was silent again. Katherine refused to take the credit this time, no matter how often she was looked at beseechingly by Dimitri's servants, as if she could do something about his most recent foul mood. All she had done was refuse to have dinner with him. That couldn't possibly account for such surliness on his part. He hadn't even appeared interested when he invited her and seemed totally unmoved when she declined. No, they weren't going to place the blame on her shoulders this time.

But what if you're wrong, Katherine? What if a simple little overture could make a difference and relieve some of the tension? Even Anastasia has been quiet and subdued. And you have been meaning to speak to him about his library.

She made up her mind that morning, and an hour later knocked on Dimitri's door. Maksim opened it and quickly exited as soon as she entered the room. He was surprised to see her, but no more than Dimitri. The Prince immediately straightened his posture and smoothed back his hair, then caught himself doing it and slumped back in the chair behind his desk. Katherine didn't notice. She was staring at the papers strewn across the desk and wondering what could keep Dimitri occupied on such a long voyage. She would have been intrigued to know he was presently reviewing proposals from numerous factories and mills in the Rhineland that he was considering buying. Analyzing tedious reports was just what Katherine excelled at.

She finally glanced up at him and was disappointed to see such an inscrutable look returned, beautiful, but utterly devoid of emotion. She became nervous, wishing she had never come up with the idea of imposing on him, even if it was for something so minor.

"I hope I'm not disturbing you." She looked quickly away from him toward the wall of books. "I couldn't help noticing . . . before . . . I mean when I was here before, your extensive collection—" *For God's sake, Katherine, why are you stammering like a ninny?* "Would you mind if I borrowed a book or two?"

"Borrow? No. The insulation in here keeps them from being ruined by the sea air. But you are welcome to read anything you like in here."

She swung around too quickly, revealing her surprise and unease. "In here?"

"Yes. I wouldn't mind the company, even silent company—unless you're afraid to be in the same room with me."

She stiffened. "No, but—"

"I won't touch you, Katya, if that is what worries you."

He spoke sincerely, his expression blasé. He didn't care, she realized. He had made just a simple offer and a reasonable one. She hadn't even thought of the sea air which could indeed ruin an expensive book.

Katherine nodded and approached the bookshelves, trying vainly to pretend she was alone in the room. After several moments she made her selection and moved to the white satin sofa to make herself comfortable. The book was a short commentary on Russia by a French count who had spent five years there. Katherine would have loved reading it, to give her more insight into these people, and she could read French as easily as English. But today she might as well have been blind.

More than an hour passed, and Katherine still wasn't able to digest even a single word. It was impossible to concentrate in the same room with Dimitri, wondering if he was watching her, too nervous to look up and find out. Even without looking at him, she could feel his presence dominating her, working strangely on her senses. She felt warm and hot by degrees, while the room was actually pleasantly cool. And her nerves were definitely frazzled. The slightest noise made her start and her heart pick up its beat.

"This isn't working, is it, Katya?"

God, what a relief to have him put an end to this torture. And she didn't need to ask him to explain his statement. Had it been just as difficult for him to concentrate with her there? No, that was silly. He had probably just sensed her discomfort.

"No, it isn't," she answered with some embarrassment.

She closed the book in her lap before she looked up at him. It was a mistake. What his voice hadn't revealed his eyes did. They were that certain shade of velvety brown she had come to associate with his passion, lustrous, almost black, and so intense. They seemed to strip her naked, to probe into her soul for an answering chord of feeling she didn't dare give into.

"Your options are limited at the moment," he said quietly, his voice so contrary to the emotion in his eyes. "Either get into my bed or take the book and leave. But do one or the other—now."

She was unable to resist a glance toward his bed. God, the temptations this man threw at her one after another. She had thought there would be no more. *Wrong again, Katherine.*

"I—I think I had better leave."

"As . . . you . . . wish."

The words struggled out of him. It was all Dimitri could do just to remain seated, when every muscle screamed to leap up and stop her from fleeing. What kind of masochist was he to inflict such torture on himself? It was hopeless. She wasn't going to change. Why did he persist?

Katherine leaned back against the closed door, her heart still hammering, her cheeks flushed, and she was clutching the book so tightly to her chest that her fingers hurt. She felt as though she had just escaped her execution. Perhaps she had. Dimitri threatened her beliefs, her principles, her self-esteem. He was capable of destroying her will, and then what would be left of her?

But she had so desperately wanted to walk to that bed. And if he had gotten up, if he had made one move toward her . . . She had seen in the last glance she had stolen in his direction what it had cost him not to move: the clenched fists, the straining muscles, the grimace etched on his features.

God, what madness to have sought him out. She should have remembered it wasn't safe to be alone with him. But she had thought he had lost interest. Couldn't she even assume the obvious where he was concerned?

Katherine walked away, lines of worry creasing her brow once again. But the melancholy that had been dogging her lately was gone.

Chapter Twenty-one

The carriage sped along at an alarming rate, the view through the window nearly a blur. Katherine had developed a headache from trying to distinguish anything of the passing scenery and gave up. At any rate, her main concentration was in trying to keep her seat.

Anastasia laughed at her gasps and cringes. "This is a normal ride, my dear, nothing to be alarmed about. Wait until winter, when the wheels are exchanged for runners. Then the *troika* really races along."

"You mean you turn carriages into sleighs?"

"Of course. We have to with so much snow and ice covering the roads for most of the year. I know in England you usually keep a sleigh just for when it snows. We could do the same, only in reverse, but instead of storing a *troika* for only a few months' use, we convert it. Much more economical, don't you think?"

Katherine had to smile, quite sure that Anastasia had never once concerned herself with economics, at least not on a personal level. But the smile didn't last. The carriage turned abruptly, and she lost her grip on the seat and slammed into the side wall, which was fortunately well padded with a thick gold velvet. Unhurt, she started to laugh, seeing that Anastasia had also bumped shoulders with the wall, and the younger girl joined her. She could see how Russians might enjoy such rides if they grew up with them. A child, she imagined, would be thrilled by such an experience.

When Anastasia regained her composure, she said, "We are almost there."

"Where?"

"Didn't Mitya tell you? He has decided to leave me with our older half-sister, Varvara, and her family. She rarely leaves the city, except to escape for a while the damp of autumn. I don't mind at all, even though St. Petersburg is so boring in August, with everyone off to their summer palaces on the Black Sea coast or traveling. But this will keep me out from under Aunt Sonya's thumb for a while more, which suits me perfectly."

"And where is Dimitri going?"

"To Novii Domik, our country estate, and he's in a terrible hurry." She frowned. "He won't even stop to see Varvara, which is really too bad of him. But I'm sure he will see you safely settled first, probably with one of the families associated with the British Embassy. I wish you could stay with me. I'm sure Varvara wouldn't mind. But Mitya said it wouldn't be convenient at this time. Do you know why?"

"I'm afraid I haven't spoken to him at all."

"Oh—well, I wouldn't worry about it. Mitya must know what he's doing. But you will promise to visit me as soon as possible. I want to show you everything."

"Princess, I think there's something you should know about—"

"Oh, here we are! And look, there's one of my nieces. How she's grown!"

The carriage stopped before a huge house that in England would have been termed a palace, but then it seemed as if every other building Katherine had seen on this wild ride through St. Petersburg had been either a palace or a barracks. But she wasn't surprised. She did know something of Russia's history, in particular that Peter the Great, who had built this jewel of a city with the forced labor of his serfs, had also forced his nobles to build stone mansions here, with the threat of exile or execution if they refused.

Anastasia immediately jumped out of the carriage, but the many footmen in red-and-silver livery who had come running down the steps made sure she didn't fall. Katherine watched as two of them practically carried her up the stairs, a hand on each elbow as if they thought she couldn't maneuver a few steps by herself. And then the little golden-haired niece was in her arms, clamoring for a generous hug.

A homecoming. It made Katherine's throat tighten. When would she have hers? She should have said something to Anastasia sooner. The girl was the only one who could really help her, the only one who would consider defying Dimitri. There was still time, but only a few minutes.

Katherine reached for the door, but was knocked back against the seat as the carriage took off again. Frantically she stuck her head out the window, but the most she could do was return Anastasia's wave. She was already too far away to hear her calling goodbye.

For the first time, she now noticed Dimitri's Cossacks trailing behind the carriage. To escort her to the Embassy? Somehow she didn't think so. Blast and bloody hell! Why had she waited so long to tell Anastasia the truth? *Because you came to like the silly girl, that's why, and you didn't*

*want to hurt her by telling her what a bastard her
brother really is. Now what's to do? You wait and see,
that's what. He can't keep you isolated from other
people now. Somehow you'll be able to talk to someone
who will help.*

Encouraging thoughts, so why didn't they
cheer her? Because she had been locked in her
cabin today just as she had been every other time
the ship had put into some port for supplies on
this long voyage. She had waited and waited,
and thought night would never come when she
might be let out. And it didn't come. She finally
realized that Russia must be similar to those few
other northern countries that had no night in
summer; St. Petersburg, at least, was almost on
a parallel with Denmark, Sweden, and Norway.
It had been late when Vladimir took her off the
ship and placed her in the carriage with Anastasia. And now she was being taken where?

It wasn't long before the carriage stopped in
front of another palace, this one even more impressive than Varvara's. But no one came to open
the door for Katherine, so she assumed she
wasn't destined to be left here. She was correct.
After about a minute, the huge doors opened at
the top of the wide stairs and Dimitri appeared
and came directly down to the carriage.

Katherine was too tense to be cordial when he
took the seat opposite her. "I don't appreciate
being whisked around by a mad driver in a city
I don't know at God knows what hour, and
furthermore—"

"What did she say when you told her?"

She glowered at him for the interruption.
"Told who? What?"

"Don't be tedious, Katya," he sighed. "Nastya. You did tell her your sad story, didn't you?"

"Oh—actually, no."

His brow rose sharply. "No? Why not?"

"There wasn't time," she replied stiffly.

"You have had weeks—"

"Oh, shut up, Dimitri. I was going to tell her, don't think I wasn't. She ought to know what a despicable cad you are. And I started to, but we arrived at your other sister's home too soon, and Anastasia was excited and left so quickly . . . Don't you dare laugh!"

He couldn't help it. He hadn't seen her like this since the beginning of the voyage, with such fire in those lovely blue-green eyes. He had forgotten how delightful she could be in her fury. And she had put his last worry to rest. Anastasia could have caused a problem if she had decided to champion Katherine's cause. He had become too lax in thinking that if Katherine hadn't told her by the end of the voyage, she wouldn't tell her at all. He hadn't realized until after the travel arrangements had been made and the two women were given a carriage to themselves that the last minute would be the opportune time to enlist his sister's aid. But Katherine had failed. Intentionally? Sweet Christ, he would like to think so.

"It is as well you didn't tell her, Katya," he commented as he settled back in the luxurious seat.

"For you," she retorted.

"Yes, it does make things easier."

"So now what?"

"You will remain with me for a while more."

He had attended to all his immediate business in the city that afternoon. Servants had been dispatched ahead to inform his aunt that he was back and would soon be home. Others had been sent out to locate Vasili, and of course, Tatiana. He still didn't want to think about resuming his courtship, though he knew he would have to soon. But now his thoughts were filled with Katherine and the week ahead. He would have her more to himself with Anastasia left behind in the city. There was no telling what that might lead to.

"Can't you just send me home now?"

The wistful note in Katherine's voice annoyed Dimitri, but he shrugged it off. "Not until I hear that the Tzar has concluded his visit to England. But come now, surely you will want to see some of Russia as long as you are here. You will enjoy the trip to Novii Domik. It is about two hundred fifty miles east of here in the province of Vologda."

"Dimitri! That's practically the full length of England! Are you taking me to Siberia?"

He smiled at her natural ignorance. "My dear, Siberia is across the Ural Mountains, and the Urals are a thousand miles away. Have you really no concept of the size of my country?"

"Apparently not," she mumbled.

"You could probably fit a hundred of your Englands into Russia. Novii Domik is hardly any distance at all in comparison and will take less than a week to reach, what with the extra daylight hours we have to travel in during this season."

"Must I go? Can't you leave me here?"

"Certainly, if you want to remain behind a locked door for a month or more. In the country, Katya, there are no English." He didn't have to explain the significance of that. "You will have much more freedom and more to do. You did say you were adept at numbers. My bookkeepers have no doubt been lax while I've been away."

"You would trust me with your accounts?"

"Shouldn't I?"

"No, actually—blast it, Dimitri, you really think you're going to come out of this without the least consequence, don't you? You think I'm such a faint-hearted ninny that I won't see you pay, that I won't do *something* to cause you grief? You never did comprehend what you've done to me *and* my family, or rather, you don't care. You've ruined my reputation by dragging me here without a proper chaperon. I'll have to literally buy a husband when I'm ready for one, because I'm too honest not to admit what I'm now lacking, thanks to you. My sister's life is probably ruined now too, which you are also responsible for, because I wasn't there to prevent her from eloping with a fortune hunter. My brother wasn't ready for the responsibility my absence has no doubt forced on him. And my father—"

Katherine's tirade was cut off abruptly when Dimitri leaned forward, grabbed her shoulders, and dragged her across the carriage into his lap. "So I have wronged you. I am the first to admit it. But your situation is not as bad as you would make it, Katya. I will buy you a chaperon who will swear she was with you every minute and won't change her story on threat of death. As for your lost virtue, I will give you a fortune to buy this husband you want, if you insist on having one, but it will also enable you to live independently if you would rather, without a husband or any man to answer to. And if your sister has married this fellow you object to, I can make her a widow—it is that simple. As for your brother . . . How old is he?"

"Twenty-three," she answered without thinking, too stunned at the moment to do otherwise.

"Twenty-three, and you're worried he can't shoulder a little responsibility? Give the boy a chance, Katya. As for your father, I don't wish to discuss him. If he misses you, he will certainly better appreciate you when you return. Let me tell you instead what else I have done to you."

"Don't."

"Ah, but I insist." He chuckled when she tried unsuccessfully to leave her new seat. "I forced you to take a vacation, which you sorely needed if even half of the things you claim are true. I have given you adventure, new friends, new places to see, even a new language—yes, Marusia has told me how quickly you mastered Russian with her help." His voice suddenly deepened. "I have also forced you to experience new and wonderful feelings. I introduced you to passion."

"Stop it!" Her eyes flared as she pushed against his chest to keep him from drawing her closer. "You think you have all the answers, but you don't. First off, a chaperon means nothing when my disappearance without a word speaks for itself. And I won't accept your money. I've told you that repeatedly. My father is wealthy, extremely wealthy. I could live quite comfortably for the rest of my life on my dowry alone. If you want to give away a fortune, give it to Lord Seymour—he needs it, I don't—and I certainly wouldn't let you kill him, for God's sake, no matter how much misery he will cause my sister.''

Before she could say another word, Dimitri defied the push of her hands and kissed her. It wasn't exactly an ardent kiss, just enough to stop the flow of her words—at first. It became much more than that after only a few seconds. His kisses were a drug, a potent tranquilizer. Katherine became all weak and malleable—and heard him groan.

''Sweet Christ!'' And then his eyes looked into hers, those dark, hypnotic eyes. ''We don't need a bed. Say we don't need a bed, Katya.''

His fingers were stealing under her skirt as he spoke. She put her hand down to block the way.

''No.''

''Katya—''

''No, Dimitri!''

He leaned back, closing his eyes. ''This is what I get for asking.''

Katherine didn't comment. She was so flustered that she could barely make it back to her seat when he released her.

''I had thought to share the carriage with you, but that's not such a good idea, is it?'' he continued. ''I would end up attacking you within a mile.''

''You wouldn't.''

He opened one eye with the brow sharply cocked, then the other with a sigh. ''No, but you would consider any overture an attack, wouldn't you, little one? And since I can't quite manage to keep my hands to myself, I suppose the decent thing to do is leave." He waited a moment, hoping she would contradict him. He sighed again when she didn't, long and loud. "Very well. But be warned, Katya. The time is going to come when I won't be so easily managed. You had best hope you are on your way back to England before then."

Chapter Twenty-two

*W*hen she thought about it later, Katherine was glad that Dimitri wasn't in close attendance on that long ride to Novii Domik, and not for the obvious reason. Marusia and Vladimir had joined her instead; consequently the trip became a learning experience. With Dimitri present, she would have been aware of nothing but him. But with Marusia she was able to relax. Not even Vladimir's dour company could inhibit her, nor did his tolerant silence seem to bother his wife. Marusia was informative, entertaining, talking the whole way.

Katherine learned a little more about the people, the land, and between villages and estates that were described in detail, more about Dimitri. Some things she could have done without knowing, but once Marusia started, it wasn't easy to deter her from a subject.

The countryside was breathtakingly beautiful, awash with summer colors; wild flowers, tall stands of silver birch, fields of golden wheat, and the vivid green of pines. But the villages were the most picturesque, with their blue or pink cottages, all with identical red-painted porches. Katherine thought they were quaint until she learned that such orderly villages were actually military colonies. The carriage passed close enough to one for her to see even children in uniform.

These military colonies were one of the subjects Marusia expounded on, since she had particular distaste for them. They had been started nearly thirty years ago by Alexander's order. The provinces of Novgorod, Mogilev, Kherson, Ekaterinoslav, and Slobodsko-Ukrainski were soon housing one third of the army in these new camps. The process was simple. A regiment was moved into a district, and automatically all the inhabitants of that district became soldiers, reserves for the unit settled on their soil. The old villages were torn down to be replaced by symmetrical cottages. The serfs' new role was taught with blows of the stick. Everything became military, even to plowing the fields in uniform to the sound of a drum.

"What about the women?" Katherine wanted to know.

"The Tzar's idea was to keep soldiers with their families when they weren't off fighting his wars, but also to combine the work of the soldier with that of the serf, who would be given military training. So the women are an important part of the colonies. Marriages are decided upon by the military authority. Not one widow or old maid is overlooked, and none has any choice. They have to marry the man they are ordered to marry and produce children. And fines are imposed if they don't give birth often enough."

"And the children?"

"Enrolled among the army children at the age of six to begin training. And everything is done by regulation: the caring of cattle, the washing of floors, the polishing of copper buttons, even the nursing of children, everything. For the least infraction—the cane."

Katherine was incredulous. "And the people just went along with this?"

"The *people* were serfs. They simply went from civil obedience to military obedience. But no, many protested, entreated, fled, or hid in the forests. There was even a full-scale rebellion in the colony of Chuguyev, which reached such proportions that many death sentences were pronounced by the military tribunal. These were carried out not by shooting but by having the condemned pass under the rod twelve times between the rows of a battalion of a thousand men. More than one hundred fifty men died under the blows."

Katherine looked to Vladimir to confirm this appalling story, but he was studiously ignoring both women, considering the subject highly inappropriate for female discussion. But his wife was in her element when she was gossiping, especially when she had such an avid listener. And she had a flair for drama. He didn't have the heart to curb her enjoyment.

"Alexander loved his colonies," Marusia continued. "Tzar Nicholas loves them as well. But then he is even more of a military man than his brother was. He insists on order, neatness, and regularity, and so he naturally feels most at ease among army officers. The Prince said the Tzar even sleeps on an army bed in his palace and when he travels through his empire, inspecting his troops and institutions. Prince Dimitri had to accompany him several times on these inspections when he was in the Imperial Guard."

Katherine knew nothing about this most elite unit of the military or that Dimitri had at one time belonged to it, but Marusia was quick to change that. And so the talk had come around to Dimitri, and Katherine's interest picked up, as did Vladimir's disapproval of their choice of topics. It was one thing for his wife to gossip about the Prince with the other servants, all loyal to Dimitri, but something else again for him to be discussed with an outsider, and this one in particular.

After describing his illustrious if short military career, Marusia went on to proudly delineate his ancestry, swearing it could be traced back to Rurik, the very man hailed as the founder of the Russian state. "Rurik was one of a group of Varangians from Scandinavia who settled along the Dnieper River in the ninth century, taking over the leadership of the Slav robber bands already established there."

"You mean Vikings?" Katherine now made the connection, only surprised she hadn't before. Dimitri could in fact have been a Viking of old. "But of course, I should have realized. The height, the coloring—"

"Vikings, Varangians, yes, they were kinsmen, but not many in Russia are as tall as our prince. The royal family, yes. The Tzar himself is more than six feet."

In the days that followed, confined to the carriage and each other's company, Marusia and Katherine touched on every possible subject at least once. Katherine learned about the rest of Dimitri's family: about the oldest brother, Mikhail, who had died; about his two sisters, Varvara being one, and their families; about all the illegitimate children, who were as close and as well cared for as the legitimate ones; and about Dimitri's Aunt Sonya, who according to Marusia was a female tyrant. No subject was sacred, even the Alexandrovs' financial status. Textile mills, a glass factory, copper mines, as well as vast estates in the Urals with more than twenty thousand serfs, the summer residence on the shores of the Black Sea, the palace on the Fontanka in St. Petersburg, another in Moscow, Novii Domik—and these were just some of the family holdings.

Apparently Dimitri also had his own personal fortune, inherited from his mother, and numerous businesses scattered across Europe, which Marusia didn't know much about. Vladimir, who did know, wasn't volunteering any information. She mentioned only his ships in some detail—not one, but five—a castle in Florence, a villa in Fiesole, and a country manor in England, and the fact that Dimitri, until Mikhail's death, had spent more time out of Russia than in it.

When they discussed serfs, Katherine discovered that use of the cane was not exclusive to the military colonies; even a torturing spiked collar was used by some landowners to enforce obedience in their serfs. She came to understand why the Alexandrov serfs were so fiercely loyal, and why they preferred to be owned than set free to earn dirt-poor wages in deplorable working conditions in the cities.

"Do you know what year this is?"

Marusia laughed, not needing an explanation for Katherine's ridicule. "The tzars have talked of abolishing serfdom. Alexander wanted to. Nicholas too. How could they not when they see how backward we are in comparison with the rest of the world. But always they are given reasons why they should not, why this is not the time, why it is not possible—so many reasons."

"You mean they succumb to pressure from the landowners, who refuse to give up their slaves," Katherine sneered.

Marusia shrugged. "The *aristos* . . . It is their way of life. People fear change."

"But Dimitri is different," Katherine remarked thoughtfully. "He's not a typical Russian, is he?"

"No, and that is his mother's doing. She influenced his younger years, at least until his father's sister, Sonya, moved in. Then he had his very Russian aunt pulling him one way and his very English mother the other. And the two women hated each other, which only made matters worse. The Prince was raised in Russia, but he has never really forgotten his mother's teachings, especially on the abomination of serf-dom. Here is Russia, trying in every way to be westernized, yet clinging to the ancient custom of slavery, and it is not even a Russian custom. There were always peasants, true, but it was Ivan the Terrible who first bound them to the land so thoroughly that they lost the freedom to leave it at will."

Katherine had much to think about during the trip, mostly that Russia was nice enough to visit as long as you didn't see the cruelty and injustice beneath the surface. To have so much power in the hands of so few, and the vast majority tolerant of subjugation was inconceivable in this day and age. Good Lord, her father would have been in his element if he could have worked toward reform here. So much needed changing, too much for one person—no, that wasn't true. The

Tzar was an absolute ruler. If one man could turn thousands into serfs, another could free them.

It gave Katherine a headache to think about Russia. If this had been her country, she would have gone mad from the impotence of being able to do nothing about the conditions here. But then, if this were her country, she would probably have a different outlook. It was just fortunate she wouldn't be here long. Why she had to stay at all was becoming a question she asked herself repeatedly. Just because Dimitri said so? Ha!

At the first posting house, where the horses were changed, Katherine reviewed her options on slipping away unnoticed. It wasn't heartening to find there were none. Vladimir had obviously been given the responsibility of keeping her in his sights and out of the public eye as much as possible, and he took his duty seriously. Whenever he wasn't around, Marusia or Lida or one of the other servants was.

There was even less opportunity for escape the few times they spent the night at a country estate belonging to acquaintances of Dimitri's. There Katherine slept in the servants' quarters with a half-dozen other women, on a hard pallet on the floor. She could have slept in the main house in a comfortable bed, though probably not alone. Dimitri did make the offer. But after learning the true plight of Russian servants, and feeling a new and unbridled anger that Dimitri had placed her in the same class, Katherine turned stubborn. If she was no better than the other servants, why should he make an exception for her? She wouldn't have it. She would either be given her due or demand consistency. No more half measures. She had too much pride to accept the crumbs of his generosity, knowing what he really thought of her.

It felt good to pit herself against Dimitri again and have her will prevail. This high and mighty prince was not going to have *everything* his way. He might drag her off to the country and keep her prisoner there, but he couldn't control her behavior. She was still Katherine St. John with a mind of her own, not some lackey afraid to disagree with him.

Chapter Twenty-three

Similar to the country estates passed along the way, yet on a much grander scale than anything Katherine had seen so far, Novii Domik, or New Cottage, was a surprise and a delight. She had almost been expecting some colossal mansion, considering what she now knew of Dimitri's wealth, yet the Alexandrovs' country home was not in the least pretentious. Half-hidden amidst a grove of trees, it was a sprawling two-story manor with wide-flung wings, the veranda and balcony supported by massive white columns. Typically Russian was the fretwork on the eaves and window shutters, an example of the most beautiful carving Katherine had ever seen.

Approaching the house, Katherine could see an avenue of lime trees leading to an orchard of apple, pear, and cherry trees. Closer to the house were flower gardens, a riot of color in late-summer bloom. In the back, beyond her view, a vegetable garden separated a variety of outbuildings from the house, and less than a half-mile away was the village.

Dimitri had not ridden ahead, though he had spent most of the trip on horseback and was impatient to be home. For the last several miles he had ridden alongside Katherine's carriage. It was the most she had seen of him since they left St. Petersburg. Even at the posting houses he had managed to avoid her. She didn't mind. She had become used to not seeing him on the ship. And whenever she did see him, she always experienced that rush of feeling that she could certainly do without.

Was he still displeased with her for insisting on sleeping with the servants again last night at his friend Alexey's house? Of course he was. He was so easy to read when he was angry: the deep scowl, the tight-set lips, the little muscle that ticked along his jaw as he ground his teeth together, and the murderous look in his eyes when he happened to glance her way, as if he would like to wring her neck.

No wonder his servants feared him when he was like this. Katherine supposed she ought to fear him as well, but she couldn't help being amused instead, at least in this instance. Dimitri was so like a little boy in his temper. He reminded her of her brother Warren when he was a child and the tantrums he would throw when he didn't get his way. Ignoring Warren had broken him of the habit. Ignoring Dimitri wasn't quite so easy. It was in fact impossible to ignore such a man. She could pretend to, but the truth was she was always aware of him, vitally aware. Even when she couldn't see him, she knew when he was near.

When they reached the house, Katherine became uneasy, seeing so many people waiting there to welcome the master home. Worse, out of the four carriages in their cavalcade, hers had to be the one to stop directly in front of the house. Worse still, Dimitri ignored everyone, even his aunt waiting on the veranda, to open the carriage and drag Katherine out, up the stairs, and into the house. This is what she got for being amused by his temper—mortification.

In the wide entrance hall, Dimitri swung Katherine around to face him before he let go of her wrist. "Not a word, Katya!" he cut her off when she opened her mouth to protest such bizarre behavior. "Not a single word. I have had enough of your stubbornness, enough of your contrariness, and most definitely enough of your arguments. Here you will sleep where I put you, not where you want, not with the servants, but where I put you. 'Vladimir!'" Dimitri shouted over his shoulder. "The White Room, and see that she stays there!"

Katherine was incredulous. He actually turned his back on her then and walked back to his aunt. Dismissed. Treated like a child again—worse than a child!

"Why you—"

"Sweet Mary, not now," Vladimir hissed in her ear. "He got it out of his system. His temper will improve now, but not if you challenge him again."

"His temper can rampage perpetually for all I care," Katherine hissed back. "He can't order me about like that."

"Can't he?"

She started to contradict him, but snapped her mouth shut. Of course Dimitri could order her about. As long as she was in his blasted power, he could make her do anything he pleased. And out here in the country, surrounded by his people, she was most certainly in his power. Intolerable. Frustrating beyond belief. But what could she do?

Ignore him, Katherine. His behavior is beneath contempt anyway and not deserving of a reaction. Pa-

*tience. Your time will come, and when it does, Dimitri
Alexandrov will rue the day he met you.*

Dimitri already rued the day he met Katherine.
No woman had ever caused him such exasperation, and he couldn't even claim that she made
up for it in other ways. And there was little
doubt that she did it deliberately, took pleasure
in annoying him, delight in spiting him, and she
did it so well. Ungrateful wench. But he was
tired of humoring her and tired of losing his reason and control where she was concerned. He
had only to glance around him to see what a fool
he had just made of himself.

But he had actually done more than that,
though unintentionally. One look at Marusia's
disapproving face told him he had also diminished Katherine's worth in the eyes of everyone
there. At the moment he didn't care. It was just
as well anyway. It was time her little game was
over. Marusia and the others treated her with too
much deference. They fostered her delusions,
which made her think she could get away with
anything. Humoring her himself hadn't helped
either. But no more.

Seeing his aunt's bemused expression, Dimitri
realized he had marched past her without a
word. He greeted her properly now, but Sonya
Alexandrovna Rimsky was not known for being
circumspect.

"Who is she, Mitya?"

He followed Sonya's gaze to see Katherine
walking behind Vladimir up the stairs. Head held
high, shoulders thrown back, skirt lifted just so
high, and only the slightest sway of hips. It ir-

ritated him no end that she even walked like a
lady.

"She isn't important, just an Englishwoman
returned with us."

"But you put her in your private wing—"

"For now," he interrupted curtly. "Don't concern yourself, Aunt Sonya. I will find something
for her to do while she's here."

Sonya started to protest, but thought better of
it. She was a tall woman, nearly six feet, and
narrow in build. A widow whose marriage had
lasted less than a year, she hadn't mourned her
overbearing husband's death and had refused to
remarry and suffer the indignities of the marriage bed with yet another man. Her life, fraught
with one disappointment after another, left little
tolerance for the baser urges men were cursed
with. Her own brother had gone so far as to
marry an Englishwoman simply because he
couldn't have her any other way, and now the
Alexandrov bloodline would be forever tainted.
If only Misha hadn't died, or if he had at least
left an heir, a legitimate heir . . .

A brief look of disgust crossed Sonya's features as she drew her own conclusions about
Dimitri's companion. So now he was bringing
sluts into his home. He couldn't be discreet like
his brothers and father and just tumble a willing
serf now and then. He had to bring one back
from England. What was he thinking of? But she
didn't ask him. His mood was not conducive to
criticism at the moment, if his terseness was any
indication. And she didn't want any more dis-
graceful scenes for the servants to witness.

She waited while Dimitri had a few words with
everyone who had turned out to welcome him

home. It was ridiculous really, this respect he paid mere servants, but his mother could be thanked for his peculiarities, and he was really too old to try and change him. Tatiana would be a good influence however. The one thing Sonya had no complaints over was Dimitri's choice of a bride. But this long absence hadn't helped his suit. He had no time to waste, certainly no time to waste on an English peasant.

Belatedly Sonya noticed her niece's absence. "Didn't Nastya return with you?"

"Yes, but I left her to visit with Varvara for a while." The truth was she had become much too attached to Katherine, which could cause endless problems he didn't need.

"Is that wise, Mitya? St. Petersburg is not without its social gatherings at this time of year, even if it is almost deserted. Or did I misunderstand your message when you rushed off to bring the girl home?"

"You understood. But you needn't worry about her much longer. She has agreed to marry as soon as we can agree on a suitable husband."

Sonya's blue eyes flared in surprise. "You will give her a choice?"

"She's my sister, Aunt Sonya. I would like to see her happy in a marriage. You weren't given a choice, and look how that turned out."

Sonya drew herself up stiffly. "We needn't discuss that. Nastya is fortunate that you are so indulgent, but only an exceptional man will put up with her willfulness. There is no telling what ideas she has brought back with her from England. She never should have been allowed to visit there, but then you know my feelings about that."

"Yes, Aunt," he sighed.

He knew only too well. She had been ardently opposed to her only brother marrying a foreigner and resentful when he did so anyway. She had never forgiven Petr, and war between the two women broke out immediately when Sonya was forced to return home after her husband died. Jealousy prevented her from seeing the goodness in Anne. As far as Sonya was concerned, everything Anne did was wrong, her views outlandish, and with Anne's death, these feelings were transferred to England in general. Dimitri was certain the only reason she kept up a correspondence with the Duchess was the pleasure she got in pointing out all of Dimitri's and Anastasia's faults, which she attributed solely to their mother, though she refrained from mentioning *that* to Anne's mother.

"Well, whatever scandal Nastya stirred up in England won't follow her home, thanks be to God," Sonya remarked as they passed into the drawing room. "She can make a good marriage here. And speaking of marriage, have you seen Tatiana Ivanova yet?"

A one-track mind. Dimitri was only surprised she hadn't asked sooner.

"We've only just returned, Aunt Sonya, and I came here directly from the ship. But I have my people looking into her whereabouts."

"You need only to have asked me. She is in Moscow presently, visiting her married sister. But she hasn't exactly pined away while you were gone, Mitya. I have heard that Count Grigori Lysenko began paying his suit as soon as you left, and the rumor is that she favors him."

Dimitri shrugged, not particularly concerned. He had never liked Lysenko, not since they had been in the same unit in the Caucasus and he had had the misfortune to save the Count's life, taking a minor wound himself in the process. His gesture would have been nothing, forgotten, except that Lysenko hadn't been in the least appreciative, had in fact resented his help, and thereafter had set out to prove himself the better man at marksmanship, hunting, everything. So he wasn't surprised that Lysenko had set his sights on the lovely Tatiana. But he wasn't worried. The Count had yet to prove himself anything but a fool.

"I will send word to her that I have returned."

"Shouldn't you go in person, Mitya?"

"And appear overanxious?"

"She will be flattered."

"She will be amused," Dimitri countered, becoming annoyed by her single-mindedness. "Constant attendance didn't sway her before I left. It will not hurt to let her wonder for a while if I am still interested."

"But—"

"No buts!" he snapped. "If you don't think me capable of winning the fair lady on my own, perhaps I should cease to try."

It was a warning, plain and simple, and Sonya was wise enough to heed it. Tight-lipped, she turned and left the room.

Dimitri headed for the liquor cabinet and splashed vodka into a glass. He didn't need his aunt to tell him that he should resume his courtship immediately, but he simply didn't have the patience for it right now and wouldn't have until he had released some of this sexual tension that had him so short-tempered. There were a number of women here that he could relieve his pent-up desires with, but as great as his discomfort was after so long at sea, he didn't want just anyone. He wanted Katherine. Damn, but it always came back to her.

Furiously Dimitri threw the still-full glass into the fireplace and stalked out of the room. He found Katherine in the White Room, staring uninterestedly out the window. Boris, just bringing in her trunk, hurried the task and left when he saw Dimitri waiting to speak with her.

"I won't ask if you find the room to your liking. You will just tell me no, and then—"

"Then you will have another one of your fits," Katherine supplied as she slowly turned to face him. "You know, Dimitri, these tantrums are becoming quite tiresome."

"Tantrums!"

"Is this going to be another one?" she asked with wide-eyed innocence.

He clamped his mouth shut. She was doing it again, deliberately provoking him so that he couldn't think, couldn't remember why he had sought her out in the first place. But he didn't forget this time. And two could play her game.

"You fail to mention your own temper."

"Me? Have a temper?"

"No, of course not," he jeered. "You just scream and shout because it's good exercise for the lungs."

She stared at him incredulously for a moment and then began to laugh—warm, honest laughter that filled the room and surrounded Dimitri with enchantment. He had never heard her laugh before, not like this. It made him realize there was an aspect of her personality he had overlooked—a sense of humor or even, possibly, mischievousness. If he thought about them, many of the things she had said to him, things that had annoyed him, could actually have been gentle teasing.

"Oh, God," Katherine sighed after a moment, wiping tears from her eyes. "You are priceless, Dimitri. Exercise my lungs—I'll have to remember that when my brother complains that I'm a tyrant. I do lose patience with him occasionally."

He didn't want to break this mood. "And with me."

"Most certainly with you."

But she was smiling as she spoke, and he was filled with a curious pleasure. Why had he come? To lay down new rules. To hell with that. He didn't really want to change her or take away her pretenses, which she so obviously enjoyed. If only he weren't so sensitive where she was concerned! But if she had simply been teasing him, even just half the time . . .

"There must be some way we can fix it," Dimitri said as he casually moved closer.

"Fix it?"

"Yes, fix it—your lack of patience, my lack of patience, our mutual flaring tempers. They say lovers never find time to argue."

"Are we back to that?"

"We have never been far from it."

Katherine warily backed up when he got too close. "Actually, I've heard lovers have the most violent arguments."

"Perhaps some do, but certainly not often. Yet when they do, they have the most delightful way of making amends. Shall I tell you how?"

"I can—" Her retreat ended against the wall, and she finished with a gasp. "Guess."

"Then why don't we make amends for a change?"

She had to press her hands against his chest to hold him back. *Concentrate, Katherine. You've got to distract him. Think of something!*

"Dimitri, did you want to see me for a particular reason?"

He smiled at her effort and caught her hands in his. "I'm getting to the reason, little one, if you'll just shut up for a moment."

She became lost in his smile, and in the kiss that followed. This was no ravaging assault meant to overwhelm her. His passion had been mellowed by their talk, but it was still there, communicated in a gentle exploration by his lips and tongue that was as intoxicating as anything that had gone before. He was sharing, giving of himself, and for heavenly long moments Katherine took all he had to offer—until he became more demonstrative, and she could no longer ignore the hard bulge that pressed against her belly.

She tore her mouth away, breathless, panicky now. "Dimitri—"

"Katya, you want me." His voice was so husky it seemed to reverberate through her. "Why do you deny us?"

"Because—because . . . No, I don't want you. I don't."

His look was so skeptical, he was calling her a liar without words. She wasn't fooling him, or herself. Oh, why couldn't he understand her position? Why did he have to assume that just because they had made love once, she would be willing to again? Of course she wanted him—how could she not? But to give in to that desire was unthinkable. One of them had to be sensible, to consider the consequences. He obviously wasn't going to or just didn't care.

"Dimitri, how can I make you understand? Your kiss was pleasant, but for me it ends there. For you it ends in bed."

"And what is wrong with that?" he said defensively.

"I'm not a whore. I was a virgin until I met you. And no matter how much you kiss me, no matter how much I might . . . like it, I can't let it go beyond that. For me it has to end there. So—"

"End there!" he cut in sharply. "A kiss on the hand ends there. A kiss on the cheek ends there. But when you press your body to mine, by God, that is an invitation to make love!"

Heat stained Katherine's cheeks with the realization she had done just that. "If you would have let me finish, I was going to suggest that it would be prudent of you to refrain from kissing me again, so that we might avoid these unpleasant arguments."

"I *want* to kiss you!"

"You want more than that, Dimitri."

"Yes! Unlike you, I have never denied it. I want you, Katya. I want to make love to you. For you to suggest I not even try is absurd."

She looked away from him. His anger was just another form of his passion and it was too potent while she was herself emotionally charged.

"That you feel so strongly about it is what I don't understand, Dimitri. Do you realize we have never talked, just talked, to learn about each other, about our likes and dislikes? Everything I know about you I have learned from your servants or your sister. And you know much, much less about me. Why can't we talk for once, without these tensions getting in the way?"

"Don't be naive, Katya," he said bitterly. "Talk? I can't think when you're near me. You want to talk? Write me a goddamn letter."

When she looked up, he was gone, and the room, as large as it was, suddenly seemed small. Was she wrong? Could there be any future for her with such a man? If she gave in, wouldn't his interest wane? His sister had predicted as much. So why should she open herself to an emotional involvement that couldn't possibly last?

Who are you kidding, Katherine? You're already emotionally entangled up to your ears. You want the man. He makes you feel things you never thought you could feel, believe in things you always scoffed at. What are you holding out for?

She wasn't really sure anymore. And each time she had one of these encounters with Dimitri, she was even less sure.

Chapter Twenty-four

*I*t was an agonizingly long day for Katherine, that first day at Novii Domik. Depression settled in after Dimitri had left her, and she couldn't shake it. She could have explored the house for distraction. No one told her she couldn't. Dimitri's shouted order to Vladimir when they arrived—"The White Room, and see that she stays there!"—was certainly no deterrent. But she was still embarrassed over their arrival and wasn't up to putting on a brave pretense when she simply felt like hiding. And she didn't dare chance running into Dimitri again when she was so close to abandoning her resolve.

Good Lord, would there never be an improvement to this situation? Was it just going to get harder and harder, the temptation ever more enticing?

When she stood back and looked at the overall picture, she thought she must be crazy. Here she was tucked away in the country, ensconced in a room that was so opulently luxurious it defied description, and desired by the most handsome man alive. This was the stuff that dreams were made of. What woman in her right mind would bemoan the fate that provided a real-life fantasy?

But Katherine did. And she needed to blame someone for her predicament, tired of blaming herself. Not surprisingly, she found ample scapegoats. Her sister, for being so secretive and forcing Katherine to follow her that day. Lord

Seymour, for that matter, for losing his inheritance and becoming an unsuitable match. Even her father could be blamed. He could have accepted Lord Seymour and helped him to recoup his losses. Then there was Anastasia, for creating the scandal that brought Dimitri to England. The Dowager Duchess of Albemarle was also at fault for sending for Dimitri instead of handling Anastasia's problem herself. And of course Vladimir took top honors for his rash decision to resort to kidnapping. Every one of them could have acted differently and prevented this intolerable situation from ever coming about.

And it was more intolerable than ever. Katherine was wavering. She was getting too close to sacrificing her principles, to succumbing to what amounted to the most primitive motivation. And she knew giving in was only a matter of time now. There lay the cause of her depression. She didn't want to be just another of Dimitri's conquests. She didn't want just a few weeks of devotion. She wanted more than that. Her pride demanded more.

Katherine knew she was in a sorry state when she noticed her dinner tray that evening but couldn't remember it being brought in. She rallied, annoyed with herself for wallowing in self-pity for half the day. She hadn't even unpacked, but then she had lived out of a trunk for so long that it didn't really matter. But she could have been doing something constructive. Dimitri had mentioned his accounts. Vladimir could have fetched them. She hadn't even examined her new quarters.

She did that after dinner while her bath was being readied. That several servants were waiting on her was noted and wondered about, but then there were probably so many here at Novii Domik that a few could be spared even to attend her.

They were strangers to her and uncommunicative, seemed in fact resentful in their attitude, but maybe that was their normal disposition. Katherine couldn't blame them. Servants in England could leave if they found their employment too tedious. These people could not.

The room was magnificent in its appointments, pristine in its whiteness. The name was certainly appropriate. White carpeting, drapes, and wallpaper, though the paper did have a very light gold pattern, barely discernible, but enough to offset the heavy brocade drapes. All the furniture was painted white with gold filigree: the tables, the bedstead, the wardrobe and vanity; even the mantel was white marble. The sofa and chairs were a soothing contrast in gold and powder blue, the thick bedcovering as well.

It was a woman's room in color and simplicity. The vanity, the delicate lacy knickknacks placed throughout, the pictures on the walls, oils and perfumes in the separate small bathchamber, all confirmed it. It was an extremely comfortable room. Katherine was almost glad Dimitri had insisted she have it until she opened another door, a connecting door, and saw that it led straight into the master's chamber, the master being Dimitri.

Katherine slammed the door shut as soon as she saw Maksim laying out Dimitri's clothes. Her face flamed and then grew even hotter as the two maids turning down the bedcovers glanced at her smugly. Good Lord, and the whole household knew that he had put her here, next to him, in the room that was obviously designed for the master's wife, or in her case, the mistress! Even his aunt knew. What must that poor woman think? What else could she think?

"It's not true," Katherine said in Russian so that both servants could understand her. But all she got was a giggle from the younger girl and a smirk from the other, which ignited her temper out of proportion to the provocation. "Get out! Both of you, out! By necessity I've become accustomed to attending myself. I don't need your help. Out!"

When they just stood there, struck dumb by her outburst and a little wary now, Katherine stalked into the bathchamber and slammed yet another door shut. She tore off her clothes, unmindful of buttons that didn't give way soon enough, and prayed the bath would relax her. It didn't.

How dare he do this to her? How dare he let everyone here think she was his mistress, actually announce that fact by stipulating where she would sleep, at the top of his lungs no less, so that even the deaf would hear it? He might as well have told Vladimir to install her in his own room!

She was too agitated to remain in the porcelain tub. A silk robe had been laid out, and she yanked it on, not even bothering to towel herself dry first or wonder whose robe it was. The peach material stuck to her instantly, but she didn't notice that either.

He wasn't going to get away with this. She wanted the matter put straight immediately. And she would *not* remain in the White Room even for one night. A barn would be preferable, a simple pile of hay, a pallet on the floor, even another hammock, anywhere, as long as it wasn't near Dimitri's bedroom.

The servants were gone when she left the bathchamber as forcefully as she had entered it. The bedroom was empty, her dinner tray gone. A small fire had been banked in the fireplace, a cooling breeze from the windows stirring the embers and causing the few lamps about the room to flicker. Smoke spiraled up from one that had gone out.

Katherine stared at the smoke for a few moments, trying to concentrate, trying to compose herself into a more reasonable frame of mind. Her efforts were useless. She had to have it out with Dimitri before she could even hope to calm down. And with that thought she jerked open the connecting door again, intending to have Maksim find Dimitri for her. But the valet had gone. Seated at a small table, finishing a late dinner, was her nemesis himself.

Katherine was thrown off track for a moment, enough to say automatically, "I beg your pardon," and in the next breath, outrage recalled, "No, I don't. You've gone too far this time, Alexandrov." She pointed a stiff finger behind her. "I will not stay in that room!"

"Why?"

"Because it's right next to yours!"

Dimitri set down his knife and fork and sat back, giving her his full attention. "You think I will come uninvited into your room, when I have had the opportunity to do so ever since we first met?"

"That wasn't my thought, no. I just don't want that particular room."

"You haven't told me why."

"I did. You weren't listening." She began pacing in front of the door, arms crossed beneath her breasts, body stiff, her hair whipping about each time she turned. "If I have to be more specific, it's because that room is part of this one, it's part of the master suite, and I don't belong in it. The implication is unacceptable, and you know *exactly* what I mean!"

"Do I?"

Her eyes stabbed him briefly at this impassive reaction. "I'm not your mistress! I'm not going to be your mistress, and I won't have your people thinking I am!"

Instead of replying, he simply stared at her. He was too nonchalant. Where was the anger that always arose when she defied his wishes? He had wanted her in the White Room. Why wasn't he arguing with her about it? For that matter, what had happened to mollify his temper since their last meeting? He usually brooded for days after their more heated encounters. Here she was itching for a fight, her blood racing with the need, and he wouldn't oblige her.

"Well?" she demanded.

"It's too late to consider moving you tonight."

"Nonsense—"

"Believe me, Katya, it's too late."

There was innuendo in his tone that indicated she should know why it was too late. She stopped, eyes narrowed on him, anger increasing because he was being so ambiguous. Couldn't he see she was in no condition to play word games? She was so furious she could barely think straight, could barely stand still. She was so furious that she could feel heat radiating from her body, hear her heart pounding in her ears, sense the blood pulsing through her veins. And he just sat there staring at her, waiting, yes, waiting, as if some miraculous understanding would suddenly dawn on her.

It did. As she tried to remain still, she found it impossible, literally impossible not to move in some way. She had felt this way once before, and anger hadn't caused those exaggerated symptoms any more than it did these.

In shock, Katherine took a step toward Dimitri, then fairly jumped back, realizing she didn't dare get too near him now. Oh, God, she could almost wish for ignorance, for the bliss of not knowing what was going to happen next. But she did know, knew there was nothing she could do to stop the maelstrom that was already building inside her and would soon change her personality and have her groveling at his feet.

Katherine recoiled from the thought, exploding in a burst of righteous fury. "Damn you, Dimitri, *you* did this, didn't you?"

"I'm sorry, little one."

He was. There was regret in his expression, even a flash of self-contempt. It didn't appease her in the least, made her even more enraged, if that were possible.

"Blast you to hell and back!" she screamed "You told me I would never be given that foul drug again! You told me to trust you! Is this how I can trust you? *How could you do this to me!*"

Each word stabbed into Dimitri's conscience. He had already agonized over that same question a hundred times today. He had found enough answers for himself while his temper still raged, then had gotten drunk when the answers didn't hold up once he cooled off.

"I gave the order in a moment of anger, Katya, and then left. I returned to Alexey's house, where we stopped last night. I drank myself into oblivion. I wouldn't be here now if one of his servants hadn't dropped a tray outside the room where I was sleeping it off."

"Do you think I give a bloody damn whether you are here now or not?"

He flinched under her scorn. "You would rather go through this alone? I won't let anyone else near you," he warned.

"Of course you won't. That would defeat the purpose, wouldn't it?"

"I tried to return in time to cancel the order, but as I came up the stairs, your dinner tray was just being removed."

"Spare me your excuses and lies. There is nothing you can say—"

Katherine stopped as a wave of heat seemed to roll over her, making her nerve endings vibrate. She bent over, arms wrapped around her middle, trying to hold back the turmoil inside her. She groaned, knowing she couldn't.

Hearing Dimitri rise in concern, she lifted her head and impaled him with such a look of loathing that he didn't move further. "I hate you for this!"

"Then hate me," he replied quietly, regretfully. "But tonight—tonight you will love me."

"You're crazy if you think so," she gasped, backing slowly toward the door. "I'll get through this on my own . . . without . . . any assistance . . . from you."

"You can't, Katya. You know that. That's why you're so angry."

"Just stay away from me!"

For long moments Dimitri stared at the closed door, and then the emotions he had held in check were released as he toppled the table in front of him, scattering food and drink across the room. The outburst didn't help.

He couldn't believe he had done this to her. She would never forgive him. Not that it should matter—Sweet Christ, it did matter. He should be horsewhipped. He could have had a woman at the snap of his fingers. He had no excuse for forcing this one, even if he was certain that she desired him and all she needed was an incentive to admit it. He couldn't even do as she asked now and stay away from her. How could he? To let her suffer needlessly was unthinkable. But he would take no pleasure for himself. It was what he deserved, to see her in a constant state of arousal and do nothing to appease his own desire. To see her willing and deny himself.

Determined to keep that resolve if it killed him, Dimitri quickly disrobed and entered Katherine's room. She was already on the bed. Her robe was thrown off, her skin too sensitive now to bear even the slightest touch that didn't offer relief. And her body was twisting, undulating. Only the green satin sheets were missing for a reenactment of that first night in London.

His feet moved automatically toward the bed, his eyes transfixed by the curve of a thigh, the taut thrust of a breast, her belly turned to him now, now the smooth slope of her back. She was the most exciting, sensual woman he had ever known, and he ached for her, his body cried for her. He had been in a state of arousal ever since he saw her tray coming out of her room. He might despise himself now for what he had done, but his body had reacted to what it knew would happen, and now, now he must be mad to put himself through this torture with no hope of relief. He was on fire, had never wanted a woman so much in his life. And he couldn't have her. He had set his own punishment.

"Dimitri, please!"

She had become aware of him. His eyes flew to hers and he groaned, seeing the wild plea reflected there. She had forsaken her pride already. He could do no less.

"Shh, little one, please. Don't say anything. It will be all right, I swear. You don't have to let me love you tonight. Just let me help you."

As he spoke, he eased onto the bed, careful not to touch her until, with his eyes locked to hers, he slipped his hand between her legs to find the core of her agony. Her climax was immediate: her hips shooting off the bed, her head thrown back, a sharp cry—half pain, half ecstasy—on her lips.

Dimitri closed his eyes and kept them closed until he felt the tension drain out of her. When he opened them, it was to find her staring at him, her eyes inscrutable now, her features so relaxed that she could have been sleeping. He knew she was fully conscious, her mind clear and active while her body was temporarily free from the slavery of the drug. At this moment she was capable of any reaction, any normal reaction that was in character. In fact, he anticipated another lacerating tirade, not the calm question she finally asked.

"What did you mean, I don't have to let you love me tonight?"

"Exactly that."

He was leaning beside her; she had only to glance down to see his state of arousal. "You would let that go to waste?"

Dimitri nearly choked, seeing where her eyes were fixed. "It won't be the first time."

"But it isn't necessary this time. I don't have any fight left in me."

"That's the drug. I won't take advantage of it."

"Dimitri—"

"Katya, please! I only have so much control, and this discussion isn't helping."

She sighed in exasperation. He wasn't listening. He was so set on getting her through this trial without deriving any pleasure from it himself that he couldn't hear what she was really saying. The drug had nothing to do with her surrender. It had just hurried it along. But she wanted him to take advantage of it. *She* wanted to take advantage of it. Why did he have to turn noble *now*?

There was no time to convince him that she wanted him, with or without the drug. It was starting again, the fire rushing through her veins, the ache deep down in her loins.

"Dimitri, make love to me," she cried.

"Oh, God."

He kissed her to shut her up, bruisingly, exquisitely, but he didn't make love to her. He frustrated her efforts each time to draw him closer. The only parts he would allow to touch her were his lips and his hands, his magical hands. Her climax was swift and intense, but without the sharing, there was no true satisfaction.

When her pulse quieted and her breathing returned to normal, Katherine made up her mind that she wasn't going to have any more half measures. To go through hours of this kind of sensual torture when it wasn't necessary was crazy. Even worse was Dimitri's resolve to deny himself when his need was so obvious. True, she had been furious with him. She didn't like being manipulated. But she understood his motivation. Thinking about it, she was even pleased that he could be so desperate to have her that he would do something like this.

"Dimitri?"

He groaned. His body was half twisted, his forehead pressed on his arm, his eyes tightly closed. For all the world he seemed like a man in the grip of mortal pain. Katherine smiled, mentally shaking her head.

"Dimitri, look at me."

"No—at least, give me a moment to—"

He couldn't finish. Katherine watched the muscles straining in his neck, his hands close into fists. His body was sheened with moisture, flushed with exertion. All that power working to resist a most natural inclination. And she might have been in the same state if the drug hadn't made it impossible for her to resist.

She turned on her side toward him and said with calm deliberation, "If you don't make love to me, Dimitri Alexandrov, I swear I will rape you."

His head shot up. "You will *what*?"

"You heard me."

"Don't be absurd, Katya. It isn't possible."

"Is that so?"

She touched his shoulder, letting her fingers trail down his arm. He caught her wrist instantly, tightly, and held it away from him.

"Don't!"

His sharpness didn't sway her. "You can capture my hands, Dimitri, but what about my body?"

Katherine threw a leg over his hip. Dimitri's reaction was to leap off the bed. Katherine was momentarily distracted by this full, unhampered view of him. God, he was glorious in his nudity, the firm musculature so in evidence, powerful, beautiful in symmetry.

"Stop it." He scowled as she looked over every inch of his body.

She glanced up, amusement entering her eyes now. "Will you blindfold me too? And perhaps tie me down? After all, you did promise to help me, but you can't if you won't come near me, and I won't promise not to touch you."

"Damn it, woman, I don't want you to hate me!"

"But I don't," she said with some surprise. "I couldn't."

"You don't know what you're saying right now," he insisted. "Tomorrow—"

"Blast tomorrow! Good Lord, I can't believe I'm arguing with you about this. Scruples don't become you, Dimitri, not in the least. Or are you punishing me, because I took so long—"

"Sweet Christ, no!"

"Then don't make me beg . . . Oh, God, it's starting again. Dimitri, no more foolishness. You have to make love to me. You have to!"

249

He joined her on the bed and gathered her tightly into his arms. "Oh, God, Katya, forgive me. I thought—"

"You think too much," she whispered as she wrapped her arms about his neck, reveling in the total contact with his flesh.

His lips ravaged her face, and then he was kissing her, his tongue plunging in deeply, mercilessly, the full force of his passion released in an explosion of longing. When he entered her seconds later, it was bliss, purest bliss as he quenched the fire; it was what she needed—to be completely possessed. And the sweet throbbing that followed was all the sweeter because he came with her.

Dimitri had only just begun. This was his fantasy come true, what he had dreamed about for so long: to have her needing him, wanting him with the same intensity that controlled him. And he took full advantage of it, now that the madness of his restraint was defeated. While she lay dazed from the power of her release, he worshipped her with his mouth and hands, unable to stop loving her even for a second.

Katherine smiled, feeling the warm, gentle tugging on her breasts, the strong fingers that skimmed over her skin with such tender caresses. She might be exhausted for the moment, only the moment, but her mind was working just fine.

And in that moment, Katherine knew she loved him.

Chapter Twenty-five

The morning light turned the White Room into a brilliant display of diamond-bright jewel tones. Through the open windows sunlight spilled across the carpet but didn't quite reach the bed. Like minuscule suns, dust motes danced and swirled with each gust of warm breeze or disappeared beyond the sunbeam.

In the large bed Katherine stretched luxuriously, consciousness slowly creeping up on her. There was something important—ah, yes, last night. She smiled as the memories flitted across her mind. A happy sigh escaped her just before she opened her eyes.

She was alone. A quick glance about the room. She was still alone. She shrugged and let her head sink back into the pillow.

What did you expect, ninny? Just because he was there that other time when you woke up, doesn't mean he will be every time. He's got things to do, people to see. After all, we arrived here only yesterday, and according to him, he left soon after and didn't return until last night. There's no doubt a multitude of things he has to attend to.

But there was no denying it would have been nice to have woken up beside Dimitri. She was eager to let him know that she remembered everything and to assure him that everything she had said last night still held true this morning. And if he had been here now, she could have told him—yes, there was no reason to keep it a secret—she could have told him she loved him.

Katherine smiled as she felt a rush of warmth spreading through her just from the thought. She still couldn't quite believe it. She had fallen prey to that most silly of emotions. Her? Incredible. But love wasn't silly after all. It was real, powerful, glorious. And this was one mistake Katherine was delighted to own up to.

She lay there thinking about this new emotion for nearly an hour before she suddenly leaped out of bed, unable to contain it any longer. She had to find Dimitri and tell him what she was feeling. What she didn't realize was that her driving need was actually to hear that her feelings were returned.

She dressed in haste, with only a quick glance in the vanity mirror to assure herself that all her buttons were done up properly. She had long since given up trying to do anything with her hair. It was something she had never had to attend to herself, and something she had not been able to master from necessity. As long as it was neatly tied back with a ribbon, as she had worn it aboard ship, she was satisfied she looked demure, if unfashionable.

The most likely place to look for Dimitri first was his room, and so she knocked on the connecting door, and when she got no answer, she opened it anyway. She didn't stop to think that even yesterday she wouldn't have been so brazen. In her mind she had accepted Dimitri as her lover, and that gave her certain privileges that she wouldn't have dreamed of taking otherwise. Unfortunately he wasn't at the desk she had noticed last night, as she had hoped. He wasn't there at all, nor was Maksim, who could have helped her locate him.

Impatiently Katherine crossed Dimitri's room to get to the hallway instead of going through her own room. So it was with some surprise that she came face to face with Dimitri's aunt when she opened the door.

Sonya had been about to knock. She was given a start by finding Katherine coming out of Dimitri's room, when she had distinctly heard the order for her to be placed in the White Room. If she had needed further evidence of what the woman was doing here, she had it now. And her disreputable appearance was a wanton announcement of her calling. A woman did not wear her hair down except in the bedchamber. That this one was about to leave with her hair flowing down her back only increased Sonya's sense of moral indignation.

Katherine recovered first, enough to take a step back so that she wouldn't have to crane her neck to look up at the imposing woman. She started to smile, but blushed instead on noting the censure in the older woman's cold blue eyes. Good Lord, *that* was something she hadn't considered in her newfound happiness, but here it was in abundance. Of course her new relationship with Dimitri was scandalous. She would have been the first to admit it if she hadn't been one of the parties involved. Anyone else would say so without hesitation.

And yet she had made her decision, or rather, it had been made for her. She loved the man. And she was sure that he felt rather strongly about her as well. So she didn't have a ring on her finger—yet. She had high hopes that the matter would eventually be rectified. After all, this was not a schoolgirl infatuation that she had succumbed to. For her, this was an everlasting commitment. She had fought against it too long not to fight for it now.

Unconsciously Katherine stiffened her backbone, assuming a pose that was inherently regal. Sonya saw it as haughtiness and was outraged.

"I am looking for my nephew."

"So am I," Katherine replied politely. "So if you will excuse me . . ."

"One moment, miss." Sonya's tone was commanding, her *miss* derogatory. "If Dimitri is not here, what are you doing in his room alone?"

"As I said, looking for him."

"Or taking this opportunity to steal from him."

The accusation was so incongruous that Katherine couldn't take it seriously. "With all due respect, madame, I don't steal."

"I'm to take your word for it? Don't be absurd. The English might be so gullible, but we Russians are not. You will have to be searched."

"I beg your pardon."

"You'll do more than that if we find anything of value on you."

"What the—" Katherine gasped as Sonya began to drag her down the hall.

She tried to shake off the woman's grip, but it was as if talons had hooked into her arm. Sonya was nearly a foot taller than her, and her spare frame was deceptively strong. Katherine found herself being pulled down the stairs, where several servants had stopped in the hall to gape at yet another spectacle she was involved in.

*Keep your temper, Katherine. Dimitri will
straighten this out. After all, you haven't done anything that he would object to. His aunt is just being
bitchy. Didn't Marusia warn you she was a tyrant,
that Dimitri's personal servants stayed well out of her
path?*

In the large entrance hall, Katherine was
pushed into the hands of the nearest footman.
Older than the others, but the more thickly built,
he seemed genuinely nonplussed about what he
should do with her.

Sonya was quick to clarify. "Search her for
anything of value, and be thorough. She was
found unattended in the Prince's chamber."

"Now just a minute," Katherine said with
forced evenness. "Dimitri wouldn't stand for
this, madame, and I believe you know that. I demand that he be sent for."

"Demand? Demand!"

"Your hearing is quite excellent," Katherine
cut in sarcastically.

She probably should have resisted the gibe, but
then she was really angry now, her diplomacy
gone by the wayside. The witch had no right to
charge her with any wrongdoing. There was simply no basis for the accusation. And for her to
presume to treat Katherine like one of her serfs
was the outside of enough.

For Sonya, Katherine's sarcasm was the last
straw. No one had ever spoken to her with such
lack of respect, and in front of the servants. It
couldn't be allowed.

"I will have you—" Sonya began in a shout,
then seemed to recollect herself, though her face
was suffused with angry color. "No, I will let

255

Dimitri attend it, then you will see that you mean nothing to him. Where is the Prince?'' She rounded on the servants, who were watching this scene in fascination. ''Come now, someone must have seen him this morning. Where is he?''

''He's not here, Princess.''

''Who said that?''

The girl almost didn't step forward. To have attention drawn to her when the mistress was in one of her rages wasn't the greatest piece of wisdom. But she had opened her mouth. She had already put her foot in it. She was damned already and couldn't do worse by telling all.

Katherine thought the girl was Lida at first glance, but she was younger, and lacking Lida's confidence, seemed actually frightened. What did *she* have to be frightened about? Katherine was the one in a pickle here.

''My sister woke me before dawn, Princess, to say goodbye,'' the girl explained, her eyes trained on the floor. ''She was in a rush because the Prince had already left, and she and the rest of his entourage had to hurry to catch up.''

''Never mind all that!'' Sonya snapped. ''Where has he gone?''

''To Moscow.''

There was a moment's silence, and then Sonya's lips turned up at one corner as her cold eyes fastened on Katherine. ''So he takes his duty seriously after all. I shouldn't have doubted him. I should have known he would leave in all haste to resume his courtship of the Princess Tatiana. But he's left you behind for me to deal with. I should just put you out.''

''A capital idea,'' Katherine said tightly.

She was still angry enough not to be bowled over by this bit of news. Dimitri gone? Just like that? And to secure himself a fiancée? No, that was his aunt's assumption, not fact. *Don't you dare jump to conclusions, Katherine. There's probably a very good reason for him leaving without a single word to you. And he'll be back. You'll have answers, the right answers, and you'll laugh that you even doubted him for a second.*

"So you would like to be on your way?" Sonya broke into her thoughts tersely, her moment of improved humor past. "Then perhaps I should keep you here. Yes, Dimitri might have forgotten your existence already, but his man, Vladimir, isn't so lax, though apparently he was so harried this morning he overlooked leaving instructions concerning you. But there must be some reason you have been left behind, so I suppose I must make certain you are still here when they return, much as I would wish it otherwise."

"I can tell you exactly why I am here," Katherine retorted indignantly.

"Don't bother. Anything your kind says must be held in doubt."

"My *kind?*" Katherine fairly shrieked.

Sonya didn't elaborate. Her expression and the way she looked Katherine up and down said it all. Her eyes narrowed. She was queen bee again, through with her fury, under control, and every bit the dried-up old tyrant Marusia had called her.

"Since you are to remain at Novii Domik, you must be taught the proper conduct. Disrespect is not allowed here."

"Then you could use a few lessons in courtesy yourself, madame, because I recall being quite polite to you until you made your unfounded charge against me. You, on the other hand, have been insulting from the start.''

"That will do!'' Sonya shouted. ''We will see if a visit to the woodhouse doesn't curb your insolence. Semen, take her there immediately.''

Katherine almost laughed. If the witch thought locking her up in the woodhouse was going to make one whit of difference, she was sadly mistaken. She had just spent endless weeks confined on the ship. A few more days' confinement until Dimitri returned wouldn't bother her at all. And she could spend the time envisioning Dimitri's high rage over his aunt's tyranny.

Even the servants could envision it, Katherine thought rather smugly. The fellow holding her— Semen was it?—had hesitated a full five seconds before he began to tug her toward the back of the house. The others who watched them registered expressions from shock and amazement to outright fear.

Katherine was marched outside and over to one of the outbuildings she had noticed on her arrival. From the back of the house she had her first view of the village nearly a half-mile away, and the endless acres of ripening wheat, like a sea of gold in the morning sunlight. Funny that she could appreciate what a splendid scene lay before her while she was on her way to being locked up. But she could. It was the quest for new sights, new experiences, that made this whole trip an adventure that satisfied a longing she had long held dear.

The woodhouse was a small shedlike structure where cut wood was stored. Windowless, floorless even, Katherine's first look inside took a chink out of her smugness.

Buck up, Katherine. So it's not going to be pleasant. All the more reason to expect profuse apologies from Dimitri when this is over. He'll make it up to you, see if he doesn't.

Besides Semen, the brawniest of the footmen had also accompanied her at a nod from Sonya, as had Sonya herself. The four of them were now inside the woodhouse. Ample sunlight spilled in from the open doorway to light the stuffy room. But instead of being released and left alone, Katherine was handed over to the younger, more muscular fellow who gathered both of her hands in his and held them tightly in front of her.

"Am I to be tied up too?" Katherine sneered at this. "How quaint."

"There's no need for ropes," Sonya said condescendingly. "Rodion here is quite capable of restraining you for however long it takes."

"However long what takes?"

"You will be caned until you are ready to beg my pardon for your insolence."

The blood momentarily left Katherine's face. So that's what a visit to the woodhouse meant! Good Lord, this was right out of the Dark Ages!

"You're out of your mind." Katherine said each word slowly, clearly, as she turned her head to glare at the older woman, who now stood behind her. "You can't get away with this. I'm a member of the British peerage, the Lady Katherine St. John."

Sonya was given a start, but only for a moment. She had already drawn her conclusions about Katherine, and serfs weren't the only ones who clung tenaciously to first impressions. The woman was of no account. Dimitri's treatment of her proved it. It was Sonya's duty to break such haughtiness before it spread to the other servants.

"Whoever you are," Sonya said coldly, "you must learn some manners. You may determine yourself how long it will take for you to improve your disposition. You may beg my pardon now—"

"Never!" Katherine spat. "I give respect only to those deserving it. You, madame, have only my contempt."

"Begin!" Sonya screeched, her face livid with rage once again.

Katherine's head swung back, her eyes impaling the footman whose hold had tightened on her wrists with the order. "Release me this second."

There was such authority in her voice that Rodion's hold actually loosened. But the Princess was standing right there. Katherine saw the fellow's dilemma, saw the indecision and worry cross his craggy features, and knew the moment the Princess won out.

"You had better hope you're not around when the Prince finds out about—"

Katherine stopped, steeling herself, hearing the horrid whish of the cane just before it struck. The pain was worse than anything she could have imagined. The breath hissed through her teeth. Her mind shrieked. That first blow brought her to her knees.

"Tell her what she wants, miss," Rodion whispered imploringly, looking down at her.

He was the only one to see her face when the cane struck, and then the second blow, even worse for landing in the same spot, and then the third, striking her lower back. Her hands trembled. Blood appeared on her lip where her teeth had dug in. She was so tiny, so delicate, not a hardy peasant whose body would have been conditioned by hard labor to undergo such punishment. A few blows of the cane was nothing to a serf. But this was no serf. Whoever she was, she couldn't take this kind of abuse.

"Let me go" was all Katherine replied to Rodion's entreaty.

"Sweet Mary, I can't, miss," he said miserably as Semen wielded the cane yet another time.

"Then don't . . . let me . . . fall."

"Just tell her—"

"I can't," she gasped then swayed forward under the next blow. "St. John pride . . . you know."

Rodion was incredulous. Pride? And she was serious! Only the aristos let pride rule their actions. Dear Sweet Mary, what was he a party to here? Could she have been telling the truth about who she was?

It was with the greatest relief that he was able to say a moment later, "She's fainted, Princess."

"You want me to revive her?" Semen asked.

"No," Sonya said testily. "Stubborn woman. It obviously won't do any good to pry an apology out of her. But administer a few more strokes, Semen, for good measure."

It was Semen who protested this order. "But she's unconscious, Princess."

"So? She won't feel it now, but she will when she wakes up."

Rodion flinched with each subsequent blow of that accursed cane, wishing he were taking the punishment instead. But at least he held the woman up, supporting her by her forearms. She didn't fall, as she had feared, though what was the sense of that he would never know.

"Search her" was Sonya's last order.

Semen bent to do so, looking up after a moment, shaking his head. "Nothing, Princess."

"Well, it didn't hurt to be sure."

Rodion and Semen exchanged a glance at that. But Rodion, tight-lipped as he carried the woman out of the woodhouse, was feeling all the impotence and rage that only someone under the yoke of serfdom could feel. Didn't hurt? The Englishwoman would think differently.

Chapter Twenty-six

"*O*h my God!"

Katherine leaped off the slab she had been lying on the moment she realized what it was. The effort brought a loud moan to her lips. She crouched, out of breath, glaring furiously at the thing. It was one thing to wake up in an unfamiliar place, but quite another to find yourself roasting over coals.

"A stove! They put you on a bloody stove, Katherine! They're crazy. They're every one of them crazy!"

"*Zdravstvui, Gospozha.*"

"Like hell it's a good morning!" Katherine rounded on the woman who had come up soundlessly behind her. Seeing her back up with a start, she switched to Russian. "Were you planning on serving me for dinner?"

The woman broke into a toothy smile when Katherine's meaning became clear. "The stove isn't lit," she assured her. "It makes a nice warm bed in winter for the children and the older ones. That is why it is so big, you see. But in summer it is too hot and the baking is done outside."

Katherine gave one more fulminating look at the stove. It was huge, about five feet long and four feet wide, indeed large enough to accommodate several people as a bed. But if it wasn't lit, why did she feel as if she had just been burned?

"You shouldn't be moving about yet, miss," the woman said more seriously now, drawing Katherine's attention back to her.

"I shouldn't?"

"Unless you feel able, of course."

"Of course."

Katherine's reply was testy for lack of explanation, but it was accompanied by a shrug, which was the worst thing she could have done. Her eyes flared wide, then squeezed shut as the breath whished out of her. Unfortunately she tensed against the fire whipping down her back, and that just made it worse. She moaned pitiably, unable to resist, uncaring who heard her.

"That—bloody—bitch!" she hissed through her teeth, bent over further now in her pain. "She actually . . . unbelievable! How could she dare?"

"If you mean the Prince's aunt, she governs here in his absence, so—"

"What blasted excuse is that?" Katherine snapped.

"Everyone knows what you did, miss. The mistake was yours. We learned long ago what attitude to adopt when in her presence. She is of the old order, you see, those who demand total subservience. Show a little fear and the utmost respect, and she is more than benevolent. No one is caned here anymore—you, of course, being the exception. You just have to know how to handle her."

Katherine would have liked to handle her all right, with a torch and a whip. But she didn't say so. She was doing her best to try and will the pain away. If she didn't move a single muscle, it wasn't quite so agonizing.

"How bad is it?" she asked hesitantly.

She wasn't wearing her own clothes, so someone had undressed her, and she had to assume it was this woman. The dress that had been put on her was of coarse cotton, cool, but scratchy in the extreme. It had probably been donated by that female despot who called herself a princess. It certainly didn't belong to this woman, as she was rather on the plump side, and the dress, while uncomfortable, at least fit Katherine.

"Do you bruise easily?"

"Yes," Katherine replied.

"Then it is not so bad, I think. Many welts and bruises, but at least no broken skin or ribs."

"You're sure?"

"About the ribs, no. You could better judge. They wouldn't call a doctor, even when your fever was so high."

"I had a fever?"

"For a day and a half. It is why you were brought here. Fevers I know about."

"Where is here? Ah, I don't know your name. Mine is Katherine, by the way."

"Ekaterina?" the woman smiled. "That is a fine name, an imperial name—"

"Yes, so I have been told," Katherine cut in, exasperated with yet another version of her name. "And your name?"

"Parasha, and you are in the village, in my home. Rodion carried you down yesterday. He was most concerned. It seems the Princess had assigned no one to watch over you, even though she was aware of your fever. And with such deliberate neglect on her part, no one was willing to offer their services, leery of being associated with anyone in the Princess's bad graces."

"I see," Katherine said tightly. "So in fact I could have died?"

"Goodness, no," Parasha replied. "Your fever was just caused by the beating. It was not serious, the fever that is. Rodion, however, didn't realize that. As I said, he was most concerned. He seems to think the Prince will be displeased when he learns what happened."

At least something she had said made an impression on the man. But a lot of good Dimitri's predicted fury had done to prevent the beating from occurring in the first place. And she was only assuming that he would be furious. What if he wasn't? What if he couldn't care less?

That possibility brought a tight knot to Katherine's throat, which eased only with a concerted effort to direct her thoughts elsewhere. "Do you live here alone, Parasha?"

The woman seemed surprised by the question. "In such a big house? No, no, there is my husband, Savva, his parents, our three children, and room for more, as you can see."

It was a big house, built of wood, since wood was so plentiful in this area. It was only one story, but spread out, and certainly larger than anything Katherine had seen in the many villages she had passed on the way here. She had assumed these log cabins would be one-room affairs, but this one had several rooms, she could see at least another room beyond the kitchen door, which had been left open. The kitchen itself was roomy, uncluttered; a large table was the focal point, as well as the monstrous stove. A finely carved cupboard, more beautiful than any she had ever seen, held an assortment of wooden utensils.

The house was quiet, no sign of anyone else around at the moment. "Is everyone working in the fields?"

Parasha smiled indulgently. "Until harvest, which will start soon, there is little to be done in the fields. There is still work, of course, weeding the vegetable patches, sheep-shearing, butchering, and preparing for winter, but nothing like planting and harvest time, when we are lucky if we work only sixteen hours a day. But today is Saturday."

She spoke as if Katherine should know what that meant, and in fact Katherine did, thanks to the long conversations with Marusia on the way to Novii Domik. On Saturdays, all across Russia whole villages would converge on the communal bathhouse, where steam was created by throwing water on a large brick stove. Bathers lay on shelves lining the walls, the higher the hotter, some beating themselves and one another with birch twigs for greater effect, and to top it off, they then jumped into a frigid river or stream, or in winter rolled naked in the snow. Incredible, but Marusia had assured her the experience was truly invigorating; until she had tried it herself, she shouldn't judge out of hand.

"You're missing the steam bath yourself, aren't you?" Katherine commented.

"Ah, well, I couldn't leave you here alone when you had yet to wake from the fever, though it passed during the night. I would have had Savva carry you to the bathhouse, for the steam would have done you good. But the Prince's brother Nikolai showed up last night and spent the night with his mother here in the village, so he will probably be there. And I didn't think you would want to be pestered by him when your senses returned, at least not until you were more recovered.''

''Why would he pester me?''

''He pesters all women.'' Parasha chuckled. ''He is fast following in his brother's footsteps where women are concerned. But he is not so particular as the Prince. Any and all is his motto.''

Katherine didn't know whether to feel insulted or not. In the end she said nothing in reply. She knew who Nikolai was, Nikolai Baranov, natural son of Petr Alexandrov and one of the village serfs. His mother had been given her freedom on his birth, but she had never taken advantage of it, had stayed at Novii Domik and eventually married one of the villagers. Yet Nikolai, like all the other bastards of the Alexandrov men, was raised in the bosom of the family, with a whole bevy of servants to attend and spoil him.

How Lady Anne, a proud Englishwoman, could have tolerated such blatant proof of unfaithfulness, was beyond Katherine. Nikolai was in fact only seven months younger than Dimitri. And yet, according to Marusia, Lady Anne had never complained, had loved Petr faithfully until the day he died.

Katherine knew she couldn't be so understanding. However, she was realistic. She knew men were governed by their bodies, that even the most adoring of husbands were bound to commit indiscretions. That was a fact of life. She had seen and heard too much to doubt it. She had always firmly believed in the old adage that what you didn't know couldn't hurt you, and had believed that when she eventually married, as long as she didn't hear about her husband's indiscretions, she would blissfully ignore the probability of unfaithfulness.

That was how she had thought she would feel when she eventually married. Now she wasn't so sure. She hadn't counted on falling in love. She wasn't so sure she could blissfully ignore anything Dimitri did, and she would have to assume that he would be unfaithful if he was away from her for any length of time. The possibility hurt. A confirmation would be devastating. How could she deal with that when they were married? How could she deal with it now?

He was gone, supposedly to court another woman. She didn't believe that for a moment, but he was still away in Moscow, where any number of women would attract his eye. Of course she was assuming that he cared for her. She was assuming a lot.

Blast, why did Parasha have to remind her of the Alexandrov men's predilection for womanizing and siring bastards? Marusia had never mentioned that Dimitri had any, but that didn't mean he didn't or that he wouldn't in the future. Look at Misha, thirty-five when he died and his oldest bastard eighteen years old now.

She ought to just forget Dimitri. He was too handsome, too enamored of women in general, according to Anastasia. He wouldn't know how to be faithful to any one woman, even if he did love her. Did she need that? Certainly not. She needed to get away from him before what she felt became so overpowering that she wouldn't care what he did as long as he gave her a few crumbs of affection. And if she was going to leave, she had better do it while he wasn't around and while Vladimir wasn't there to watch her every move.

Chapter Twenty-seven

Katherine crouched in the shadows beside the house and took a moment to absorb the pain that just a little movement caused her. But she had made it this far. She had a sack of food she had hastily gathered, and she wasn't about to let a little thing like painfully bruised muscles stop her now.

She had waited impatiently while Parasha and her family had prepared for church this morning. There had been a moment of panic when the kind woman had started to insist that Savva would be happy to carry Katherine to church, that it was unthinkable to miss Mass, but Katherine had moaned and groaned so much when Parasha had tried to help her from her bed, which was still atop the stove, that she had given up the idea.

Katherine had met the rest of the family yesterday, and they had spent the evening singing the praises of their Prince and his family, who they considered part of their family. She came to realize that the happiness and welfare of the serf depended entirely on the character and wealth of his master. Under a good master he felt as if he had a home and was protected against bad fortune in a relationship that was almost like the feudal system of old. Under a cruel master his existence was more like a living hell of beatings and forced labor, in which he lived in constant dread (or hope, for that matter) of being sold, traded, lost on the turn of a card, or worse, sent off to military service for the next twenty-five years of his life.

Dimitri's serfs were all content with their lot and fully aware of their good fortune. The thought of freedom was abhorrent to them because they would then lose the protection and generosity that allowed them to prosper as well as the land they thought of as their own. In their behalf, Dimitri sold the goods they made over the long, idle winters. In Europe they fetched a much better price than in Russia, and it showed in the higher standard of living here at Novii Domik.

Fine clothes were donned for church, a custom the same everywhere it seemed. The men wore colored shirts, red being the favorite, instead of the loose shirt belted round the waist worn on ordinary days. The trousers were of finer cloth, but still baggy in the style inherited from the Tartars centuries ago. Top boots of a good quality were worn instead of the summer wear of most peasants, which was bare feet or the typical birch-bark boots. The Russian high hats of felt completed their outfits, and for some, the long overcoat, or caftan.

Women also put on a fine showing, exchanging the universal head-kerchief for a *kokóshnik*, a tall headdress richly decorated according to the means of the wearer, Parasha having pearls and gold ornaments on hers. The festive dress was sleeveless, known as a *sarafán*, and was made in soft materials and numerous colors, as Katherine saw from watching the many women passing by outside the window.

A Sunday here was like a Sunday in England, a day of relaxation after a long Mass, and Kath-

erine was counting on today's being at least two
hours long, as she had heard some were. Afterward the young people would play games, as the
children had excitedly informed her, while the
adults visited and gossiped. How English that
sounded! But Katherine didn't expect to be
around to watch or join the festivities. She hoped
to be far away before her absence was discovered.

It would have been easier, not to mention less
painful, if she could have had a few more days
to recover before making her escape. But the moment she had noticed the horse kept in the animal shelter next to the house, one of several in
the village, she knew she had the means to get
away. After hearing that no one, absolutely no
one in the village missed going to church unless
they were bedridden, she knew Sunday gave her
the only opportunity she was likely to get. She
wasn't about to wait a full week until next Sunday, when it was possible that Dimitri would be
back.

Parasha had told her it took about as long to
reach Moscow as it did to reach St. Petersburg,
Novii Domik being between the two though far
to the east. Dimitri had already been gone three
full days, not counting today. Also, he hadn't
waited on the carriages transporting his servants,
which would take five days at the least to drive
one way. He had ridden ahead, could cut down
his traveling time considerably if he was really in
a hurry. She wasn't taking the chance.

There was also the possibility that Princess
Sonya would remember that she had promised
to keep Katherine here until Dimitri returned. At
present, in view of her condition, what Kath-

erine was attempting would be thought impossible, no doubt the reason why no one had been sent down to guard against her escape. Once she had time to recover, even just a few more days, there was every likelihood that someone would be sent to watch her, or worse, she might be installed back in the big house, perhaps even under lock and key, and lose this opportunity altogether.

This was her chance, probably her only chance, with the village deserted, everyone congregated in the little church, and no one there aware of the true situation: that Dimitri actually wanted her kept prisoner at Novii Domik for the remainder of summer. That was her trump card; for now, they were all ignorant of why he had brought her here. His aunt might even say good riddance when she learned that Katherine had vanished.

She moved cautiously toward the little shed, keeping her eye on the church at the end of the road. It was distinguished from the village houses only by the belfry with a large blue onion-shaped dome atop it, characteristic of every other church Katherine had seen since arriving in Russia, except that this one, being small, only had one dome, whereas some she had seen had as many as seven or nine, all painted different bright colors, or intricately carved or shingled.

The steady drone of prayers, she hoped, would mask any sound the horse made. But then everything was down to hope now: that she could get away from Dimitri's estate without being seen, that she could remember the way back to St. Petersburg without getting lost, that no one would bother to come after her, and that she would be safely ensconced in the English community in St. Petersburg before Dimitri even knew she was gone.

She wouldn't even mind seeing him again, once she was safely out of his power and they were finally on equal ground. But all she really wanted now was to return home and start forgetting him. It was better that way. It *was* better that way, wasn't it? Of course it was.

Liar! What you really truly want is for him to come after you, to beg you not to leave, to swear he loves you and wants to marry you. And you'd do it to, ninny that you are, marry him in a minute, no matter how many good, solid reasons there are not to.

Katherine was almost thankful for the agonized wrenching of her muscles while she readied the horse and mounted him, for it got her mind back on track. Getting away now was all that was important. She needed Dimitri to see her as his equal, and he wouldn't until she could prove who she really was. And she couldn't do that here. She would worry later about his reaction and what he would do about her escape.

Riding the horse slowly away, she had her first taste of what the ride was going to be like, and all she wanted to do was scream, she hurt so badly. Never in her life had she experienced anything like this pain. If she had a gun, she wouldn't be riding away from Novii Domik but toward it, for at the moment she wanted nothing more than to find that bastard Semen and shoot him. He could have gone easy on her. He could have tempered his strength instead of putting it all into each stroke of that blasted cane. But no, show off for the Princess, follow her orders to the letter, that's what the dolt had done. Katherine was surprised he hadn't broken every bone in her back.

She had to circle around the big house to get to the road, and she did this swiftly, giving it a wide berth. Once on the road, she set off at a gallop, which was actually easier on her than a slower canter, but still had her wincing and groaning every few seconds, loudly now, for there was no longer any need for quiet. She kept up that pace off and on for four hours, or what she assumed was four hours, for she didn't have a watch, until she passed the estate where she had spent the last night on the way to Novii Domik and where Dimitri had returned the next day to get drunk.

She intended to stop at the other places where they had stopped before, for she had no money and would need food, and the servants knew her. They weren't likely to deny her a meal, even though she was now alone. They might think it strange, her traveling alone, but she could spin a tale if she had to. But she wouldn't spend the night at any of those estates. She didn't dare. It would be too easy to get trapped if someone did come after her. And there were plenty of forests where she could bed down for a few hours' sleep safely away from the road and any pursuers. Her pursuers might even pass her by, and that would serve just as well.

Right now she didn't need to stop, had enough food to last until tomorrow, and wanted to put as much distance as she could between her and Novii Domik. She was also afraid to stop, afraid that if she got off the horse now, she wouldn't have the will to get back on, or the ability for that matter. She would wait until night, when she could rest and recuperate a little before facing another day of endless pain.

Katherine almost pulled the horse to a halt when it dawned on her what she had overlooked in her perfect plan. Night. She had forgotten that there was no night at this time of year, or very little of it. And there was no way she could keep on riding, even if she didn't have a bruised, swollen back. She would have to stop, but she wouldn't have the cover of darkness to help conceal her in the forest. She would have to go further into the forest, further away from the road, just to hide. A total waste of time, but what other choice did she have?

Several hours later, she finally left the road and found a sheltered spot in which to collapse, and she literally did just that, falling off the horse when her muscles refused to help her dismount gracefully. She didn't even have enough stamina left to arrange her limbs in a more comfortable position, but lay exactly as she had fallen, mindful only of keeping the reins balled tight in her fist, since she couldn't secure the horse properly, before she simply passed out.

Chapter Twenty-eight

"So you are the little pigeon who flew the coop."

A nudge against Katherine's foot accompanied this statement so that she would be sure to hear it. She opened her eyes, disoriented, and saw him standing at her feet in an arrogant stance, hands on hips: her golden giant. Here? So soon? Her heart plummeted, then in the breath of a second, rose giddily.

"Dimitri?"

"Ah, so it is you." He grinned down at her. "I wasn't at all sure. You are not exactly what I expected someone of Mitya's—ah—acquaintance to look like."

Her heart sank again. He wasn't Dimitri, and yet he might have been his twin. Well, not quite. The same body and height, yes, exactly. The same golden hair and handsome countenance. But the forehead was perhaps a little broader, the chin a little more square, and the eyes were the giveaway. She should have noticed right off; they were not the dark velvety brown she was used to but a clear, stunning blue, sparkling, merry.

"Nikolai?"

"At your service, pigeon."

His good humor was annoying under the circumstances. "What are you doing here?"

"That question would be better put to you, yes?"

"No. I have a very good reason for being here. You don't, however, unless you were sent after me—"

"But of course."

Her eyes narrowed a fraction. "Then you've wasted your time. I'm not going back."

Katherine started to rise. This lying on the ground at his feet wasn't conducive to arguing, and she was most certainly going to argue her case. But she had forgotten her condition. Her shoulders were no more than an inch off the ground when she groaned, tears springing to her eyes.

"You see what happens when you try sleeping on the hard ground instead of the soft bed you deserted," Nikolai admonished gently as his hand fastened on her wrist and he pulled her to her feet. Her scream of pain shocked him and he released her instantly. "Sweet Christ, what is wrong with you? Did you take a fall from the horse?"

"You idiot!" Katherine gasped, half her concentration devoted to remaining perfectly still, the other half fixed on her anger. "Don't pretend you don't know. Everyone at Novii Domik knows, and you were there."

"If everyone knows, then they managed to keep it from me, whatever it is you are talking about."

Her eyes, shot more with green than blue at the moment, fixed him with a steady glare. He was pale, his expression concerned. He was telling the truth.

"I'm sorry," she said after a sigh, "for calling you an idiot. If I am a little sensitive and sore at the moment"—she smiled to herself at her choice of words—"it's because I was caned rather severely."

"Mitya wouldn't!" Nikolai was appalled and, truth to tell, incensed by this slur on his brother.

"Of course he wouldn't, you—" She stopped short of calling him an idiot again, but her moment of dispassion was gone. "He doesn't know, and there will be hell to pay when he does. Your blasted aunt did this to me."

"I don't believe it," Nikolai snorted. "Sonya? Sweet, agreeable Sonya?"

"Look you, I have had enough doubt and aspersion cast on my word these last months to last me a lifetime. But this time I have the bruises on my back to prove what I say, and your *sweet, agreeable* aunt is going to pay for every one of them when I reach the British Embassy. The English Ambassador happens to be a good friend of my father's, who happens to be the Earl of Strafford, and if Dimitri's abduction of me doesn't stir the pot to boiling, this latest outrage certainly will. I have half a mind to demand your aunt be exiled to Siberia! And you can stop looking at me as if I had turned into a turnip," she added testily. "I'm not crazy."

Nikolai snapped his mouth shut, blushing slightly. He had never been treated to such a scathing tirade before, not by a woman at any rate. Now, Dimitri had been known to lay into him on occasion—Sweet Christ, they were alike, these two. Such fire! Did she behave like this with his brother? If so, he could understand now what Dimitri had found intriguing about her, whereas otherwise she was not his type at all. Nikolai was himself intrigued.

He grinned boyishly. "You have quite a way with words, pigeon. And such emotion in such a little package." Her fulminating glare made him chuckle. "But not too little, eh? Full-grown and put together nicely, very nicely." His warm blue eyes moved appreciatively down her length and back. "And it is convenient that you have found this private bower, so secluded. We could—"

"No, we couldn't," she cut in sharply, easily reading his mind.

He was undeterred. "But of course we can."

"No we cannot!"

Parasha had been right about this one. Here she looked her very worst, wearing the most unbecoming dress, even worse than Lucy's black shroud. Her hair was in tangles and full of pine needles. The kerchief she had purloined from Parasha so that she wouldn't look conspicuous in her peasant garb (once again she had worried about getting a disguise perfect) was hanging at the back of her neck, having worked its way loose while she slept. She didn't know it, but her face was coated with a fine layer of dust, streaked in places from sweat and tears. And this man, this dolt, was suggesting they make love here in the woods, in broad daylight, at this moment, complete strangers as they were. Incredible.

"You're sure, little pigeon?"

"Quite."

"You will let me know if you change your mind?"

"Indubitably."

"Such a way with words." He grinned.

Katherine was relieved to see that he was obviously not in the least upset by her refusal to bed down with him. How different from his brother that was!

"I suppose you're in love with Mitya," he continued, sighing. "It's always the same, you know. They see him first, and"—he snapped his fingers—"I might as well be invisible. You can't imagine how depressing it is to be in the same room with him at a party or ball. The women look at him and they are ready to fall at his feet. They look at me and want to smile and pat my head. No one takes me seriously."

"Perhaps because you don't want to be taken seriously?" Katherine suggested.

He grinned again, widely, his eyes crinkling with laughter. "How astute you are, my pigeon. That little confession usually works to my advantage."

"Which proves what an incorrigible cad you are."

"So I am. And since you're on to me, we might as well be off."

"We aren't going anywhere together, Nikolai."

"Now don't be difficult, pigeon. Beside the fact that it would be unthinkable for me to leave you here alone, I also have my orders from the old lady to think of. Not that she isn't easy enough to get around, but she does control the purse strings when Mitya is away, so it's always best to stay on her good side. And she was rather up in arms about your running off."

"No doubt," Katherine retorted. "But she can turn purple with rage for all I care. I'm not going back there to be subjected to any more of her tyranny. Dimitri didn't leave me there to be abused."

"Of course he didn't. And you won't be, even if I have to protect you myself. Really, pigeon, there is nothing for you to fear at Novii Domik."

He still couldn't believe that Sonya, sweet old Sonya, had ordered a caning. It was inconceivable. The woman had probably fallen and hurt herself, and for some reason wanted to blame Sonya for her pain, and was intelligent enough to make her story sound convincing. At any rate, he had been sent to bring her back, had come this far, and having found her, saw no good reason not to carry out his mission. Besides, she had Savva's horse. What would the man think if he had to tell him he just let her go on with it? He certainly wouldn't believe that Nikolai hadn't been able to find her. Neither would Sonya. *He* would end up having to replace the horse and have the old woman peeved with him too.

"You know, Ekaterina—it is Ekate—"

"No, by God, it's Katherine, good old English Katherine, or even Kate or Kit—God, to hear myself called Kit again!"

"Very well, Kit." He smiled indulgently, though the name didn't sound at all the same in his French-Russian accent. "Mitya will straighten out this misunderstanding once he returns, and you do want to be there when he returns, don't you?"

"Would I be heading for St. Petersburg if I did? Besides, it could be weeks or longer before Dimitri gets back. No, it's out of the question. But then—" She paused thoughtfully, running over her options since he was proving so difficult. "Since it will in fact take Dimitri to unravel this misunderstanding, as you call it, why don't you take me to him instead? That I wouldn't object to.''

Nikolai laughed delightedly. ''A splendid idea, little Kit, as long as you realize the consequence of traveling alone with me such a long way.''

''I assure you my reputation couldn't be in worse ruin.''

''And I assure you I couldn't take you all the way to Moscow without bedding you, will you, nil you. *That* is the consequence I refer to. To Novii Domik I can manage to control myself, since it is only a short distance away.''

''The devil it is!'' she returned, furious with him for toying with her. ''I must have ridden fifty miles yesterday.''

''More like twenty, pigeon, and it wasn't yesterday, but this morning.''

''You mean—''

''It's only nearing evening now. We can be back in time for dinner, if you will stop putting up such a fuss about it.''

''All right!'' she stormed. ''Fine! But if that witch you call an aunt ends up killing me in her madness, it's going to be *your* fault, you—you lecherous womanizer, you! And don't think I won't haunt you for it, that is, if I get the chance, because Dimitri will probably kill you first when he learns you're responsible for my demise!''

She had more to say, but she turned her back on him to mount her horse unassisted. She would scratch his eyes out if he offered assistance. And it wasn't easy. God, each little movement hurt! But she did it on her own with the help of a large rock. And he just stood there, watching her in amazement, and feeling a trifle, no, actually more than a trifle guilty as he caught a word here and there.

"You couldn't be a gentleman, no, that would be asking too much, wouldn't it? That's something that doesn't run in your particular family, I've learned to my detriment. Kidnapped, drugged, used, imprisoned, those are run-of-the-mill niceties for the Alexandrovs. Heaven forbid that one of you should have a conscience!"

She squeezed her eyes shut for a moment. She wasn't going to succumb to this pain. She wasn't.

"Why? Why me?" Nikolai heard that plainly. "Why did he have to drag me with him all the way to Russia? Why did he have to keep after me until . . . until . . . Good Lord, you'd think I was a blasted beauty, when I know perfectly well I'm only passing fair. Why was it so important to him to—"

Nikolai wished to high heaven that she would have finished that particular statement, but she didn't. She had groaned when she nudged the horse forward, bent over in obvious pain, and he was assailed by doubts, not about letting her travel in her condition, but about her actual importance to Dimitri.

"Kit, pigeon, perhaps—"

"Not another word from the likes of you," she said with such contempt that Nikolai cringed. "I'm going back to face that bitch, but I don't have to listen to any more drivel from you in the meantime."

She rode away, and he had to make haste to catch up with her, doing so only when she reached the broken shrubs at the side of the road that had led him to her in the first place. Damn, but he was in a quandary now about what to do. Keeping Aunt Sonya happy was one thing. Raising Dimitri's fury was quite another. And trying to talk to this quarrelsome woman now was something else again. In the end, he decided that if she really was important to Dimitri, then his brother would want her to be where he left her, not in St. Petersburg where he would have to search for her. That is, if he wanted to find her. Sweet Christ, it would be nice to know the actual truth about what was going on here.

Chapter Twenty-nine

*D*imitri stared at the empty room: the bed smoothly made, nothing out of place, sterile, like a white tomb. A feeling that it had been like this for days made him rush to the wardrobe and throw open the doors. The clothes were all there, even the black cloth purse she had tried to brain that annoying fellow with the first time he had ever seen her.

He let out his breath, unaware that he had even been holding it in. Katherine wouldn't leave without that purse, would she? It was all she had left that was actually hers. So where was she, then?

Irritation swiftly took hold. He had steeled himself to face her. For hours, as he raced the last miles to Novii Domik, he had been working himself into a numbed state of mind in which he could accept anything she might say to him, and he expected the worst. Now he felt like a condemned man who had been given a short reprieve when all he wanted to do was get his execution over.

He had expected to find her in the White Room, reading a book perhaps, or primping at her vanity, or even curled up in bed eating bonbons. *That* was how he had always found Natalia when he deigned to visit her. He had even thought to find Katherine pacing the room in a fury of boredom. So much for what he expected.

It wasn't that late in the evening when he had rushed into the house and straight up the stairs without a word. Two footmen in the entrance hall had stared at him in amazement. A maid in the upstairs hall had gasped upon seeing him. Usually the household had warning of his coming. But Dimitri hadn't been doing anything in the usual way lately.

He hadn't even returned with his servants. For that matter, they had been far behind him on his mad dash to Moscow, and when he had turned around, wanting to speak to Katherine, only a day and a half short of the city, and finally came upon them almost halfway there, he had sent them on. After all, Moscow was still on the agenda, Tatiana still needed a visit from him. Only two Cossacks had kept up with him, and even they had fallen behind today.

It wasn't like Dimitri to do anything in such a hurry. His race to Moscow certainly did not come from any wild desire to see his intended future bride. She had been the farthest thing from his mind, no more than the vague reason he had set off for Moscow instead of in some other direction. Actually any direction would have served for his cowardly leave-taking. That was exactly how he had thought of himself after the mad panic to be gone had worn off. The reason for his rush had been to get away from Katherine, to be far away when she woke up after their night together, to avoid the contempt and loathing she was bound to feel, despite her words to the contrary while she was still under the drug's influence.

He had come to his senses halfway to Moscow. So he had made a mistake. It wasn't the first time. So this was a particularly bad mistake. It would just take longer to break down Katherine's anger this time. She had been furious with him before and he had gotten around it, or rather, she had cooled off on her own. She was a sensible woman. She didn't hold grudges. That was one of the things he liked about her, besides her spirit and defiance and passion and a dozen other things.

He had gone on in a much better frame of mind, satisfied that the hole he had dug for himself wasn't *that* deep. He had even begun to wonder if he could somehow talk Katherine into staying in Russia. He would buy her a mansion, fill it with servants, shower her with jewels and the most expensive clothes. Tatiana was for getting him an heir. Katherine was for loving, and he wove a fantasy that had her placed firmly in his future.

And then he had remembered how he had departed, without so much as a word to her. He hadn't even made sure that she would still be there when he returned, assuming she wouldn't have the courage to venture forth alone in an unfamiliar land. But if she was angry enough, she might well do anything. And in boredom, she had nothing to do but gnaw on the bone of her anger.

He had turned around immediately. Tatiana could wait. He had to settle things at home first, even if it meant facing Katherine's fury sooner than he had planned, before she had a chance to calm down. Then again, she wasn't likely to calm down until she had something to occupy her mind with besides murdering him.

Now, as before, he wanted the worst over and done with so that he could go on from there. He also had an overwhelming passion just to look at her again, to see if the worst of his obsession was over. He had been gone for five days. If the first thing he wanted to do when he saw her was make love to her, then he was right back where he started, and his foolishness in drugging her would have been for nothing.

Dimitri left the White Room and marched back down the hall. The maid he had seen earlier was gone, but another was coming up the stairs with a tray piled high with food, no doubt meant for him. It didn't take long for the news of his unexpected return to spread.

"Where is she?" he asked the girl abruptly.

"Who, my lord?"

"The Englishwoman," he replied impatiently.

She seemed to cower away from him. "I—I don't know."

He passed her by, calling out to one of the footmen while he was still descending the stairs, "Where is the Englishwoman?"

"I haven't seen her, my prince."

"And you?"

Semen, who had known Dimitri all his life and who knew his rages were for the most part harmless bursts of emotion, was suddenly so frightened that he couldn't find his voice. It wasn't that the Prince had come in and gone straight to the White Room, which Ludmilla had whispered as she rushed past on her way to spread the news of his return. Nor was it that he was asking for the woman, not having found her where he obviously expected to find her. It was his anxious expression, and the remembered words he had heard whispered to Rodion: "You had better hope you're not around when the Prince finds out about—" She hadn't been able to finish. He had cut off her words with the first lash of the cane. *He* did that.

"Where's your tongue, Semen?" Dimitri snapped into his thoughts.

"I—believe she was seen in the kitchen—earlier." Dimitri had reached the hall, was only a foot away, and Semen seemed to shrink in his boots. "Right now—" He had to clear his throat, not once, but twice. "Right now, I don't know, my lord."

"Who would know?" got Dimitri only shrugs.

Playing dumb? Since when did his people play dumb with him? What the hell was going on here?

He scowled at each man before starting toward the back of the house, bellowing, "Katherine!"

"What are you shouting for, Mitya?" Sonya asked, coming out of the drawing room just as he passed it. "Really, you needn't shout to let us know you have returned, though why you have come back so soon—"

He rounded on his aunt. "Where is she? And if you value peace and quiet, don't ask me who *she* is. You know perfectly well who I'm talking about."

"The Englishwoman, of course," Sonya replied calmly. "We haven't misplaced her, you know, though she did run away once, stealing one of the villager's horses. It was fortunate that Nikolai was here at the time to fetch her back."

Several emotions washed over Dimitri simultaneously. Surprise that Katherine *had* tried to leave, when that hadn't been his main worry.

Relief that she was here somewhere, even if he was having trouble finding out exactly where. And jealousy, bright, hot, and absurd, that one of his handsome, woman-chasing half-brothers—Nikolai in particular—had met his Katherine.

"Where is he?" Dimitri asked tightly.

"I do wish you would be more precise, my dear. If you mean Nikolai, he didn't stay here long. He came to welcome you home as soon as he heard you were back and has gone on to Moscow with the same intent. Obviously you missed each other on the road."

Dimitri brushed past her into the drawing room, heading straight for the liquor cabinet. Possessiveness was a new experience for him. He didn't like it. For a moment he had actually thought about throttling his brother just for doing him the favor of fetching Katherine back here—no, not for that. For being out in the countryside alone with her, giving him the opportunity to do what he did best. If Nikolai so much as touched her . . .

"I suppose you are tired, Mitya, and that is why you are behaving in this boorish manner. Why don't you get a good night's sleep, and we can talk in the morning about why you have returned so soon."

He downed a short vodka before fixing her with his dark gaze. "Aunt Sonya, if I don't get some answers here very quickly, you're going to think my present behavior is on the right side of saintly. I came back here to see Katherine and for no other reason. Now, where the hell is she?"

Sonya had to sit down after those terse words, but to her credit, her voice didn't sound at all as

292

shaken as her insides. "I imagine she has retired for the night."

"I checked her room. Where is she sleeping, then?"

"With the servants."

Dimitri closed his eyes. *Those* tactics again. Trying to make him feel guilty for all the times he had thrown her origins at her and also making a statement that was quite clear. The meanest bed was preferable to his.

"Damn her, I should have known she would pull something like that as soon as I was gone!"

Sonya blinked in surprise. He was angry with the woman, not her. This was more than she could have hoped for, considering she had realized her mistake the moment he had shouted for his whore. Perhaps she could increase that anger.

"She is the most haughty, insulting woman I have ever met, Mitya. I put her to work scrubbing floors to see if that would humble her a little, but I doubt anything will."

"She agreed to that?" Dimitri asked incredulously.

Sonya could feel the color rising in her cheeks. Agreed? Agreed! He would have let her refuse? Didn't he hear her? She had been insulted. What was he thinking of to spoil that creature so?

"She didn't object, no."

"Then it seems as if I have wasted my time in coming back," Dimitri said with bitter asperity, not even looking at his aunt now. "So she wants to scrub floors now! Well, if she thinks that little piece of work is going to make me feel any more guilty, she's sadly mistaken."

He snatched up the bottle of vodka before angrily stalking out of the room. Semen and the other footman had to move quickly away from the door, where they had been eavesdropping before he burst out of the room and practically ran up the stairs.

Sonya poured herself a glass of sherry and smiled as she took a sip. She hadn't understood Dimitri's last comments, but that didn't matter. He would return to Moscow now and Tatiana, and probably be gone for months, forgetting about the Englishwoman completely.

Chapter Thirty

Nadezhda Fedorovna watched the English-woman covertly, blue eyes narrowed with resentment and loathing. And the more she watched her pushing her brush around the kitchen floor, ignoring everyone around her as if she were too good to associate with the kitchen servants, the more Nadezhda's resentment festered.

Who was she, anyway? Nobody. She was small, so small she could have passed for a child, while no one could mistake Nadezhda's full figure for anything but a woman's. Her hair was a dull, nondescript brown, while Nadezhda's was a flaming red, glossy, thick, her best feature by far. The only thing the foreigner had to recommend her was unusual eyes. In fact, there was nothing about her that should have attracted someone like Dimitri Alexandrov. So what had the Prince seen in her that no one else saw?

Nadezhda wasn't just prejudiced. Everyone had asked the same question. But for Nadezhda, who had had one glorious night with the Prince years ago, but had never been able to entice him again, the question was a burning one.

It was something she had never been able to get over, her failure with the Prince. She had had such wonderful plans. She would bear the Prince a son, elevating her stature enormously, assuring herself a life of ease.

She had not conceived from her one night with Dimitri. Some were beginning to think he was impotent, herself included. At the time she was wise enough to realize that she could still claim a child as his if she could get pregnant soon enough after she had been with him. With a little help from the lustier of the footmen, she had done just that, and was so happy, so proud of her accomplishment, that she had to boast of it to her sister, who betrayed her to their father, who beat her so badly for planning to deceive the Prince that she lost the baby. Nadezhda had wallowed in her bitter failure ever since.

Now here was this foreigner, this ugly interloper that the Prince had brought here and put in the White Room. The White Room! And she would have everyone believe that the Prince really cared more about her other than to bed her at his convenience.

Nadezhda had laughed when she heard that Princess Sonya had ordered her caned for her insolence. She had been delighted to see her put to work in the kitchen at the meanest tasks. She wasn't so haughty now. And the Prince hadn't come to remove her from her drudgery either, as half the household had anticipated, foolishly believing that he wouldn't like the way his aunt had treated the woman. But he *had* brought her here. And he *did* leave her here, instead of sending her on her way after he was done with her. And he had also looked for her last night as soon as he returned, news Nadezhda had received with rancor, until she later learned he was now furious with the woman, no doubt for showing such disrespect to his aunt.

No one had told the Englishwoman that the Prince was back. The other servants were in fact purposely keeping the news from her in a ridiculous attempt to spare her feelings. She didn't even notice the whispering and sympathetic looks, she paid so little attention to what was going on around her. It would serve her right to find out the Prince had been here after he was gone again, but Nadezhda couldn't wait that long. No one had told her the subject was prohibited. And the woman ought to be made to see that she had fooled no one with her delusions about *their* Prince Dimitri.

Nadezhda was only surprised that Princess Sonya hadn't been the one to tell her. It had been plain to see she hadn't been pleased yesterday morning when the woman didn't protest against her new position of floor scrubber. No doubt the Princess, like Nadezhda, had been hoping for resistance so that she could punish her again.

At least Nadezhda had been there to witness that humiliation. And she had been quick to inform the woman how lucky she was to be getting off so lightly after running away, stealing a horse, and putting the Prince's brother to the trouble of fetching her back, that she should have been caned again instead. And what did that bitch reply to Nadezhda's thoughtful disclosure?

"I'm not a serf, you fool, I'm a prisoner. It's perfectly natural for a prisoner to try and escape. It's expected."

Such impudence. Such ingratitude. Such pretension. It was as if she thought herself so superior to them all that she was incapable of being humbled by anything they did or said to her. But

Nadezhda had the means to bring her down a peg or two now, and if no one else had the gumption or desire to do it, she certainly did.

Katherine should have been warned by the malicious looks being cast at her by the flame-haired Nadezhda that she was in for more unpleasantness, but she hadn't thought the girl would be so spiteful as to pass her and deliberately spill a full bowl of wet breakfast scraps, pretending she had tripped. If Katherine hadn't moved quickly enough, the wastes would have landed in her lap instead of just spattering her knees and arms.

"How clumsy of me!" Nadezhda proclaimed loudly before dropping to her knees as if she meant to clean up the pile of oatmeal, rotten tomatoes, sour cream with bits of eggs, onions, mushrooms, and caviar oozing in it—Russians loved caviar with their *blini*, the pancakes served every morning at Novii Domik.

Katherine sat back, waiting to see if the girl really would wipe up her mess. But all she did was shove the now-empty bowl in front of Katherine.

"It's silly of them to make you scrub the floor over and over again, when it is already spotless," Nadezhda murmured snidely. "I thought I would give you a little something to make your efforts worthwhile."

So she was done pretending this was an accident. "How benignant of you," Katherine replied without expression.

"Benignant?"

"Forgive me. I sometimes forget myself when speaking to an ignoramus."

Nadezhda didn't know what *ignoramus* meant either, but she did know when she was being subtly insulted. "You think you are so clever with your fancy words, eh? Well, Miss Clever Bitch, what do you think of Prince Dimitri's return and his avoidance of you?"

Katherine's expression became an open book filled with excitement. "Dimitri's back? When?"

"Early last evening."

Early last evening Katherine had been dead to the world after twelve hours of drudgery. She wouldn't have heard anything if the house had fallen down around her ears, so she certainly wouldn't have heard Dimitri raising hell in her defense. But then why hadn't he sought her out? The morning was hours old. Why was she still here?

"You're lying."

Nadezhda's lips tilted mockingly. "I have no need to lie about this. Ask Ludmilla there. She saw him come in. Ask anyone here. They all thought to keep it from you because of your insistence that he would be furious when he learned what had happened. Well, little fool, he was furious, to be sure, but with you."

"Then his aunt didn't tell him the truth."

"Believe that if you like, but I know differently. The conversation they had was overheard. Princess Sonya told him everything. He knows you're here scrubbing floors and he doesn't care. Stupid wench," Nadezhda spat. "Did you really think he would take your side against his aunt? He's been up for hours, making preparations to leave again today. That's how eager he is to see you."

Katherine didn't believe her. She couldn't. She was a spiteful, malicious girl, though what Katherine had done to earn her enmity she didn't know. But Rodion came into the kitchen just then, and surmising the situation, yanked Nadezhda to her feet. He wouldn't lie to Katherine. He had been nothing but kindness since Nikolai had brought her back here.

"What have you done, Nadezhda?" he demanded.

The girl simply laughed, and jerking her hand away, swayed back to her corner of the kitchen. Rodion immediately bent down to help Katherine scoop the pile of scraps back into the bowl. She didn't say anything until the messy job was done, then she asked him plainly, "Rodion, is Dimitri really here?"

He wouldn't look up. "Yes."

A full minute passed. "And he knows where he can find me?"

"Yes."

He glanced at her then, but wished to God he hadn't. Sweet Mary, he had never seen such bleak pain in someone's eyes before. The beating hadn't done it to her, but a few nasty words from that spiteful Nadezhda had.

"I'm sorry," he said.

She didn't seem to hear. She hung her head and began the mechanical motions that pushed the brush back and forth across the floor. Rodion stood up and looked about the room, but everyone suddenly seemed inordinately busy, no one even hazarding a glance in their direction—except Nadezhda, who smiled gloatingly. Rodion turned and stalked out of the kitchen.

Katherine continued scrubbing the same spot, over and over. How furious Sonya would be if she knew how beneficial this particular task was for Katherine. She had been angry when she had been given no choice but to comply and do as the witch ordered. She had discerned immediately that Sonya would have relished her refusal, so instead she refused to give her that satisfaction. She would scrub the bloody floor until it killed her, without a single complaint.

But instead of the physical labor aggravating her sore back, it had eased her condition, the constant slow moving of her arms pulling and massaging each muscle, soothing the tightness, reducing the swelling instead of inflaming it as that jarring ride had done. And after a full day of scrubbing yesterday, when she might have thought she would have to crawl to her bed in agony, she was simply worn out from the labor, a strain in her lower back, and a definite soreness in her arms and hands, but that she didn't mind at all. All movement was easier now, with only a slight twinge here and there. She could almost forget the beating, if she didn't actually touch her back.

The tears that had been gathering in her eyes spilled over. *So much for trying to distract yourself, you idiot. When was the last time you cried without some kind of pain forcing the tears out? There's no pain now, you stupid ninny. Stop it! There's no good reason! You knew all along he didn't care. Look how he left without a word, without insuring your safety. Just a few words to his aunt could have prevented that archaic beating.*

Oh, God, it hurt so much that she could hardly breathe for the choking constriction in her throat.

How could he just leave her here? He wasn't even going to come to see if she was all right after that savage beating. He cared that little. That's what hurt the most.

He had spent the night here, gone to bed knowing that his aunt had condemned her to slavery in the kitchen, done nothing to alter that fact. No apologies. No champion. And he was going to leave again. Was this his idea then of how she would be kept busy while she was here? The bastard.

And you fell in love with him, you contemptible fool, even when you knew it was an asinine thing to do. Well, you got just what you deserved. You always knew love was an insane emotion, and this proves it.

It was no use. There was no room for anger to take hold, nothing inside her but the hurt that was fast numbing her senses, until finally there was nothing left to feel but welcome emptiness.

Chapter Thirty-one

"*The* boots, man!" Dimitri growled impatiently. "I'm not presenting myself at court. They'll be covered with dust by the end of the day."

Semen rushed forward with the boots still only half shined. Why did *he* have to be at the bottom of the stairs when the Prince needed a valet to replace the absent Maksim? He was a jumble of nerves, expecting at any moment that the Englishwoman would appear and tell Dimitri the whole of the story, not just the half-truths the Princess had told him. But then she didn't even know the Prince was back. Why should she leave the kitchen? He couldn't depend on that. He wouldn't be able to relax until Dimitri was gone again, and, thank God, he was preparing to leave now.

Dimitri caught a glimpse of himself in the mirror and was surprised by the baleful stare it returned. No wonder Semen was so edgy. Had he possessed this angry look all morning? How should he know? He was still half drunk, if truth were known. Two bottles of vodka hadn't produced the desired effect of putting him to sleep. It had only made his thoughts discordant as the night wore on. And even after a sleepless night, he still wasn't tired. Sweet Christ, what he wouldn't give for a little sleep to erase the whole problem from his mind.

"You want the dress sword, my lord?"

"I suppose I should wear my medals too on the road," Dimitri snapped, but then quickly apologized for his testiness.

He had donned one of his old uniforms simply because he felt in a warlike mood. He didn't have to wear all the trappings that went with it. The scarlet jacket was still in excellent condition, the tight white trousers spotless, the knee-high boots as stiff as when they were new. If the Tzar had his way, the whole country would be in uniform, civilian as well as military. Unlike in other countries, here a man's uniforms didn't retire from active service when he did. At court, rarely anything else was worn.

The knock at the door brought a sharp "Come in!" before Semen could move to open it.

Rodion stepped into the room, looking uncomfortable when he saw Dimitri's scowling countenance. It had been one thing to think about setting the record straight for the woman's sake, but quite another actually to speak up when the Prince was looking like this.

Semen had quite literally turned ashen, guessing Rodion's intention. Rodion had gotten drunk the night the woman burned with fever from the beating. He had been the one to take her to Parasha. He had been the one to warn the kitchen workers to leave her alone. Yet he had played a part in hurting the woman just as Semen had, even if neither had had any choice. How could he forget that?

"Well?" Dimitri barked.

"I—I think there is something you should know—about the Englishwoman—before you leave, my lord."

"Katherine. Her name is Katherine," Dimitri snarled. "And there isn't anything you can tell me about her that would surprise me, so don't bother. In fact if I never hear another thing about her, it will be too soon!"

"Yes, my lord." Rodion turned to leave, relieved and yet disappointed at the same time.

Semen was just letting out his breath, some little color returning to his cheeks, when the Prince halted Rodion.

"I'm sorry, Rodion." Dimitri motioned him back, sighing. "I didn't actually mean any of that. What did you have to tell me about Katherine?"

"Just that—" Rodion exchanged a glance with Semen, but stiffened his resolve and blurted— "your aunt had her caned, my lord, so badly that she didn't awaken for nearly two days. She works in the kitchen now, but not by choice. She would have been beaten again if she had refused."

Dimitri didn't say a word. For a long moment he just stood there staring at Rodion, then he left the room so quickly that Rodion had to jump back out of the way.

"Why did you have to do that, you fool?" Semen demanded. "Did you see the look on his face?"

Rodion was not in the least sorry now. "She was right, Semen. And it would have gone a lot worse if he had found out later, after he'd left, and no one bothering to tell him while he was still here. But he's a fair man. He isn't going to blame us for following the Princess's orders. It's not who wielded the cane that will concern him but why it was done, and that's for his aunt to explain, if she can.''

From downstairs, the crash of the kitchen door could be heard throughout the whole house. Three more crashes followed, though not nearly so loud, as several women in the kitchen were so startled that they dropped what they had been holding.

Every eye was on the Prince, framed in the doorway, though a few spared a glance for the broken hinge dangling from the door. Every eye, that is, except Katherine's. She didn't bother to look up, not when he appeared so dramatically, not when he crossed the kitchen to stand above her, not when he dropped to his knees beside her. She knew he was there. His presence had always been unmistakable, even when she couldn't see him. She simply didn't care. If he had come last night, she probably would have cried on his shoulder. Now he could go to the devil. Too late was too late.

''Katya?''

''Go away, Alexandrov.''

''Katya, please—I didn't know.''

''Didn't know what? That I was here? I happen to know otherwise. I happen to know that witch relative of yours told you everything.''

She still hadn't looked up at him. Her hair, loose beneath the kerchief tied round her head, fell forward over both shoulders, partially concealing her face as she bent over still scrubbing the floor. The dress she wore wasn't hers and was so filthy that it reeked. Dimitri felt like killing someone, but first he had to take care of Katherine.

"She told me that you were sleeping with the servants, *not* that she put you there. I thought it was your choice, Katya, just as before, that you were again refusing any amenity I offered you. She told me you had run away and she had put you to work here. She said you didn't refuse the work. Again I thought it was your choice."

"Which shows what you get for thinking, Alexandrov, a total waste of time for you."

"At least look at me when you insult me."

"Go to hell."

"Katya, I didn't know you were beaten!" he said in exasperation.

"It's nothing."

"Must I strip you to see for myself?"

"All right! So I have a few bruises. It doesn't hurt anymore, so your concern is a bit late, not to mention rather dubious."

"You think I wanted this to happen?"

"I think your concern was aptly shown when you didn't bother to explain to your aunt why you brought me here. *That*, Alexandrov, sums it up nicely."

"Look at me!"

She tossed her head back, her eyes cutting into his, bright, glassy, very close to betraying her. "Are you happy? Let me know when you've seen enough. I have work to do."

"You're coming with me, Katya."

"Not on your life." But Katherine wasn't quick enough in moving back from him. Dimitri pulled her to her feet and just as swiftly had her up in his arms. "My back, you beast! Don't touch my back!"

"Then hold onto my neck, little one, because I'm not putting you down."

She glared at him, but it was useless. She had gone through too much pain to put up with any more if she didn't have to. She wrapped her arms around his neck and he immediately lowered his arm to her hips, supporting her firmly there and beneath her thighs.

"I'll have you know this means nothing," Katherine hissed as he started out of the kitchen. "If I weren't afraid of hurting myself, I'd clobber you."

"When you are feeling better, I will remind you. I will even have a cane fetched and stand fast while you do your worst. It's no more than I deserve."

"Oh, shut up, shut up—"

Katherine didn't finish. The tears had started again, and she squeezed Dimitri's neck tighter, hiding her face in the curve.

He stopped by the broken door, and there was a world of difference in the tone of his voice as he rapped out an order to two maids. "I want a bath and brandy in my room immediately."

Katherine stirred herself enough to protest that. "I wouldn't be caught dead in your room, so if that's for me—"

"The White Room," Dimitri corrected himself sharply. "And a doctor here within the hour. You and you"—he fixed the two maids with his hard gaze—"come with me to assist her."

"I can assist myself, Dimitri. I've been doing it long enough now to have got the hang of it nicely, thank you."

He ignored her, as did the maids who jumped to follow his orders. There was a collective sigh in the kitchen once the Prince was gone. There were also a lot of "I told you so" expressions on those who had tended to believe the English-woman. Nadezhda wasn't one of them. She demolished the lump of dough she had been kneading, incensed by the scene she had just witnessed. But ruining the dough got her a scolding from the cook, which she replied to sharply, which got her a slap, which was silently applauded by one and all, for no one particularly cared for Nadezhda and her surly ways.

Upstairs in the White Room, Dimitri gently set Katherine down on the bed, receiving no thanks for his care. The maids hurried to fill her bath, the one thing she wasn't about to refuse, not having had a decent bath since Dimitri had gone. The brandy was refused, however, the glass shoved away with annoyance, and she was most certainly annoyed.

"I don't know what you think you're proving with all this attention, Alexandrov. I would just as soon you had left me where I was. After all, kitchen work is just another new experience for me, and you have pointed out how you are responsible for all my new experiences since I met you. How much I have to thank you for."

Dimitri flinched. He could see now that in this sarcastic mood of hers, trying to talk to her would be useless. He could have told her it was his base cowardice in not wanting to face her after their night together that had led to his thoughtless flight. But that night was the last thing he wanted to remind her of now. That would only be adding fuel to the fire.

"The bath is ready, my lord," Ludmilla offered hesitantly.

"Good, then get rid of that rag she is wearing and—"

Johanna Lindsey

"Not with you in here!" Katherine cut in heatedly.

"Very well, I'll leave. But you will let the doctor examine you when he arrives."

"It isn't necessary."

"Katya!"

"Oh, all right, I'll see the blasted doctor. But don't bother coming back yourself, Alexandrov. I have nothing more to say to you."

Dimitri went through the connecting door to his room, but just before he closed it, a gasp from one of the maids made him look back, and he was treated to the sight of Katherine's dress falling to her waist. Bile rose up in his throat. The full view of her back was literally a maze of blue, brown, and yellow, with deepest purple in long straight lines where each blow had welted her.

He shut the door, his head leaning against it, his eyes tightly closed. No wonder she had refused to listen to him. What she must have suffered, and all because of his neglect! And she had let him off easily. She hadn't even screamed at him. Oh, God, he wished she had screamed at him. At least then there might have been some hope of reaching her, making her understand that he would do anything to turn back the clock, to take away her pain, that the last thing he wanted was to hurt her. Sweet Christ, all he had ever wanted to do was love her. Now he had sunk so far beneath her contempt that he wasn't even worthy of her hate.

Dimitri found his aunt in the library. She was standing by the window looking out at the orchard, her back tense, her hands clasped tightly before her. She was expecting him. Nothing escaped her notice in this house, and he knew she had probably been told word for word everything he and Katherine had said to each other in the kitchen. She was anticipating the worst. But Dimitri's anger was deep and self-directed. Only a small portion was reserved for his aunt.

Quietly he moved up beside her and stood looking out at the same view, but without seeing it. The tiredness he had hoped for earlier surrounded him now, weighing down his shoulders.

"I leave a woman here in the security of my own home and return to find she has been put through hell. Why, Aunt Sonya? Nothing Katherine could have done could have warranted such treatment."

Sonya was relieved by his soft tone, and deceived into thinking he wasn't as upset as had been reported. "You told me she wasn't important, Mitya," she reminded him.

He sighed. "Yes, I did say that, in anger, but did that give you the right to abuse her? I also told you she wasn't your concern. Why in God's name did you involve yourself?"

"I found her coming out of your room. I thought she might have stolen something from you."

He turned toward her incredulously. "Steal from me? Oh, Christ! Steal from me! She has refused everything I have tried to give her. She spits on my wealth."

"How could I have known that? I only wanted to have her searched. The matter would have ended there if she hadn't turned so belligerent about it. How could I ignore such rudeness to me in front of the servants?"

"She is a free woman, an Englishwoman. She isn't subject to the archaic rules and customs of this country."

"Who is she then, Mitya?" Sonya demanded. "Who is she besides your mistress?"

"She's not my mistress. I wish she were, but she's not. I don't really know who she is, probably some English lord's bastard, but that doesn't matter. She plays the role of a grand lady, true, but I tolerate it. She had no reason to suppose she need modify her attitude here, even for you. But most important she was under my protection. Sweet Christ, Aunt Sonya, she is such a tiny, delicate woman. Didn't it occur to you that such a beating could have damaged her permanently? Crippled her even?"

"It might have, if she had shown even a modicum of delicacy, but she didn't. Just three days after her beating she was racing across the countryside on the back of a horse."

"An act of desperation."

"Nonsense, Mitya. It was only a little beating. If she had really been hurt by it, she wouldn't have been capable—"

"Not hurt!" he exploded, finally giving Sonya a glimpse of his true emotional state. "Come with me!"

He took her wrist and pulled her behind him up the stairs and into the White Room, where he threw open the door to the bathchamber. Katherine shrieked, sinking down into the water, but Dimitri crossed to the tub and firmly lifted her up, presenting her back to Sonya. He got a soapy washcloth slapped across his neck and chest for the trouble.

"Damn you, Alexandrov—"

"I'm sorry, little one, but my aunt was under the illusion that she hadn't really hurt you."

He set her back down in the water and quickly closed the door, though he could still hear Katherine's furious disclaimer. "I'm fine now, you dolt! I told you that! You think a St. John can't tolerate a little pain?"

He didn't have to labor the point with Sonya. She had paled as much as he had upon seeing the result of her handiwork. He took her elbow and led her out of the room, but stopped at the top of the stairs.

"It was my intention, Aunt Sonya, to leave Katherine here at Novii Domik for several weeks until—well, the reason isn't important. But that is still my intention. Under the circumstances, I think it would be best if you visited one of your nieces for a while."

"Yes, I'll leave today . . . Mitya, I didn't realize. . . . She seemed so sturdy, despite . . . I know that is no excuse—" She hurried away, unable to finish, unable to face Dimitri's condemnation a moment longer.

She was like so many nobles of the old school, committing atrocities in a moment of anger, regretting it later, when it was too late.

"No, that is no excuse, Aunt Sonya," Dimitri murmured bitterly to himself. "There is no excuse."

Chapter Thirty-two

Monday

My Lord Prince,

As soon as you departed for Moscow, the young miss left her bed and would not return to it under any circumstances (her words, my lord). She spent the remainder of the day in the garden, pruning and weeding and cutting flowers for the house. The flowers are everywhere now, in every room. There are none left in the garden.

Her attitude has not changed. She will not speak to me at all. She speaks to the maids only to tell them to leave her alone. Marusia has had no luck either in getting her to talk. She wouldn't go near the account books you left for her to work on.

Your servant,
Vladimir Kirov

Tuesday

My Lord Prince,

Nothing has changed, except she did explore the house today, although she asked no questions, not even about the family portraits she found in the library. In the afternoon she walked to the village, but found it empty, since the harvesting has begun. She refused the use of one of your horses for this excursion. Rodion accompanied her, since she seems less hostile to him than anyone else. The purpose of her visit was to apologize to Savva and Parasha for taking their horse.

Your servant,
Vladimir Kirov

Wednesday

*M*y Lord Prince,

This morning the young miss took two books from the library and spent the remainder of the day in her room reading. Marusia still cannot get her to talk, and she looks at me as if I'm not there.

Your servant,
Vladimir Kirov

Thursday

*M*y Lord Prince,

She stayed in her room the entire day reading, not even coming out to eat. When Marusia took her meals to her, she reported that the miss seemed more distracted than usual.

Your servant,
Vladimir Kirov

Friday

*M*y Lord Prince,

Today the young miss disturbed the entire household with her demands. She wanted every servant brought before her to relate his or her duties and when she was finished, she informed me that Novii Domik has too many servants doing useless jobs and that I should find them more worthwhile employment.

Her attitude is much improved, if you can call a return to her imperious nature an improvement. Marusia swears her depression is finally over. Even her peculiar habit of talking to herself has returned.

Your servant,
Vladimir Kirov

Saturday

*M*y Lord Prince,

The young miss spent most of the day watching the villagers work in the fields and even tried helping, though she stopped when she realized she was only in the way. When Parasha invited her to the communal bath, she declined, yet on returning to the house, she made use of your steamroom and even had cold water poured on her afterward. Her laughter over this experience was contagious. Nearly everyone was seen smiling afterward.

Your servant,
Vladimir Kirov

Sunday

*M*y Lord Prince,

After church, your account books were delivered to the young miss's room at her request. You were right, my lord. She couldn't resist the challenge for long.

Your servant,
Vladimir Kirov

Monday

*M*y Lord Prince,

I am sorry to inform you that my wife had the misguided notion that the young miss would be pleased to know about the daily reports you requested. That was not the case. She has let me know in no uncertain terms what she thinks of my spying, as she calls it. Furthermore, since she knows that I won't end the reports at her request, she said that when I write tonight, I should tell you that although she hasn't tallied any exact figures yet, in glancing through your account books, she has already surmised that four of your investments are worthless, a steady drain on your capital that you can't hope to see a profit from in the near future, if ever. These are her words, my lord, not mine. If you ask me, it is impossible for her to have drawn these conclusions in such a short time, if she even knows what she's talking about.

Your servant,
Vladimir Kirov

Dimitri gave a short bark of laughter after finishing this letter. Two of those bad investments Katherine had found were no doubt the factories he considered his charities, for each year they fell just short of breaking even. Yet they each employed a large work force, and he couldn't see himself closing them down and putting all those people out of work. He had planned to make the necessary changes eventually, to make the factories self-supporting as well as profitable, even if he had to change the goods manufactured. He had just never found the time to devote to such an undertaking.

He had known Katherine would discover the loss from those factories easily if she was as good as she claimed to be at figures. But the other two? He wondered if he should write her to discuss them? Would she even read a letter from him? Just because she had deigned to go over the account books when she had said she wouldn't touch them, did not necessarily mean she was ready to forgive him. She had made it quite clear before he left that she would be most happy if she never laid eyes on him again.

"So I have finally tracked you down. I tried every club, every restaurant, every party currently in progress. Never would I have thought to find you at home—"

"Vasya!"

"And attending to correspondence, no less," Vasili finished with a grin, coming forward to clasp Dimitri in a powerful bear hug.

Dimitri was delighted by the surprise. He hadn't seen his friend since early March. Before he had left for England, he had been so tied up in his courtship of Tatiana that he had found little time for Vasili, a mistake he wouldn't let happen again. Of all his friends this one was the most dear, the one who most understood him. Not quite as tall as Dimitri, with coal black hair and light blue eyes, a devilish combination according to the ladies, Vasili Dashkov was the charmer, the carefree soul, exactly the opposite of Dimitri. Yet they were so attuned, they could read each other's minds more often than not.

"So what took you so long? I have been back for nearly a month."

"Your man had a little trouble finding me, since I was with a certain countess on her estate and didn't want to be found. Couldn't have it getting back to the husband that she was entertaining without his knowledge, now, could I?"

"Of course not," Dimitri said in all seriousness as he resumed his seat.

Vasili chuckled, plopping himself down on the corner of Dimitri's desk. "At any rate, I stopped by Novii Domik first, thinking to find you there. And what the devil is wrong with that bear Vladimir? He wouldn't even let me in your house, just told me I'd find you here and sent me on my way. And what's he doing there anyway, when you're here? I've never known him to be out of shouting distance from you."

"He's keeping an eye on something for me that I couldn't trust being left unguarded."

"Ah, now my curiosity is whetted. Who is she?"

"No one you know, Vasya."

"Yet a treasure that must be guarded, and by your most dependable man?" Vasili's eyes widened. "Don't tell me you've stolen someone's wife."

"That's your department, I believe."

"So it is. All right, talk. You know I won't let up till you do."

Dimitri wasn't being evasive. He wanted to talk to Vasili about Katherine. He just didn't know how to go about it, how much actually to explain.

"It's not what you're thinking, Vasya. . . . Well, it is, but . . . No, this situation has got to be unique."

"Let me know when you make up your mind."

Dimitri sat back, giving his friend a quelling look. "I am utterly obsessed with this woman, yet she wants nothing to do with me. She actually hates me."

"That *is* unique, and not to be believed either," Vasili scoffed. "The ladies don't hate you, Mitya. They might become annoyed with you, but they don't hate you. So what did you do to get on the wrong side of this one?"

"You're not listening, not that I haven't done everything conceivable to earn her enmity, but she wanted nothing to do with me from the beginning."

"You're serious, aren't you?"

"You could say we met under the worst circumstances," Dimitri replied.

Vasili waited for him to go on, but Dimitri had turned pensive, remembering, and Vasili exploded, "Well? Must I drag it out piece by piece?"

Dimitri looked away, not very proud of his part in this. "To be brief, I saw her on the London street and wanted her. I thought she would be available, so I sent Vladimir after her. Everything went wrong from there. She wasn't for sale."

"Sweet Christ, I see it already. Resourceful Vladimir got her for you anyway, didn't he?"

"Yes, and slipped an aphrodisiac into her food. I end up with the most sexy, sensual virgin God ever created, and the most memorable night of love I have ever experienced. But the next morning, in full possession of her faculties again, she insisted on having Vladimir's head for abducting her."

"She didn't blame you?"

"No, actually, she just couldn't wait to get away from me. The trouble was, she made certain threats about going to the authorities, and what with the Tzar's scheduled visit, I thought it prudent to remove her from England for a while."

Vasili grinned wryly. "I don't suppose she was delighted with that plan?"

"She is possessed of a glorious temper, which I have been treated to more than once."

"So you have this lovely wench still under wraps, and still wanting nothing to do with you. Does that about sum it up?"

"Not quite," Dimitri replied quietly, his expression bleak. "I made the mistake of leaving Katherine at Novii Domik, and I returned to find my aunt had abused her. If she didn't hate me before, she does now."

"This time she blames you?"

"With good reason. I didn't insure her safety as I should have. I left rather quickly, for reasons I am too ashamed to repeat."

"Never say you . . . No, you wouldn't have raped her. That's simply not your style. So you must have had her drugged again."

Dimitri gave Vasili a disgusted look for his perception. "I was angry."

"Naturally." Vasili chuckled. "You've never come up against a female who wasn't seduceable before. It must have been most trying."

"Stow the sarcasm, Vasya. I'd like to know what you would do faced with similar circumstances. Katherine is the most stubborn, argumentative, pretentious woman I know, and yet I can't be in the same room with her without wanting to carry her off to the nearest bed. And the most irritating, the most frustrating thing about it is, I know she isn't completely immune to me. There have been stolen moments when she returns my passion, but she always comes to her senses before I can take full advantage of them."

"So you are obviously doing something wrong. Is she holding out for marriage, do you think?"

"Marriage? Of course not. She has to know that isn't possible—" Dimitri paused, frowning. "On the other hand, with her delusions, she just might think it is possible."

"What delusions?"

"Didn't I mention she lays claim to being Lady Katherine St. John, daughter of the Earl of Strafford?"

"No, but what makes you think she isn't?"

"She was found walking the street, in the dress of a commoner, and without escort. What conclusion would you draw, Vasya?"

"I see your point," Vasili said thoughtfully. "But why would she make this claim?"

"Because she knows enough about the family to get away with it. It's quite likely she's the Earl's natural daughter, but that still doesn't make her marriageable."

"So, if marriage is out of the question, what is the second thing she could want?"

"Nothing. She wants absolutely nothing from me."

"Come now, Mitya, every woman wants *something.* And it sounds to me as if this one just wants to be treated like a lady for a change."

"You mean I should pretend I believe her?"

"I wouldn't go that far, but—"

"You're right! I should bring her to the city, take her to parties, escort her—"

"Mitya! Am I mistaken, or are you here in Moscow because Tatiana Ivanova is in Moscow?"

"Damn!" Dimitri slumped back in his chair again.

"That's what I thought. So shouldn't you get a firm commitment from the Princess before you are seen adoring someone else? After all, it is expected that you will have your mistresses, but not while you are pursuing your future bride. I don't think Tatiana would take too kindly to that. What are you doing home, anyway, when she is at the Andreyev party tonight, and with your old friend Lysenko? For that matter, what is she doing with him, when you are back?"

"I haven't gone to see her yet," Dimitri admitted.

"How long have you been here?"

"Eight days."

Vasili's eyes shot to the ceiling. "He's counting the days. For God's sake, Mitya, if you miss your Katherine that much, send for her, keep her here under wraps until you have Tatiana's answer.''

Dimitri shook his head. ''No, when Katherine is around, she's all I can think about.''

''It seems to me she's all you can think about whether she's here or not. You've been procrastinating, Mitya.''

''What I have been, Vasya, is miserable, and no fit company for anyone. But you have made your point. I need to get this marriage business out of the way first before I can resolve anything with Katya.''

Chapter Thirty-three

"Grigori, isn't that Prince Dimitri just coming in?" Tatiana asked as they waltzed across the dance floor.

Grigori Lysenko stiffened, turning Tatiana around so that he could face the entryway. "So it is," he replied tightly. "I suppose you will no longer be available, now that Alexandrov is back?"

"Whyever would you say that?" She smiled up at him innocently.

"You haven't accepted my proposal, my dear. It is the general consensus that you have only been waiting for Alexandrov to return."

"Is it?" Tatiana frowned, unaware of this.

"But it is too bad of him not to have sought you out until now, when everyone knows he has been in Moscow for a week," Grigori added deliberately.

Tatiana set her teeth. She didn't need to be reminded of that, which she *was* aware of. Her own sister had pointed out that Dimitri's obvious lack of eagerness to see her was rather insulting. Tatiana had been furious. And now Grigori said much the same thing.

"It has been wondered if he hasn't changed his mind about offering for you."

"So what if he has? Do you think I really care?"

But she did care. She cared too much. All she had wanted was to have Dimitri exclusively to herself for a while, and she could count on that only during their courtship. Once they were married, he was bound to lose interest, bound to go his own way, as every other husband did. There would be other women who would claim more of her husband's time than she would, for she would be the woman he had already won, safely stored away at home to visit or not as he chose, while the excitement of the chase would be elsewhere.

It didn't occur to her that she could make his life so interesting at home that he wouldn't think to wander. Tatiana was of the opinion that all men were alike, a general misconception shared by most women. She was also quite selfish when it came to her own needs, and had thought nothing of Dimitri's frustration while she had played him along.

Now she wasn't so sure her strategy had been at all wise. Was it too much to ask to have Dimitri's complete attention for a few months? Had she made him wait too long? If he was no longer interested, she would be made to look a fool, whereas before she had been the envy of every woman in Russia.

It couldn't be borne. To have people whispering behind her back, pitying her, or worse, thinking she had got no more than she deserved. Everyone knew Dimitri had asked her to marry him, she had made sure of that. Everyone knew she had made him wait for her answer. They wouldn't blame him for withdrawing his proposal. She had kept him dangling for months. It would be her fault, all her fault.

Of course she had Grigori here, and half a dozen other admirers to fall back on, all of whom professed to love her madly. But that wouldn't be any consolation if Dimitri no longer wanted her.

Tatiana waited, waited for Dimitri to notice her, waited for him to cut in on her dance with Grigori. He didn't come forward. He did notice her and nodded in her direction, but went right on conversing with Prince Dashkov and several other men who had greeted him when he came in.

As soon as the dance ended, Tatiana leaned closer to her partner to whisper, "Grigori, would you take me over to him?"

"You ask too much, Princess." Grigori could no longer conceal his disappointment. "I am not a graceful loser."

"Please, Grigori. I think you will be pleased with what I have to say to him."

He stared at her for a moment, noting her anxiety, her heightened color, and also the determined gleam in her eyes. She was so ethereal in her loveliness. He had set out to win her in order to steal her from Alexandrov, but had made the mistake of falling in love with her in the bargain. What could she tell his rival that would please him? Or was she just using him? He had to know one way or the other.

Nodding curtly, he took her elbow and led her over to the group of men who parted and drifted away when they saw who she was, all except Alexandrov's closest chum, Dashkov. He just stood there grinning, not trying in the least to conceal his interest in this reunion.

"Mitya, how good it is to see you again." Tatiana smiled up at Dimitri.

"Tatiana. Lovely as ever, I see," Dimitri replied, accepting her proffered hand and brushing a light kiss against the knuckles.

She waited, waited again for him to make some indication, to say something, anything, that would tell her he still wanted to marry her. He said nothing, not an apology for not seeking her out sooner, not that he had missed her, not that he was delighted to see her, nothing. He left her no choice.

"I believe you know Count Grigori, my fiancé."

"Fiancé?" Dimitri repeated, one brow raising the tiniest bit.

Tatiana moved closer to Grigori, who had the sense to put his arm about her waist, confirming this surprising news. "Yes, I do hope you aren't too disappointed, Mitya. But when you left so suddenly, sending me that short little missive saying you didn't know when you would be back, what was I to think? A lady can't be expected to wait forever."

Dimitri nearly choked on that one, but didn't want to insult the lady. "Then I must simply congratulate you both, I suppose."

He offered his hand to Grigori, the gentlemanly thing to do under the circumstances, but the man couldn't resist saying, "Too bad, Alexandrov. The best man won, eh?"

"If you think so, Lysenko."

That was all, Tatiana realized. No anger, no jealousy. She had done the right thing. He wouldn't have asked her to marry him again. She had lost him before he had even returned to Russia. But this way, she wasn't made to look a fool. She had prevented that, even if it was by committing herself to a man she didn't love. Then again, she could always get out of that commitment later.

"I'm so glad you understand, Mitya" were Tatiana's last words before dragging Grigori away.

"You know you could have prevented that, don't you?" Vasili said from beside Dimitri, his voice heavy with disgust.

"You think so?"

"Come off it, Mitya. She stood right there and waited for some sign of affection from you. You know damn well she hadn't accepted his proposal before that very moment. You saw the look of surprise on his face. It was as much news to him as it was to you."

"So it was."

Vasili grabbed Dimitri and turned him so that they were face to face. "I don't believe it. You're relieved, aren't you?"

"As a matter of fact, my shoulders do feel much lighter." Dimitri grinned.

"I don't believe this," Vasili repeated. "Six months ago, you tell me that she is the woman you are going to marry before the year is out, that you'll have your heir by next year. Nothing was going to stop you, you said. You made an all-out campaign to win her and became enraged because you couldn't pin her down to an answer. In fact you were in a constant rage over her vacillation. Am I right or am I wrong?"

"You needn't labor the point, Vasya."

"Then would you mind telling me why you're so delighted she has thrown you over? And don't you dare tell me it has anything to do with that wench you're pining over. Marriage has nothing to do with love. Tatiana was a most suitable match for you. You didn't have to love her. Sweet Christ, she is the most beautiful woman in Russia! She could have a pea for a brain and still be desirable. And her bloodline is impeccable. She was perfect for you. Your aunt thought so too.''

"Enough, Vasya. You're acting as if *you* have just lost her.''

"Well, damn it all, if you had to get yourself married, I wanted you to have the best. I thought that was your intention as well. Or is it no longer imperative that you marry and produce an heir? Have you heard something about Misha, that perhaps—''

"Don't tell me you're still hoping for the impossible. Misha's dead, Vasya. It's been too long to hope otherwise. And no, nothing has changed. I still need a wife. I just don't need this one. To tell you the truth, the reason I was dragging my feet about resuming this courtship was I couldn't see myself starting all over again, having to go through months of evasion and procrastination again just to get a simple answer, and being expected to dance attendance on the lady while she kept me waiting. I have better things to do than waste my time like that.''

"But—''

"Vasya! If you think she's such a prize, *you* marry her. Personally, I find I don't want to be tied down to a woman who doesn't know her own mind. I have discovered how refreshing forthrightness can be.''

"Your English wench again?'' Vasili sneered, only to gasp, "You're not thinking—''

"No, I haven't lost my reason, though I can't deny I wouldn't mind being tied down to her.''

Dimitri grinned, before sighing, "But there are plenty of other suitable women available, ones who won't hesitate with an answer, so I can get this business over with. Any suggestions?"

"None that you wouldn't find some fault with, I'm sure."

"Perhaps Natalia can recommend someone. She's an incorrigible matchmaker, so keeps abreast of such things."

"Wonderful. A mistress choosing a wife," Vasili said dryly.

"I thought it was rather a brilliant idea." Dimitri chuckled. "After all, Natalia knows my likes and dislikes very well, so she wouldn't suggest anyone that I won't get along with. She can make this chore much easier for me."

"You don't even know where she is at this time of year," Vasili pointed out.

"So I will just have to track her down. Really, Vasya, I would like this matter over, but I'm not in *that* much of a hurry. I do have other things to keep me occupied in the meantime."

When Dimitri returned home, there was another letter waiting for him, this one from his sister . . . and not at all welcome.

Mitya,
    You must come immediately to keep your promise. I have met the man I want to marry.
                                                    Anastasia

What promise? He had never promised he would be quick to approve her choice of husband. But if he didn't, no doubt the minx would

331

find a way to marry without his approval. What was her rush?

Damn, just when he thought he had arranged everything perfectly to give him more time with Katherine before he must send her home, or at least offer to send her home. The more he thought about it, the more he wished he could come up with an adequate reason to keep her here longer. He was fine at coming up with reasons to put off another courtship. Why couldn't he think of something that would prevent Katherine sailing out of his life?

Chapter Thirty-four

"*M*y lady?" Marusia stuck her head in at the door. "A messenger has finally come from the Prince. We are to leave immediately to join him in the city."

"Moscow?"

"No, St. Petersburg."

"Do come in, Marusia, and close the door. You're letting in a draft," Katherine said, pulling her shawl closer about her shoulders. "Now, why St. Petersburg? I thought Dimitri was still in Moscow?"

"No, not for some time. He has been to Austria on business and has only just returned."

Typical, Katherine thought. Why should she be told he had left the country? Why should she be told anything? He just stuck her in the country for months and forgot about her.

"Has the Tzar returned at last? Is that why we go to St. Petersburg?"

"I don't know, my lady. The messenger just said we were to hurry."

"Why? Blast it, Marusia, I'm not budging until I know what to expect," Katherine said irritably.

"I imagine that if the Tzar has returned and the Prince plans to send you home, it would have to be done soon, before the Neva freezes and closes the harbor."

"Oh." Katherine slumped back in her chair by the fire. "Yes, that would explain the hurry," she added quietly.

Where did that leave her? Arriving home with a stomach ballooned with pregnancy and no husband to show for it. Not if she had anything to say about it. She couldn't do that to her father. Disappear for half a year and then bring home an even worse scandal? No and no again.

She had planned to tell Dimitri about her condition when he returned to Novii Domik. She had planned to demand that he marry her. But it had been nearly three months since she had seen him. Summer had vanished quickly. Autumn was gone as well. She hadn't planned to spend the winter in Russia, but she was *not* going home without a husband. If Dimitri thought he was going to stick her on a ship and have done with her, he was crazy.

"Very well, Marusia, I can be ready to leave tomorrow," Katherine conceded. "But as for rushing, you can forget it. No more flying carriages for me, thank you, and you can tell your husband I said so."

"We won't be able to return as quickly as we got here anyway, my lady, now that the nights are longer."

"That can't be helped, but I was referring to the daytime traveling. No more than twenty or twenty-five miles a day. That should assure us a more comfortable ride."

"But that will take twice as long."

"I'm not going to argue about this, Marusia. That river can surely wait a few more days before it freezes over." She hoped not, but then that was the whole point of delaying her arrival in St. Petersburg, that and making sure her baby wasn't jostled about by the mad Russian drivers.

* * *

Dimitri had a fit when he got Vladimir's message. Katherine insisted on traveling at a snail's pace. They probably wouldn't arrive for nearly a week yet. Damn, this was not supposed to happen.

His idea of stranding her in Russia because of the weather had had its drawbacks from the beginning, mainly that he would have to forego seeing her for several months, until winter arrived. But he had known that once summer ended, she would be constantly demanding to know when she could leave. So he had had to avoid her, to avoid her questions, to get through autumn and hope winter would come early this year.

Sitting it out in St. Petersburg had been a long and depressing wait, especially through the cold and damp of autumn. And he hadn't even had a wedding to plan for his sister which could have kept him occupied. As soon as he arrived, she had informed him that *that* particular young man wouldn't do after all. Dimitri had nothing to do but attend to normal business, which he had grossly neglected of late, the proof being in the account books Katherine had sent on to him, revealing not four companies nearing ruin but five. There were a few friends to visit, but most avoided the city in autumn as well as summer, and were only just returning now for the winter season. Natalia had finally shown up last week and had promised to give his problem of who to choose for a bride immediate thought, even if he didn't care to think about it himself.

The most irritating, depressing, and outrageous thing about this time he had deliberately stayed away from Katherine was that he had remained celibate—he, who had never gone three nights without a woman when it wasn't necessary. And it wasn't necessary. There were women wherever he went who made it quite clear they were available. But they weren't Katherine, and he was still in the throes of his obsession with his little English rose. Until he got her out of his system, no one else would do.

The very minute the ice started forming on the Neva, Dimitri sent for her. After all this time, he was madly impatient to see her again. So what did she do? She deliberately delayed her arrival! So like her. Anything to defy and aggravate him. Vladimir was so right. She had returned wholeheartedly to her normal contrariness. But that was certainly preferable to the silent contempt she had treated him to when they last parted. Anything was preferable to that.

So Dimitri waited again, but took advantage of the time to perfect the excuses he planned to offer Katherine for not getting her out of Russia in time. She was going to be furious, but he hoped it wouldn't take her too long to accept the inevitable.

Katherine was thinking exactly the same thing as the carriages rolled along the one-hundred-foot-wide streets of St. Petersburg six days later. Dimitri was going to be furious with her, and rightly so, for missing her ship. The best way to get around his anger, she had found, was to attack on some different front. She had a store of grievances to choose from, all insignificant in light of her condition and what she now wanted, but all ready weapons she could make use of.

The vast openness of St. Petersburg was an amazing sight for someone used to the congestion of London. Katherine enjoyed her first real look at Russia's window on the western world, for she hadn't really seen anything on her whirlwind arrival here.

Everything was so monumental in this city of grandeur. The Winter Palace, a Russian baroque edifice of some four hundred rooms, was perhaps the most impressive sight, but there were so many palaces and other buildings of immense size, so many public squares. And the nearly three-mile-long Nevsky Prospeckt, the city's main street, with its many stores and restaurants. She had a glimpse too of the Peter and Paul Fortress across the river, the prison where Peter the Great had sent his own son to his death.

The open-air market held the most interest for Katherine, distracting her enough to forget for a few moments her final destination. Great piles of frozen animals were brought here on sleds from all over the country. All manner of things frozen were used to preserve freshness for the cows, sheep, hogs and fowls, butter, eggs, fish.

And the delightful oddities. Bearded merchants in robelike caftans of drab colors next to their gaily dressed wives in brocaded smocks and tall, brightly colored headdresses that formed a shawl nearly touching the ground. Befurred Bashkirs. Turbaned Tartars. Holy men in their ankle-length tunics, with long, flowing beards. Katherine was able to distinguish some of the many different nationalities that comprised the Russian people.

Here were housewives carting away their purchases on little sleds, while street musicians in long coats and fur hats entertained them with a *gusli* or a *dudka*, and street vendors hawking *ka-*

Johanna Lindsey

lachi, twisted loaves of bread made from the finest flour, tried to tempt them to part with a few more kopecks.

This was the Russia she had seen so little of, the people, the differences, the beauty of so many cultures that all blended together. Katherine made a mental note to have Dimitri bring her here when there would be time to see everything instead of just riding slowly past—but then she was reminded again of where she was going.

She could have recognized Dimitri's palace as they drew near, but it wasn't necessary to try. He was outside on the steps, which had been brushed clean of the falling snow, and at the carriage the moment it stopped, opening the door, reaching in to take her hand.

Katherine had been extremely nervous on this last leg of the journey as they neared the city. After all, she had been particularly unkind and unforgiving when they were last together, refusing to listen to anything Dimitri had to say, letting her hurt develop into one of the worst pouts she had ever indulged in. Now her nervousness brought her defenses to the surface. Not that she wasn't stunned by the sight of him, so dazzling in his splendid Russian uniform that her heart was racing at double time. But she no longer had just herself to think of. Her senses might be devastated, but her mind was quite ready for battle.

He drew her forward and lifted her to the ground. "Welcome to St. Petersburg."

"I've been here before, Dimitri."

"Yes, but for too short a time."

"You're right. Being whisked through a place doesn't give one time to appreciate it. My arrival, slow and leisurely as it was, was much more pleasant than my departure.''

"Am I to apologize for that too, when I have so much more to apologize for?''

"Oh? You don't mean to tell me *you* have done something to apologize for? Not you, surely.''

"Katya, please. If you want to cut me up into little pieces, can it at least wait until we go inside? If you haven't noticed, it's snowing.''

How could she not notice when her eyes were fascinated watching each little white flake melt on his face? And why wasn't he screaming at her for taking her sweet time in getting here? He seemed to be making an extreme effort to be pleasant, too pleasant, when she had been expecting the worst. Hadn't the river frozen over yet? Was she too early after all?

"Of course, Dimitri, lead the way. I am at your disposal, as usual.''

Dimitri flinched at her tone. Katherine's mood was worse than he had expected, and she hadn't even been told she was stranded yet. What then could he expect when she learned of her new situation?

He took her elbow and ushered her up the steps. The large double doors opened as they reached them and closed immediately after they had stepped inside, opening again a moment later to admit Vladimir and the others carrying in some of the baggage, closing again immediately. This opening and closing of doors, as if she didn't have hands of her own to do it, had annoyed Katherine before, but not since the cold arrived, for the quickness of the footmen certainly kept cold drafts down to a minimum.

Used to the quiet elegance of Novii Domik, Katherine was momentarily amazed by the opulence of Dimitri's city residence. Polished parquet floors, wide marble stairs thickly carpeted, paintings in gilt frames, a mammoth chandelier of crystal suspended in the center of this enormous room, and this was just the entry hall.

Katherine said nothing, but waited until Dimitri led her into another overlarge room, the drawing room, scattered with furniture in marble, rosewood, and mahogany, the chairs and sofas upholstered in silk and velvet in muted shades of rose and gold, blending well with the Persian rugs.

A large fire was crackling in the hearth, surprisingly warming the entire room. Katherine settled herself in a chair big enough only for one, a defensive move noted by Dimitri. Sitting, she untied the heavy cape Marusia had lent her and tossed it back over the chair. Nothing that Dimitri had bought her in England was fit for a Russian winter. That would quickly be rectified. Her winter wardrobe was ordered and nearly finished. A servant had already been instructed to take a dress to the dressmaker for adjustments to the measurements as soon as her luggage was unpacked.

"Would you care for a brandy to warm you?" Dimitri asked, taking the seat opposite her.

"Is that a Russian cure-all too?"

"Vodka is more appropriate here."

"I've tried your vodka, thank you, and didn't particularly care for it. I'll have tea, if you don't mind."

Dimitri waved a hand, and Katherine glanced up to see one of two footmen standing by the door turn and leave the room.

"How nice," she said tightly. "Now I get a chaperon. Rather late, don't you think."

Dimitri waved his hand again and the door closed, leaving them alone. "The servants are always so underfoot, after a while you don't notice them."

"Obviously I haven't been here long enough then." Katherine opened the door to what was on both their minds, but quickly, cowardly, closed it again. "So, Dimitri, how have you been?"

"I have missed you, Katya."

That was *not* the turn the conversation was supposed to take. "Am I supposed to believe that, after you disappear for three months?"

"I had business—"

"Yes, in Austria," she interrupted curtly. "I was told, but only after you sent for me. Before that, you could have been dead for all I knew." Oh, God, her resentment over his long neglect was showing. She hadn't meant him to know how much she had missed him too.

The tea arrived, obviously prepared ahead of time. Katherine was saved from making a further blunder and given time to get her thoughts back under control. She poured the tea herself, taking her time over the ritual. Brandy had been brought for Dimitri, but he didn't touch it.

When Katherine remained quiet, sipping her tea, Dimitri realized she was done taking him to task for the moment. But he wanted the worst over.

"You were right, you know," he said softly, drawing her eyes back to his. "I should have sent you word before I left for Austria. But as I said earlier, I have much to apologize for. I also should have left Austria sooner, but unfortunately the business took longer than I expected and . . . Katya, I'm sorry, but the harbor is now closed. There will be no sea travel from here until spring."

"Then I can't go home?"

He expected her to respond that the whole country couldn't be closed off, and indeed it wasn't. Dimitri had more lies ready to convince her that the open ports were not for her. Her simple question threw him, however.

"Why aren't you upset?" he demanded.

Katherine realized her mistake. "Of course I'm upset, but I was afraid this would happen when it started snowing on the way here. I have had days to accept the idea already."

Dimitri was so delighted that she was already resigned to staying that he nearly smiled, ruining the contrition he was supposed to be feeling. "Of course the southern ports are open, but a thousand miles away and a grueling trip this time of year even for a Russian used to the weather."

"Well, that is certainly out of the question for me," Katherine replied quickly. "I practically froze just coming here."

"I wasn't going to suggest it," Dimitri assured her. "There is also the western route overland through to France." He failed to mention all the open ports along the coasts between here and there, but then he was counting on her not thinking of that. "But again, it is not a trip recommended for winter."

"I should think not," Katherine replied. "I mean, if Napoleon's undefeated army could be defeated by a Russian winter, what chance would I have? So where does this leave me?"

"Since this is my fault—after all, I did promise I would have you on a ship back to England before the river froze—I can only hope you will accept my hospitality until the ice melts in the spring."

"In the same capacity?" she inquired. "As prisoner?"

"No, little one. You will be free to come and go as you like, to do as you like. You would be my guest, no more."

"Then I suppose I have no choice but to accept," she said, sighing. "But if I'm no longer to be watched and guarded as before, aren't you afraid I'll denounce you for a kidnapper to the first person I meet?"

Dimitri was flabbergasted. This was too easy. In all the hours he had spent going over his plan, imagining her reactions, this quick acceptance was not one of the responses he had anticipated. But he was not one to bemoan good fortune.

He grinned at her. "It will make a most romantic tale, don't you think?"

Katherine blushed. Dimitri, seeing the warm color spread across her cheeks, recalled other times she had looked just so, times when she had been more receptive to him. He was so moved that he forgot his resolve to go slowly with her this time and immediately closed the space between them, proving that Katherine's defensive tactic of sitting in a small chair so as to remain far apart from him was pointless. He lifted her, seated himself, and tugged her gently onto his lap.

"Dimitri!"

"Hush. You protest before you even know what my intentions are."

"Your intentions have never failed to be improper," she retorted.

"You see how well we suit, little one? You already know me so well."

He was teasing her, and she didn't know quite what to make of it. But there was nothing teasing about his hold on her. It was firm and intimate, one arm pressing her tightly to his chest, the other draped across her lap, the hand boldly caressing her hip. Warm feelings spread along her nerve endings. She hadn't felt so alive in months. He had always been able to do this to her, always stirred her in a purely physical way . . .

"I think you had best let me up, Dimitri."

"Why?"

"The servants might come in," she offered lamely.

"If that is your only reason, it won't do. No one will open that door on threat of death."

"Be serious."

"But I am, little heart, most serious. We will not be disturbed here, so come up with another reason, or better yet, don't. Just let me hold you for a while—Sweet Christ!" he gasped. "Don't wiggle around so much, Katya!"

"I'm sorry. Did I hurt you?"

He groaned, settling her in a less crucial spot. "It's nothing that you couldn't take care of if you only would."

"Dimitri!"

"Forgive me." He grinned as the bright spots appeared on her cheeks again. "That *was* rather crude of me, wasn't it? But then I never could think very clearly when you were near, and right now is no exception. Why do you look so surprised? You didn't really think that I would stop wanting you just because I have been away from you these three months?"

"As a matter of fact—"

Dimitri couldn't contain himself a moment longer. That she had let him hold her this long gave him such encouragement that he was on the brink of ripping her clothes off. He kissed her, so intensely, so thoroughly, that the result was inevitable, though he didn't know it yet. His hand came up to caress her breast, and he groaned, feeling the hard, tiny nub forming beneath the material.

Her moan was caught in his mouth, trapped with his. Oh, God, she had missed him, missed the way his kisses turned her to jelly, missed the way his hands set her afire, the way his eyes could thrill her with a look. And his body, his beautiful, hard, exciting body, and what it could do to her. She had missed that too. There was no point in denying it any more. She loved making love with him. And she wanted to now.

"Dim—Dimi—Dimitri! Let me catch my breath."

"No, not this time."

He continued kissing her fiercely, and Katherine felt warmed all over from the sheer joy of realizing that he was afraid, this powerful, strong man, afraid that she wanted to stop him. She cupped his face in her hands gently to hold him back, her eyes smiling into his.

"Take me to the sofa, Dimitri."

"The sofa?"

"This chair is a mite inconvenient at the moment, don't you think?"

As understanding dawned on him, such a look of wonder and pure delight crossed his face that Katherine nearly cried. She thought she was going to be dumped on the floor, he stood up so quickly, but no, she was held firmly in his arms and a moment later, laid carefully down on the velvet sofa, which was as comfortable as any bed.

On his knees beside her, already fighting the buttons on his jacket, Dimitri paused only once. "You're sure, Katya—no, no, don't answer that."

He kissed her again before she could, but Katherine gave him an answer anyway by wrapping her arms around his neck and returning his kiss with total abandon. She knew exactly what she was doing. Drugs weren't needed to stimulate her desire. Dimitri did that all on his own. He was the man she loved despite all misgivings, the father of her unborn child, the man she was going to marry. The particulars could be worked out later. There was plenty of time. Now was the time for their reunion.

Chapter Thirty-five

With snow whirling outside the windows and the fire burning in the great hearth, the large drawing room seemed more like a cozy nook, especially with the sofa facing the fire, close enough to receive its warmth directly. It was late afternoon, according to the clock on the mantel. Distantly there was the sound of a cat mewling, a door closing somewhere in the house, a carriage whisking by out front. Close up was only the sound of the fire crackling and Dimitri's heart beating.

Katherine was in no hurry to disturb the intimacy of the moment. She lay half on the edge of the sofa and half on Dimitri. There wasn't very much room, but she didn't feel as if she would fall. Far from it. Dimitri's arm around her back, holding her close to him, was warm and secure.

At the moment, he had taken her hand from where she had been idly tracing a path through the mat of golden hairs on his chest and was kissing each finger, an erotic experience, since he also chose to nibble and suck on them as well. Katherine simply watched him, her eyes half closed, fascinated by what his tongue and lips and teeth on her sensitive fingertips were making her feel.

''If you don't stop it, little one, I am going to have to make love to you again.'' Dimitri startled her with his husky voice.

''Me? What am I doing?''

"Looking at me with those sensuous eyes of yours. That is really all it takes, you know."

"Nonsense," Katherine scoffed, but she couldn't help smiling. "And what about what you're doing? If you don't stop it"—she gave the same warning—"I'm going to have to—"

"Promise?"

Katherine laughed. "You are incorrigible."

"What do you expect when I have denied myself this pleasure all these months?"

"Now why do I believe that?" Katherine said in some surprise.

"Because it's true . . . and because I have quite proved to you these last few hours how great was my need. Haven't I? Or do you need more proof?"

"Dimitri!" She giggled as he rolled her beneath him. But she found he wasn't teasing as he entered her, quickly and deeply. "Dimitri." His name was a sigh now, just before she reached up to capture his kiss.

When Katherine's breathing returned to normal awhile later, she was about to make a comment on Dimitri's insatiability, but he beat her to it.

"You are going to be the death of me, woman."

"There you go exaggerating again." She laughed. "Why, I can recall two separate occasions when your stamina was quite remarkable."

He glanced down at her in surprise. "And appreciated, perhaps?"

"At the time, certainly, which isn't to say I couldn't have done without such experiences. I much prefer my own spontaneity and freedom of choice."

He couldn't believe what he was hearing. *She* had brought up the druggings and without the slightest trace of anger. She had forgiven him. And she was admitting that this time was by her choice. She was admitting she had wanted him.

Sweet Christ, how many times he had fantasized about hearing just such a confession from her. "Do you know how happy you make me, Katya?"

It was Katherine's turn to be surprised, he sounded so sincere. "Do I?"

"For so long I have wanted to hold you like this, to kiss you." He did. "I have ached with the need to touch you, to love you. This is where you belong, Katya, here in my arms. And I am going to do everything in my power to persuade you to remain in Russia permanently. I will do anything to convince you that you belong with me."

"Is—is that a proposal?" Katherine whispered hesitantly, incredulously.

"I want you with me always."

"But is that a proposal, Dimitri?" she asked more firmly.

Damn! "Katya, you know I can't marry you. You know what it is I am asking."

Katherine tensed, feeling as if the air had been knocked out of her. Having her temper rear its ugly head while she was in this intimate position didn't help.

"Let me up, Dimitri."

"Katya, please—"

"Blast you, let me up!"

She pushed hard enough to slide out from under him and scrambled to a sitting position. Her hair hit him in the face when she swung around to face him again. Her nudity and vulnerability were her least concern.

"I want my children to have a father, Dimitri," she said without preamble.

"I will cherish your children."

"That's not the same thing, and you know it. I'm good enough to be your mistress but not your wife, is that it? Do you know how insulting that is?"

"Insulting? No, not when I couldn't care less about a wife, when she is only the means to get an heir and fulfill my obligations. You I care about. I want you to be part of my life."

She glared at him, but her anger was slipping away. God, he knew just what to say to tug on the strings of her heart. She loved him. What he wanted was what she wanted, to be a part of his life. His callousness about a wife was . . . well, she would pity his wife—if that wife wasn't herself. She wasn't giving up. She had five months until spring to become necessary to him, to make him more than care about her, to make him love her so much that he would defy the society that said a prince couldn't marry a commoner, as he thought her to be. Let him be surprised later to find she was his social equal.

She reached out a hand to touch his cheek, and he caught it, kissing the palm. "I'm sorry," she offered softly. "I forget you have your obligations. But when my first child comes along, Dimitri, I intend to be married. If not to you, then to someone else."

"No."

"No?"

"No!" he said with finality, drawing her tightly to him. "You aren't marrying, ever."

350

Katherine said nothing to such fierce possessiveness. She just smiled, glad now that she hadn't told him that she was already expecting her first child, though he would be able to figure that out for himself very shortly. And when he did, let him remember what she had said, that she *would* have a husband, one way or another. A nice bluff, but of course he wouldn't know that.

Chapter Thirty-six

The ball gown was exquisite, like nothing Katherine would ever have chosen for herself. A dark, lustrous turquoise satin, with a white lace insert in the bodice and hundreds of pearls running in streamers down the bell-like skirt. It was flamboyant, a deeply scooped neckline ending off the shoulders, the lace draping over little puffed sleeves. It wasn't Katherine. She felt like a fairy princess wearing it.

Her hair had been parted in the middle and pulled back sleekly to side ringlets in the current style, with pearl ornaments attached. Every accessory had been included: the long white gloves, the satin shoes in the same shimmering turquoise, even a white lace fan to dangle from her wrist. And Dimitri had come in earlier to hand her a jewelry case containing the pearl-and-diamond necklace, earrings, and ring she now wore, as well as another collection in sapphires and emeralds, so that she would have a choice, he said. Trifles, he called them. He said the same of her winter wardrobe. Several gowns had arrived today along with the ball gown, the rest to be delivered soon.

He was treating her like a mistress already, she realized, but the thought didn't disturb her. It wouldn't be long before none of the clothes he had ordered for her would fit, and then she would be amused to see how he would treat her. She turned around before the full-length mirror, taking particular notice of her waistline. It was still as slim as ever, and in that she was fortunate, being three and a half months along. Only her breasts had filled out a little, but again, nothing noticeable yet, nothing to alert Dimitri that he would soon have one of the children he claimed he would cherish.

Oh, you are in for a surprise, my prince. Soon you will know why my sentiments have changed so drastically.

Of course she wouldn't be so blasé about her situation if she were home in England. That would be a different story entirely. But as long as she was here, why couldn't she enjoy herself for the time being? After all, she no longer had to worry about getting pregnant.

Katherine smiled to herself, glancing about her new bedroom once more before she left it. Once again she had been given the room that would normally belong to the lady of the house, and it was pure luxury in every detail. But she had not slept here last night. Her smile widened. She doubted she would sleep here tonight either.

Oh, it had been heaven, sheer heaven, spending the whole night with Dimitri, sleeping in his arms and waking to find him still beside her. And to be greeted by one of his devastating smiles before she had even cleared the sleep from her eyes, and a kiss, which led to other things . . . She had no doubt that she had made the right choice. She was happy. That was all that mattered for now.

He was waiting for her at the bottom of the stairs, holding out a magnificent white ermine cloak lined in white satin, which he draped around her shoulders before handing her the matching muff.

"You're spoiling me, Dimitri."

"That is the idea, little one," he replied quite seriously, his smile warm, his eyes dark in appreciation of the picture she presented.

He was resplendent himself in another uniform, this jacket white, with heavy gold epaulets on his shoulders, gold-embroidered collar, and the blue cordon of the Order of St. Andrew draped across his chest, the medal worn for no reason other than to impress Katherine. Yet Dimitri was the one impressed, and he couldn't take his eyes off her as he helped her out to the carriage and as they drove the few blocks to the ball he was taking her to.

She was exquisite in her finery, and he was vividly reminded of the portrait Anastasia had painted of her, which now hung in his study and which caused him such unease every time he looked at it. No one was going to mistake this woman for a servant, actress, or whatever she was—not looking like this. Nor would he have formed his conception of her status if he had first seen her like this, which made him realize that it was no more than clothes and circumstances that had convinced him she was not who she claimed to be. And what if he was wrong? A tight knot of misgiving formed in his belly. No, he couldn't be. But perhaps it wasn't such a good idea to take Katherine to such a large gathering this first time she was appearing in public.

He had wanted to please her, to show her off, to do as Vasili had suggested and treat her like a lady instead of keeping her hidden behind closed doors. But suddenly he was afraid to share her. Suddenly he wanted to keep her locked away all for himself.

"I assume you will introduce me to people, Dimitri. So tell me, who am I to be?"

Had she read his thoughts? "Who you say you are—Katherine St. John."

"That isn't exactly how I would put it, but if that is how you intend to introduce me, then I suppose it wouldn't be polite to correct you."

She was teasing him. Why was she teasing him, and about her identity, of all things? "Katya, are you sure you wish to go to this affair?"

"And not show off this divine gown? Why, it's been ages since my last ball. Of course I want to go."

There she was again, dropping little tidbits about her life that couldn't possibly be true, yet she said such things spontaneously, without thought, without reason, just in the natural course of a conversation. The carriage stopped before he could make up his mind whether to disappoint her and take her home or hope for the best. Knowing Katherine's outspokenness, she was bound to step on a few toes tonight, and speculation about her was going to run rampant. What if she lost her temper here?

"You do know how . . . I mean, you wouldn't cause—"

"What are you worried about, Dimitri?" Katherine grinned at him, having an idea what was suddenly bothering him.

"It's nothing," he replied evasively, lifting her down to the ground. "Come along. I don't want you catching cold out here."

He ushered her inside a huge mansion, where they turned their furs over to a waiting footman,

then mounted an ornate double staircase to the
ballroom upstairs. If there had been a reception
line, it had been dispensed with by this hour.
Their hosts were the first to greet them, stopping
them just inside the wide doorway, and as Dimitri had warned, he introduced her as Katherine St. John.

Katherine was impressed when she got a moment to look around. The room was tremen-
dously large, an actual ballroom rather than
several rooms converted into one, and a half-
dozen chandeliers created a dazzling display of
light, reflecting on what surely must have been
several million rubles' worth of jewelry. Out of
some two hundred guests, half were dancing,
others gathered about the sides of the room,
talking in groups or pairs, or wandering to and
from the refreshment tables set up at the end of
the long room.

A liveried servant came by with a tray of
drinks, but Katherine declined for now. Dimitri
took one and drained it, setting the empty glass
back on the tray. Katherine couldn't help smiling.

"Nervous, Dimitri?"

"What could I possibly be nervous about?"

"Oh, I don't know. Maybe that I might embarrass you here among your friends. After all,
what could a simple peasant possibly know about
comporting herself in such august company?
Dress her up in a pretty gown, but she is still just
a peasant, right?"

He didn't know what to make of her mood.
She wasn't angry. Her expression was lit with
humor. But her teasing was drawing blood nonetheless.

"Mitya, why didn't you tell me you were coming tonight? I would have—oh, am I interrupting?"

"No, Vasya, nothing that can't wait until later," Dimitri replied with relief. "Katherine, may I present Prince Vasili Dashkov?"

"Katherine?" Vasili gave her a brief glance, then his eyes widened considerably as he turned back to Dimitri. "Not *the* Katherine! But I was expecting . . . I mean . . ." At Dimitri's scowl, he stopped altogether, flushing.

"You've rather put your foot in it, Prince Dashkov, haven't you?" Katherine said pointedly. "Let me guess. Since Dimitri has obviously told you about me, you were expecting someone with a little more brilliance to her plumage perhaps? But then we can't all be ravishing beauties, my lord, more's the pity. Your amazement at Dimitri's interest in me is no greater than my own, I assure you."

"Katya, please, you'll have my friend here cutting out his tongue in a minute to satisfy you. He doesn't realize you're teasing him."

"Nonsense, Dimitri. He knows I'm teasing. He's just embarrassed for dismissing me at first glance."

"A mistake I would never make again, dear lady, I swear to God!" Vasili assured her emphatically.

Katherine couldn't help herself. She laughed delightedly, enchanting Vasili into a new awareness of her. Dimitri was likewise affected by the merry sound. He loved to hear her laughter, even if it did fill him with a warmth that was wholly out of place here.

He drew her near to him, his arm fitting snugly around her waist, and whispered huskily into her ear, "Any more of that, little heart, and you will have me in the predicament I usually find myself in with you—wanting a bed with none near at hand."

She looked up at Dimitri, surprised to see that he was serious, and blushed so becomingly that he bent to kiss her, uncaring of where they were and who was watching. Vasili's dry wit stopped him.

"I'm going to save you from making a lovesick fool of yourself, Mitya, by dancing with your lady. That is, if you don't mind?"

"I do," Dimitri said tersely.

"But I don't," Katherine added, stepping out of Dimitri's embrace to smile warmly at Vasili. "However, I must warn you that certain people would tell you I can't possibly know *how* to dance, Prince Dashkov. Are you willing to risk your feet to learn the truth of the matter?"

"With utmost pleasure."

Vasili drew her onto the dance floor before Dimitri could protest again. He stared after them, unaware that he was scowling, making every effort not to go after Katherine and yank her back to his side, as was his first inclination. It was only Vasili, he had to remind himself. Vasili wouldn't make any advances toward her, knowing how Dimitri felt about her. But he didn't like seeing another man's hands on her, even his friend's.

Ten minutes later, when Vasili returned alone, Dimitri exploded. "What the devil do you mean you turned her over to Aleksandr?"

"Easy, Mitya," Vasili said, taken aback. "You saw that he cornered us before we left the floor. What could I do when she agreed to another dance?"

"You could have damn well warned him off."

"He's harmless, and—" Vasili had to jerk Dimitri around when he started for the dance floor. He pulled him to the side, away from curious ears. "Are you mad? You would cause a scene just because she's dancing and enjoying herself? For God's sake, Mitya, what's wrong with you?"

Dimitri stared hard at Vasili, then let his breath out slowly. "You're right. I—oh, hell, lovesick was putting it rather mildly." He smiled in apology.

"Haven't you won her yet?"

"Why? You think that will lessen this obsession? I assure you it won't."

"Then what you need, my friend, is a distraction. Natalia is here, if you haven't noticed."

"I'm not interested."

"No, you dolt, I know that," Vasili said impatiently. "But she has narrowed down the field and finally has a name for you, or so she confided to me earlier. Your perfect future bride. Remember you asked her—"

"Forget it," Dimitri interrupted curtly. "I have decided not to marry."

"What?"

"You heard me. If I can't marry Katherine, I'm not marrying at all."

"But you can't be serious!" Vasili protested. "What about the heir you need?"

"Without a wife, it will be perfectly acceptable for me to adopt any children that Katherine gives me."

"You *are* serious, aren't you?"

"Quiet," Dimitri hissed. "Aleksandr's bringing her back."

For the next hour, Dimitri didn't let Katherine out of his sight, and she loved every minute of it. He danced with her again and again, teasing her mercilessly about stepping on his feet, when she didn't, not once. He was in such good humor, and she was having the most marvelous time of her life—until he left her in Vasili's care while he went to fetch them a cooling drink, and Vasili was immediately commandeered by a brazen countess who wouldn't take no for an answer and dragged him off to the dance floor. If Vasili had still been there, he would have taken Katherine out of earshot of the group of gossips standing behind her, who didn't seem to care that she *was* within listening distance. She should have moved away on her own, but at first she was amused, hearing:

"But I told you, Anna, she's English, one of his relations from his mother's side. Why else would Mitya guard her so closely?"

"To make Tatiana jealous, of course. Didn't you see her come in with her fiancé?"

"Nonsense. If he were going to make Tatiana jealous, he would be staying close to Natalia. She's here too, you know. After all, Tatiana knows Natalia is his mistress and has no doubt heard that Mitya has been visiting her again since Tatiana chose Count Lysenko over him. Did you hear how furious he was about that?"

"Not furious, Anna. The poor boy has been so depressed that he came straight to St. Petersburg and has rarely left his house these last three months."

"Well, he certainly seems to have gotten over his depression tonight."

"Of course. You don't think he wants Tatiana to know how miserable he's been, do you? It was really too bad of her to end their courtship by introducing her fiancé to him. And after Mitya came to Moscow only to resume their courtship."

"Then you think he still loves her?"

"Don't you? Just look at her, over by the orchestra. Tell me what man wouldn't love her?"

Katherine couldn't help herself and looked at Tatiana as well. She quickly turned away, and walked away too until she could no longer overhear the comments. But the damage was done. The Princess Tatiana was the most beautiful woman Katherine had ever seen. Did Dimitri still love her? How could he not?

He's used you, Katherine, and lied to you about being out of the country. Why? Was he so upset over his princess that he simply forgot to send you home in time? Why does he bother with you? Why this grand pretense of wanting you when you can't hold a candle to such a gorgeous creature as Tatiana Ivanova?

"Lady Katherine?"

She almost didn't turn around, it had been so long since she had been addressed so. But she did, recognizing the voice. She groaned inwardly, and then saw, out of the corner of her eye, that Dimitri had returned. But he halted in midstride only a few feet away, his face gone deathly pale on hearing the man address her. She couldn't worry about him now. She had the Ambassador to deal with first, her father's dear friend—good Lord, how could she have forgotten the possibility that she might meet up with him here?

"What a surprise, Lord—"

"*You're* surprised! I couldn't believe my eyes when I saw you dancing past a while ago. I said no, that can't be little Katherine, but it is you, by God. What the devil are you doing in Russia?"

"It's a long story," she replied evasively, immediately changing the subject. "I don't suppose you have heard from my father recently?"

"Indeed I have, and I don't mind telling you—"

"Did he mention anything about my sister—a marriage perhaps?"

This time Katherine managed to distract him. "As a matter of fact, Lady Elisabeth has eloped with Lord Seymour. Remember him? Nice enough chap. But the Earl was furious, of course, until he found out that some information he had on young Seymour was all wrong."

"What!" Katherine fairly shrieked in her surprise. "You mean it was all for nothing?"

"What was? Don't know anything about that," he said gruffly. "Your father only mentioned your sister's marriage in telling of your own disappearance, because you both vanished the same day. George was expecting an elopement, you see, so for a while he simply thought you had gone with them as chaperon, you know. It wasn't until the newlyweds returned home some two weeks later that he learned otherwise. They think you're dead, my lady."

Katherine groaned miserably. "My—ah, my letter explaining everything must have been misplaced somehow. Oh, this is terrible!"

"Perhaps you should write your father another letter," Dimitri said tightly, coming forward at last.

Katherine turned to see that he had recovered completely from his shock. In fact, if his current expression was any indication, it looked as if his famous temper was about to explode. Now what the devil did *he* have to be angry about?

"Dimitri, my boy. That's right, you know Lady Katherine St. John, don't you? Saw you two dancing earlier."

"Yes, Lady Katherine and I have met, and if you will excuse us, Ambassador, I would like a few words with her."

He didn't give anyone time to protest, least of all Katherine, as he literally dragged her out of the ballroom, and out of the house. On the stairs outside she caught her breath, but as she was about to upbraid him, she was pushed into a carriage, and Dimitri got the first word in.

"So it is all true! Every bit of it true! Do you know what you have done, *Lady* Katherine? Do you have any idea of the repercussions, the—"

"What *I* have done?" she gasped incredulously. "What the devil are you raving about? I told you who I was. You are the blasted know-it-all who wouldn't believe me."

"You could have convinced me! You could have told me what an earl's daughter was doing on the street, dressed in rags, alone."

"But I did tell you. And those were not rags I was wearing, but my maid's uniform. I told you!"

Johanna Lindsey

"You did not!"

"Of course I did. I told you I was in disguise so that I could follow my sister, because I thought she was eloping. And you see! Elisabeth did elope. And I could have prevented that if not for you!"

"Katya, you told me none of that."

"I tell you I did. I must have." At his continued glower, she snapped uneasily, "Well, what's the difference? I gave you my name, my status. I even gave you a list of my accomplishments, some of which I have since proved nicely. But to this day, you were still too pigheaded to accept the obvious. Good Lord, Marusia was right. You Russians take top honors for inflexibility of first impressions."

"Are you finished?"

"Yes, I believe I am," she replied tightly.

"Very well. Tomorrow we will be married."

"No."

"No?" he shouted again. "Just yesterday you wanted to marry me. You were even furious when I explained that it wasn't possible."

"Exactly," she retorted, her eyes glittering suspiciously with moisture. "Yesterday I wasn't good enough for you. Today suddenly I am? Well, no thank you. I won't marry you under any circumstances."

He turned away, glaring murderously out the carriage window. Katherine did likewise. If she had known Dimitri better, even just a little bit, she would have realized that his anger wasn't so much for her as for himself. But she didn't know that. And she took his castigation to heart. How dare he blame her for this? How dare he offer to marry her *now*, when he didn't love her, when it

364

was only to satisfy some misplaced sense of atonement? She wouldn't have it. She didn't need his pity. She didn't need a husband to marry her because he felt he *had* to. She had more pride than that, by God.

Chapter Thirty-seven

*T*he smooth blanket of snow, unmarked as far as the eye could see, gave an impression of a land untouched by man, empty of life, desolate, or reborn, washed clean of all the ravages of civilization. It was so blindingly beautiful, this scene—bushes turned into little hills with heavy white coats, naked birches thrusting dark fingers into the overcast sky—so silent, so peaceful to a troubled mind.

Dimitri stopped on the road, or what he assumed to be the road, for the snowstorm that had blown through this area had obliterated it as well as any landmarks that might tell him he was still on the right track. He had been warned by his host, Count Berdyaev, not to venture out this soon, that he should stay over another night just to be certain the storm had really passed. Dimitri had refused.

What had begun as the simple need to get off by himself for a while so he could think without Katherine's distracting presence nearby, had turned into nearly a week's absence from St. Petersburg. He had been on his way back from an aimless three-day ride when the storm arrived so unexpectedly, forcing him to spend several more days as the Count's guest. Now he was in a welter of impatience to be home. Katherine had been left alone too long as it was, and his running off the very night of their argument didn't help.

There was another incentive for his leaving Berdyaev's as soon as the storm let up. Tatiana Ivanova had shown up there in a party of ten, which included Lysenko, needing shelter from the storm just as Dimitri had. The situation in the house was intolerable, made worse when he had the misfortune to witness Tatiana breaking her engagement to Lysenko. If looks could talk, the fellow obviously blamed Dimitri for this turn in events.

In the stillness, the report of a gun was deafening. Caught off guard, Dimitri tumbled backward as his horse reared. His landing was cushioned by a half-foot of snow, but the wind was knocked out of him for a moment. When he glanced up, it was to see his frightened horse disappearing into the distance, but that wasn't what concerned him.

He rolled over into a crouch and scanned the forest behind him. He saw Lysenko immediately, for the man made no effort to hide himself. Dimitri's heart stilled. He was in the process of raising his rifle for another shot—yet he hesitated. Their eyes met across the distance, and the anguish Dimitri saw gave him pause. Then Lysenko lowered the weapon and jerked his horse around, riding hellbent back the way he had come.

What devils could drive a man to do something like this? Dimitri was afraid he knew. Tatiana. Lysenko obviously thought Dimitri was responsible for his losing her.

"What's wrong with you, Mitya? The man just tried to kill you, and you're standing here making excuses for him." He sighed disgustedly.

"Sweet Christ, now I'm talking to myself like she does."

He turned to see if his horse had stopped down the road, but it hadn't. It was nowhere in sight, though easy enough to follow. Dimitri sighed again. Just what he needed: a long walk through the snowdrifts. But at least he was able. That idiot had had a clear shot, but hadn't taken it. He supposed Lysenko had a conscience after all.

Dimitri changed that opinion when he found his horse an hour later with a broken leg and had to dispatch it. He was left with the annoying suspicion that Count Lysenko had known exactly what he was doing. Unfamiliar with the area, hours away from Berdyaev's, with no houses or villages in sight, and the sky looking uglier by the minute, Dimitri had the feeling that he wasn't only stranded but also in danger of being caught in another storm without shelter. His chances in that case were none.

He set off immediately in the direction he had been heading. He had come too far from Berdyaev's to try and make it back there, so his only hope of finding shelter before nightfall was to continue on.

It wasn't long before the cold seeped through the leather of his gloves and boots, and his extremities grew numb. His fur-lined coat was some help, but not when the temperature dropped as evening approached. But at least the snow had held off. And just before the last of the daylight dimmed completely, he found a little shed, an indication that he had drifted onto someone's property. As much as he would have liked to find the owners of the property, with no house in sight he didn't dare. His strength was too depleted from trudging through the snow all day, and the light was gone.

It was apparently an abandoned shed, perhaps used for storage at one time, but empty now, too completely empty. There wasn't a single item that Dimitri could use to start a fire, unless he wanted to tear down boards from the walls and lose what little insulation from the cold they offered. It wasn't much. The cold still managed to slip in through cracks in the walls, though most of the wind was kept out. Still, it was better than nothing, and once morning came, he would be able to find the house that had to be near.

Dimitri curled up on the cold dirt floor in a corner, wrapped tightly in his coat, and went to sleep, wishing he had Katherine's warm body beside him—no, he had better reserve his wishes for simply being able to awake come morning, for that was one of the bitter results of being exposed to Russia's icy weather: falling asleep in it and never waking up.

Chapter Thirty-eight

Katherine came to him out of the fog, warm and sultry, and she wasn't angry with him anymore. She didn't blame him for the ruin he had made of her life. She loved him, only him. But the snow fell again and she began to fade. He couldn't see her through the snow, couldn't find her, no matter how far he ran, no matter how loudly he called for her. She was gone.

When Dimitri opened his eyes, the sight that greeted him made him so certain he was dead that he might have had a heart attack if he didn't as quickly see Anastasia and Nikolai too. His eyes came back to the apparition.

"Misha?"

"You see, Nastya." Mikhail chuckled. "I told you there was no need to wait until he recovered more."

"You didn't know that for certain," Anastasia protested. "He could have had a relapse. I know I would have, confronted with a ghost."

"Ghost, am I? I'll have you know—"

"Sweet Christ!" Dimitri exhaled sharply. "Is it really you, Misha?"

"In the flesh."

"How?"

"How?" Mikhail grinned. "Well, I could tell you how my cowardly comrades left me with three saber wounds to let my blood nourish the earth. Or I could tell you how the Armenians dragged me back to their camp to make sport of me before I died.'' He paused here for effect, his blue eyes crinkling. ''Or I could tell you how the chief's daughter took one look at this notorious Alexandrov face of mine and badgered her father into giving me to her.''

''So which will you tell me?''

''Don't let him rib you, Mitya,'' Nikolai put in. ''All of it's true, if we're to believe him, and I suppose we must, since he brought that same Armenian princess home with him.''

''Is it too much to hope that you married her, Misha?'' Dimitri ventured.

''Too much to hope?''

Nikolai laughed. ''He *would* find that of particular interest, since Aunt Sonya hasn't let up on him ever since you were reported dead, Misha. There was nothing for it but for poor Mitya to marry and get himself an heir before there were no Alexandrovs left.''

Dimitri scowled at this brother. ''Trust you to find humor in that. I assure you I didn't.''

''Well, you can relax now,'' Mikhail informed Dimitri proudly. ''I not only married her, but she's already given me a son, the reason why I was so long in returning. We had to wait until the boy was born before she could travel.''

Dimitri did relax, but in simple weakness. ''Since your ghostly appearance has been explained, would someone mind telling me what you three are doing surrounding my bed and how the devil I got here? Or did I only dream of being stranded—''

''It was no dream, Mitya.'' Anastasia sat down on the bed to offer him some water. ''You have been so sick that for a while we weren't sure you would recover.''

"You're ribbing me again?" But not one of the three faces was smiling. "For how long?"

"Three weeks."

"Not possible!" Dimitri exploded.

He tried to get up, but was assailed with dizziness and sank back onto the pillow, closing his eyes. Three weeks of his life gone, not remembered? The emotions that possibility stirred overwhelmed him.

"Mitya, please, you mustn't get upset," Anastasia insisted with a worried frown. "The doctor said that once you regained full consciousness, you would have to remain undisturbed and progress slowly."

"You've had a rough time of it," Nikolai added. "You were burning with fever most of the time, though there were several occasions when you awoke and seemed perfectly normal, making us think it was over, but the fever came back again."

"Yes, I've told you three times myself how you got here and what was wrong with you," Anastasia said. "You were awake enough to make demands, give orders, and be a nuisance. Don't you remember?"

"No." Dimitri sighed. "How did I get here, if you wouldn't mind telling it again?"

"Some soldiers found you while out searching for a runaway serf," Anastasia explained. "They thought they had him when they saw your tracks leading to that shelter you were in. How long you had been there is anyone's guess, for you were already delirious and couldn't say. You couldn't even tell them who you were."

"They took you back to their barracks, and fortunately someone recognized you and sent word to us," Nikolai continued. "When Vladimir got there, you were just lucid enough to demand he take you home."

"Which was a mistake," Anastasia added. "You were caught in a storm that had apparently already struck in that area several days earlier, and it took days to get you here. By then you were so much worse, we feared for your life."

"Women," Mikhail grunted. "They don't realize a man isn't going to let a little thing like a cold end his days, not when there are so much more exciting ways—"

"Spare me your gory adventures for now, Misha," Dimitri said tiredly. "When did you get here, anyway?"

"About a week ago. Here I was expecting a glorious homecoming, and everyone is sitting around here with long faces, worrying about you."

"Everyone?" His spirits rose. "Katherine too? Was she worried?"

"Katherine? Who is Katherine?"

Nikolai chuckled. "He means the little wench—"

"Lady Katherine St. John." Dimitri glared at him.

"Really? You mean she was telling the truth, even about Sonya?"

"Yes, and that reminds me: What happened when you found her?"

The question, put in that tone, had the power to make Nikolai step back, even though he had nothing to fear from Dimitri at the moment, as weak as he was. "Nothing. I assure you I never even got near her."

"Will someone tell me who this Katherine is?" Mikhail asked again, and again got no answer.

"Where is she?" Dimitri demanded, first of Nikolai, whose blank look made him turn to his sister next. "Nastya? She *is* here, isn't she?"

"Actually—"

She got no farther, her uneasy look warning him that she was withholding bad news. "Vladimir!" He turned to Nikolai, frantic now. "Where is he? Get him for me." And again: "Vladimir!"

Anastasia pushed him down on the bed as Nikolai rushed out of the room. "You can't do this, Mitya! You're going to have a relapse—"

"Do you know where she is?"

"No, I don't, but I'm sure your man does, so if you will just calm down and wait until he gets here—"

"My lord?" Vladimir appeared, hurrying toward the bed, already apprised of the reason for Dimitri's distress. "She went to the British Embassy, my lord."

"When?"

"The day after you left. She is still there."

"You're sure?"

"I posted a man to keep watch, my lord. He has yet to see her leave."

The tension drained out of him, leaving Dimitri so weak that he could barely keep his eyes open. As long as he knew where she was . . .

"Now will someone tell me who this Katherine is?" Mikhail demanded.

"She's going to be your sister-in-law, Misha, just as soon as I am on my feet again. Good to have you back, by the way," Dimitri added, just before sleep claimed him.

"I had the impression he wasn't too keen on marrying." Mikhail glanced at his siblings questioningly.

Nikolai and Anastasia were both smiling as they moved quietly out of the room, but it was Nikolai who suggested, "I guess someone changed his mind."

Chapter Thirty-nine

"Lady Katherine, are ye receivin' this mornin'?"

Katherine glanced up from the tally books with a sigh. "Who is it this time, Fiona?" When would her neighbors stop being so blasted nosy?

"She said she was the Duchess of Albemarle."

Katherine simply stared at the girl while the color slowly receded from her face. Dimitri's grandmother? Here? Did that mean . . . No, if Dimitri were in England, he would have come himself. Wouldn't he?

"My lady?"

Katherine focussed on the maid again. "Yes, I'll see her. Show her into the— Wait, she is alone, isn't she?" At Fiona's nod, she said, "Very well. On second thought, show the lady in here. My office is more informal. And bring some refreshments too, Fiona."

Katherine didn't move from behind her desk. She sat there, worrying the tip of her quill between her teeth, and growing more and more nervous by the second. Why was Dimitri's grandmother coming to see her? There was no way she could know anything. No one knew the truth, not even her father.

The Earl had been so understanding in the one letter she had received from him before she left Russia, but that was in answer to the letter she had sent him, which was composed of elaborate lies meant to calm his concern and assure him she was fine, just not ready to come home yet.

She couldn't tell him the truth, for a father's duty was to avenge his daughter's honor, and she wanted none of that.

The tale about being kidnapped by mistake and ending up in Russia was as close as she came to the actual truth. She made use of the excuse she had given the Ambassador by claiming that she *had* written immediately upon reaching Russia, but the letter must have become lost and she had only just learned that no one knew what had happened to her. And then in her indomitable way she informed him that as long as she had been forced on this trip, she was going to take advantage of it and travel a while more. He wasn't too happy about that, but he wished her well and had included a tidy sum to see to her expenses.

Yes, he had understood, until she had arrived home with Alek three weeks ago. Alek he didn't understand at all, nor why she refused to make excuses for him, saying simply that she had fallen in love and children were the usual result of such happenings. The biggest bone of contention between them was that she wouldn't name the father, said only that she had met him while traveling through Russia, and no, she simply didn't want to marry him. What were they to tell people? Absolutely nothing.

Katherine wasn't the first to bring home a baby from her travels, but she wasn't about to claim it was an orphan she had found. That excuse had been given so often by other highborn ladies that it simply would not have been believed. Since Katherine St. John wasn't considered the type to indulge in an affair, she trusted that the rumors and speculation about her wouldn't be too damaging. She was proved right. The general opinion, though she wasn't aware that dear Lucy had started the rumor, was that she was a widow now, so devastated by her husband's death that she refused to talk about him.

This amused her. It allowed her to ignore all inquiries about her son's father without the least bit of embarrassment. Not that she was ashamed. She was, in fact, so proud of her son that she delighted in showing him to anyone and everyone who asked to see him. But anyone and everyone did not include Dimitri's grandmother.

Alek unfortunately had that notorious Alexandrov face, as well as his father's coloring. Not that Katherine wasn't delighted with the way he looked, but he was too obviously Dimitri's son. The Duchess would have only to look at him to see the resemblance. In some future meeting between Dimitri and his grandmother, Katherine's remarkably Alexandrov-looking son would be mentioned, and then Dimitri would know that she had left him, knowing she carried his child; that she had refused to marry him, knowing she might be denying him his heir. He wouldn't take too kindly to that. He might even try to wrest Alek from her. She could not take any chances.

At the sound of a throat being slightly cleared, Katherine jumped to her feet nervously. "Your ladyship, please come in." She indicated the chair opposite her desk. "I understand you are acquainted with my father. He's in London, if you came to see—"

"I'm here to see you, my dear, and please let us dispense with formalities. I would like it if **you** would call me Lenore."

Lenore Cudworth wasn't anything like Katherine might have expected, though what she had really expected she didn't know, except that some ladies of the Duchess's stature and age clung to the old ways, even to wearing outdated clothes, some even still powdering their hair. Lenore was dressed in a stylish traveling suit, vivid in color, her only concession to her age being her hair, which was done up neatly in an older style that quite suited her. It was silver-gray, though her face bore few wrinkles. She was still a very handsome woman, and Katherine was unnerved to see from where Dimitri got his dark brown eyes, for hers were exactly the same, if a little warmer, with infinitely more laugh lines surrounding them.

"You mustn't be nervous."

"Oh, I'm not," Katherine quickly assured her. Blast, she was off to a bad start. "And please call me Kate. My family does."

"And what does Dimitri call you?"

Katherine's eyes flared, giving her away before she could ask, "Dimitri who?" "Why have you come here?" she asked instead, bluntly, fearfully now.

"To meet you. To satisfy a curiosity. I have only just learned that you have returned to England, or I probably would have come sooner."

"I wouldn't have thought you the type to sniff about for a scandal, your ladyship."

Lenore laughed despite herself. "Oh, my dear Kate, how delightfully refreshing to meet someone who doesn't mince words. But no, I assure you I'm not a scandalmonger. You see, I received a rather long letter last year from Dimitri's aunt on his father's side—we will agree you

379

know my grandson?'' When Katherine didn't so
much as blink, Lenore smiled, undeterred.
''Well, at any rate, Sonya, Dimitri's aunt, does
so love to complain to me about his many amo-
rous peccadilloes. For years she has written, undoubtedly trying to disillusion me into believing
the poor boy is a lost cause, which I have never
believed for a moment. I would have discouraged her letters if they weren't so amusing. But
this particular letter wasn't amusing at all. She
told me that Dimitri was now bringing his . . .
women, shall we say? That he was bringing his
women back from England now and that he had
gone so far as to install one in his own home.''

Katherine had gone quite pale. ''Did she happen to mention her name?''

''I'm afraid she did.''

''I see.'' Katherine sighed. ''She never understood why I was there, you know. It certainly
wasn't what she thought. And I doubt Dimitri
ever did own up—oh, this is beside the point.
You—you didn't bring this information to my
father, did you?''

''Whyever would I do that?''

''To relieve his mind. For a while after I disappeared, he thought I was dead.''

''You mean . . . I'm sorry, dear, I had no idea.
I was aware of your absence from England but
not that George had no clue to where you were.
It was assumed you had gone on a tour of Europe. But wasn't that rather thoughtless on your
part? I realize Dimitri is quite the ladies' man, but
to just run off with him—''

''I beg your pardon,'' Katherine interrupted
sharply, ''but I didn't happen to have a choice in
the matter.''

The Duchess actually blushed. "Then I truly am sorry, my dear. And it appears I have come here under the wrong impression. I thought— rather I assumed—that you had had an affair with my grandson and that the son you came home with might be his. You see, I have heard about the child, and I had hoped, actually I still do . . . What I mean to say—"

"Alek is not Dimitri's son!"

Lenore sat back, surprised by the emphatic denial. "I didn't mean to imply . . . Well, yes, I suppose I did. Forgive me. But considering most women find my grandson rather irresistible, it was natural to assume . . . Oh, dash it all, Kate, I would like to see the boy."

"No. I mean, he's sleeping and—"

"I don't mind waiting."

"But he hasn't been feeling well. I really don't think it would be a good idea to disturb him."

"Why are you putting me off? This is my great-grandson we are talking about."

"He isn't," Katherine insisted angrily, not at all liking this corner she was backing into, but quite unable to think clearly in her anxiety. "I told you Dimitri isn't his father. Why, he left me at Novii Domik for months. Do you know how many men there are at Novii Domik? Hundreds. Need I say more?"

Lenore smiled. "All you needed to say, my dear, was that you had never been intimate with Dimitri, but you didn't say that, did you? No, and you won't convince me you are the type to go flitting from one man to another either, so don't bother trying. The boy doesn't know, does he? Is that what you're afraid of?"

"Your ladyship, I'm going to have to ask you to leave," Katherine replied stonily.

"Very well, my dear, you win for now." Lenore's voice was still pleasant. She didn't succumb to emotion the way the young so often did. Yet she was quite firm in her added prediction. "But I'll see your Alek eventually. I won't be denied my first great-grandchild, even if I have to bring his father here to settle the matter."

"I wouldn't advise that," Katherine replied, exasperation taking over. "Do you realize how furious he would be if you brought him here for nothing. And it would be for nothing."

"Somehow I doubt that."

Chapter Forty

"Well?" Dimitri demanded.

Vladimir entered the dining room with considerable reluctance. "She wouldn't accept the flowers, my lord, or your letter. Both were returned to me, the letter unopened."

Dimitri slammed his fist down, spilling his wine and knocking over the candelabrum in the center of the table. A footman rushed forward to grab it before a fire started. Dimitri didn't even notice.

"Why won't she see me? What have I done that was so terrible? I asked her to marry me, didn't I?"

Vladimir said not a word. He knew the questions weren't being asked of him. He had heard them asked a hundred times before. He had no answers anyway. He didn't know what the Prince had done, unless it was the same thing he had done, and Sweet Mary, how often he had asked himself how he could have been so stupid, so blind, so incredibly perverse in his judgment. How Marusia had rubbed it in and gloated, because she had known all along, while he had doggedly stuck to his misconceptions about Lady Katherine.

"Perhaps if you—"

Vladimir got no further, the footman at the door interrupting with the announcement: "The Dowager Duchess—"

That fellow got no further either, as Dimitri's grandmother pushed him aside and entered the room. That she was quite out of sorts was obvious, though Dimitri, rising swiftly, didn't notice in his surprise.

"*Babushka!*"

"Don't you '*Babushka*' me, you thoughtless, irresponsible man," Lenore said tartly, slapping away the arms that tried to embrace her. "Do you realize what an embarrassment it was for me to be asked what you were doing back in London so soon when you had been here only a few months ago, and I didn't know you were here now or then? What do you mean by coming to England and not paying me a visit, not even telling me you are here, not once, but twice?"

Dimitri had the grace to flush. "I owe you an apology."

"You owe me more than that," she retorted. "You owe me an explanation."

"Certainly, but sit down. Take a glass of wine with me."

"I'll sit, but no wine."

And she did, and immediately began drumming her fingers on the table, waiting, angry, impatient. Dimitri waved the servants away and returned to his seat, feeling quite put on the spot. What could he tell her? Certainly not the truth.

"I was coming to see you, *Babushka*," he began.

"Three weeks late?"

So she knew he had been here that long. He was just wondering what else she knew when she added, "I wrote you no more than a month ago, and I know very well you couldn't have received my letter yet, so that isn't why you're here. Now, out with it. What are you doing here, and why must I be the last to know about it?''

"You wrote me? Was it anything important?''

"You're not putting me off, Dimitri. I demand to know what you're up to. Why, you have my own son keeping secrets from me. He must know you are here, or you wouldn't be using the townhouse.''

Dimitri sighed. "You mustn't blame Uncle Thomas. I asked him to say nothing for the present, because I knew you would insist I join you in the country for a visit. But what I am doing is just too important . . . I have to stay in London, *Babushka*. I have to make sure she doesn't disappear again.''

"Who?''

"The lady I want to marry.''

Lenore's brow shot up. "Oh? As I recall, you said you would be married by the end of last year. When that didn't come about and when I received your news about your half-brother's return from the dead, I assumed you were no longer in any great hurry to tie yourself to any one woman.''

"That was before I met Katherine.''

"Not Katherine St. John!'' Lenore gasped.

"How did you know? No, don't tell me. I suppose I have made a complete fool of myself. With as many times as I have been turned away from her door, the whole town must know. And chasing her down Piccadilly was a piece of lunacy, especially when she managed to elude me anyway.''

"Very well, I take it you have followed Lady Katherine here, and that's why you're here now. But what about earlier this year?"

"I was looking for Katherine then too. I thought she had returned here, but I was mistaken. The most I could find out then was that she was supposedly traveling on the Continent, where, no one knew exactly."

"You could have at least come to see me for a day or two, as long as you were here," Lenore complained.

"I'm sorry, *Babushka*, but I wasn't very fit company at the time. I was in fact quite out of sorts when I found Katherine wasn't here, as I thought she would be, and I had no idea where to look for her next."

"Desperate, were you?" Lenore smiled now for the first time. "If I didn't know better, I might think you were in love."

Dimitri frowned. "Is that such an impossibility?"

"No, of course not. It's just that I've met Lady Katherine and she's a formidable lady, for all that she comes in such a small package. You won't find her jumping to do your bidding, my boy. You won't find her agreeing with your every opinion either. She's been too long running things her own way and won't be easily adaptable to a subservient role, if indeed she is adaptable, which I highly doubt. She's a lady who knows her own mind, not exactly the type I would have expected a man of your temperament to want for a wife."

"You're not telling me anything I don't already know."

"I'm not, eh?" Lenore chuckled.

She could tell him a thing or two, but she decided not to. Why give the boy ammunition he didn't need? He had had things too easy all his life. It wouldn't hurt him to have to put forth a little effort to get what he wanted this time, and if little Kate gave him a hard time of it, so much the better. Of course if he failed to win the lady in the end, that would be a different story. Lenore was *not* going to be denied her first great-grandson.

"You say Katherine won't see you?" Lenore asked now. "Why is that?"

"I wish I knew. When we were last together, we argued, but then we often argued, so that was nothing out of the ordinary. She had just become my—well, that is neither here nor there. The point is, she ran away, disappearing completely, and now that I've finally found her again, she refuses to speak to me. I have much to make amends for, certainly, but she won't even give me the chance. It's as if she's afraid to see me."

"Whether she is or isn't is beside the point. If she's the one you want, my boy, you'll just have to find a way, won't you? And I think I'll remain in London awhile to keep tabs on your progress. You will of course remember to invite me to the wedding, if there is to be one."

Dimitri remained where he was after his grandmother left him, her humor much improved, his much worse. If only he didn't have the feeling that she knew something he didn't.

Chapter Forty-one

"*K*it? Are you up?" Elisabeth knocked on the door, then was startled to have it open so quickly. "Oh, I see you are."

"Of course I am. The question is, what are you doing up this early?"

"I thought we might go out together this morning, riding, or shopping, you know, as we used to."

Katherine headed down the hallway, her sister beside her. "That would be nice, but I really have too much—"

"Oh, come on, Kit. I only have these two days to visit while William is away on business. As it is, he thought it was silly of me to spend the weekend here, when our townhouse is just a few blocks away."

"So it is," Katherine agreed, smiling.

"Nonsense. I just wanted it to be like old times once more, before you . . . that is . . ."

"Before I what?"

"Oh, you know."

"Beth," Katherine said warningly.

"Oh, before you get married too, or something like that, and—"

"I'm not getting married, Beth, and what the devil made you think I was?"

"Now don't get all huffy. What was I supposed to think? It's no secret, you know, what's been going on here. Your servants are absolutely thrilled about it, it's so romantic, and they of

388

course told my maid everything. You have the most handsome man in the world beating on your door twice a day, sending you gifts and flowers and letters—''

''Who said he's handsome?''

Elisabeth laughed. ''Honestly, Kit, why are you so defensive? I have seen him of course. A Russian prince is naturally a curiosity.'' They had reached the dining room, where the Earl was having breakfast, but Elisabeth didn't end the conversation. ''He was pointed out to me several weeks ago, and I just couldn't believe that you actually know him. And then I heard how persistent he has been in trying to see you. It's so exciting! How did you meet him? Please, Kit, you must tell me everything.''

Katherine sat down, ignoring the look her father gave her. He too was waiting to hear her answer, but she was firm in keeping the truth to herself.

''There is nothing to tell,'' she said nonchalantly. ''I simply met him in Russia.''

''Nothing to tell!'' George St. John snorted. ''He's the one, isn't he?''

''No, he is not,'' Katherine repeated, having answered that same question a half-dozen times in the last three weeks.

''You mean Alek's father?'' Elisabeth gasped.

''Oh, do be quiet, Beth. It makes no difference who he is. I don't want anything to do with him.''

''But why?''

Katherine stood up, giving first her sister and then her father a look that said she had had quite enough. ''I'm taking Alek to the park. When I get back, I don't want to hear that man mentioned to me again. I am quite old enough to make my own decisions, and I have decided I never want to see him again. That's all there is to it.''

When she left, Elisabeth glanced at her father, whose look said he was suffering from his own bout of exasperation. ''What do you suppose he did to make her so angry with him?''

''Angry? Do you think that's all it is?''

''Of course. Why else would she not even want to talk about him? Have *you* talked to him?''

''I'm never here when he comes around,'' George admitted. ''But I suppose I should pay him a visit. If he is Alek's father—''

''Oh, no, you wouldn't force them to marry, would you? She'd never forgive you for that, unless of course she makes up with him. But how can she do that if she won't see him?''

Katherine strolled along the edge of the trees, keeping in the shade. She also kept her eye on Alek cavorting on his blanket in the sun, even though his nurse, Alice, sat beside him. It was the middle of September, but after spending an entire winter in Russia, England's sun even at this time of year made Katherine uncomfortable if she stayed out in it too long. But Alek loved it and loved watching the autumn leaves blowing past him.

At four and a half months, he was becoming much more active and was much more of a handful. His present joy, now that he had discovered it, was rocking back and forth on his hands and knees. The next stage, according to his nurse, would be crawling. Katherine wished she knew more about babies. But she was learning, and delighting in each new phase of Alek's learning process too.

"Katya?"

Katherine spun around, instantly infuriated, eyes flashing, but after one look at Dimitri, the heated words stuck in her throat. It was as well. She didn't want him to know he could still ignite her emotions. He was staring at her, not a glance at Alek. She had nothing to fear, yet.

She was proud a moment later when her voice came out so calm. "Surely this is no coincidence."

"I don't leave such things to chance."

"No, you wouldn't. Very well, Dimitri, since it appears you won't give up and go home, do tell me what is so important that you must—"

"I love you."

Oh, God, fantasies again, vividly clear, in broad daylight. She had to sit down, quickly, but with no benches near (she was *not* going to collapse at his feet), the nearest tree trunk had to do, and she walked toward it unsteadily, gratefully leaning against it. Maybe he would just fade away, as fantasies were wont to do.

"Did you hear me, Katya?"

"You don't."

"Don't what?"

"Love me."

"More doubt." His voice turned sharp, but she wouldn't look up at him. "First my grandmother, now you. Sweet Christ, why is it so impossible to believe that I could—"

"You've seen your grandmother? . . . Oh, what a silly question. Of course you must have. Did she tell you she came to see me recently?"

Dimitri stared hard at Katherine. She was avoiding meeting his eyes, looking from one side of him to the other, anywhere but at him. What was wrong with her? He hadn't seen her for nearly a year. A year! He had to fight the urge to crush her in his arms. And she, she changed the subject when he tried to tell her he loved her. She didn't care. She honestly didn't care. It was like a knife gutting his insides, but instead of blood, rage spilled out.

"Very well, Katya, we will talk about my grandmother," he said icily. "Yes, she mentioned that she had met you. She also thinks we won't suit, as you apparently do."

"Well, we wouldn't."

"You know perfectly well we would suit!"

"You don't have to shout!" She glared up at him. "Did I shout at you? No, I did not, even though *I* have every reason to. You used me, Alexandrov. You used me to make your Tatiana jealous. You never went on that Austrian trip. You were in St. Petersburg all along, moping about with a broken heart because your princess chose another man instead of you."

"Where did you hear such nonsense?" he demanded furiously. "It's true I didn't go to Austria. That was simply the excuse I needed for not sending for you in time to take ship for England. But I lied because I couldn't bear for you to leave me. Sweet Christ!" he exploded. "Do you think I would have stayed away from you at Novii Domik all those months for any other reason? I needed that excuse to keep you from sailing out of my life. What is wrong with that?"

"Nothing, if that were the truth, but I don't believe a word of it," Katherine replied doggedly. "You just wanted me around to make Tatiana jealous. She's the one you love, and yet you would have married me anyway. Well, I don't need such grand gestures from anyone, thank you. And for your information, you would have married me for nothing. I returned home without the slightest scandal attached to my name, so I didn't need you to sacrifice yourself on my account. If anyone talks about me, it's to sympathize. You see, it got around somehow that I eloped at the same time as my sister did, which threw our father off the track, so to speak. But where she has a husband to show for it, I unfortunately lost mine."

"A widow!" Dimitri snorted. "You are believed to be a widow!"

"I haven't encouraged that assumption, but that is beside the point. The point is my reputation is still intact. You've wasted your time tracking me down, Dimitri, if you thought marriage would clear your conscience."

"Is that really what you think? That I would sail all the way to England just for a troubled conscience, not once but twice?"

"Twice?"

"Yes, twice. When I couldn't find you anywhere in St. Petersburg, I had to assume your friend the Ambassador had gotten you out of the country. I was ready to thrash the man for his insistence that he hadn't even seen you again after the night of the ball."

"Oh, you didn't!" she gasped.

"No, I spent my anger elsewhere, on a fellow equally deserving."

Katherine shivered at the glint of satisfaction that appeared in his eyes for a brief moment, pitying the man responsible for it. "Is the fellow still living?" she asked in a small voice.

Dimitri laughed wryly. "Yes, more's the pity. And I think he might even marry Tatiana after all. You see, she thought we were fighting over her, the foolish woman. And when I didn't come to claim her as the victor, she went to console the loser. But he's welcome to her, Katya, as far as I am concerned. I don't love her. I never loved her. I was in fact immensely relieved when she chose Lysenko over me. He didn't believe that, of course, being in love with her himself. The idiot blamed me when she broke off with him, and thought if he got rid of me, he could win her back."

Katherine turned pale suddenly. "What do you mean, get rid of you?"

"Concern, little one? You will understand if I find that difficult to—"

"Dimitri! What did he do?"

He shrugged. "He was responsible for my being stranded in a snowstorm, which cost me a month and a half in bed. During which time, I might add, you conveniently left the country."

"Is that all?" she asked in relief. "He didn't wound you or anything?" At his black scowl, she smiled weakly. "Sorry. I didn't mean to make light of . . . A month and a half? That must have been a dreadful cold." His scowl grew worse. "Well, if you must know, I didn't leave the country, not until this summer anyway."

"The devil you didn't. I had people looking for you everywhere, woman. I had the Embassy watched, the Ambassador followed, his servants bribed—"

"But he was telling you the truth, Dimitri. He hadn't seen me. Oh, I did go to the Embassy when I left your house, but before I could see the Ambassador, I met Countess Starov. She is such a nice woman and so easy to talk to. When I mentioned that I was in need of a place to stay for a while, she very generously opened her home to me."

"You don't think Vladimir was so lax that he didn't have you followed that day, do you?"

"On the contrary," she retorted. "That was exactly why the Countess suggested I exchange clothes with her maid. I left the way I came in, with no one the wiser, and I spent the remainder of the winter with Olga Starov. Do you know her? She's such a dear lady, if a trifle on the eccentric side, and—"

"Why did you feel you had to hide from me? Do you know I nearly went out of my mind worrying about you traveling in that weather?"

"I didn't hide," she protested, only to correct herself. "Well, perhaps at first I did. I was—" No, she wasn't going to admit that she was afraid that if she saw him again, all her firm resolutions would fall by the wayside, not to mention that her condition would have been exposed. "Let us say I was still quite angry over—over—"

"Yes? My using you? My lying to you? My being in love with another woman?"

The caustic derision in his tone scalded her. Hot color seeped into her cheeks. Had she really believed all of that? Hadn't she suspected on the day he had shown up at Brockley Hall, making her panic and race off to London, that he wouldn't have been there if he loved another woman?

Think about it, Katherine. You haven't been able to face him these last weeks because you knew you might have been wrong. You also knew he would be furious with you for keeping Alek from him. You were afraid, pure and simple.

But not once had she thought he might love her. She had relegated that possibility to the realm of make-believe. Could such dreams come true? But she was forgetting his reaction when he had learned the truth about her identity.

"You didn't want to marry me, Dimitri. You were enraged when you thought you would have to. You were so angry you left the city. Do you know how that made me feel?"

"For an intelligent woman, Katya, you show a marked lack of sense sometimes. I was angry with myself, not you. That very night, before I knew who you were, I told Vasili I had decided not to marry anyone if I couldn't marry you. And the irony is that less than a month later, Misha came home with a wife and a son."

"But I thought—"

"We all did. But he wasn't dead. And his return freed me from my obligations. I could have married you then, Katya, regardless of who you were. But that night of the ball, all I could think about was how I had wronged you and how you couldn't possibly forgive me. I was appalled by my own behavior, especially since I had seen the truth in Nastya's portrait of you but stubbornly ignored it just so that I could retain a measure of control over you. To admit who you were was to risk losing you, and I couldn't bear that. But I lost you anyway."

"Dimitri—"

"Lady Katherine, Alek's cheeks are turning pink," Alice interrupted. "Do you want me to move to the shade, or should I take him home now?"

Katherine groaned inwardly, glaring at the woman, wanting nothing more than to throttle her for bringing Alek this close to his father. But Dimitri barely spared the nurse and child a glance. He simply looked at Katherine questioningly, as if he assumed—what, she didn't know. However, before she could say something, answer the nurse, give him some lie or even the truth, Dimitri must have thought over the nurse's question and reached the truth on his own.

He turned sharply, fixing his eyes on Alek with an intensity that paralyzed Katherine. Then he took the boy away from the nurse, staring at him, noting every little detail, and Alek stared back quietly, fascinated as always by something new. And his father was certainly new to him.

"I'm sorry, Dimitri," Katherine said in a small voice. "I was going to tell you when I joined you in St. Petersburg. I really was. But after what you said on that first day, I decided to wait, and then . . . after the ball, I was too upset, angry, and—and hurt. I wanted to marry you, but not if you felt you *had* to marry me. And—and I wasn't hiding from you. After several months had passed and you didn't find me, I went out often. I even passed your house. But I suppose you had already left the city."

He glanced up at her only then, to remind her, "Looking for you."

"I realize that now. But at the time, I gave up, deciding it was for the best that we didn't see each other again. So I came home as soon as

Alek was old enough to travel. You have the right to know about him. I'm not denying that. And I would have written to you to tell you. But you showed up here so quickly. I was only just settled in, home only a month."

"When I couldn't find you here, I returned to Russia. And when I still couldn't find you there, I came back here. I could think of nothing else to do. But you have had ample time to tell me since I arrived. I have called on you daily."

"I know, but—I was afraid."

"Of what? That I would take him from you? That I would be angry? Katya, I am overjoyed. He is—he is incredible! The most beautiful baby I have ever seen."

"I know."

She couldn't help smiling at the pride in his eyes as he put his cheek to Alek's and gently squeezed him close before handing him back to the nurse. "Take him home," he told the woman. "My man will escort you, and your lady will return shortly."

At Dimitri's wave, Katherine noticed the carriage parked behind her own and Vladimir stepping down from it to meet Alek's nurse. Dear old Vladimir. Always there when needed, always resourceful. If not for him, Katherine would never have met Dimitri, never have borne Alek. And to think how much she had resented him at one time.

Dimitri said nothing until his carriage had driven away and then he turned to Katherine, his eyes expressing all the tenderness inside him. "I love you, Katya. Marry me."

"I—"

His finger touched her lips. "Before you say anything, be warned, little one. If I don't like your answer, you will probably find yourself abducted once again, you and the boy, and there will be no escaping me this time."

"Is that a promise?"

He gave a shout and picked her up in his arms, swinging her once around before letting her slide slowly down his body and fastening his mouth to hers. In his kiss was all the aching loneliness of so many months. And as usual, there was no bed around.

Chapter Forty-two

_V_ladimir was waiting for them in the entryway when Dimitri returned Katherine to her home. In his exuberance Dimitri clasped his longtime servant in a bear hug, leaving the poor fellow breathless.

"She said yes, Vladimir!"

"I gathered as much, my prince. Congratulations, and to you, my lady."

"Thank you, Vladimir." Katherine nodded regally. "And you needn't be so stiff. Just because I'm going to be your new mistress, doesn't mean there will be _that_ many changes. I'm a very forgiving sort, you know. I promise to have you whipped only on Saturdays."

Dimitri chuckled at the slow flush creeping up Vladimir's cheeks. "He doesn't know you're teasing, Katya. You really must choose your targets with more care."

"Nonsense. He knows very well. He just has a guilty conscience. Isn't that right, Vladimir?"

"Yes, my lady."

"Well, you can put it to rest, my friend." She grinned at him now. "I have a lot to thank you for, if truth were known."

Katherine turned away, removing her bonnet and gloves, and only Dimitri heard Vladimir sigh. He smiled to himself, shaking his head. His soon-to-be-wife was going to be a holy terror in his household. His people would never know when to take her seriously and when not, but it would certainly keep them on their toes. And then he realized the same went for him and his smile widened. He didn't care. As long as she was always near and happy and loving him, she could tease to her heart's content.

He turned to Vladimir. "The Duchess is expecting me for lunch. You'll have to inform her . . . No, better yet, bring her here. Is that all right, Katya?"

She grimaced. "Of course, but I feel I should warn you, Dimitri. She isn't going to be too pleased with your news. She and I didn't get on too well together at our first meeting. I'm afraid I refused to let her see Alek, and she didn't take too kindly to that."

"You mean she knew?"

"She knew I came home with a son. She only suspected he was yours. Sonya had written her complaining about me, you see."

He gave a short bark of laughter. "Why that old . . . I knew she was keeping something from me. But you're wrong, you know. She greatly admires your spunk, as she calls it. And she was quite as determined as I was to see us reconciled. Now I know why. She wants to coddle her great-grandson."

"Oh, it's you, Kate." George St. John appeared at the top of the stairs. "I thought I heard voices, but I couldn't understand a word of such gibberish. Practicing your French again, are you?"

"Come down, Father. I want you to meet your future son-in-law."

"The Russian?"

"Yes."

"So it *was* him," George said with a smug amount of satisfaction.

"Yes, it was him."

Katherine spared a glance at Dimitri to see if he was getting annoyed that they were speaking in English. He wasn't. But this was going to get difficult. Her father didn't speak French.

"Don't know why it took you so long to own up to it," George said when he reached the bottom of the stairs. "I could have got him for you sooner, you know."

"I got him for myself, thank you, without any help."

"And here I thought I had done the catching," Dimitri said in perfect English, and to George: "It's a pleasure to meet you, my lord."

Katherine turned on him, eyes narrowed and sparkling. "Why, you—you—"

"Dolt? Fiend? Scoundrel? Oh, we mustn't forget blasted lecher. And those are only a few of the names you have called me when you thought I didn't understand a word of English."

"Was that fair?"

"Fair, little one? No. Amusing? Yes. You are absolutely adorable when you mumble to yourself in a fit of pique."

"Isn't she though," George agreed. "I always thought so. Got the habit from her mother, you know. Now there was a woman who could carry on the most interesting conversations, all by herself."

"All right." Katherine grinned. "I give up." And then to change the subject, hopefully, "Is Warren or Beth in? They'll want to meet Dimitri."

"It'll have to wait until tonight, Kate. Your sister said something about shopping, and Warren's off at his club, I believe. And I was just leaving, too. You will come for dinner, won't you?" He directed this to Dimitri. "Need to discuss the wedding arrangements, you know."

"I wouldn't miss it," Dimitri assured him.

The front door opened just as George reached it, and Elisabeth stepped in. "Back so soon?" George greeted her. "So's your sister, and she has some news for you, I believe."

"Oh?" Elisabeth glanced over his shoulder and then gasped, seeing Dimitri and Katherine standing close together. "Oh!" And she rushed forward, leaving her father chuckling as he left.

Katherine made the introductions and explained her happy news. But her sister didn't seem to be listening. Seeing Dimitri up close for the first time, she could only stare at him, spellbound. Katherine had to jab her in the ribs to bring her to her senses.

"Oh! I'm sorry." Elisabeth recovered, blushing. "I'm so happy to meet you at last, not that I've heard much about you. Kit has been so close-mouthed and . . . Does this mean you're going to take Kit off to live in Russia? It's so cold there."

"On the contrary." Dimitri smiled. "I imagine we will spend most of our time traveling to inspect my many business ventures." Here he glanced at Katherine. "I have been warned what happens when I don't watch over my investments."

Elisabeth missed the byplay between them. "But that's wonderful! Kit always did want to travel. And she has such a flair for business. You will let her help, won't you?''

''I wouldn't have it any other way. But now, as much as I want to get to know her family better, I must ask you, little Beth, if you will excuse us for a short time. Your sister has only just agreed to marry me, and I still have much to say to her.''

''Of course!'' Elisabeth agreed eagerly, but then she would have agreed to anything he asked, she was so mesmerized. ''I have things to put away and—and I'll see you later, I hope.''

Katherine was amused by her sister's behavior, but not at all surprised. How many times had she been thrown into a jumble of confusion herself when Dimitri looked at her with those sensuous dark eyes. She was, in fact, still in a pleasant state of shock from which she doubted she would ever truly recover. This man said he loved her. *Her.* It was so inconceivable. How did she get to be so lucky?

A moment later, with Elisabeth disappearing up the stairs, Dimitri put his arm around Katherine's waist and steered her into what looked to be the drawing room. It was.

''You didn't have other plans for tonight, did you?'' Katherine was saying. ''I mean, my father did put you on the spot there.''

''All my plans revolve around you, little one,'' he replied.

His closing the door behind them was Katherine's first warning of his immediate plans. The look in his eyes confirmed it.

''Dimitri!'' She tried to sound shocked, but the smile curling her lips belied her. ''This isn't your house, you know. Here servants think nothing

of opening doors and barging right in.'' He
solved that problem by grabbing the nearest chair
and bracing it against the door. ''You're terribly
wicked.''

''Yes,'' he agreed, taking her in his arms,
where she pressed her body close, closer. ''But
so are you, my love.''

''That's nice,'' she murmured against his lips.
''Say it again.''

''My love. You are, you know. Without you,
there is no joy in my life.''

*Did you hear that, Katherine? Do you believe it
now?*

She did. This fairy tale had come true.